To Jonathan and Olivia

SUNLIGHT ACROSS THE PLAINS

Catherine Dunbar

Hodder & Stoughton
LONDON SYDNEY AUCKLAND

First published in 1994 by Hodder and Stoughton
A division of Hodder Headline PLC.

10 9 8 7 6 5 4 3 2 1

British Library Cataloguing in Publication Data

Dunbar, Catherine
Sunlight Across the Plains
I. TItle
823.914 [F]

ISBN 0-340-59441-1

Typeset by Hewer Text Composition Services, Edinburgh
Printed and bound in Great Britain by Mackays of Chatham plc.

Hodder and Stoughton Ltd
A Division of Hodder Headline PLC
338 Euston Road
London NW1 3BH

Acknowledgments

I would like to thank all those who gave so generously of their time to share with me their recollections of Kenya and in particular: Dennis and Charlotte Mayers, Juanita Carberry, Arthur Wolseley-Lewis and Sheila Nicoll.

PROLOGUE

From where he sat on the wide verandah of his bungalow, Edward Sinclair had a powerful sense of being watched. Beyond the parched lawn, among the tinder-brittle long grass which bordered it, a movement caught his eye. A ripple, almost imperceptible in the moonlight, but there all the same.

Even now, after all his time in Kenya, he found himself tensing with anticipation. Once he would have snatched up his rifle and rushed down the verandah steps, alert with curiosity, but the years had tempered his impetuous nature. Wait and see, that was the way here among the Kikuyu.

He leaned back in his chair, his fingers tightening around the half-full whisky glass. It seemed almost a part of him these days. He knew he drank too much and didn't need Juma's daily chastising to remind him. Nowadays he hardly recognised the face which stared back at him from the bathroom mirror. He could no longer pretend it was age alone which had caused such destruction. Every line of him proclaimed the coarsening of a face that had been enviably handsome in his youth, the disintegration of a once fine body.

He shrugged and took another gulp of whisky. He felt no self-pity. He could have left long ago, sold up and returned to England, but the land had held him fast: demanding, cruel even, yet inescapably beguiling.

Whatever the heartbreak, whatever the price he'd paid, he still loved the place and what had lured him out here nearly thirty years before still bewitched him, as it had others of his kind: the restless, the unconventional, the enterprising, the adventurous – those who like himself had come out to fulfil a dream. To create a farm out of nothing. To hew out of the rocks and bush some sort of home, to coax out of the earth a crop or two. To survive against the elements.

He sighed and stretched out to refill his glass. Juma had grudgingly placed the whisky bottle on the glass-topped table beside him. The sudden movement caused a stirring in the long grass. He lifted his head, all at once alert. He had forgotten his uninvited visitor: a leopard, perhaps, or a scavenging hyena? He stood up, a little unsteadily, and crossed over to the wooden railings of the verandah, peering out into the darkness. Usually such a bold display was enough to put the animal to flight; but not so tonight. He vaguely wondered if it might be the rogue baboon which had pestered them a few weeks before, intent on wreaking havoc amongst his small livestock again. But almost as the thought came to him he heard a soft cough, and knew it to be not savage at all, but human.

'Come on out!' he called, first in English and then in Swahili. 'Show yourself, do you hear me!'

His gravelly voice cut across the soft stirrings and insect calls of the night. Loud and ferocious, it worked its trick in an instant. Something moved just beyond the bubble of light from the verandah lantern, then the darkness seemed to part for a moment as a young *toto* moved out of the shadows towards him. The child, about ten years of age, was large-headed, skinny-limbed, velvet-eyed and now, face to face with the old man *Bwana* Sinclair, not at all sure of himself.

Fidgeting from foot to foot he gave a shy, lopsided grin.

Edward shot him a look of practised severity. 'You should be at home asleep in your hut,' he told the boy shortly. 'What would your parents think if they were to wake and find you gone? That the leopards have taken you, eh? And so they might, if you are foolish enough to wander around at night all alone . . .'

The boy seemed not in the least daunted by such a reprimand. The mention of leopards only made him smile the more. *Bwana* Sinclair had a reputation amongst the villagers of being able to rid them of the most troublesome marauders. He beamed at the old man, as if in silent tribute to those past courageous deeds.

'So, what are you doing skulking around my house?' Edward demanded, unmoved by the cherubic face.

The *toto* gave a light shrug of his thin shoulders and looked away.

'Well?' Edward's voice was irascible, for he thought he knew only too well the reason for the boy's visit. Yesterday, foolishly as he could now see, he had tried to distract one of the young *totos* who was having a particularly nasty burn dressed by showing him his soda syphon.

The ploy had worked only too well; the syphon had caused a sensation. To the child it had seemed that the water bubbling out into the mug which *Bwana* Sinclair held was possessed of a most lively ebullient spirit. The boy had immediately stopped his wailing and drawn back in fascination. How, he had asked Sinclair solemnly, did the spirit live in the bottle?

Now, of course, Edward realised the implications of his rash deed. The *toto*, burns duly dressed, had returned to his village and told all his friends about the spirit which *Bwana* Sinclair kept locked in a bottle. The boy standing before him now, Sinclair suspected, was the first of a steady stream of young hopefuls who would venture up to the house for many months to come, on the chance of catching sight of the wondrous spirit.

And yet, even knowing the consequences, Edward was tempted to show his latest visitor the syphon; it had been a brave act to come up from the village in the dark alone, and Sinclair always found courage hard to resist.

'You wish to see the spirit in the bottle, do you?' He was careful to keep an edge of severity to his voice. 'He may be angry, you know, at being disturbed so late at night . . .'

The boy's eyes widened but he did not draw back. Edward found himself scarcely able to resist a smile at such determination.

'What's your name, child?' he asked, gesturing for the boy to step forward to the verandah.

'Ndwetti, *Bwana*.'

'Then, Ndwetti, step a little closer. Are you sure you wish to see this spirit?'

'Yes, *Bwana*.' The boy's brown eyes met Sinclair's gaze unflinchingly.

'You will not cry out in fear if he comes?'

Indignantly, Ndwetti puffed out his chest. 'No, indeed, *Bwana*.'

Edward smiled. 'Then you are a brave boy, Ndwetti. Courage should always be rewarded. I'll let you see the bottle. But after you have seen how it makes the water whisper and dance you must go straight back to your village, do you hear?'

'Straight back,' repeated Ndwetti dutifully.

'Good. Now wait here.'

Ndwetti stood, fidgeting with anticipation, as Edward went up the steps into the house.

At last Edward came down the steps clutching a mug in one hand and the syphon in the other.

'You may hold the mug if you like, but you must keep it steady, do you understand?'

Ndwetti hesitated for only the briefest moment, then he took it, both hands encircling the mug.

'Are you ready then?' Edward asked him with a smile of encouragement.

Silent now, as if realising that the auspicious moment had indeed come, Ndwetti could only nod.

'Well then . . .' Slowly Edward depressed the silver handle at the top of the bottle. With a sudden spurt the effervescent water shot out of the nozzle. Startled, the boy drew back so quickly that the water fell onto the parched lawn. It made a faint hiss, seeming to dance on the surface for a moment, then disappeared into the ground. Just as Edward thought the *toto* would drop the mug and make a run for it, Ndwetti seemed to steel himself, and, steadying his hand, held the cup out to catch the remaining stream of water.

'Well done,' said Edward softly.

Ndwetti held the cup up against his ear and gave a beaming grin. 'They are wrong, *Bwana*. This spirit is not angry. I can hear it laughing. And see, it plays games against my cheek.' He indicated with long fingers the tickling motion which the bubbles made against his face as they burst. 'You see, *Bwana*, how right I was not to be afraid of it . . .' He puffed out his chest with an air of self-satisfaction.

'Yes, Ndwetti, you were right not to be afraid,' conceded Sinclair. 'And because you were such a brave fellow, I shall tell you a secret. There is no spirit in the bottle.'

Ndwetti's eyes widened slightly, then he gave a little shake of his head. 'But I have seen it,' he said slowly.

'No. There is no spirit in the bottle,' Edward told him again. 'Come here and I will show you . . .' He beckoned the boy closer.

'See,' he said, lifting the cap to the silver top in which lay hidden the soda syphon bulbs. 'These are what make the water sparkle and dance.'

Ndwetti regarded the black bulbs solemnly. The concept of these tiny objects working such magic was much harder for the boy to fathom than any idea of a spirit existing in a bottle. He hesitated, stretched out to touch it, then, shaking his head, drew back.

'It's true,' insisted Edward. 'And if I were to remove the black bulbs the water would not sparkle. It couldn't. Look, I'll show you.' The bottle was almost empty anyway. He squirted the last drops onto the lawn and then unscrewed the top. 'Run up to the verandah, Ndwetti. You'll find one of these bulbs on the table there. Bring it down, and the jug of water, too.'

Ndwetti sped up the steps and returned a few moments later, hands full. Edward took the jug from him and carefully filled the glass bottle.

'See Ndwetti, the water doesn't sparkle yet,' he said. 'But when I put in the black bulb, so . . .' He screwed it into the head of the syphon. 'You see.'

Ndwetti's eyes widened as he saw the bubbles running into the bottle. Edward gave the syphon a vigorous shake. 'Now the water sparkles!'

Edward gave the wire-covered bottle one last shake and then depressed the handle again. Immediately the syphon sprang into life, the water spluttering onto the lawn.

Ndwetti crouched down, his chin sunk down between his scabby knees, poking at the water with one long thin finger, watching as it bubbled momentarily on the surface before sinking away into the earth. He nodded his head, as if satisfied at last that the old man spoke the truth.

'Now you must go home, Ndwetti,' Edward told the boy. 'You must tell the other children in the village that they must not come up here, do you understand? The bulbs will run out if they are used too often, and then the syphon will not work.'

Ndwetti's countenance brightened. This seemed to be altogether what he had expected to hear. He gave Sinclair a wide smile. 'I understand, *Bwana*. The syphon will grow tired if it is disturbed too often. It will grow angry and refuse to work, is that not so?'

Ndwetti's logic seemed indisputable. 'Yes, that is so,' Edward agreed, laughing out loud. What point was there trying to refute such a deduction?

Ndwetti seemed pleased that he and the old man at last understood each other. 'I shall tell them, *Bwana*,' he announced importantly. 'I shall tell them that it will grow angry and refuse to work.'

'You do that,' Edward said, taking the mug back from the boy. 'Now back to the village with you. Before the lions get you . . .'

Ndwetti flashed his large white teeth in one last beaming smile then slid away into the darkness.

Edward stood on the lawn for a moment watching the boy's willowy form merge into the night. The darkness closed in about his shadow with a completeness which Sinclair found disconcerting. One moment the boy was there, the next nothing. It was almost as if he had never been.

That was what it was like in Africa. One could never escape the feeling of isolation, of the precariousness of one's own existence, the sense of utter blankness on all sides.

When Edward had first arrived out here before the Great War, when he had trekked with his wife and two children from Nairobi in a rumbling oxen-drawn cart through roadless terrain to this piece of land, the vastness of the country had dawned on him only slowly. A mountain which looked close never seemed to get any closer, and beyond each range of hills lay another far horizon, stretching on and on forever.

There seemed no break, no order, just the same endless landscape, the pale-brown grass and bush and stunted thorn tree, the rocky mountains and sunlit plains. There had been no towns, nor dwellings, nor signs of past existence.

He had found that eerie at first: that generations of people had lived there, lived and died, and yet left no visible trace behind. No tombs or burials mounds even, let alone ruins of cities or temples. He had known then that this country was harsh and destructive, still very much its own master. The enormity of his task had struck him with a vengeance. Yet he had never thought of giving in. It wasn't in his nature.

Would he have turned back if he had foreseen how hard an existence it was to be? Probably not. He was a determined man, never one to choose an easy path when a more adventurous one beckoned. The trouble was he had taken with him those less able to face the challenges, and had lost them in consequence. His wife, Amelia, and young son, Harry, long since dead; and Sarah, his daughter, as good as dead to him . . .

Edward sighed into the darkness. Memories. How long ago it all seemed, and yet, how strange it was that little inconsequential incidents would suddenly come back to him. He could remember that first journey as if it were yesterday. Every detail. Most of all, if he closed his eyes, he could see his darling Amelia perched precariously on the front of the low wagon, a mushroom-brimmed hat and green-lined parasol protecting her face from the sun.

Not once had she complained. Not of the heat, nor the dust, nor the ticks and flies; her buoyant mood had carried them all, even when the wagon had become bogged down crossing a river and every last piece of their possessions had had to be unloaded to enable the oxen to be moved on. Amused, not annoyed – the reaction was typical of her. And if he concentrated very hard he could almost hear the sound of her laughter now . . .

He stood stock still, hearing only the low mocking bark of a jackal.

Sweeping up the whisky bottle as he passed he climbed the verandah steps, pushed open the screen doors and went through the dark hallway to the drawing-room beyond.

An ancient copy of the London *Times* lay crumpled in the armchair beside the flickering lantern. Unceremoniously, Edward thrust it aside as he slumped down into the well-worn seat.

Damn! It was the boy's visit which had unsettled him – the sudden void after company had cast him into melancholy mood. He poured himself another whisky and settled back even further into the chair, his great bulk threatening to overflow its edges. He had always been of a generous size but, unlike the Kikuyus who seemed to shrivel up with age, he had spread even further. His hair, silvery white, was now wild and wiry, and with his dark complexion, hooded grey eyes and large hooked nose, he had about him an air of a ferocious pirate which his cantankerous nature did nothing to dispel.

He turned his head to look at the photographs arranged on the polished mahogany table by the window. Old photographs, all of them. One of Harry in his mother's arms, another of him on his prized chestnut pony – taken, Edward reflected grimly, just before the blackwater fever killed him – and behind that one of his daughter, Sarah, taken just after they had arrived out here. Even at thirteen, she showed signs of her later beauty and elegance.

Sarah. The one whose loss he regretted most of all. How lethally and completely she had cut herself off from him. He had never even seen his granddaughter, Alexandra.

Once, years ago, Sarah had condescended to post out from England a photograph of the child, a peach-skinned, tousle-haired, wide-eyed moppet of about four. But he was never to have the grandfather's privilege of dandling the darling upon his knee, or know the joys of sharing childish secrets. And now it was too late. Alexandra was eighteen. Too old for such indulgences.

Occasionally, in his more sentimental, alcoholic moments, he had started to write to her; but the letters had never been sent. In the light of day he recognised there was something pathetic in his barely disguised pleas for forgiveness and friendship.

Forgiveness? How could he hope for that from a child of Sarah's? And without that, what hope was there of friendship?

And yet he could not forget the photograph. There had been something compelling about the child's face. The eyes that had stared out at him had been as bright and as steadfast as boot-buttons and there had been more than a hint of challenge in the tilt of her chin. It was a lively face, intelligent, but what had so caught his attention was its look of unmistakable determination.

He had sensed then that Alexandra was a child after his own heart. And that, had they met, they would have found themselves kindred spirits.

He emptied his glass and lurched ponderously to his feet, putting out a hand to the back of the armchair to steady himself. What he would give to see his granddaughter. Just once.

He hesitated, as if momentarily disorientated. Then, straightening, he made his way over to the walnut secretaire in the corner of the room. He flopped down on the ribbon-backed chair in front of it and pulled open the desk with a swift, clumsy movement.

He knew what he must do.

It was just after midnight that Juma, the houseboy, found Edward slumped over the desk, an empty whisky bottle beside him. He clicked his tongue against his teeth. As a Muhammadan he would not touch wine or spirits and it went against the dryness of his Somali mind to see the havoc that drink had brought upon a once-respected proud man.

He bent over and tried to stir his master, turning him slightly so that he could slip an arm under the old man's shoulders in an attempt to raise him. But tonight Edward was out to the world, and Juma, strong as he might be, was too slight to carry his dead weight alone to the bedroom.

He let Edward sink forward again then left the room for a moment before returning with a light rug. He gently covered the slumbering body, almost as if he were dealing with a child, then he straightened slowly, staring down with dark concerned eyes. He clicked his tongue again, this time with distress.

He couldn't bear to see a man of Edward's repute let himself sink so low. Yet he knew why. One incident – so long ago, it had almost been washed away by time. But like the sting of the snake, the venom had slowly seeped through, gradually poisoning them all.

If only . . . Juma stopped. Almost unconsciously he tightened his lips. No, he must not think about it. He had been sworn to secrecy and Sinclair had said that if he so much as hinted at what had happened he personally would skin Juma live. Juma believed him, such had been Sinclair's temper that night.

He bent over the old man again with a sigh, checking he was as comfortable as possible.

It was as he was tucking in the corner of the rug that he caught sight of the letter, the top edge protruding from under Sinclair's head. Juma stretched forward and carefully eased it out. It was sealed and addressed. Juma squinted in the darkness to make out the writing: Miss Alexandra Drayton. Sinclair's granddaughter . . .

He glanced down at the old man. By rights he should return the letter to its place, but past experience had taught him that letters such as this one invariably found their way to the rubbish bin in the morning. Why, he did not truly understand – for in his experience a letter was a precious thing. Certainly the few that Sinclair had received had obviously been so, for he had carried them around in his pocket for weeks, as if not trusting himself to let them out of his sight for a moment, taking them out from time to time to read again, until the creases were so worn that Juma had thought they would split in two.

He sighed. He knew how much Sinclair loved his granddaughter and sensed what the letter would contain. Somehow he could not bring himself to return the envelope to the desk.

He was not a man of impulse but it seemed to him fortuitous indeed that he had found this letter before the old man had had a chance to destroy it. Subterfuge was not in Juma's nature, yet he knew now what he must do. Tomorrow, the Burtons would call on their way to Nairobi, as they did on the first Thursday of every quarter, to enquire whether Sinclair needed any stores. The letter could be safe in their keeping and well on its way to Nairobi before Sinclair awoke and thought of destroying it – if indeed he even remembered writing it.

Juma wasted no more time. Turning, he clasped the letter to his chest and walked determinedly back to his quarters.

1

Alexandra, really you're impossible! I don't believe you've heard one word I've said!'

Alexandra Drayton lifted her head from her book and gave her mother an indulgent smile. 'Yes, I have, Mother,' she returned brightly. 'You've been exhorting the charms of my blue dress.'

'The cinnamon georgette,' Sarah Drayton corrected her daughter with an exasperated sigh. Transforming Alexandra into a fashionable young lady was proving to be a more difficult task than she had ever imagined. Clothes were a topic which left her daughter cold and she made little effort to hide the fact. Undeterred, Sarah tried again. 'Don't you agree it would be perfect for tonight?'

Alexandra turned another page without looking up. 'Perfect.'

'And the shoes, what about the gold kid?'

'Shoes?'

'Darling, yes, shoes . . .' Sarah Drayton raised her green eyes heavenwards. 'Really, Alexandra, you might try and show an interest. This evening is important.'

Every evening was important to her mother, Alexandra reflected matter-of-factly. The endless round of house parties, garden parties and dinner parties – each one had to be planned for with something akin to military precision. She sometimes thought her mother must have been born clutching the latest copy of the *Tatler* and discussing what hat to wear to Ascot.

She sighed and stretched, book in hand, while her mother turned her attention to the pressing question of jewellery. It seemed to Alexandra that at this time of economic instability her mother's need to keep up appearances had become almost obsessional. They had to be seen everywhere, seen in splendour too. As if by wearing the latest Schiaparelli creation one could dispel the rumours that Sir George Drayton had lost a considerable fortune on the stock exchange following the Great Crash of '29.

It was too silly. Everyone knew. Everyone knew because everyone else was in the same situation as far as Alexandra could see. Very few of their friends and acquaintances had escaped the reverberations from the slump in America. Some, like her mother's close circle, tried as far as possible to pretend that it hadn't happened. Others, like Winston Churchill – who had just embarked on a lecture tour of America to recoup his losses – were more open about their misfortunes and quite determined to redress the balance.

She knew which camp she would fall into. At eighteen, Alexandra Drayton was a very positive young woman.

She shifted restlessly on the padded window seat and turned to stare out of the window. Down below in the busy London street fog-banks were gathering, thickening and spreading across the garden square. There was a faint blue tinge to the afternoon light, the promise of frost to come.

She was dimly aware that her mother was speaking to her.

'Alexandra, do you hear me? I said, I thought the pearls would be appropriate . . .'

Alexandra shifted her copy of *The Waves* slightly, as if she were trying to set up some sort of wall against the conversation.

'The pearls, the choker, whatever you think, Mother,' she murmured with a little shrug. 'After all, it doesn't really matter does it? It's not as if I'm about to emulate Unity Mitford and turn up wearing a pet grass snake around my neck, is it?'

'Alexandra!' There was genuine reproach in her mother's voice.

Instantly Alexandra regretted her flippancy. She'd meant no harm by her light remark but she should have guessed what reaction it might cause. Her mother was so tetchy lately. A sunny mood could break into a storm at the slightest word, not like in the old days, in the calm of financial certainty. Poor Mama: she, more than anyone, liked things to be safe and secure, to know exactly where she stood. A reflection on Kenya, perhaps, where her mother had known no real security.

'I'm sorry, Mother,' she apologised a little ruefully.

'You've been out of sorts all week,' her mother accused her, still unappeased.

'I haven't.'

'Yes, you have. Look at you now. Argumentative.' She gave an aggrieved lift of her shoulders and bent to pick up a cigarette from the onyx box on the table. 'Ever since that wretched letter arrived . . .'

Ah, Alexandra had wondered when they would come to that. Perhaps, from the very beginning, this was where the argument had been heading.

'Mother, really!' she protested, putting aside her book. 'The letter has nothing to do with this.'

'Hasn't it?' Sarah Drayton took a long draw on her cigarette and glanced across at her daughter. The family likeness between them was striking. The same almond-shaped green eyes, the same high cheekbones and straight nose. The same stubborn jaw. Alike in character in some ways too – although Alexandra, at that youthful stage of intensity and challenge would not see it. As a child Sarah too had been headstrong, reckless, ready to pursue a dream . . .

She flicked the cigarette into the onyx ashtray, her whippet-thin body tensing slightly. The letter had been secretly unsettling. After all these years, how had her father dared to write begging for Alexandra to come out to Kenya? What loyalties did he misguidedly think were due to him?

'You're not going,' she reiterated firmly, not quite able to meet her daughter's watchful gaze. 'I shan't allow it.'

'But I don't understand why not. He's your own father. You're awfully hard on him you know.'

'Hard?' Her mother stopped rearranging the ornaments on the walnut console table beside her. 'If you knew him you wouldn't say that.' Her voice was defensive.

'But I don't know him, do I?' Alexandra threw back. She knew confrontation wasn't the way to win her mother over. But she wanted desperately to go, wanted to savour the sweetness of independence, of excitement, wanted terribly to meet her enigmatic grandfather. 'Why won't you let me go? Think of how lonely he must be, Mother.'

'He deserves to be.' There was a small icy pause in which her mother seemed to catch her breath. 'Everything that has happened to him, he has brought on himself. The ruination of the estate, the loss of his family, his own . . . degradation. How can you be sorry for a man who has drunk and gambled his way to his own destruction?'

'Father says it was the untimely slump in coffee prices which finished him off,' Alexandra pointed out. She, like her father, was prone to giving people the benefit of the doubt.

'It was the gambling debts which did that,' her mother returned unremittingly. 'Without those he would not have been forced to sell off the best part of the farm and he would still be financially sound now. No, Alexandra, don't be tempted to give him your sympathy. Save it for those who worked day after day to help him build up the estate. Save it for my poor mother who struggled against all odds for his sake, struggled until she could bear it no longer. You were too young to remember her, of course, but all I can say is it was a mercy I was able to offer her a home here away from it all.'

Granny Sinclair. Vaguely, so vaguely that it was only an illusion of frailty and the sweet smell of rosewater, Alexandra *could* remember her. She had since learnt that Granny Sinclair had come for what was supposed to be a short holiday, but, on finding a safe haven in England, she had chosen to spend her remaining few years away from the hardship of the farm life and her husband's increasingly erratic behaviour. She had never again returned to Kenya. Never again had she seen Edward Sinclair, despite his pleading letters.

In the frosty silence, Alexandra watched her mother stretch over and stub out her cigarette with sudden venom.

'Why must he write now?' her mother demanded, her voice almost an angry growl. 'It's typical of him to suppose he can play on our sympathy and worm his way back into our lives after all that's happened!'

'Mother, please don't,' said Alexandra quietly, hating to see her so bitter. 'There wasn't one hint of "my last dying wish" in the letter, you know . . .'

'He knew better than to try that!' Her mother gave a tight little laugh. 'And don't be fooled by him, Alexandra. He's as cunning as a fox when it comes to getting round people.'

He *had* been cunning, Alexandra had to give him that. No mention of his loneliness, of his wanting to see her. Just a wonderful description of the country, so evocative that she could almost smell the dusty pungency of the land. And the gentle, but urgent, wish that she should see it, not him. He had painted a tempting picture, designed to lure a restless soul. It was as if he knew instinctively of her rebellious streak. And in that one letter he had formed a link between them, an understanding that they were like minds and like spirits.

There was a flat, weighted silence. Her mother seemed to marshall her forces. 'And what about Charles?' She sounded less strained now. 'I thought there was an "understanding" between you both. How on earth can you consider becoming engaged to someone one minute and the next tell me you want to go gallavanting off to Kenya . . .'

'Charles wouldn't mind.'

'You seem very sure of him. Is that wise?'

Alexandra's eyes flicked across to her mother, watching as she took another cigarette from the box and slid it into her jade holder. There had been mistrust in her voice, but why? Against Charles? Or a cry from longer ago, against Papa? No, surely not. It was quite obvious that her father still adored her mother, even after all these years; and he was so gentle, so patient, it seemed unimaginable to her that he ever could have caused her mother pain.

Against Grandfather then? It was obvious that her mother felt he had betrayed them all. It had coloured her life. But Alexandra was determined she would not allow the feelings of another generation to dominate her own life, or affect herself and Charles . . .

She closed her eyes for a moment. Charles. Even her mother grudgingly approved of him, though she only saw him as his outward image presented itself: the son of Lord Kildare, wealthy and well-connected, possessing all the attributes which her mother's ambitions for her had extended to year by year.

But Alexandra saw a different side to Charles. It was what had made him stand apart from the 'chinless wonders' her mother had foisted upon her that season.

In Charles she had sensed a similar disinclination to conform. He had refused to join his father's bank, willy-nilly, and she admired him for that, and although his plans for freedom were amorphous at the moment, they were there. As was the undercurrent of adventure. The same fast-beating pulse that flowed through her veins ran in his and she couldn't believe he would try and dissuade her from visiting Kenya. Rather, he would greet the idea with unfettered boyish enthusiasm. Might even be persuaded to come too. Charles would encourage her to go, knowing that an opportunity such as this, the chance to test herself, didn't come often in the confined and protected world she knew.

She pushed her dark hair back from her face with a casual hand and looked across at her mother. She looked so brittle, so frail, standing there that impulsively Alexandra went over to her and kissed her cheek. Her mother meant well, surely, and if she seemed overprotective and anxious it was only for love's sake. Alexandra had no wish to quarrel with her, only to be forced to accept her very different ideals and lifestyle. Thankfully, Charles was the one thing they seemed to agree upon.

'Oh ye of little faith,' said Alexandra softly, kissing her again. 'You don't think Charles would let such an amazingly delightful creature such as me slip through his fingers, do you?'

The tension left her mother's face, the silvery beauty returning in an instant. It was easy to see now why men's heads turned when she entered a room. She smiled and put her hand out to her daughter. 'No, darling,' she declared. 'Not unless he's a fool. Which I take it he's not . . .'

'You know he's not!' Alexandra gave a twirl so that her skirt fanned out around her slim legs. Charles might have obtained only a passable degree from Cambridge but that was due to lack of application rather than brain-power.

'So . . .' Sarah Drayton leaned forward and stubbed out the partially smoked cigarette. 'What time is he due here tonight?'

Alexandra smiled, glad that the mood had eased between them. 'Actually, he rang just after lunch to say that he'd go straight to the theatre. One or two things have cropped up so he might be running a bit late.'

Sarah looked across at her daughter. 'Too much to hope for that he might be trying to find himself some sort of occupation, I suppose?' Purposely she kept her voice light, knowing the ground she walked on was as dangerous as quicksand.

'Oh Mother! He doesn't have to work!' Alexandra protested with a smile.

'Not financially, perhaps. But it doesn't do for a young man to be rich and have time on his hands, Alexandra. I wish he'd at least have given his father's bank a try.'

'It would suffocate him, Mother,' said Alexandra, repeating

Charles' own words. 'You must see that, surely? Oh, I know most of the people you knew in Kenya worked all the hours God gave them, but it doesn't mean you have to wish that on everyone else.'

'I don't.'

'Well then. Please give Charles a chance,' she urged, defending his freedom of spirit as if it were her own. 'Let him have some fun. Think about when you were eighteen. I bet you didn't plan ahead then. I expect you were as frivolous as any of us, a gay young thing with no thought for the future . . .'

Her mother stood before the mirror, back to back with herself, suddenly small and vulnerable in her rose silk dress. 'I expect I was,' she murmured. There was a change in her voice but Alexandra, too busy thinking of Charles, failed to notice.

'You see!' she cried with a teasing smile, a hint of triumph in her tone. 'And you wouldn't have missed those adventures for anything, would you? I expect you still even think of them sometimes, even now. Those heady, glorious moments . . .'

'Not really.'

Alexandra looked disappointed. 'Too busy, I suppose. Poor Mama.'

'Too sensible,' Sarah declared, putting her arms around her daughter's slim waist. 'And if you were *half-way* sensible you'd have been up those stairs half an hour ago starting to get ready.'

Alexandra smiled. 'But you know it doesn't take me more than a few minutes to get changed!'

'Well it should!' chided her mother gently. But she was smiling. Alexandra had the maddening ability to throw things on and still manage to look fetching. It was a quality which did nothing to help Sarah Drayton's uphill struggle to turn her daughter into a lady of fashion, though secretly she couldn't help admiring her. It took a certain confidence to refuse to bow to conventional pressure. 'Now go on with you,' she said, waving her out of the room. 'Upstairs.'

'See, I'm going. Just for you,' returned Alexandra easily, surreptiously bending down to pick up her book. In truth, she had no intention of getting ready yet and was merely taking herself upstairs to read for a while longer in peace, but she wanted to please her mother with appearances of compliance.

'We're due out at seven,' her mother reminded her. 'Don't forget.'

'I won't.' Alexandra turned for a moment. 'Are you coming up too, Mother?'

'In a moment. You go on ahead.'

As soon as she heard her daughter's footsteps on the stairs Sarah turned from the door and went over to stand by the fire which blazed so comfortingly in the hearth.

It was a lie, of course. She did remember those heady, glorious moments. The tantalising images of her youth had sprung readily to mind. Every one of them. The duck shoots on Lake Naivasha in the still of the early morning, the noisy camp-fire safaris, the bustling dinner dances at the Norfolk, the moonlit rides . . . And that first New Year's Eve party at the Muthiaga Club. That, above all, she remembered.

She gave a little shiver and moved closer to the fire. A few small words, that was all it had taken. A few small words and a long-buried memory, like a sleeping snake, had lifted its head and stirred.

2

Charles Montague opened one eye and closed it again with a groan. His head ached and his tongue felt too large for the dry mouth that contained it. Why, oh, why, had he been fool enough to drink all those concoctions on top of the quantity of champagne he'd consumed earlier in the day?

He lay still for a while, trying to gather his senses. There was a slight movement beside him, the soft rustle of silken sheets. He opened his eyes drowsily and rolled his head sideways on the pillow to take in the creamy white curves of the body beside him. He sighed. God! Now he remembered. Kitty.

He hadn't meant to come here at all. But somehow after lunch at the Club with Monty Buckmaster, after a drop too much of champagne, he'd sort of drifted up this way. Kitty always sprang to mind when he'd had too much to drink. She was always so welcoming. So deliciously accommodating.

He slid from the bed and went to the bathroom to splash down his face, his bare feet padding against the thick wool carpet.

'Darling! You're not going!'

Kitty, lying curled up on the outside of the ruffled white sheets like an exquisite pearl in an oyster shell, was affording him her most beguiling pout.

She stretched out one thin white arm and beckoned him back with a carefully manicured finger. 'Come back to bed,' she purred softly, arching her back and stretching like a bored feline. 'Come and warm me up.'

'Kitty, I can't,' Charles protested. 'I'm late as it is!'

He was sorely tempted though. Kitty lying there in all her luminous beauty was hard to resist. Dear Heaven, if the critics could see her now. Kitty Marsden, up-and-coming actress. A girl of great promise whose small part at the Adelphi in Cochrane's *Ever Green* had earned her rave reviews. Charles had been there on the first night – though he had been careful not to acknowledge her for Alexandra had been with him – and many times since. But it was her looks which had won her the most praise, that wonderful translucent skin, that flowing mass of copper-red hair. She was twenty-four, two years older than himself, and yet she looked not a day over nineteen.

Considering how little care she took over herself – and of how much she drank and swallowed pick-me-ups – Charles was amazed that she showed no sign of her hard living. It seemed hardly fair that a girl who indulged so heavily in all the vices could appear so youthful and pure.

The cold water on his face was beginning to have effect at last. Slowly he was starting to feel half-way human again. He came back into the bedroom and began to pick up his clothes which lay scattered across the floor.

He glanced at Kitty. 'Shouldn't you be getting ready, old thing?' he enquired, seeing she had made no move. 'You've a show to do in an hour, don't forget.'

She stretched, divinely supple. 'I've plenty of time.' She looked across at his taut body and sighed. 'So have you, if you had half a mind . . .'

'Kitty, don't start!' Charles was having difficulty finding his shirt. He found it stuffed behind the coffee table.

'You're a beast, Charlie,' Kitty admonished him, helping herself to more champagne. 'You're neglecting me, you know.'

'I'm not.'

'You are. I need pampering and attention.' The voice had become faintly kittenish. Charles knew where this was all leading.

'You're a vixen, Kitty,' Charles pronounced helplessly. He looked at his watch and groaned. He still had to drive home, get changed and be at the theatre at a quarter to eight. 'I've got to drive like Hades as it is,' he said, struggling into his socks.

Kitty's cupid mouth puckered. 'You don't deserve me, Charlie!' she declared petulantly. 'I've a good mind to find myself another lover. Someone more considerate . . .'

Charles laughed. 'You already have other lovers, Kitty.'

'Darling! What a thing to suggest!' protested Kitty, opening her china-blue eyes very wide.

But they both knew he was right. A girl like Kitty couldn't help but waver occasionally. Besides, who could blame her? She was much too clever to suppose that their relationship had any lasting quality about it. Charles had been very careful not to promise her anything – remembering how Viscount Renton had been well and truly sewn up by his pretty little actress and had had to pay a small fortune to extricate himself from the mess.

So, if she had other lovers, although he did not exactly like the thought, it was almost a relief. It would make the break, when it came, easier. And regrettably, that evil day was coming. He'd put it off as long as he could, but with his engagement to Alexandra about to be announced he would have to get shot of Kitty. Not yet, though, he thought glancing across at her looking so utterly delectable on the bed. Not quite yet.

He stretched over to pick up his roll-collared waistcoat which lay crumpled beside the bed. Kitty grabbed his wrist and pulled him across towards her.

'Stay,' she whispered into his ear, her tongue flickering against his skin.

He groaned. Really she was insatiable. 'Can't,' he said, but he allowed her to go on kissing him.

'Then come back later,' she said softly.

'I've got a dinner afterwards.'

'After that.' She pulled his face down towards her again, her thin arms tightening about his shoulders. 'Some close friends are coming back here after the show. A small party. Exclusive. It'll be fun, Charlie . . .' She pushed him away gently and stretched out to pour herself another glass of champagne. 'Lots of lovely women, Charlie. Lots of lovely drink.' She took a sip from the glass, all the while her eyes tempting him across the rim. 'And I've got a little surprise for you . . .'

She had his attention now. She saw his head jerk up.

'What sort of surprise?'

She laughed. Charlie was so predictable. He hated not to be part of the excitement.

'Wait and see,' she said, purposely tantalising. She dipped her red-taloned finger into the champagne and then sucked it slowly, suggestively, her eyes never leaving his face. 'You won't be disappointed.' She felt him waver. She smiled. Tempting Charlie was so simple. 'Now don't be a spoil-sport, Charlie. Do come. It'll all be such fun . . .'

She watched him slip his thick tweed coat over his shoulders. He looked rumpled, boyish, still a little worse for wear, but appealingly handsome all the same. She smiled again. 'Don't let me down, Charlie. I'm relying on you.'

'I shouldn't, Kitty,' he said, pulling on his gloves. A lock of brown hair fell across his face and he blew it upwards ineffectually. 'I probably won't come.'

But even as he opened the door to leave she knew that he would. Charlie was always so easy to manipulate.

Outside in the street below Alexandra could hear the first rumbling of morning traffic. London slowly coming to life. She yawned and stretched, for a moment loath to leave the warm comfort of her bed. It was early and the room was still cold, despite the newly lit fire which glowed invitingly in the grate.

She pulled the covers more tightly about her and with one arm behind her head lay back against the superfluity of pillows, staring up at the corniced ceiling above her.

It had been a strange evening last night. She had never known Charles to be so restless. He had been like a cat on a hot tin roof throughout the play. Admittedly the speeches to mark the opening of the theatre had been tediously long but since he had arrived late he had been saved most of the torture. Besides, even from the moment he had sat down he had seemed distracted, only half listening to the play, despite an outstanding performance by John Gielguld as Malvolio and Ralph Richardson's amusing Sir Toby Belch.

He hadn't even shown much amusement when Lilian Baylis's speech after the play had turned into such a fiasco. Who on earth had been fool enough to give Miss Baylis that huge basket of fruit before she had made her speech? Alexandra smiled at the recollection. It had had disastrous consequences. She'd been hampered by such a burden from the beginning; but worse, as she swept out her arm impulsively to emphasise the point of her argument, pieces of fruit began to drop out of the basket onto the stage; first an apple – which she had tried to cover with her long robes – and then a pear, until the solemnity of the occasion had been irrevocably shattered and the audience had collapsed into fits of laughter.

Even that diversion had not been able to change Charles's mood. As the evening wore on he had become more and more distant, until finally, at the Fitzherberts', he had made his excuses and left early. So unlike Charles, who was usually the life and soul of the party. She regretted his premature departure, not only because she missed his amusing company, but because she had hoped to be able to talk to him about Kenya before her mother managed to corner him and make her feelings against such a venture known. Still, she thought, stretching lazily, they were due to meet for lunch at the Ritz today so at least she'd get a chance to talk to him then.

She stretched again and tossed back the covers, sliding her feet gingerly out into the cold. She was not one to lounge in bed when awake and preferred to take breakfast amid the bustle of the house downstairs.

She crossed over into the bathroom and turned on the taps to fill the huge white enamelled bath. There was a pause, then with a strangulated gurgle the hot water spluttered out reluctantly. The plumbing in the house was not perfect but it was certainly an improvement on the travesty in their house in the country. It was one of the reasons why her mother, despite the elegance of the Drayton family seat, preferred to spend most of her time down in London.

The other reason, Alexandra reflected as she climbed into the bath, was the sheer vitriolic domination of Grandmother Drayton, who, despite having been removed to the Dower House, still regarded Drayton Hall and its estate as hers and guarded her domain with the fierceness of Cerberus. How anyone as easygoing and charming as her father had ever been a child of her loins, Alexandra could not fathom. No wonder Grandfather Drayton had given up the ghost long ago. Sheer exhaustion from dealing with his wife's constant demands, of fencing against her acid squibs, had surely taken its early toll.

A force to be reckoned with then, Grandma Drayton. She had made life impossible for Sarah Drayton, making no bones about the fact that she regarded her as a usurper to the throne. Her own choice for her darling son had been Lord Brackley's daughter and she hadn't taken too kindly to George's insistence on making his own match, particularly since Sarah had little to offer except her beauty. But George had held firm, refusing to be bullied by his mother, and eventually Grandma Drayton had had to capitulate and withdraw her opposition.

She had never ceased to let Sarah know she was not her own choice though, and the situation was aggravated by Sarah's inability to produce a son and heir for the first ten years of her marriage. An unforgivable shortcoming in Grandma Drayton's eyes, that. And although Hugh's arrival into the world eight years ago had rectified that position, she still seemed to hold Sarah personally responsible for making her wait so long for her grandson, even now relishing the chance to send her way a barbed dart to that effect.

She was nothing but an old tyrant, thought Alexandra, watching the steam rise from her bath. Thank heaven she seemed to approve of Charles, for she would have stirred and interfered mercilessly had she not. Age had not seemed to diminish her need to be all-powerful – if anything, it had increased it.

A telephone began to ring downstairs, its shrill note cutting through the silence of the house. Alexandra lifted her head, half expecting it to be Charles – he was prone to reorganising lunch dates at the last minute – but no footsteps came her way, so she continued to luxuriate in the warm rose-scented water.

A few minutes later, splashing the last of the soap from her face, she climbed out of the bath and briskly rubbed herself dry. She crossed back into her bedroom and pulled on a pair of dark-blue flannel trousers, a white silk blouse and her favourite Schiaparelli *trompe-d'oeil* sweater. Then, with only a quick glance in the mirror to ruffle her hair vaguely into place, she started to make her way down to the morning-room.

As she was coming down the stairs she heard the sound of agitated voices from the library. Angry voices. She paused, one hand going to the banisters, hesitating.

'I shall not have it, do you hear?' Her mother's voice, stripped of any sweetness, rose up to her. 'The humiliation of it all . . .'

'The situation is only as humiliating as we allow it to be,' she heard her father say, his voice low and insistent. 'I understand your anger, of course I do. But the whole episode was nothing more than an unfortunate accident. It'll blow over. These things always do.'

'And what about Alexandra?' Her mother's voice was fierce, protective. 'Have you thought how this might affect her?'

At the mention of her name, Alexandra stiffened. What was going on? If this concerned her she had no intention of staying here on the stairs, skulking furtively like a recalcitrant child.

She sped downstairs and pushed open the panelled library door. Across the space of the room she saw her mother standing sideways in the curve of the window. She looked poignantly frail standing there, her thin shoulders hunched slightly forward as if the burden she was carrying was much too great for her.

Both her parents seemed to start as she came in.

'Alexandra!' Her mother's head jerked up at the sight of her. 'I thought you were still upstairs.'

'I heard voices,' Alexandra replied, half accusingly. 'What on earth is going on?'

Her mother broke away from the window and came towards her, arm outstretched. 'Darling, now is not the time . . .'

'The time for what?' Alexandra broke in, sensing she was about to be unceremoniously dismissed. 'If this concerns me, I have a right to know, surely.'

She saw her mother hesitate. 'Darling . . .' Sarah Drayton ran an unsteady hand through her daughter's hair. 'Daddy and I need time to talk first. After all, we only heard about all this a few minutes ago . . .'

'About all what?' Alexandra's voice was quieter now. A slow niggling fear started to dig at the pit of her stomach.

There was a silence of such intensity that she thought the room would snap.

'About all what?' she repeated. She turned to her father imploringly. 'Daddy, please. I'm not a child.'

'I don't think . . .' her mother began, then stopped as Alexandra's father halted her with a quick gesture.

'Sarah, she's right. She's not a child,' he said. 'She should know the truth.' He spoke, as always, in that calm patient way of his. As if nothing could ruffle him. 'Besides, if there are plans to be discussed, she ought to be part of them. It's her future we're talking about after all, not ours.'

'I know but . . .' Sarah stopped and turned to look out of the window. She shook her head and sighed. 'Oh, what on earth possessed Charles to be such a fool . . .'

'Charles?' Alexandra picked on the word. Fear sent a shiver down her spine. 'Something's happened to him, hasn't it? An accident . . .'

'Yes,' said her mother, the word so soft it was barely audible.

'No,' insisted her father, almost sharply, his voice overriding Sarah's. 'At least, not in the sense you mean.' He looked directly at Alexandra, his grey eyes unflinching. 'I think perhaps you ought to sit down.'

She did so, perching uneasily on the edge of the button-backed chair, the obvious gravity of the situation momentarily unnerving her.

Her father came to stand in front of her, his tall spare shape daunting despite its familiarity. His hand slid inside his jacket pocket to draw out a cigarette case. 'So, Alexandra, the facts.' There was a pause as he lit a cigarette. 'I fear your young Charles has got himself into a bit of a fix,' he said gently, his eyes flicking over her to see her reaction. 'It seems that after he left the Fitzherberts' last night he went on to a party at a . . . a friend of his. An actress. It turned into a rather wild affair, it appears.' He took a long slow drag at his cigarette, his eyes never leaving hers. 'And to cut a long story short, some damn fool brought along some drugs to the party. Cocaine, I believe.'

Her father hesitated. Alexandra glanced up at him. She could deduce nothing from his expression which was almost studiedly impassive.

'And?' she urged.

'There was an accident.'

'Go on,' Alexandra prompted.

'It involved one of the girls.' He hesitated. 'The actress. Apparently she took an overdose of the damn stuff. Been drinking all day, evidently, then took a veritable cocktail of drugs. By the time they got her to hospital it was too late.'

'Too late?'

'They didn't realise what was happening you see. Thought she had just gone to the bedroom to sleep it off.' Her father gave a helpless gesture with his hands. 'When they discovered her she was already unconscious.'

'Oh, God!' Alexandra's voice sank to nothing beneath the weight of the moment.

'She was dead by the time they got her to the hospital apparently. Nothing they could do to save her . . .' Her father watched as she pressed her hands tightly together, struggling to gain mastery of herself. 'But the point is,' he continued evenly, 'there'll have to be an inquest. Charles most probably will be expected to appear.'

'Charles?' She looked up at him, slightly startled. 'But why?' She hesitated, a ghastly, terrible thought coming to her. 'They don't hold Charles responsible, do they?'

'No, not at all.' Her father came to her side and took her hand in his. 'But it's what the papers will make of it, my darling.' He stood there, looking down at her, wondering how much he ought to tell her. 'She was quite a promising young actress I believe, the darling of the Press, and once they know that Charles was there at the party, you know what they'll try and insinuate. The up-and-coming actress and the Lord's son. They'll have a heyday.'

It was taking a while for it all to sink in. 'But Charles can deny all that surely?'

She could see by his face that something was wrong.

Her father ran his hand through his dark hair. 'Charles knew her quite well, I believe,' he said, at last. The nuance was unmistakable.

'Oh, I see.' Alexandra closed her eyes briefly, tried to steady herself. 'I see.' A terrifying sense of unreality swept over her. She dropped her head to her hands.

The telephone in the hallway started to ring. A maid came in to whisper something to her mother. The Press? God, let it not be them just yet . . . She watched her mother leave the room and the hidden implications of Charles's actions last night began to dawn on her.

'So . . .' She raised her eyes up to her father's aquiline face, a myriad of emotions threatening to overwhelm her. 'What's to be done?'

Her father lowered himself onto the arm of the chair and gave her hand another squeeze. 'Don't be too down-hearted, darling,' he said softly, bending forward to kiss her forehead. 'This thing'll blow over pretty soon, you'll see. In the meantime I suggest we postpone the announcement of your engagement for the moment. Lord Kildare has arranged for Charles to go up to their Yorkshire estate until the inquest. Thinks it's prudent for him to be out of the way for the time being. I agree. Then the idea is that Charles will go over to New York for a few months, work with one of the banks there, until it all dies down a bit.'

'I see.'

'And I think it would be wise for you to leave London for a while too. Perhaps you could go up to Drayton Hall for a time . . .'

'Daddy!' To be stuck miles from anywhere with Grandma Drayton would be a fate worse than death. She looked up at him and saw he was smiling. The ploy to get some reaction from her had certainly had its effect.

'Well, then. Where would you like to go? Venice?'

She leant into the crook of his arm. 'Actually, before all this happened, I was thinking of going to Kenya. To see Grandfather . . .' It had been merely an idea once. Now it was a lifeline.

'You know what your mother thinks about that?' Her father shifted his position slightly to peer down at her.

She nodded. 'But you could make her change her mind,' she said confidently. He was capable of anything, her father.

'If that's where you really want to go.'

'It is.' She lifted her head at the sound of the door opening.

Her mother came back into the library. She looked calmer now, more positive. 'That was Lord Kildare on the telephone,' she announced. 'Charles is leaving for Yorkshire immediately. He asked if he might be allowed to see Alexandra before he left. I've agreed to a short meeting . . .' Her eyes swept over Alexandra's face, betraying a flicker of concern. 'But you don't have to see him, darling, if you don't want to . . .'

'Of course I want to see him, Mother,' Alexandra insisted. 'This doesn't alter my feelings for Charles, you know.' Her voice was forthright, steady, but in truth she'd been shocked by the news. And not just by the tragedy. Of course she wasn't so naïve as to believe that Charles's past was blemish-free. But being presented with the facts so brutally and publicly had thrown her.

She looked up to see her mother regarding her with sad understanding. As if she herself knew the inner turmoil and confusion Alexandra was going through at this moment. Impossible, of course: what would her mother know of scandal? Her life had been secure and comfortable with her father. She had never known this feeling of being cast adrift, of discovering that life was nothing more than a fragile layer of ice covering the dark lake of uncertainty.

She heard the sound of a car drawing to a halt outside the house and stiffened, despite her intentions suddenly unprepared for the encounter.

'Chin up,' whispered her father, giving her arm an encouraging squeeze.

She brushed an imaginary particle from her dark trousers and stood up determinedly. But for all her steely resolve she felt like Theseus about to enter the dark, forbidding labyrinth. And as she made her way towards the morning-room and Charles, she forced herself to remember that, despite the hazards of the maze, Theseus had won through in the end.

In the event her meeting with Charles was not nearly as difficult as she had imagined. He had come into the room looking so utterly subdued and forlorn that she had forgotten her anger and hurt; she had held out her arms to him and he had fallen into them, pulling her head against his shoulder.

'I'm so sorry,' he'd said, his voice little more than a whisper. 'So desperately sorry. I wouldn't have dragged you into this for the world . . .'

And she'd known it to be true. He'd stood there suddenly looking so young, so totally unprepared for life, real life, that it had frightened her a little. His face was white, his eyes circled by great bluish shadows, and all the vibrant energy and power which had exuded from him in the past had been extinguished.

She was not used to seeing Charles as a little boy lost, so hopelessly without direction: it unnerved her slightly as if she were looking at a stranger standing there before her.

'It doesn't change things between us, Charles,' she'd told him, knowing how much he would need her reassurance of loyalty. And she had been rewarded by a look of such naked relief that she'd realised then how desperately afraid he'd been that he might lose her.

They'd sat down then and talked, trying to bring some sense of normality back into their lives. But all the while Alexandra had been conscious of the sound of the engine running outside the house, the gentle purr of the chauffeur-driven car, waiting to take Charles up to Yorkshire. It distracted her and she'd barely listened as Charles, in halting sentences, had told her about Kitty, about the party. In truth, she hadn't really wanted to hear the details but she'd let him ramble on, knowing it to be a need for absolution.

'Try and forgive me,' he'd asked her, when he'd finished. And when, looking down at her, he'd seen that she had done so long ago, she had heard him breathe out a grateful sigh of relief. He'd closed his eyes then, letting himself feel a brief moment of forgetfulness in her arms.

She'd been strong then: but now, standing by the window watching the long polished black nose of the Rolls Royce pull away from her sight and glide ponderously on its way to Yorkshire, she felt some of Charles's vulnerability and uncertainty gain hold of her. She felt empty, alone, as if in a way his banishment was hers also.

'Bearing up, little one?'

She turned to find her father standing behind her.

'Sort of.' She couldn't admit to more.

Then her father's comforting arms were round her shoulders, and she turned a little towards him.

'I know this may not be the right time to say such a thing, darling,' he said quietly, 'but you know, this catastrophe may be the making of young Charles. I regret the way this has happened, of course, but it's no bad thing for a man to be tested from time to time. It's how a man deals with his failures and disappointments that shows him for what he is. It's easy to swim with the tide, not so easy to swim back against it.'

She lifted her head up towards him. 'You're not suggesting Charles isn't capable of facing adversities, are you?'

'No, of course not,' he reassured her gently. 'But life has always been so easy for Charles. He's never had to cope with anything he didn't want to in his life. Until now.'

Alexandra looked away from him, fingering the petals of an enormous arrangement of hot-house flowers which adorned the walnut table. He saw that his remarks had hit home.

There was a pause. 'I meant to tell you,' he said, changing tack. 'I've had a word with your mother about Kenya . . .

She lifted her head at that. 'Have you?'

'She's agreed to let you go.'

The colour came back to her face. 'However did you contrive to arrange that?' She even managed a smile.

'With difficulty,' he admitted with a boyish grin. The tension between them seemed to ease. 'Anyway,' he said, moving to stand before the fire, 'it's all settled now. Lady Sharp's sister is going out there later this month, so we're hoping she can accompany you, at least as far as Nairobi. And we'll sort out some friends for you to stay with out there. You probably won't want to stay with Grandfather all the time, you'll want to see as much of the country as possible. Besides, you know he's not been well, you may even find he's not up to having you to stay for long.' He hesitated a little awkwardly, thrusting his hands into his pockets. They both knew he was talking about Grandfather's drinking bouts. No one quite knew what state he'd be in.

For a moment Alexandra was silent. She concentrated on the delicate pale leaves of the cyclamen.

'Daddy, do you know much about Grandfather?' she asked, at last.

'A bit, why?'

'What's he really like?'

Her father half turned from the fire. His grey eyes seemed to look beyond her, as if searching back in time to distant memories. He smiled. 'Well, from all reports I'd say a beguiling character,' he said. 'Apparently, he was the sort of man who'd come into a roomful of people, stir them all up, and leave totally unaware of the havoc he'd wreaked. He was domineering, uncompromising, yet had such unbridled enthusiasm that he would sweep anyone and anything along in his tide. Most of the people I met who knew him described him as the most captivating of men.'

Alexandra picked up the cushion from the sofa beside her and started playing with the braid which edged it. 'Then why does Mother talk about him in such disparaging terms?' she asked. 'She's so bitter about him. Has she always hated him so?'

'Oh, my darling, how little you understand!' said her father, giving her a look, half sad, half amused. 'She adored him, don't you see? Idolised him.' His hands went on in an expansive gesture. 'He was like a god to her. And when he ruined the estate – and himself – she felt betrayed by him, let down.' A smouldering log stirred in the grate, threatening to tumble forwards; her father leant forward and pushed it back into place with a gentle nudge of his shoe. 'I could have warned her. Told her. It doesn't do to make mere mortals into gods, you know. They have a habit of falling from the pedestals on which they've been forced to stand.'

So many pieces were tumbling into place. 'So, in a way, all these years she's been punishing Grandfather for not living up to her own expectations of him,' Alexandra said slowly. She thought of Charles and of how easy it was to demand too much of other people, how easy to let disappointment turn to anger.

'You mustn't blame your mother,' her father said quickly, careful as always to exonerate Sarah's actions. 'It couldn't have been easy to watch someone you love so completely gradually destroy himself . . .'

'I can see that,' admitted Alexandra. She put the cushion back on the sofa, guiltily aware that she had almost demolished the braid thread by thread. She grimaced. There was still one piece of the jigsaw, though, that was missing. 'But why did Grandfather go to pieces like that? What started it? Self-destruction doesn't sound like the action of the man you described earlier.'

'Perhaps it was sheer loneliness,' her father said quietly. 'He'd lost Sarah, remember. She'd come over here and married me, and Amelia had come over too, never to return. But who can tell?' He gave a slight shrug. 'Sometimes a small, seemingly unimportant rock can start a landslide, can't it?'

'I suppose so.' There was a hint of disappointment in Alexandra's voice. She had put her grandfather down as a fighter.

'But whatever,' her father was saying, 'I think he's been punished enough, don't you? I think it's time for a little forgiveness.'

'Yes.' She thought about Charles again, of his pale, drawn face pressed close against the window of the Rolls Royce as it edged its way remorselessly northwards. 'Yes,' she said again, 'I do.'

'And I'm glad you're the one to carry the olive branch out to him, Alexandra.' Her father stretched out an arm to her. 'I have a feeling you and he will understand each other well.'

'So do I.' She laughed. She knew her father was referring to their wilful natures.

Seeing that smile, that toss of the head, George Drayton was struck anew as to how like her mother she was. It brought back to him most poignantly the Sarah he had first met in London all those years ago. For a moment he wondered if he were doing the right thing in allowing Alexandra to go over to Kenya. He knew how much Edward Sinclair had adored his daughter, had missed her when she had gone. He worried that Alexandra's arrival would serve as a cruel reminder of all those years he had lost. Could it not reopen old wounds, emphasising what might have been?

He closed his hand over Alexandra's. 'If it doesn't work out, you'll come straight home, won't you?' he said, suddenly serious.

Alexandra laughed, dismissing his fears with the confidence of youth. 'But of course it will work out,' she protested, her green eyes bright with certainty.

'But if it doesn't,' he persisted. 'You will leave straight away, won't you? Promise me . . .'

Something in his face, in the tone of his voice, made her look up. She was aware of a hint of warning in his tone. There was no flippancy in her reply this time. 'All right,' she said, with unaccustomed caution. 'I promise.'

3

Low voices carried across the early morning calm as the *Empress* steamed its way past palm-fringed cliffs into Kalindini harbour. Alexandra, leaning against the railings of the promenade deck, watched with growing excitement as the low green island of Mombasa unfurled before her like a languid leaf against the sunlight.

Now that her destination was in sight, all her fears of being disappointed by this strange country – or worse still of hating it on first sight – seemed as flimsy as thistledown, instantly dispelled by the sheer exotic brilliance of the scene before her.

Nowhere but in Africa could there be such shades of colour. Flame-trees threw umbrellas against the torrential light, bougainvillaeas were everywhere – cherry red, brilliant orange; hibiscus twined with oleanders, while the delicate creamy flowers of the frangipani stood out against the dark foliage of the mango trees like shy bridesmaids at a wedding. The riot of colour had an intensity that overwhelmed the distant forms of the white lime-washed houses and red-tiled roofs, even the tall scarred walls of Fort Jesus which stood solemnly guarding the harbour.

'Hard to believe we're actually here, isn't it?'

At the sound of a girl's voice, Alexandra turned to find the tall dark-haired figure of Jane Stanhope crossing the scrubbed deck towards her. Jane came up beside her and draped her long arms over the railings, stooping a little to rest her chin against her hands.

'Heavens, what a relief it is to think we shall be on dry land soon,' she continued with an expressive grin. 'I swear I never want to see another deck quoit again as long as I live, do you?'

'Absolutely not.' Alexandra laughed as their eyes met. 'How

can such a preposterous game be taken so seriously?' And taken seriously it had been, with fierce competitions raging almost without an interval, regardless of the heat or the surging seas.

Jane grimaced at the memory. 'Don't you remember how furious Captain Malahide was to be beaten by old Mrs Bowden in the finals?' she recalled with amusement. 'Delighted, I was. He'd been boasting all the way to Aden how easily he'd sweep the board with us.' She wrinkled her freckled nose. 'Wasn't he just the most insufferable man? So arrogant. Do you know he gave one poor cadet positive hell one morning for occupying his deckchair? As if it *mattered*! I took great delight in sitting in it the next day, pretending not to notice his fearful glares!'

Alexandra giggled. Jane had been her saviour on this voyage. Resourceful, amusing, she had proved an enlivening antidote to the tedium of the journey. They had met on the first day out of port and had taken an instant liking to each other. Jane was on her way out to join her husband of only a few months on his farm up beyond Lake Nakuru on the western side of the Aberdare Hills and knew as little of the life that lay ahead as did Alexandra. It was a comfort to them both to feel that they were not alone in their underlying sense of vulnerability. Together they could laugh about their fears, encourage and share their hopes for the future. It was a friendship formed in such raw openness that they both knew it would last a lifetime.

An easy silence fell between them as they leant against the railings watching the rugged Moorish buildings of Mombasa taking shape before them. Alexandra shielded her eyes against the glare. It all seemed more exotic than she had imagined somehow, although she had known it would be very Arab in appearance. On the voyage out a fellow passenger who had sat at her table for dinner had taken much delight in telling her of the long and bloody history of Mombasa; of the three centuries of struggle between the Arabs and the Portuguese for the possession of the island and the coast of Azania. Now she could see all too clearly the result of that struggle in the exotic blend of its buildings; she was aware too, that, even though Mombasa was a British protectorate, the Arab law continued to be practised, and the Muslim faith as well as various Arab customs was still observed.

The ship's engines shuddered and fell into a low pounding rhythm.

They were nearing the docks. It was a disappointment to Alexandra that now that the new docks were built they would not be taken ashore by the colourful dhows which long ago had carried her mother and her family to land. The staid gangplank that awaited them wasn't part of the image she had of Mombasa and its history of turmoil.

She turned her face to the wind, scrutinising the crowd which had gathered on the quayside below, wryly observing the odd mixture of culture and costumes, Arabs and Africans, white settlers and military all standing cheek by jowl.

Beside her, she felt Jane pressing hard against the railings, craning her neck even further to see across the jostling mass. She seemed to catch her breath, every inch of her body tensing.

'Oh, Alexandra, what do I do if Tom hasn't managed to find time to get away?' she asked, none of the old buoyant confidence apparent now. 'He said he'd try but . . .'

'Of course he'll come,' Alexandra said soothingly. She slipped her arm around her friend's shoulders. 'You'll see.'

'I don't think . . .' Jane began then let out a very unladylike squeak. 'Oh, Alexandra, he's here! I can see him!' Her cheeks were suddenly very pink, her brown eyes glistening. 'Oh, do look, Alexandra! There!'

She began to wave vigorously over the railings towards a slim, deeply tanned young man who, on hearing her shouts, lifted his hat to wave back with equal energy and delight.

Alexandra watched their frenzied antics for a moment then pulled back from the railings. Silly, of course, to let herself think of Charles at this moment. Impossible not to, though. Something about Tom standing there, his brown hair tousled by the wind, waving his hat with such abandon had reminded her so acutely of Charles and his unfettered sense of fun and gaiety. She drew back.

She had tried so hard not to think of Charles over these past few weeks, pushing him from her mind as best she could. But now, seeing Jane's excitement at the sight of Tom, she felt an acute sense of loss. How different her arrival here was from her frenzied departure from England. There she had been surrounded by loving friends and family – even her little brother Hugh had been allowed out from prep school for the day to see her off. Here there was no one.

She compressed her lips tight together and brought her chin up with a jerk. It would never do to start feeling sorry for herself now. She must think of what lay ahead of her, not behind. Think of the adventures, not of the disappointments.

She straightened her shoulders, suddenly conscious of Jane's excited babble beside her.

'So you will come, won't you?'

'What?'

'You haven't been listening, have you?' complained Jane with a little sigh of exasperation. 'I've been telling you that Tom wrote saying that everyone should see the old town of Mombasa before they leave. Apparently it's fascinating and there's just time before the up-country train leaves at half-past four. You've got to come!'

'Nonsense,' Alexandra protested, embarrassed lest her sense of vulnerability had shown through. 'You and Tom will want to be together. I can go with Mrs Sheldrake.'

'Mrs Sheldrake won't want to venture to the Old Town. You know very well she'll find the nearest comfortable hotel in which to decamp with her wretched bridge four and continue to play as if she's still ensconced at Eaton Square!'

Alexandra smiled at the truth of Jane's words. She had seen little of Mrs Sheldrake, her parents' chosen escort for the entire voyage. On the first day out of port Mrs Sheldrake had formed a bridge four and had hardly stirred from the first-class lounge thereafter. She had seen none of the delights of Port Said or Aden, none of the breathtaking sunsets over the wild, rocky shores of Somalia, none of the enchantments of the white-beached coastline. Certainly she would not bother with Mombasa and secretly Alexandra was convinced that Miss Sheldrake's opinion of Kenya would rest not on the beauty of the country nor the charm of its people, but merely on the success or otherwise of the rubbers she'd played.

Nevertheless, despite Jane's pearls of wisdom, she tried to stand firm. 'Listen, it hardly makes for a romantic reunion for you and Tom to have me tagging along with you both, does it?' she told her friend pointedly.

'For heaven's sake, Tom and I have years to be alone together,' returned Jane prosaically, thinking of the farm which lay miles away from its nearest neighbour. 'Come on, don't be a goose, I want you to come. Really.'

'I'm quite capable of going by myself you know.'

'I'm well aware of that,' Jane returned sweetly. 'Besides, I know for certain that if you weren't to come with us there'd be a dozen or so young cadets from the ship positively clamouring to escort you! I'm asking you because I thought it'd be fun for us all to go together.' Her hand went up to catch her hat as a sudden gust of wind threatened to blow it overboard. 'Honestly Alexandra, you do like to invent problems for yourself.'

'I most certainly do not!' returned Alexandra, indignantly, realising too late the trap she'd let herself fall into.

'Well then, that's settled,' Jane said, pushing home her advantage. 'And I promise you that if Tom is too horrified that I've invited someone else to come with us, then I'll banish you immediately! There, does that make you feel any better?'

'Heaps.'

Jane ignored the sliver of sarcasm which had penetrated Alexandra's voice.

'Good,' she purred. 'Then I'll meet you in the Customs Hall in about ten minutes.'

She might have said more but at that moment they heard the noisy rattling of the gangplank being brought into place as the ship docked against the quayside.

For a moment Jane stood stock still, almost as if she couldn't believe they had finally reached their destination, that now there was not even the smallest speck of ocean between herself and Tom. Then, forgetting all her mother's long lecture about the impropriety of any public display of emotion, she was down the gangplank with a great shout, running as fast as she could into her husband's outstretched arms.

They boarded the up-country train late that afternoon having spent a gloriously tiring day exploring. Under Tom's guidance they had weaved this way and that, in and out of the narrow winding streets, buffeted by black and brown bodies and assailed by a mixture of pungent and exotic scents: sweetened coffee mingled with spices and dried fish; the fragrances from colourful creepers and aromatic bushes wafted against the earthy odours of sweat and dung, all the smells of land and sea coming together in a powerful, heady mix, the like of which Alexandra had never before encountered.

She had been fascinated by it all, but for her the most beguiling place had been the old harbour. It had seemed like a scene straight out of the Arabian Nights, with the delicate wooden dhows lying almost hull to hull, their lateen sails furled; and fierce-looking sailors in their brightly printed *kekois* with curved Arabian daggers at their belts, cooking on charcoal braziers and chewing on betel nuts. She would have liked to have spent longer there but Tom insisted that they head back to the station for fear of missing the train.

As it happened they need not have worried. A huge piece of machinery was being loaded onto one of the freight carriages and was causing considerable chaos.

Tom cast an envious eye at the wooden crates as they walked past them.

'New farm machinery!' he remarked a little covetously. 'What I would give for that! Mine is so antiquated I think they must have been some of the original pieces from the Agricultural Revolution.' He gave Jane a wry smile. 'Well, I suppose we ought to be grateful that some lucky devil is doing well enough to afford it. Perhaps it bodes well for the rest of us!'

There was no self-pity in his voice but Alexandra sensed the underlying tension to his words.

Jane took his arm and gave it a tight squeeze. 'It'll get better, Tom!' she insisted gently. 'You'll see!'

Tom forced a smile. 'Can't get worse, I suppose. And at least those damn locusts seem to have given up on us this year . . .'

His tone was light but it had been a dreadful past few years. Apart from the locusts which, in their great black swarms, had devoured everything and anything in their path, here in Kenya the depression had its stranglehold as on everywhere else, too. The farmers' plight was almost desperate, with a whole bag of maize fetching only enough to buy one gallon of petrol, if that. He glanced quickly at Jane. He'd told her the truth before he'd asked her to marry him, told her there were long years of hard toil in front of them before they could build up the farm, but he wondered if she really understood how precarious their existence might be.

As if sensing which way his mind was running Jane looked up at him and smiled. 'Don't worry, my darling, I can take locusts and drought and whatever else might be foisted upon us,' she told him reassuringly. 'And there'll be two of us to face it now.'

'Half the worry, half the burden . . .' Tom laughed, slipping his arm around his wife's shoulder and drawing her close. He knew now he hadn't misjudged her. Pink and pretty misses were all very well but it was those with steely backbone and resolve that Kenya needed.

There was a clatter and a great shout behind them as the porters struggled with the last crate.

Tom glanced over his shoulder. 'Heaven help them if they drop that lot!' he exclaimed dryly. 'The proud owner will have been waiting for the best part of a year for it to get here and I doubt if he'll be any too pleased if it arrives in more pieces than intended!'

Aware that delays and disappointments were very much a part of the life here, Alexandra was beginning to deduce that the only way to survive them was with humour rather than irascibility.

They continued to push their way up along the platform through the jostling crowd, past beaded women thrusting bananas and oranges up at the passengers from the gravel below, past jostling Africans in tattered shirts and red blankets, past suited Europeans and their inevitable line of porters.

At last they arrived at Alexandra's carriage.

'What luck!' exclaimed Jane, glancing further down the train. 'Our compartment is only two down from yours so you've an easy escape route if Mrs Sheldrake becomes too impossibly boring.'

'Jane, hush!' implored Alexandra, only too aware that Mrs Sheldrake was already ensconced in the compartment and could probably hear every word they spoke.

Undeterred, Jane grinned mischievously. 'So, we'll give you a chance to settle in and to hear all about the wonders of bridge and then we'll come and rescue you for dinner. Is that all right?'

Alexandra laughed, despite herself. 'Perfect,' she agreed. 'And if Tom is half-way as knowledgeable about the rest of Africa as he was about Mombasa I shall arrive in Nairobi feeling quite at home!'

Tom made a wide-eyed grimace. 'God! Was I that boring on our tour?' he asked with a grin. 'There's nothing I hate more than somebody who thinks they have something to say on every subject.'

'We'll come and retrieve you in about an hour then,' Jane told her as she stepped up into the carriage. 'Or sooner if you like . . .' She gave a huge wink, implying that the delights of Mrs Sheldrake describing card by card the play of the afternoon would wear thin long before.

Which was all too possible, thought Alexandra, as she stowed her luggage away, listening with only half an ear as Mrs Sheldrake recounted the afternoon's rubber. It would mean nothing to her, it seemed, that the train on which they were about to travel had such a stirring history. It had been a most remarkable piece of engineering through near-impossible terrain. But it was not that which had captured Alexandra's imagination as a child when she had read the story – it was the amazing feat of endurance by the men who had built it, the thousands of Asians brought into Kenya for just that purpose.

Theirs had been an unhappy lot and Alexandra had devoured the tales she had been told about the man-eating lions of Tsavo who had regarded the workers as easy pickings; about the pitiless heat, or the marauding tribes who had pilfered and looted and who, worse, had slaughtered the surveyors and work parties who had been foolish enough to enter their territory. She had never quite understood the purpose of the extravagant railway which had seemed to lead through uninhabited wilderness to nowhere in particular; but then, judging by its nickname – the Lunatic Express – neither had a lot of other people.

Outside there was a buzz of frantic last-minute activity. Then the train started to pull out of the station to the accompanying shouts of the Africans crowded together into the third-class coaches behind.

Slowly, like a black snake across the sands, the train slid its way past the monstrous glistening baobabs and the brilliant creepers, past the coconuts and the cultivation, climbing all the time until at last it reached the open bush.

Alexandra stared out of the window. As far as the eye could see the countryside was featureless and flat; not even a tree was visible, and the vegetation looked twisted and stunted, as if too tired to stand up straight and lift its head. The heat-baked sand and stones gave off a faintly ghostly sheen, and she could imagine the Arab caravans of old with their haul of ivory and slaves trudging their way over this vast expanse of waste towards the Great Lakes.

It was all so barren out there; not at all as Alexandra had pictured it. There wasn't even any wildlife, as far as she could make out in the fading light. She felt vaguely cheated by it all, and told Jane as much later that evening at dinner.

'It'll be different tomorrow,' Tom assured her across the white-linened table. 'You'll see. When you wake up in the morning you'll find it positively teeming with game out there. The whole caboodle. Giraffes, gazelles, wildebeest, even some lions if we're lucky.' He took a sip of wine. 'I saw a whole pride not fifty yards from the tracks on the way down. Didn't even budge as we roared past.'

'Not like in the old days when they'd try to take a bite out of any passerby,' Alexandra remarked.

'Absolutely. Although it wasn't always that way round. When the line was first opened, if they saw an exceptionally fine specimen they'd stop the train. Once, when a particularly important official spotted one out of the window they stopped the train for hours near Tsavo while he disembarked to hunt down the lion. They arrived in Nairobi half a day late, I gather!'

'With or without the lion?' Jane enquired dryly, jabbing at a piece of mutton on her plate.

'With,' Tom replied with a smile.

He paused while an African waiter in his spotless white *kanzu* refilled his glass. 'Now the line has smartened up no end and they wouldn't dream of stopping for a lion! It's called progress, I suppose. Though I'm not so sure. Half the charm of this line was its unpredictability. Now one can be sure of arriving in Nairobi on time half the sense of adventure has gone!'

They all laughed.

'Actually I'm rather looking forward to getting to Nairobi,' said Jane, leaning back in her seat and stretching languidly.

'Don't put too much store by the place, my darling,' Tom warned her. 'For all its two cinemas and veneer of sophistication, it's still a bit like Dodge City at the end of the cattle drive!' In atmosphere at least. Last time he'd been in Nairobi, after a few drinks at the Norfolk, he and his more exuberant friends had had races up and down Sixth Avenue in 'borrowed' rickshaws.

'Like that, is it?' Jane laughed. 'Heaven help us then!' She turned to Alexandra. 'Your grandfather's going to meet you in Nairobi, isn't he?'

Alexandra nodded. 'He's coming down by car. He wired us that

I should meet him in the Norfolk Hotel rather than at the station. In case he was delayed, I suppose.'

'Infinitely sensible,' Tom approved. 'The roads can be hellish. Go too fast into a dried up *donga* and before you know it you've got to walk miles to find help, and then wait to be towed rather ignominiously home by a team of oxen!'

'That sounds distinctly like personal experience,' ventured Jane, looking across at him with a bright smile.

'It is,' he admitted dolefully. 'But I shouldn't laugh too freely, my darling, because in the wet the driving is even more precarious. You find yourself slithering all over the place, even with chains on the back wheels!'

'Then I shall develop the habit of staying at home,' announced Jane.

Tom stretched over to take her hand. He wasn't sure how much she was teasing. 'Actually, you soon get the hang of it. It's just a knack driving over these country roads,' he reassured her. 'Before long you'll be zooming your way into Kitale and Eldoret.'

'I'm sure I will,' Jane agreed emphatically. She was not one to dwell on difficulties for long.

Alexandra turned to stare out of the window. It was now pitch-black. In Africa night closed in like a shutter, quickly and absolutely; there was no long-drawn-out twilight here.

Behind them, a young official in a clean new khaki suit, perfectly pressed, shiny brass buttons agleam, appeared to be having difficulty explaining to the waiter that he had ordered something other than the steamed spotted-dick pudding which had been placed so determinedly in front of him.

It was a losing battle. The hesitant Swahili which the young man spoke quickly deteriorated into loud, verbose English and finally into the inevitable vigorous sign language. The waiter continued to looked baffled until, at last, with a smile he took the plate away. But the official's smug look of triumph at his success was cut short a few minutes later at the sight of the waiter advancing towards him with precisely the same pudding, now suitably smothered in custard.

Alexandra tried not to laugh, but there was something about the young man's pomposity which made her want to side automatically with the African waiter.

'Oh dear,' Tom said quietly finishing the last of his coffee. 'We always get one like that on these trips. Newly in from England, and quite determined that everything should run by the book. Quite hopeless, of course. The only way to survive here is to adapt and adapt again!'

'Reminds me of the odious Captain Malahide; doesn't it you, Alexandra?' asked Jane with a grimace.

'Yes,' agreed Alexandra. 'Just as tiresome.'

They fell into giggles and recited to Tom some of the more heinous of Captain's Malahide's crimes. How far away it all seemed now.

Alexandra sighed and stretched, 'I think I'd better turn in,' she said. 'It'll be a long day tomorrow.'

'For all of us,' agreed Jane. The journey up past Eldoret would take them well past nightfall.

Alexandra bid them both good night and made her way back along the juddering train to her compartment. The all-consuming blackness of the Tara Desert seemed to press against the window-panes, almost with a power of its own. She was glad of the burning brightness of her compartment when she slid back the door.

The African steward had been in while she had been at dinner and had converted the long seats into beds, neatly laying out the bedrolls. Mrs Sheldrake was already settled for the night, hair-net and face-cream in place, the thin white sheet pulled up over her plump shoulders.

'While you're up, my dear, open the window, will you?' she called across to Alexandra, glancing up from her bridge book. 'It's awfully hot in here.'

'It is, isn't it?' agreed Alexandra. 'But Tom Stanhope has just warned me that the dust from the Tara gets everywhere and it's best to keep the windows closed if you can.'

Mrs Sheldrake looked slightly put out. 'Personally, I never thought a bit of fresh air hurt anyone,' she muttered, pointedly waving her book in front of her to emphasise how hot it was. 'But I suppose if you think you know best I shall just have to swelter all night . . .'

The next morning, when Alexandra awoke, she was extremely glad she hadn't succumbed to Mrs Sheldrake's pressure. Even with the windows closed tight the red dust had insinuated its way in and a thin film covered almost everything. Had the window been open their hair and clothes and belongings would have been coated and stiff with the red powder.

But her exasperation at the dust was short-lived. Outside, as she drew back the blind, was a world transformed. Forever embedded in her memory would be that sight: the sun rising over the highveld of Africa.

Like a great copper gong it drifted above the horizon sending its thin pure light flooding out like molten gold across the grassy savannah. It picked out every fold in the surface of the plain, every weather-warped, twisted thorn tree, rolling up the long shadows thrown out by the rocks so that soon the grass and trees and bush and anthills were swathed in sunlight, springing to a new golden life of their own. And rising in silent splendour in the background Mount Kilimanjaro, majestic in its ruff of clouds. Alexandra was overawed by the sheer numbers of game which drifted like a shifting shoal across the plain. They no longer seemed perturbed by the train that rattled noisily by. Close-packed, gracefully horned gazelles grazed close to the tracks, their tails a-wag; while beyond them great shining herds of zebras and wildebeeste in their thousands unhurriedly sifted their way across the grasslands.

Even Mrs Sheldrake, for once, was overwhelmed by the sight, bestirring herself from her bed to come and stand beside Alexandra at the window.

'My dear, it doesn't seem possible, does it?' she remarked, taking off her hair-net and crimping up her curls carefully with her manicured fingers. 'So many. And last night there was nothing.'

Alexandra nodded. 'It makes it all the more startling, doesn't it?' She pressed her face even closer to the thin glass to catch sight of two dappled giraffes, tall and beautiful, as they moved off into the distance, their peculiar rocking gait making them look like two tall-masted ships upon a stormy sea.

The herds, dotted here and there, seemed to melt into the distance. But every so often some particular group or movement would catch Alexandra's eye: a pride of lions sloping off into a thick-bushed gully, a pair of lithe hunting cheetahs trailing the herds, a troop of absurd-looking warthogs with their darting run and their tails sticking straight up in the air like Roman standards held aloft; a procession of rhinos, the leader halting as he smelt the train, swinging a lowered head round to face it, looking for all the world as if he were intent on charging the train itself in sheer outraged fury at its intrusion. All these – like precious gems in an already glittering crown.

There was a knock at the door. It was Jane, looking wonderfully fresh and cool in a smart printed silk dress which Alexandra hadn't seen before.

'Are you ready for breakfast?' she asked brightly, leaning a silver-bangled arm up against the doorway.

'Not yet,' admitted Alexandra. The charm of the morning had left her in no mood to rush. 'You two go on ahead. I'll join you in a few minutes.'

'Lazy-bones!' Jane teased her. 'Well, you'd better get a move on, you know. We'll be in Nairobi before you know it.' The excitement in her voice was obvious. 'I'll see you in the dining car then. Don't be long!'

'I won't.'

After she'd gone, Alexandra sat on the edge of her bed brushing out her hair in slow, careful movements. In a few short hours she'd be in Nairobi. In a few short hours she would see the grandfather she had so longed to meet.

It was what she had wanted, what she had fought to be allowed to do. So why then was there this tightening nub of doubt in her stomach, and a niggling sense of foreboding?

The Norfolk Hotel had changed little since its first days, save for the removal of the hitching post from the front of the verandah. Approached by a long line of gum trees it was substantial and spacious and although, as Mrs Sheldrake vocally pointed out, it was not as grand as the now fashionable Torr's, nor as luxurious as the New Stanley, it was a welcome resting point for Alexandra.

There was no sign of her grandfather when she arrived and Alexandra was grateful that her father had insisted on booking a room for her, although at the time she had teased him about extravagancy. Downstairs there was a hubbub of people greeting one another after long absences or saying their farewells, groups preparing for safaris, friends just meeting for morning coffee. There was a general ebb and flow of human bodies which made the hotel seem only marginally less hectic than the station she had just left.

Upstairs, she was relieved to find, it was much more peaceful. She kicked off her shoes and walked over to the window. From here she could see down the long avenue towards the heart of town. It was not at all as she had expected it to be. It had none of the impressive presence of Mombasa, none of its sense of history.

Nairobi, despite its effort at refinement, seemed to Alexandra to betray its beginnings as a railway town, never quite escaping its image as a frontier post. Standing here, she could well imagine Lord Delamere and his cronies galloping up the street to the hotel to carry out their boyish pranks, shooting out the lights of the police station to the outrage of the law and the amusement of the settlers. It seemed just a step away.

She glanced down into the sunlit street below. Motor cars were pushing their way gingerly past the lumbering ox-carts. The scene seemed to epitomise Nairobi. It looked like a town trying to force its way into the present and European grandeur, with its Imperial National Museum; yet never quite losing its past, with its Indian quarter and the African markets and *shambas*. Imposing stone buildings and tin shanties stood side by side, banks that would not disgrace Pall Mall looking down on infinitely inferior neighbours. It seemed to Alexandra a place in the midst of change, where on one corner she could see smart glass-fronted shops, and on the next native women, scantily attired, carrying on their heads long boat-shaped hampers full of skinny hens.

She turned back from the window at the sound of a tap at the door.

'Can I come in?' Jane poked her head around the door. She had evidently finished her shopping tasks in record time. 'I've left Tom checking our supplies,' she said. 'He's having to go through every single box in minute detail so I thought I'd come on over. I'm not too early am I?'

'Not at all. Grandfather's not even here yet.'

'Good. That'll give us all the more time to talk, won't it?' Jane said with a grin, coming over to flop down on the bed. 'I was terribly afraid that your grandfather might have come and swept you away already.'

'No chance of that.'

There was a slight tension to her voice which Jane didn't miss. By means of distraction she picked up a broad-brimmed hat which lay on the bed beside her and held it clownishly aloft. 'Do look,' she insisted mirthfully. 'Tom's latest present to me. He insisted that the sun-hat I brought out from England wasn't nearly enough to protect me.' She put it on and posed, head tilted, hand tucked under her chin. 'What do you think? Not exactly *Vogue*, is it?'

'Well, I doubt Chanel will be using it for her collection next year,' admitted Alexandra. 'But it does look eminently practical.'

'It is.' Jane grimaced, and swinging her legs round to the edge of the bed, stood up. 'But not nearly so practical as the boots.'

Alexandra peered down at Jane's legs and saw only light-weight shoes. 'Boots?' she enquired, confused.

'Yes, boots,' Jane said, warming to her theme. 'I left those behind with Tom – they were so hideous. Can you imagine, there I was in my Worth silk dress standing in Eadie's Store encased in these . . . well, they were workman's boots, I swear to you.'

'Workman's boots?' Alexandra chortled. 'Good heavens, Jane, what exactly is Tom expecting you to do up at the farm?'

'Nothing,' insisted Jane glibly. 'Apparently they're to protect me from the snakes when I'm walking through the fields. Though since he also tells me that the black mamba can move faster than a galloping horse I'm not really sure what help he expects them to be anyway. If I'm going to have to run that fast, I'd have thought I'd have been better off in my plimsolls!'

They fell into shrieks of laughter. There were just too many hazards for any one alone to be taken seriously and dwelt upon.

There was a tap at the door. Alexandra opened it to reveal one of the African boys from the hotel standing there in his immaculate white *kanzu*. With great aplomb he handed her a telegram.

Alexandra took the envelope and ripped it open. 'It's from Grandfather,' she said, glancing at the name at the top. The slight sensation of foreboding she had felt on the train was beginning to gather strength.

'Don't say he's still at Thika,' exclaimed Jane, coming to her side.

'He is, I'm afraid.' Alexandra sank down onto the bed, tucking one leg under her. 'Seems there's been a problem. He's asking me to catch the next train up to Thika. Says he'll be there to meet me.'

'Oh, Lord!' said Jane gloomily. 'Do you think you ought? I mean, do you think he's reliable?'

'He sent me the telegram, didn't he?' Alexandra returned defensively. 'Besides, what else can I do?' That, of course, was much more to the point.

'Tom might have an idea,' said Jane hopefully. 'Perhaps he might know of someone going over that way . . .'

'I doubt it,' remarked Alexandra. 'Besides, by the time we've sent another telegram to Grandfather there'll be an awful confusion.'

Jane fed the rim of her hat through her fingers reflectively. 'I suppose nothing can go wrong, really, can it?' she said, at last. 'I mean, he's obviously in a position to meet you at the station, otherwise he wouldn't have telegraphed you to come up.'

'Exactly.'

'Well then, what time's the train?'

Alexandra glanced back at the telegram. 'He doesn't say. I expect reception will know. There's probably only one a day.'

'More than likely,' agreed Jane. 'I'll go and ask, shall I? You can get your bags together, just in case.'

She was back a few minutes later, decidedly out of breath. 'It leaves in ten minutes,' she squeaked. 'Just chuck your bags together. Tom's downstairs. He says he'll drive us.'

'We'll never make it!'

'Yes, we will!' Jane grabbed her bags from her and they started along the passage at breakneck speed. 'Come on.' They sped through the lobby and down the wide verandah steps to Tom's waiting car.

Somehow they negotiated their way past the pedestrians, the mule-drawn buggies and the ox-carts, the short round snout of the car edging its way past the everyday hazards of Nairobi's streets with a faintly rakish air. Alexandra, wedged in the back-seat amongst the parcels and the baggages, thought she would never emerge in one piece. The problem of catching the train dimmed in comparison to that of her immediate safety, but eventually they skidded to a halt outside the station.

It was less crowded now than when she had stepped off the Mombasa train that morning but just as noisy, full of the shriek and rattle of imminent mechanised departure. They ran along the side of the train, a porter tagging relentlessly behind until they found a promising-looking compartment.

Tom pulled open the door for her. 'Up you go,' he said, helping her on to the train.

'Don't forget to write,' called up Jane. 'And you've got to come and see us. You've got all the details, so there's no excuse!'

'I will!' It was almost impossible to hear above the noise. 'As soon as I'm settled.'

She closed the door behind her and blew Jane a kiss through the open window. The train almost imperceptibly started to move. She waved to them, leaning out of the window, calling out her farewells to them, until their figures were swallowed up by the crowds on the platform.

The artificial light of the high-roofed station gave way to the brilliant blue sky of a perfect Kenyan morning. Outside the town quickly evaporated and sun-baked Africa reasserted itself. Alexandra sat by the window, watching the pale dustladen grass and twisted trees slip past. A sense of exhilaration pushed its way through her weariness. Finally, finally, she was on her way.

It did not occur to her, as the train lumbered northwards, that her grandfather, unaware that his telegram had been delivered with such unusual promptness, was not expecting her to arrive in Thika until the following afternoon.

4

Robert Dalgleish tipped his broad-brimmed hat to the back of his head and leant one arm languidly against the station wall. It was a movement of contrived slowness which did nothing to mask the restless energy that seemed to pulse through him.

He stood a little apart from the rest of the milling crowd, his face alert, his eyes watchful. It looked as if he were appraising each and everyone of them: yet, in truth, his thoughts were miles away, back at the farm he had left more than a hour before.

He had had a hellish morning.

It had begun with the boy driving the tractor too close to the ox team and spooking them so badly that it had taken over an hour to untangle them without cutting the rawhide traces. A series of minor – but time-consuming – mishaps followed, and then his uncle had announced crustily that he had no intention of driving all the way down to Thika to supervise the loading of the new farm machinery which was due to arrive there that day.

'Too damn hot!' he had complained.

Robert would have been irritated by such peevishness had he not suspected that it was something more menacing than heat which had deterred his uncle. The scorching sun had never stopped Cameron Dalgleish from doing what he wished in the past. And he recalled that over the past few months his uncle had started to puff over short distances, pausing for breath when it seemed he had barely walked five paces.

He had tried to make his uncle see a doctor but persuading him to do such a sensible thing had proved difficult.

'My God! Can't a man grow old in peace!' he had shouted at

Robert when he had suggested that he see Dr Silvester. 'A man's entitled to slow down a bit at my age!'

Robert had dropped the subject, feeling it wiser at this stage not to point out that Cameron Dalgleish was not even nearing sixty yet. Besides, his uncle was as obdurate as an ox, impossibly so, and Robert knew from experience that he would consult a doctor when *he* thought the time was right. No amount of cajoling would persuade him otherwise.

Robert found his uncle's intractability maddening at times, but he knew that for a man to survive out here he had to have steely resolve. And Cameron Dalgleish was a survivor.

He had come out to East Africa in 1906, six years after the Uganda Railway had reached its terminus on Lake Victoria. Together with his brother, Alastair, Robert's father, he had taken a chunk of dusty wilderness and turned it into a thriving estate.

Now he was the envy of the district, expanding while others were contracting, and he'd just bought himself a sizeable plot out on the other side of the Aberdares beyond Gilgil. Though perhaps it was this latest venture which had brought him to such a state of exhaustion.

Why his uncle should resist easing up, Robert had no idea. He had nothing to prove. Or more precisely, no one left to prove it to. Perhaps he merely wanted to go down fighting. Robert smiled. He could understand that sentiment.

He straightened and pushed away from the post at the sound of the train approaching from down the valley. The two tiny brilliant fire-finches dust-bathing close to his feet stopped suddenly and with a final shake of their glittery wings flew off into the bush. Robert turned and issued a brisk volley of Swahili instructions to a group of men standing in the shade, and they came forward eagerly. The arrival of this new machinery had been a long-awaited event and they were enjoying being a part of the general excitement.

Robert followed them down to the end of the train. The two crates had been lashed to the top of the open goods truck and would need to be eased down gently. He unleashed another volley of instructions, carefully detailed so that there would be no misunderstandings. All the same, two of the men decided they should have the honour of taking what was considered the lead side and a heated exchange broke out between them.

Robert cut it short instantly. 'Wanyamo! This side – now.' Only the sharpest and most direct approach would work in this case, he knew. Exchanges could last for hours if not dealt with promptly and they were holding up the train as it was.

As sulkily as a child who has had its prized toy taken away, Wanyamo went to the other side, brightening only when Robert told him that if he did his task well he could have the lead side with the second crate.

It wasn't until they were bringing down the final crate that Robert noticed the girl. She was standing surrounded by a mound of luggage, looking a little incongruous in her blue calf-length silk dress which was infinitely more suited to Nairobi and Torr's than Thika and this dusty station.

He was conscious of her beauty. He had no idea who she was, only that she must be newly arrived, judging not only by the luggage but by her delicate skin so obviously untouched as yet by the cruel African sun.

Leaving the boys to carry the first of the crates to the truck outside, he walked over across the station towards her.

'Need any help?'

She looked up at him, striking green eyes taking the measure of him. 'No. I'll be fine, thank you.'

'Are you sure? You look a bit lost to me.'

'Really, I'm fine.' Her voice was more insistent this time. She looked faintly annoyed – Robert wasn't sure whether at him for intruding, or at whoever it was who was late meeting her. He decided it must be the latter. Lack of confidence had never been one of his failings.

'Glad to hear it,' he said affably. 'But if you do need anything, I shall be here for the next fifteen minutes or so. I'd be happy to help . . .'

'Thank you. That's very civil of you.'

Her voice seemed to have lost some of its brittleness. Encouraged, he held out his hand to her. 'Forgive my manners. Let me introduce myself. I'm Robert Dalgleish, by the way.'

Her hand seemed very small and soft against his own firm, long fingers. 'Alexandra Drayton.'

It was not a name which immediately sprang to mind. He was disappointed. He'd hoped the introduction would clear up the mystery of her identity. 'Are you going to be staying close to Thika?' he asked.

'Pretty close. My grandfather's got a farm a few miles to the north of here.' She paused looking at him. 'It's called Kirimangari. I don't suppose you've heard of it.'

There was a pause, almost imperceptible. 'As a matter of fact, I have,' he said. He tried to keep his voice light, but it was a turn of events he'd not been expecting. He kicked at a stone and sent it scuttling across the ground. 'So, Edward Sinclair is your grandfather, is he? Well, who'd have thought it?'

'What's that supposed to mean?' Alexandra queried. There was a faint tightening to her voice. He had forgotten how vulnerable she must be feeling.

'Nothing,' he said quickly. If she knew nothing about the petty feuding between his uncle and Sinclair then he was not going to be the one to bring it up. 'I suppose I was just surprised. It means we're practically neighbours.'

'Practically?' Alexandra's left eyebrow arched quizzically. 'I'm beginning to learn that in Kenya that means that you're only a hundred miles from each other, rather than five.'

He laughed. 'No, really,' he insisted amiably. 'As it happens we're very close. In fact the farms adjoin.'

'Do they?' Her face brightened. It was as if for the first time she had proof of its existence. Up until now it had been a vague name, nothing more.

'Yes. We're slightly north of you, that's all. Have to pass your turn off on the way down here . . .' He paused, glancing at her. 'In fact, if your grandfather doesn't arrive . . .'

'He will arrive,' insisted Alexandra, not allowing him to finish.

'Of course he will,' Robert agreed. He hadn't the heart to say otherwise. Her chin might be tilted in challenge but those lips looked perilously close to wavering. 'Grandfathers have a habit of turning up atrociously late, in my experience,' he added matter-of-factly. 'Unless they're military, then they have the even more annoying habit of turning up atrociously *early* for everything. We had one like that. It nearly drove my mother to distraction!'

She smiled at that. It quite transformed her, giving her face a glowing vitality, a quality of richness which was utterly captivating. For just such a smile, Robert thought, Troy was sacked.

There was a noise at the other side of the station. Robert looked up. He had forgotten about his wretched crates. The removal of them had ground to a halt, with the boys standing there, leaning against them, regarding his pursuit with wide boyish grins.

He called out an instruction to them, staccato, and they instantly feigned frenzied action.

'I'd better go,' he said to Alexandra with a grin. He pushed his hand through his thick sandy-coloured hair and replaced his hat. 'Will you be all right?'

'Perfectly.' Again that smile.

'And if for some reason your grandfather hasn't arrived by the time we've loaded up then we'll sort something out. Whatever happens, there's no need for you to be stranded here. I'm sure we can get you up as far as Kirimangari.'

She nodded without speaking. He noticed that this time she didn't refute the possibility of her grandfather not arriving.

He turned then and crossed the station with purposeful strides, wondering quietly to himself if he should mention the alternative of her staying at the perfectly comfortable Blue Posts Hotel just down the road, instead of journeying up to Kirimangari with him.

But then he remembered her smile and, whistling, walked on.

Billows of dust folded outwards from the wheels of the truck. As it bounced its way northwards along the pitted murram road, Alexandra, seated in the front beside Robert Dalgleish, had never thought it possible to be quite so shaken about.

But, despite the discomfort, despite her worries about what might have befallen her grandfather and despite the heat which seemed to sear its way through the windows of the truck, she felt excitement flow through her. She suddenly felt very much part of the country through which she was travelling, aware for the first time of its sounds and its fragrance. She had not been aware before of the dry peppery smell of the bush, nor of the rich cacophony of animal and bird calls – the coos, the squawks, the snarls, all now beginning to have an identity of their own.

A flock of weaver birds, squabbling and flapping in a flat-topped acacia tree, rose in a yellowish haze as the truck rattled past. Alexandra shaded her eyes to watch them as they flew off into the sunlight.

Beyond them, in the far distance, she thought she saw the glimmer of a snow-peaked mountain. It seemed almost a mirage in this heat.

'That's Mount Kenya,' said Robert, following her gaze. 'Beautiful, isn't it? The Kikuyus believe it to be the dwelling place of God – Ngai. They say that Mogai, the Divider of the Universe and Lord of Nature, made the mountain his resting-place. He then took the man Gikuyu to the top to point out the beauty of the land he was giving him, and told him if ever he was in need he should make a sacrifice and raise his hands towards Mount Kenya . . . It's supposed to have great magical qualities.'

He was full of these little anecdotes about the animals, about the land through which they were travelling. It was clear that he loved the place and had a strong affinity with the country itself.

She glanced at him now, stretching her toes in her too-tight shoes. He was a tall man, loose-limbed, with sandy fair hair and a classically straight nose. He was older than she'd first thought at the station, in his late twenties perhaps, and there were deeply etched sun-lines at the corners of his eyes.

He had a strong, animated face, with a wide mouth which even now had a touch of wry humour about it. He would take life as it came, she sensed, although she was keenly aware that beneath that boyish charm was something formidable, a force to be reckoned with.

As if sensing she was studying him, he glanced across at her, his eyes disconcertingly blue even from beneath the shadow of his broad-brimmed hat.

'Surviving?' he asked.

'Just about.'

'You'll find the roads in England dreadfully boring after this,' he told her, his face creasing into a smile.

'But so much faster and more comfortable!' she countered, dimpling. 'And I swear I'll never complain about the springs in Daddy's car again!'

'I bet you do!' he laughed 'So, tell me, how are the crates doing?'

She turned and looked through the back window of the truck. It was difficult to see through all the swirling dust. 'Still there, at least I think so.'

'Glad to hear it,' he returned blithely. 'I'd have hated them to have come all this way only to be floored on the home stretch.'

'They look like survivors to me!' she told him, glancing over her shoulder again. 'In fact,' she said scrutinising the crates more carefully, 'I rather think I made their acquaintance in Mombasa yesterday. Could that be?'

'More than likely. I expect they were enduring cruel treatment there as well.'

She laughed. 'They were. But I can tell you, you were the envy of all the train. I gather new farm machinery is a pretty rare sight these days.'

'It is. And I'm afraid we only have these by courtesy of the bank manager.'

'Oh! And I thought things might be looking up.'

'Not yet,' he said with a light shrug. 'But it will, soon enough. The trouble is, not everyone can hang on.'

She sensed from his wording that the Dalgleishes were in a stronger position than most.

He slowed down as they passed three women plodding alongside the road, their heavy loads suspended by leather straps around their heads. It all looked unbelievably painful to Alexandra. The loads were so weighty that the straps bit into their foreheads.

They fell into an easy silence.

'Do you see much of my grandfather?' she asked, after a while.

Robert glanced at her quickly then fixed on the road again. 'Not really. If you want the truth, he's a bit of a recluse.'

'Is he?'

'My father and my uncle and he used to be great friends years ago, though,' Robert paused, almost imperceptibly. 'In fact, I can remember your mother. She used to come over with your grandfather occasionally. I seem to remember as an eight-year-old thinking she was rather smashing!'

Alexandra laughed at his boyish phrase. 'She still is, really,' she said.

'I can imagine.' He brought his gaze up to her face and smiled, fighting the temptation to say how alike they must be. Past images sprang to mind. It was amazing what he could remember.

'So what happened?' Alexandra asked, stretching out her legs a little.

'Between my uncle and your grandfather?' She nodded. He lifted his shoulders in a shrug. 'Don't know really. I think they fell out over some land. Your grandfather was in debt . . .' He hesitated, glancing at her.

'I know. You needn't worry. My mother told me. He gambled his way into debt and then had to sell off his best land,' she said quietly.

'Well, my uncle was the one to buy the land. I don't think your grandfather was too pleased about that. Hurt his pride to have to sell it off bit by bit, I suppose.' He glanced at her, trying to read her mind. 'Anyway they don't speak now. Haven't for years.'

'I see.' Perhaps her grandfather had become a recluse from necessity rather than choice. It wouldn't do to fall out with neighbours. They were few and far between. A guinea fowl scratching in search of seeds in the earth at the side of the road alarmed shrilly at the approach of the truck, thrashing its stubby wings as it made off into the dry rustling grass.

'And what about your father?' Alexandra ventured. 'Did he fall out with my grandfather, too?'

'He died before all the fracas took place,' Robert said. 'Both my parents did. They were killed when I was ten. In England, of all places. In a car accident while there on leave.'

'I'm so sorry.' She was mortified by her blunder.

'It's all right. It all happened a long time ago,' he said. But she noticed his voice had lost its deep vibrancy.

She made a great business of getting a handkerchief out of her bag and wiping her hands with it. 'So what happened to you?' she asked, not quite trusting herself to look at him yet.

'Oh, in many ways I was lucky, I suppose,' he said. 'My uncle wanted to look after me. We filled a gap in each other's lives, you see. I had no parents, he had no children. It was an admirable arrangement. Far better than my being sent home to chilly England to live with some aged grandparents whom I'd never known. It was threatened but Uncle wouldn't allow it.'

She could tell he was eternally grateful to his uncle for saving him from such a fate. It was strange for her to hear someone talking of England with such antipathy. She had never viewed it as an alien country before, never thought of it as being cold and remote.

To her it meant the loving circle of her family; long, lazy summer days, cosy winter nights. And Charles. She let out a sigh. It all suddenly seemed so terribly, terribly, far away.

Robert glanced at her. 'Tired?' he asked, mistaking her sigh.

'A little,' she admitted.

'We're nearly there.' He nodded to the left. 'Just up there's the turn-off.'

A few minutes later they were turning off the road, passing the squatters' densely cultivated *shambas* – areas, Robert told her, given over to the Kikuyu labourers for their own cultivation. Then they came to a series of five-barred gates, which one of the boys from the back of the truck leapt down to open and close.

In the distance she could hear a dog barking. After a few more minutes they came over the rise in the terrain, and there, down on the hillside below, she could see the house at last.

Her disappointment was acute. At first she thought – *hoped* – it might be an outbuilding, so unprepossessing was it. But its lines were all too familiar to her: the grey stone bungalow with its two chimneys, unmistakably the same one as in her mother's faded photographs.

They swung to a halt in front of the wide verandah steps. Inside the house Alexandra could see a shadow move, but no one came out to greet them.

She hesitated for a moment then climbed down from the truck. She was stiff from the long journey and after the constant rattle and creaking the stillness here was profound.

There was a stirring inside the house again and this time a tall African dressed in a white *kanzu* like a surplice reaching down to his ankles, came out onto the verandah. He looked a cheerful soul, his scarlet fez contrasting vividly with his ebony skin and white teeth.

'Jambo!' Robert called out to him.

'Jambo, *bwana*,' he returned starting to come down the wide verandah steps towards them.

Halfway down he stopped. He stared at Alexandra confused, and turning to Robert broke into a rapid torrent of Swahili.

Robert listened to him without interrupting. At last she heard him say: '*Kesho?*'

'*Kesho*,' insisted the man, nodding vigorously.

She heard Robert laugh. 'It seems,' he said, turning to her with a smile, 'that you've caught them unawares. They weren't expecting you until tomorrow. That's why there was no one there to greet you at Thika.'

She pushed back her dark hair from her face confusedly. 'Tomorrow? But the telegram told me to catch the next train.'

'I know. But apparently it was delivered in half the usual time. You were just unlucky – or lucky – whichever way you look at it. It never occurred to them that you'd have time to catch this train up.'

Alexandra grimaced. 'I nearly didn't,' she admitted. 'I can't tell you the panic I had trying to get to the station on time!' She would have to write to Jane to tell her the outcome of their mad dash – she would doubtless be much amused by it.

'Well, at least it means there's nothing wrong with your grandfather,' said Robert philosophically. 'I was beginning to worry that it might be something a little more serious than just a car breaking down when we didn't see him on the road up.'

She glanced back over her shoulder towards the house. 'Where is he, by the way? Do you know?'

'Inside. Asleep. He's not been well, apparently.' He nodded towards the African on the steps. 'Juma told me that's why he couldn't come down to Nairobi to meet you.'

'Juma?' She should have known. She turned back to the African who had welcomed them. 'You were here in my mother's day, weren't you?' she asked, beaming across at him. 'How long have you have been here? It must be all of twenty years . . .'

'Twenty-four,' pronounced Juma, a look of triumph in his eyes. 'And it is very good you have come, *memsahib kadogo*. Very good. It is too long now the *bwana* has been alone.'

She heard in his voice his affection for her grandfather and smiled again. 'Yes, too long, Juma,' she agreed softly.

There was a clatter behind her as the boys swept up her suitcases and carried them up into the house.

She turned to Robert. 'Won't you come in for a drink or something?' she asked him.

'No, thanks. The machinery, remember. My uncle will have quite given up on me.'

'Of course. Well then,' she held out her hand to him. 'Thank you for being my saviour. I think Thika would have lost all its charm by now.'

'Oh, way before now!' he assured her with an easy smile. He

pushed his hat to the back of his head and started towards the truck. Then, changing his mind, he stopped and turned back to her again. 'By the way, if there is anything I can do for you while you're here, you'll let me know, won't you?' he said, his blue eyes very insistent.

'Thank you, I shall.' Alexandra bent down to stroke a large scruffy dog which had stirred from the shade of the house to come over to greet them. 'Perhaps you'd . . .'

She got no further. Her words were drowned by a loud clatter from inside the house. It sounded as if a heavy piece of furniture had fallen over.

'Damn and blast it!' roared a voice. 'Juma! Where is everybody? Juma!'

Juma seemed unperturbed by the ferocity of the blast from inside. 'Here *bwana*!' he called out, unmoved. 'With the *memsahib kadogo*. She's arrived, *bwana*.'

Another crash came from inside and then a figure appeared in the doorway. So intense was the shadow cast by the deep verandah that for a moment Alexandra had difficulty seeing beyond the stone pillars to the man who stood there. Then the figure made a great effort to straighten and her grandfather stepped out into the sunlight.

Despite his great bulk and height, despite his wide shoulders and thick limbs, he had an air of unmistakable frailty about him. And seeing him standing there, hair ruffled as if from sleep, eyes blinking against the glare, Alexandra felt a sudden, unexpected wave of protectiveness towards him.

'Grandfather!' she called up to him, her voice full of emotion.

For a moment he seemed lost, staring down at her disorientatedly. He said something under his breath which Alexandra didn't catch.

Then she saw Juma step across to him, one hand going under his elbow. 'It's Miss Alexandra,' Juma said to him. His voice was patient, almost as if he were speaking to a child. 'It's Miss Alexandra who's come.'

Her grandfather blinked again, then as he seemed to focus on her, the frown, the strange look in his eyes, cleared.

'Alexandra?'

'Yes, I'm afraid I've caused confusion by coming a day early,' Alexandra apologised. She started up the verandah steps towards him, ignoring the peeling paint which crumbled on her fingers as her hand ran up the wooden railings. 'There was some silly misunderstanding about the telegram but luckily Mr Dalgleish here was quite the knight in shining armour and was able to bring me all the way to Kirimangari.'

'Dalgleish?' The obvious hostility in his voice stopped her in her tracks. 'Did you say Dalgleish?'

'Yes.' She hesitated, suddenly unsure, the smile fading from her face. 'Mr Dalgleish . . .'

'Damn you, child!' he exploded at her, not allowing her to finish. 'Why must you torment me so!' His massive hands were gripping the railings so tight that the knuckles showed white. 'Cameron Dalgleish is not welcome on my land, d'you hear?'

'Cameron Dalgleish did not bring Miss Drayton. I did.'

Alexandra wheeled round. She had been so immersed in her own confused thoughts that she hadn't heard Robert Dalgleish come up to stand behind her on the steps. He seemed remarkably unmoved by her grandfather's outburst.

'I'm Robert Dalgleish,' he said, coming up the last of the steps. His voice was deep and rounded, almost lazy.

'Cameron's nephew?' Alexandra's grandfather pointedly ignored Robert's outstretched hand.

'Yes, I am,' Robert acknowledged, dropping his arm back to his side without any outward sign that he had noticed the insult.

'Cameron's nephew, eh? Then you'll do me the favour of clearing off my property Mr Dalgleish.' His eyes, meeting Robert's over the proud arch of his Roman nose, were unutterably cold. 'I don't want your kind here!'

'Grandfather!' cried Alexandra. 'I . . .' She felt Robert's hand gently squeeze her shoulder, warning her not to continue.

'Your quarrel is with my uncle, not with me,' pointed out Robert quietly, the merest flicker of anger in his eyes. 'And I assure you, I meant no offence by bringing your granddaughter up to Kirimangari. It just seemed to me it would have been unchivalrous indeed to have left her all alone on Thika station, with not a soul in sight.'

'Unchivalrous!' Alexandra's grandfather laughed. The short sound held all the contempt in the world. 'What do the Dalgleishes know of chivalry?'

'Grandfather, please! Please don't talk to Mr Dalgleish like that.'

Alexandra turned to Robert, her face pink with embarrassment. 'I'm so sorry, Mr Dalgleish. I would never have accepted your kind offer if I had known what friction it would lead to . . .'

'Wouldn't you?' His blue eyes met hers, full of boyish cheek. 'Then I'm glad you didn't know!' he said lightly.

His smile was so infectious that she found herself smiling back at him, despite everything.

She glanced up across the verandah to where her grandfather stood. He was sagging against the railings, as if the last burst of temper had drained every ounce of strength from him. He looked suddenly like a wilted poppy, only a semblance of his former pride and power apparent.

She turned back to Robert. 'I think you ought to go, Mr Dalgleish,' she said quietly. 'Grandfather looks far from well.'

'Are you sure you don't want me to stay?'

'No, really.'

'You'll manage, do you think?' He reached out and touched Alexandra's shoulders very lightly with the tips of his fingers as if to reassure her that if necessary she could count on his continued support.

'Quite sure, thank you. I've got Juma here, after all.'

Still he hesitated. 'All the same, I don't like to leave you . . .'

'I'll manage,' she insisted. 'Really. Besides, I think your presence might only make things worse.'

He smiled, making light of it. 'Probably.'

Alexandra started down the steps towards the truck, leading the way. 'I'm sorry about Grandfather behaving so badly,' she said.

'Quite.'

'Besides – the machinery, remember?'

'Oh Lord, that.' It would be dark before he got the wretched stuff back to the farm now. 'You're right. I'd better get a move on.'

He climbed into the truck and pulled the door to with a slam. Alexandra saw him wave jauntily out of the open window at her as he turned the truck in a half circle in front of the house. Then, with a creaking and whining, the truck pulled off down the drive again.

A great plume of murram dust rose up into the air as it sped away into the distance. Alexandra watched until it had become a mere red smudge on the horizon and then turned back to the house.

As she came up the steps she noticed that her grandfather was no longer on the verandah. Juma must have helped him inside. She walked through to the drawing-room. At first she thought the room was empty, so still was it. But then she heard a muffled rustling, a faint murmur, coming from the far corner of the room.

'Grandfather?' It was difficult to see, the shutters were closed and the light filtered. She edged forward. 'Grandfather, are you all right?'

He was on the settee, head tipped back against the velvet cushions, his boots stretched out on the worn upholstery. She thought at first he was asleep, but, as she crossed the room towards him, he turned his head in her direction and opened his eyes the merest slit.

'So you came back, did you?' he murmured, squinting at her through heavy lashes.

'I wasn't gone long,' she returned, surprised. He must have fallen asleep and lost track of the time.

'Wilful, that's your trouble. Damn women. Always so wilful . . .' His words were hardly distinguishable. He mumbled on but now she could hardly understand any of it. Something about Sarah, her mother, she wasn't sure what. All she knew was that delicacy of speech did not count for much in this household.

She bent to straighten the cushions, determined not to be put off by his abrasive behaviour, determined to smooth over this less than auspicious start. It was then that she saw that one of his hands was loosely clasped around a glass and that a half-empty bottle of whisky was tucked into the side of the settee.

She stepped back, staring down at him. So many pieces fell into place. His unsteady walk, his mumbled speech, his flushed complexion. Not a fever at all. And she, innocent fool that she was, had been about to give him sympathy.

'I don't believe you have the fever at all, do you?' she said before she could stop herself.

'What's that you're saying?' He screwed up his eyes as he tried to focus on her.

'You've been drinking . . .'

Her grandfather mustered up a look of indignation. 'Been drinking, yes. But not *drunk* . . .' He tried to prop himself up on his arm but slipped sideways again, his eyes closing with the effort of the movement.

But he was drunk, that was the trouble. Alexandra looked down at him, her cheeks flaming. How could she not have seen it earlier? True, her hitherto small world had left her unprepared for such an occurrence but Robert Dalgleish had known at once, she saw that now. That was why he had been so loath to leave her here alone. Oh, the humiliation of it all.

'Oh, Grandfather . . .' The urge to befriend him struggled against her disappointment in him.

He stared back at her with bleary eyes. 'Now, you'll not hold it against an old man that he's had a drink or two, will you?' he asked, his tone wheedling.

The whole bottle, more like. She gave a little shrug of her shoulders. How could she tell him how often she had imagined this meeting? This was not the grandfather of her dreams . . .

'Alexandra!' She could hear the pained reproach in his voice. 'Oh, but you're hard-hearted,' she heard him murmur from behind her. Hearing, too, the sound of his glass being refilled. 'Hard-hearted, just like your mother.'

She turned towards him at that. Strange how little time ago she had accused her mother of just the same thing, but now . . . 'Perhaps,' she returned wearily, 'she had every right to be.'

He pushed himself up onto his elbow, resting against it unsteadily. 'Damn you! What gives you the right to criticise, Miss Prissy?'

She fell into awkward silence, her discomfort acute.

'Quiet now, eh? Well, that's something at least.' The words were spoken with the sudden spitefulness of a petulant child. Her grandfather took a shaky swig from his glass. 'Where's the harm in a drink or two, for God's sake? Answer me that, Miss Prissy. Where's the harm?'

She should have stayed silent, of course, but somehow he'd goaded her too far this time. She shot him a level look. 'Harm enough, Grandfather, if you destroy a lifetime's work by it.'

Her dart hit its mark. He stiffened at that. 'What do you know about it?' he asked her, his face flushing deeply. 'Nothing!'

'I know that you lost your best land to Cameron Dalgleish,' she said quietly. 'Lost it through gambling and drink . . .'

Her grandfather regarded her steadily for a moment. 'That wasn't all he took,' he said bitterly. He sank back against the cushions again, head back, staring at the ceiling.

She could see that. She could see he had lost his self-respect and pride along with the land. The imploring tone in his voice made her regret her earlier sharpness. She had so wanted this first meeting to be perfect. She felt a tinge of pity for him lying there, a defeated, lonely old man. Who was she to judge, after all?

She might have gone to his side then, might have taken the hand which rested limply against his chest but at that moment the door swung open and Juma hurried in carrying a hurricane lamp in his hand.

He glanced at the two of them, sensing the tension between them. 'Your room is ready, Miss Alexandra, if you want to go through now,' he said, silently urging her to leave.

She looked across at her grandfather. He had turned his head away from her as if erecting an invisible barrier between them. She saw him reach out for his whisky bottle, clumsily clinking glass against glass. If ever she had been about to console him, to extend the hand of friendship towards him, the moment was gone.

'Thank you, Juma,' she said, weariness showing in her voice. 'I'll come now.'

She followed silently behind him, hardly aware of her surroundings.

'Don't be too hard on the *m'zee bwana*,' said Juma as he pushed open the door to her bedroom. 'He had the fever yesterday, truly he did.' He crossed the room to light the hurricane lamp on the bedside table. 'And today . . .' He hesitated. He couldn't tell her the truth of course. That the *bwana m'zee* had been scared of meeting his beloved granddaughter, scared lest she be disappointed in him. He sighed. And now look what had happened. 'Tomorrow will be different,' he insisted quietly.

She was touched by his loyalty to her grandfather. But nonetheless she was not convinced that the next day would bring any change.

After he had gone she sank down on the bed, careful to keep her shoes on – for Juma had repeatedly warned her of the perils of the jiggers which would bury under her toenails given half the chance. A heavy weariness seemed to tug at her whole body. It was hard for her to admit that she had made a mistake and yet, undoubtedly, that was exactly what she had done. She had tried to pursue a romantic dream and had ended up in the nightmare of reality.

She stood up and went to the window, hugging herself with crossed arms. Outside it was dark. Perilously dark. There was no sign of life as far as the eye could see. No distant lights. Nothing. For the first time she was aware of her own total isolation. It unnerved her a little, accentuating her own sense of vulnerability.

She crossed back over the room to her suitcase, her legs leaden, the mire of misery dragging at her feet. She would leave, of course: as soon as it could possibly be arranged. She would just have to swallow her pride and telegraph her parents' friends near Nyeri.

Outside she could hear a wild animal calling from just beyond the compound. She wasn't sure whether it was a leopard or a lion, but whatever it sounded very dangerous and, to her mind, very hungry. Worse still, it sounded very close.

She shuddered and sank back down again upon the bed, her slim body the eloquent expression of despair. It was all so strange, that was the trouble. Every sound, every smell, every silhouetted form. And suddenly, despite all her resolutions, she was longing for the warm, familiar security of home again. For her father's soft, reassuring voice, for Charles's frivolous gaiety and for his infectious laugh, which soon would have humoured her out of this dark mood.

If she sat stock still she could almost hear them now. She closed her eyes tight, trying to conjure them up. But as if to taunt her, the only sound that came through the night was the cackle of the hyena as he furtively slipped past the compound into the darkness.

5

When Alexandra awoke the next day sharp bands of sunlight were forcing their way beneath the wooden shutters of her room. She had thought never to fall asleep but already it was morning, and no longer early, judging from the hubbub and bustle outside.

She stretched, linking her fingers behind her head, and leant back against the pillow. Yesterday she had been barely conscious of her immediate surroundings; but now, looking about her, she was aware for the first time of the decoration and shape of her room, and of how delicate the pieces of furniture were here, how feminine. That little walnut secretaire in the corner, for instance, was not a piece she would associate with the man she had met yesterday at all.

That this undoubtedly had been her mother's room came to her slowly and after the first initial shock at such a discovery, a slow nub of pleasure began to grow within her at the thought.

She judged it had changed little. The worn flowery bedspread had been here then, she guessed, so too the little array of china animals standing on top of the secretaire. She glanced at the mahogany bookcase beside her bed and smiled. The uneven row of books with a miscellany of titles seemed to chart her mother's path from child to teenager and then to adulthood. She was touched by the sight of them. It exposed a gentler side to her mother, somehow, a more vulnerable part.

Alexandra hitched herself up in bed and stretched again. From outside she could hear the sounds of a house coming to life: the murmur of low voices, the clank of pails, the soft rhythmic swishing of a verandah being swept, familiar everyday sounds, reassuring against the distant shrill calls of strange and unknown birds.

She should get up, she knew, but she wasn't sure she could face her grandfather again just yet. She felt she was walking the rim of a volcano, aware of the potential danger: one false step and she would be engulfed by sparks. Yet he had to be faced, she knew.

She took a sharp decisive breath and flung back the sheet, swinging her feet onto the rush-matted floor below.

A few minutes later Alexandra was washed and dressed and following the mouth-watering aroma of frying bacon and freshly made coffee through to the dining-room. As soon as she came through the doorway she could see Juma, immaculate in his white *kanzu*, standing by the round polished table in the centre of the room. There was no sign of her grandfather.

'Jambo, Miss Alexandra,' Juma greeted her, as she crossed over to the side table where the bacon and eggs were being kept warm over a night-light. 'Did you sleep well?'

'Yes, thank you,' Alexandra returned. She began to help herself to the scrambled eggs. She had not realised until this moment how hungry she was, but then she recalled that she had eaten nothing since yesterday's breakfast on the train.

She placed three rashers of bacon on her plate and then returned to the table. 'Is Grandfather awake yet?' she asked Juma as she sat down.

'Oh yes, *memsahib kadogo*.' Juma afforded her a beaming smile. 'Up and out long ago.' The breeziness of his voice gave no hint of the struggle he'd had to get the *bwana m'zee* out of bed this morning. 'He has gone down to the nursery. Be back in an hour maybe.'

'Nursery? He's gone to see the children then?' Alexandra asked, helping herself to a piece of fresh toast that the cook, Kamau, had just brought in.

'Children? No, no.' Juma beamed delightedly at her mistake. 'The seedlings. The little coffee seedlings down by the river. That is what he's gone to see. They grow in the nursery down there.' He chuckled to himself again.

Alexandra laughed. 'Oh, I see.' She couldn't take offence at his mirth.

'But he fusses over them so, they might as well be children,' Juma pronounced, nodding happily. 'Just as much trouble.'

Kamau came back from the cookhouse with some freshly brewed coffee. He poured her a cup and then placed the pot on the coaster on the table. It was strange for Alexandra to realise that this coffee had been grown here. She paused over her cup, drawing in the rich aroma, then glanced over to Juma who was still hovering discreetly in the background.

'So my grandfather will be back in about an hour, will he?' she asked, trying not to show her relief that she had been given a few moments' grace.

'Yes, Miss Alexandra.'

'And . . .' She hesitated. 'And was he quite well this morning?' she asked, trying to word it as delicately as possible.

Juma took her meaning at once. 'Quite well,' he returned emphatically. He stood, shifting restlessly from one foot to the other. 'It is only sometimes he is like that, the *bwana m'zee*. It is only sometimes he remembers and then he remembers also that he is so alone.' Juma's mouth curled slightly. 'That is why your coming is so good. He will not be alone now.'

'No.' Her reply was automatic. She couldn't bring herself to tell him she had already decided to leave within a few days.

'So good for him to have you here . . .' Juma continued, unaware of her discomfort.

'Yes.' She had to turn her head away from his gaze. Yet, why should she feel guilty, she asked herself crossly. After all, the loneliness her grandfather felt he had brought upon himself.

She downed the last of her coffee and stood up, anxious to extract herself from this conversation.

'I think I'll take a walk around the garden while I wait for Grandfather to return,' she said, her voice stiffer than she'd intended. 'Will you tell him where I've gone, Juma?'

She was glad to step outside. It was hot already, the sunlight brilliant, not a cloud in the sky. Alexandra came down the steps, the rail warm to her touch.

The garden, for the most part, was set out to lawn. It was now showing the effects of the long dry season and was parched and brown, despite stoic attempts at watering by Njeroge, the gardener. He was out there with his hosepipe now, though Alexandra could have told him it was a hopeless task this late in the morning. The sun's rays were like blotting-paper and every particle of moisture was sucked up in a matter of seconds.

She started to walk across the lawn towards the herbaceous

border which ran along its edge like a bedraggled colourful ribbon. Butterflies flitted over the grass, settling from time to time to suck at the last of the moisture left from Njeroge's watering. They opened and shut their brilliantly coloured wings, pulsating against the dense shadows cast out by the flowering shrubs. As Alexandra came near they rose in a blue-black haze, like a misty cloud.

At the edge of the garden, Alexandra stopped. To either side of the driveway lay row upon row of carefully planted coffee trees. She was taken aback by the height of them. They stood about six feet tall, their shiny evergreen leaves supported by slender branches. She was surprised by the orderliness of it all, too. The garden might be ramshackle, but not so the coffee lines. They were nurtured and tended and seemed lush and green against the parched dryness of the earth.

A group of Kikuyu workers were busily hoeing between the lines, trying to dig out the rapacious weeds while drawing away no more soil than necessary from the stems of the trees. Just before the rains began it was doubly important to keep as much moisture as possible in the soil and they worked slowly and carefully.

Alexandra stood there for a moment, listening to the dull chipping sound of their hoes against the hard earth, hearing their soft laughter and low voices. In the distance she heard the shrill call of a bird, unseen against a starkly blue sky. It was all so peaceful here, so serene, it seemed unimaginable that last night she had had such fears.

She turned at the sound of a truck noisily grinding its way over the crest of the hill, a plume of dust smudging the horizon. Even as it jolted down the dirt track towards her she knew to whom it belonged. Robert Dalgleish. She wasn't sure whether to be pleased or alarmed that he had come back. Instinctively she glanced over her shoulder to see if her grandfather was in sight.

The two house-dogs lying in the shade of the great fig-tree in front of the house stood up and gave a cursory bark as the truck swung into the driveway, then quickly sank back again with a slow wag of their tails as the truck drew to a halt in front of the verandah steps.

'Good morning.' Robert Dalgleish's tousled fair head appeared out of the truck's window. 'I hope you don't mind my calling again so soon. I just wanted to check that all was well.'

'That was kind of you,' she said, touched by his concern.

'To be honest,' he said, pushing open the door and stepping down, 'I wasn't sure if I should have left you last night. The old boy seemed a bit worse for wear . . .' He came across the drive towards her. Even at this distance she was aware of the blueness of his eyes. They had an intensity which she found not a little disconcerting. 'You obviously survived, I see,' he said.

She liked that about him. No edge. No affectations. 'Just about,' she admitted, shielding her eyes against the sun's glare.

'I'm glad to see it.'

'But I may not,' she continued wryly, 'if my grandfather finds you here now.'

He gave a light-hearted grimace. 'That won't arise, hopefully. If my calculations are right.'

'What calculations?' Her hand went to sweep the dark hair back from her face.

'That, like any good planter, he'd be out first thing in the morning instructing his team of boys what needed to be done.'

'I see.'

'Am I right?' He raised an inquisitive brow.

'Absolutely.' She couldn't resist a teasing smile. 'So yours is not quite the daring mission I at first thought . . .'

'Heavens no!' He gave her a wide boyish grin. 'I've too strong a sense of self-preservation for that!'

'Have you now?' Her green eyes met his, serious for a moment. 'Then perhaps I ought to tell you that my grandfather will be back before too long. He's only gone as far as the nurseries, I believe. I don't think he'd take kindly to your calling again, however chivalrous your intent.'

He ducked his head towards her. 'I shall bear that in mind,' he said, but she noticed that he made no move to leave.

They stood for a moment in silence. A skink poked its scaly head out of the long grass beside the compound, then, sensing their presence, darted back in with a great rustle. Robert kicked at a stone with the toe of his boot and sent it scudding across the gravel.

'So,' he said, tipping his wide-brimmed hat back on his head. 'I take it that your grandfather's thinking of planting out more seedlings, is he? I'll say this for the old chap, he doesn't give up easily, does he?' There was a hint of admiration in his voice.

She glanced up at him. 'You sound surprised,' she said.

'No, not really.' He shrugged. 'But he's been hit quite hard over the past few years, you know. He had a bout of leaf fungus which wiped out a few good acres. Many men have given up for less.' He turned his head to look back over the coffee trees. 'But he knows his business, that much is obvious.'

'Is it?'

'Oh yes,' he continued matter-of-factly. 'You have only to look at the trees to see how well they're growing to see that. They're well pruned and you have to have a highly-trained team to do that. It's one of the keys to a successful coffee crop. If you don't prune properly you can lose half your potential harvest.'

She stood for a moment looking back over the rows of glossy-leaved trees. 'So it isn't Grandfather's mismanagement that's to blame for his downfall then,' she ventured.

'Not as far as I can see,' said Robert, glancing back across the fields. 'Seems pretty well run to me. In fact, seeing how efficient he is, I have to admit I can understand why the old chap was so galled to have lost that land to my uncle. If he still had it, he would be in quite an enviable position now.'

Alexandra smiled rather bleakly. It was what her mother had told her a hundred times. 'Well, what's done is done.' She gave a little shrug. 'Nothing can change all that now.'

'No,' Robert agreed, looking down at her. For a moment she thought he was going to say something more but then he thrust his hands into his pockets and said: 'I'd better be on my way, I suppose. I only called to make sure you'd lasted the night.'

She laughed. 'I did. Though thank you for your concern.'

They fell into step as they started back towards the truck. 'Have you decided how long you're going to stay yet?' Robert asked as they came back under the cool shade of the fig-tree.

'Not really.' She lifted her shoulders slightly. 'A week, ten days. Something like that.'

'I see.' Their eyes met. She knew very well that on the journey up from Thika she had told him that she was coming out for six months or so. Her change of plan could only indicate one thing. 'Are you sure you really want to stay here?' he asked gently. 'Do you want me to drive you back to Thika?'

'Oh no!' she insisted, slightly embarrassed that he should see how woefully unprepared she had been for the state of things here. 'I'll manage. Really. It all takes a little getting used to, that's all.' Whatever else, she could last the few days until she arranged her journey to Nyeri.

He lingered for a moment by the truck. Standing there in the brilliant sunshine she saw again how the fair hair and skin had somehow perfectly accommodated to the sun.

He leant against the truck, surveying her candidly across its dust-covered roof. 'I was thinking,' he said, after a while. 'There's a polo match at Stuart Avery's place next weekend, perhaps you would like to come? It's just a local friendly match, that's all. But it'll probably be the last before the rains come.'

'I'm not sure it would be wise . . .' she hesitated.

'Because of your grandfather?'

She nodded. 'I'm not sure how far this feud extends, you see. Is it just on this property that he won't abide the Dalgleishes or does the hostility extend beyond his own perimeters?'

'That I can't answer I'm afraid,' admitted Robert. 'To be honest, until yesterday, I hadn't seen him for years.'

She glanced across at him, sensing that for all his outward calm of yesterday he had been as taken aback as she had been at her grandfather's enmity towards him.

'Listen,' he said. 'As far as I can see, the best idea would be to get Stuart to send you and your grandfather an invitation to the match and you can see what reaction it provokes. You might be pleasantly surprised. Your grandfather might even want to come, you know. He used to be a dab hand at polo in his day.'

'Did he?' She tried, but failed, to hide her surprise. Thinking of the inebriated hulk on the settee last night, it was something she could hardly imagine.

'Yes. His team nearly beat the K.A.R.s for the Connaught Cup one year. Quite the little demon. Had a wonderful Somali-Abyssinian cross which could turn on a pin. Extraordinary pony. I've been trying to match that mare for years.' He opened the truck door and climbed in. 'And my uncle won't be at the match, if that's any consolation, so there won't be a chance of a fearful confrontation.'

That was cause for solace, at least. She imagined their meeting would be like the clash of the Titans.

'Try and come, won't you.'

She laughed at his insistence. She could see he was a man used to getting his own way. 'All right, I'll see if I can,' she said. 'If I'm still here by then, that is.'

He seemed not to have heard her last remark. He put the truck into gear and started to ease forward, then changing his mind, stopped. 'By the way, I couldn't help noticing as I came up here, some of the trees in the top field look as if they're getting a touch of the mealy bug . . .'

'Which is to be discouraged?'

'Most definitely.' He gave her a dry smile. 'After a dry spell like this there's no predators around, you see. They'll multiply like mad given half the chance.'

'I see. So I should tell Grandfather then?'

'Probably worth it.' He tried to make his voice sound casual. He had no wish to be thought to be interfering. Though the trees had been banded with grease, in some cases it had not proved effective in stopping the bugs. 'He's probably noticed it, of course. But if he hasn't been up in the top fields for a few days, he might just have missed them. Sly little devils they are!'

'I see. So, what do they look like?' Their eyes met. It was quite clear that if she were to mention the bugs to her grandfather she would have to pretend that she had discovered them herself. She could hardly mention Robert Dalgleish's presence at the farm again. 'I mean, would I really have noticed them?'

'With such observant green eyes, yes!' he said with a teasing smile. 'You'd have seen them around the flower buds and growing tips. They're like a white mealy mass. Just tell him you've seen them and ask him what they are. He'll know what to do.'

'I will then. Thank you.'

'My pleasure.' The truck began to judder forward again. 'I'll see you next weekend then.'

She didn't bother to refute his statement. He gave her a quick farewell salute out of the open window and then the truck rattled laboriously up the driveway to the top of the hill and out of sight.

There was a silence for a moment, then she heard the verandah door being opened behind her. She spun round quickly to find Juma standing at the top of the steps looking down at her.

'*Memsahib kadogo!*' he called softly down to her. His tone was hushed, anxious. 'Miss Alexandra, your grandfather he is coming back now!'

That Juma had been watching out for his return all the time Robert Dalgleish had been there was obvious now. She grinned up at him, acknowledging their conspiracy. 'Thank you, Juma. I'll come up straightaway.'

'Hurry, Miss Alexandra, do. He mustn't know. To think that Dalgleish had been here again would anger him greatly.'

Alexandra sped up the steps. She had no wish to provoke her grandfather into the sort of temper she had seen last night. She was only too aware of the fragility of their relationship.

She was sitting quietly reading one of the books from his small collection when he came into the sunlit drawing-room. She lifted her head at his entrance, a little wary lest his mood be uncertain.

But he seemed cheerful enough as he crossed the room towards her. 'My dear child, forgive me for not being here earlier. What must you think of me?'

She was surprised at how spritely he was, as he walked across to kiss her upturned cheek. Last night she had thought him frail and unsteady, but now she saw that it was only the whisky which had made him appear so. He moved easily, not a hint of aged bones in his stride.

'You slept well, I trust?' he asked, lowering himself into the chair beside her.

'Perfectly, thank you,' she said. 'Last night I was a little weary, I confess.'

'Last night we were all a little weary, my dear,' he pronounced heavily. He met her gaze without flinching. No apology for his behaviour. No excuses. His cloaked admittance of it was as far as he was prepared to go.

He shifted his position slightly so that he could see her more clearly. 'So, my dear, how is the family? You must tell me everything. I get so little news these days . . .' He turned his head as Juma brought in a jug of lemonade and two tall glasses on a wooden tray. 'And you must tell me about yourself. Your mother wrote saying that you were keen to come out here before becoming engaged to some young chap or other. Some eminently suitable fellow, your mother said . . .'

Alexandra lifted her head at that, relieved. The rattle of spilling beans had seemed ominously close at one point. Her mother had told him nothing, then. 'His name is Charles Montague,' she said, and just the mention of his name made her spirits lighten a little.

'Charles Montague, eh?' Edward Sinclair's eyes twinkled at the way the mere mention of that name had brought a glow to his granddaughter's face. 'And may I be permitted to hear all about him?' he asked, almost gently.

'You might be sorry you asked me,' Alexandra warned him, knowing that once she got started she might ramble on for hours.

He smiled again. 'Never.' All his charm was in that smile.

They fell into easy conversation. He seemed genuinely interested in Charles and for her part she hadn't realised how much she had wanted to talk about him to someone else. How much she needed to. It brought him closer somehow, so that the aching loss she had felt was momentarily stemmed.

Her grandfather listened attentively, prompting her only occasionally. 'And so,' he said at last, 'you're to spend six months apart . . .'

'Yes.' Her voice faltered on the word.

'Your choice?' he asked. The directness of his question threw her for a moment.

'No. Not exactly.'

'Ah. So your mother thought you were too young to become engaged, then?'

She wasn't sure what to say. 'It was a little bit of that, I suppose.' She hesitated. She looked across at her grandfather. That he would understand that Charles had made a mistake and had been forced to pay the price of it, she was certain. He might even sympathise with Charles and his predicament. But still she did not feel close enough to him to confess the truth to him.

Her grandfather's greenish-grey eyes scanned her face, watchful. He must have sensed that there was something beyond what she had told him, but he made no sign that he suspected anything was amiss. Made no move to delve and dig as others might have done.

'So,' he said, making a great business of pouring himself another glass of lemonade, 'you were saying you like to ride . . .'

'Very much, yes.' She smiled at him, grateful for his tact in changing the subject.

'Well then, perhaps we can take out the horses and see round the farm later on this afternoon,' he suggested. 'When it's a bit cooler. Would you like that?'

'Most definitely.' Her enthusiasm was genuine. She could think of nothing more pleasant. She stretched out her legs and took another sip of lemonade. She was beginning to feel more comfortable with him now, more relaxed.

'I'll get the horses saddled up for this afternoon then,' he said. 'You can ride Pashka, he's as old as the hills but very sure-footed and willing.' He was silent for a moment and then he said: 'He was your mother's horse, you know . . .'

There was a slight change in his voice, a tightening, which made her look across at him. His head was bowed and he was staring absently down at his hands.

Without looking up he asked quietly: 'How is she? You haven't said yet.' The wistfulness was unmistakable. The pain.

She saw now what she had been too blind to see at the beginning. That this was all he had wanted to hear about: Sarah. All he had wanted to know, but had been too proud to ask. And like a lion he had had to make several circles around his prey, feigning disinterest, before he had been confident enough to close in.

'Mother? She's fine.' The words fell limply between them. The trouble was, she couldn't think of what to say exactly. The wealth of details seemed suddenly to slip from her at the crucial moment.

'She's happy?'

'She and Daddy are blissfully happy,' she said, sensing, correctly, what he wanted to know. 'Daddy simply adores her, even now, after all these years . . .' It came easier then. She knew now what it was he wished to hear. Little snippets, long since tucked away, were plucked from the past and placed before him, given to him like sips of water to a thirsty man on a desert trail.

After a while he said a little distantly: 'You're very like her, you know.'

'Am I?'

He nodded. 'Very. She'll miss you . . .'

'Oh, she has Daddy,' returned Alexandra brightly. 'And, of course, there's Hugh. He'll keep her busy . . .'

'Hugh?'

'Yes, Hugh.' She gave him a teasing smile. 'Honestly, Grandfather, don't say you've forgotten your own grandson!'

'Grandson?'

'Yes, of course. Don't say . . .' She stopped. One look at his face was enough. He didn't know. He hadn't even been told he had a grandson. Now she knew why she hadn't seen any pictures of Hugh in the sitting-room. She had thought to find them elsewhere in the house. Now she knew there were none.

'Grandfather . . .' She put her hand out to his arm, but he shook it off, standing up so abruptly that the chair jolted backwards. 'I'm sorry, I didn't know . . .'

He went to stand at the window, his back firmly towards her, head bowed. Looking at the sagging shoulders she thought that Prometheus himself had never carried so heavy a burden.

'I didn't realise,' she blundered on, mortified. She sat there wretchedly, watching him. 'It never occurred to me that you hadn't been told . . .' Why on earth hadn't her mother warned her?

The vast expanse of back didn't move. She didn't know how to approach him, how to comfort him.

Alexandra sat there in silence for a moment. After a while she said: 'There's some photographs in my case, if you'd like to see them, Grandfather. I meant to bring them out earlier. Some of the family . . . and of Hugh, of course – ' She paused. 'There's one taken on his last birthday – he's eight now . . .' she added quietly. Even these basics he wouldn't know, she supposed. She hesitated. 'Would you like me to get them for you?'

'Please.' It was all he could manage.

She stood up and went back to her room. The photographs were still packed at the bottom of her case. There was an album and a few loose prints which she had flung in at the last minute. Her father had teased her about taking so many but she had held firm. Now she was inordinately glad she had.

When she came back into the sitting-room her grandfather was still standing at the window, but she sensed a strengthening in him. The shoulders were set squarer, the head not so bowed. Even so, he still avoided turning to face her.

'I'll just leave these on the table, Grandfather,' she called out, trying to keep her voice light.

She hoped he might say something then but the silence was absolute. She stood there uneasily, twisting her fingers together. Finally she cleared her throat.

'I'll be in the garden if you need me.' Already it seemed to have become her refuge.

She didn't wait for his acknowledgment but slipped quietly out onto the verandah. The sun was hot, the shadows short and dense. Behind her she heard the sound of her grandfather stirring at last, his footsteps reverberating against the wooden floor. Then she heard the sound of a drink being poured, the chink of glass against glass. Not lemonade this time, she was sure. And yet, could she blame him? Until this moment she had never fully realised the extent of her mother's bitterness.

She wished she had been forewarned. She might have been able to handle the situation with a little more sagacity then. The hidden complexity of emotions, the secrets, had taken her by surprise. If only she had a girlfriend to talk to. She sighed. If only Jane lived close by. Jane would have offered her sound advice.

She started down the steps into the garden, glad to leave the chilly gloom behind her, to feel the warmth of the sun on her back. So what had happened all those years ago to cause this rift, she wondered. Some deep-seated instinct told her it was something more than just the farm. But what?

The answer lay here at Kirimangari, she was sure of it. It teased her like the missing piece of an intricate jigsaw. And she knew now she couldn't leave until she'd found out the truth.

6

While Alexandra was struggling with her conundrum at Thika, Jane Stanhope was battling with her own problem in Eldoret.

Standing in the courtyard opposite the farmhouse in the cool of the morning, she watched with more than a little trepidation as Tom fought to unlock the surgery door. Last night, when he had looked so exhausted, it had seemed a sensible suggestion for her to take over the morning's 'sick list'; but already she was regretting her hasty offer, woefully aware that her medical skills until this moment had extended little beyond dabbing disinfectant onto a child's grazed knee.

'Are you quite sure that it's safe for me to administer all this willy-nilly?' she asked Tom a little gingerly, as he showed her the shelves laden with neatly labelled bottles.

'Of course. I had even less experience than you and I still managed,' he returned cheerfully. He sounded confident enough but Jane noticed that all the time he was speaking he was carefully moving the cattle medicine a safer distance away from those for human consumption. 'Besides,' he continued airily, 'don't forget those books I gave you. Indispensable for reference . . .'

The books: Jane smiled. *Black's Directory* and a government booklet entitled *Medical Hints for the Settler* had appeared over breakfast that morning. They had done little to boost her confidence. Flicking through the pages she'd been appalled by the range of diseases one could catch out here, little encouraged by Tom's insistence that most could be cured with a good dousing of Condy's, or a decent dose of castor oil or quinine. Listening to his cavalier attitude, Jane had vowed silently that if she were ever to become ill she would head straight for the nearest doctor at Eldoret rather than let Tom get his hands on her.

She watched him now as he drew out a large tin box marked with a red cross and unlocked it. Inside was a mass of small bottles and vials.

'Now this one's opium,' he said, holding up one of the small bottles. 'It's the only anaesthetic we have, so remember where it's kept, won't you?'

His words, coupled with the sight of the scalpels in oiled silk and the forceps and surgical needles, made all her doubts start anew.

'Tom, I really have no idea what I'm doing.'

'You'll be fine,' Tom insisted, grey eyes steady. 'It's common sense mostly. And if there are any really difficult cases, then leave those until I get back. But there won't be. Honestly. It'll be things like minor burns, stomach-aches, problems like that . . .'

From the corner of his eye Tom saw the head boy Mwangi, standing on the pathway, his hat in his hand, and his stick of office tucked respectfully under his arm. 'Listen, darling, I must be on my way,' he said apologetically. 'I'm late as it is. But don't worry. I'm not expecting you to be a Harley Street surgeon in just one day!'

'No, perhaps you ought to make it two!' she rejoined dryly.

'Slow learner, eh?' he teased. He bent over to kiss her. He hesitated, knowing that she wanted him to stay, but also knowing that he couldn't. There was just too much to be done this morning.

'You'll cope admirably,' he told her, giving her an encouraging smile. Then, catching up his hat from the scrubbed table, he was gone.

Jane stood in the doorway, trying to adopt her best Florence Nightingale pose of efficient calm as she watched him head towards the maize fields, Mwangi at his side. A tiny nub of resentment started within her which she quickly quelled. Silly to care that they had had so little time together, she told herself sharply. On the boat out with Alexandra she might naïvely have imagined life would pass at a leisurely pace here, although Tom had told her truthfully, on the train up from Mombasa, that running the farm would be a full-time job, and she must try not to mind.

She'd been warned, but all the same she had still foolishly envisaged that she would have time to acclimatise on her first day. She had pictured them taking a leisurely breakfast together, then walking, arms linked, as he'd shown her the outbuildings and the *shambas*; then she had seen them saddling up to ride further afield to inspect the rest of the farm and to see the waterfall which she had heard so much about, returning tired and happy to sit on the verandah, feet up, drink in hand, to look down across to the purple hills beyond.

Instead she had awoken at the jingling sound of the *tenkele* to find that Tom had already gone through to breakfast. She had had to bolt hers down in order for them to come down to the surgery together before Tom had hurried off to the fields. She knew he wanted to get everything as straight as possible before the rains came, but, even so, she could have done with a little more indulgence on her first morning.

To be fair, Tom had told her exactly what to expect. But words and reality had seemed worlds apart when she arrived here late last night. The house, which Tom had described as sparsely furnished, had turned out to be utterly cheerless, with bare walls and cold concrete floors, warped boards and flimsy curtains. There was no bathroom as such, and the water had to be brought up in buckets from the iron drum outside the kitchen. But she could see that Tom was inordinately proud of what he had built here and she had taken great pains to hide her disappointment, mentally making a note to send to England for some hangings for the walls, and some rugs and cushions, and anything else she could think of to brighten the place up.

Last night she had thought it odd that Tom hadn't been conscious of the sparseness of his surroundings all these years. Now she knew the reason: he'd been simply too busy. And acknowledging that, she knew that if his time was going to be so occupied, so must hers. There was nothing quite so conducive to loneliness as boredom.

She squared her shoulders determinedly and turned her mind back to the surgery. Already the line outside had increased considerably. She smiled to herself, remembering Tom had told her to expect more than the usual quota today. Many would have nothing wrong with them at all but would have come down to inspect the new *memsahib*. She wondered if they would have been so eager to have joined the queue if they had guessed at her inexperience.

From across the courtyard she saw Meru, the houseboy, coming to join her, the wide legs of his faded khaki shorts flapping around his skinny knees. She could barely disguise her relief at the sight of him. At least he would know something of the medicines to be used for he had helped Tom regularly in the surgery in the past.

'Common sense, that's all it is,' Jane repeated to herself forcibly under her breath. But all the same she had to thrust her hands into the deep pockets of her beige printed cotton dress in an attempt to hide her nervousness as she called in her first patient.

It was one of Tom's *shamba* boys. She didn't even have time to examine him or to ask him what was the matter, for Meru handed the quinine tablets almost before the boy had stepped inside.

This then, was what malaria symptoms were like, Jane thought to herself as she gave the boy his daily dose of quinine. She'd have to remember those. Malaria was a particularly common problem here and she suspected there would be several more cases amongst the 'sick list' waiting outside.

The next boy to come in was the colour of Meru's khaki shorts. He looked so wracked with pain as he hobbled in clutching his stomach that Jane at first feared it to be an attack of appendicitis. But on further questioning by Meru it turned out to be an acute case of nothing worse than constipation. She gave him a four-ounce dose of castor oil which, although it seemed excessive, Meru insisted was the quantity Bwana Stanhope issued for such severe cases. Tom, she gathered, went for quick and dramatic cures.

She stopped the cork back tightly into the bottle and then called for the next patient. This time it was merely a mild abrasion on a boy's foot and she quickly dabbed it clean and applied some antiseptic cream, covering the area with some liniment and tape.

She was beginning to feel more confident now. The walking wounded which she had half expected had failed to materialise.

And so the morning went on. There was only one case which caused her to be grateful for the relative lack of daylight in the room. A young mother brought her *toto* in with an ulcerated leg oozing with pus. Jane had never seen such a repulsive sight before.

'How on earth did it get like this?' she asked Meru in hushed tones as she tried to get most of the putrid flesh away with corrosive sublimate. 'She must have seen how bad it was, surely?'

'But of course,' Meru agreed cheerfully as he handed her another swab. 'But first they think they must try their own remedies before they come to us.'

'I see.' She turned her head away; the smell was quite appalling. 'And what sort of remedies would she have used on this? It seems only to have aggravated things.'

Meru gave a little shrug of his shoulders. The answer was probably that the mother had used a healing plaster made of certain leaves and warm cow dung, but he thought it inadvisable to say as much to the new *memsahib*.

Jane caught the look on his face and probed no further. She took the wet lint which he held out to her and bandaged over the sore, telling him to instruct the mother and child to come back every day until the ulcer was completely healed. Whether or not they would, she wasn't sure. Tom had warned her that they were a law unto themselves.

She glanced down the line of patients, feeling more relaxed now. Only a few more to go. She should be finished soon.

It was just as she was calling in the next patient that there was a loud shout from outside and a young boy burst into the surgery in great agitation.

'*Nyoka! Nyoka!*' he cried out, waving his arms frantically.

Jane stiffened at his wailing. 'What is it, Meru?' she asked, turning to him hurriedly. 'What's he saying?'

'A snake, *memsahib*,' Meru told her, turning back to the boy to catch the rest of his jumbled words. 'There is bad trouble. A snake has bitten his sister. She will die, he says . . .'

'*Mbaya sana*,' the boy repeated dully.

'She is very bad,' Meru said.

'Oh God!' This was exactly the kind of disaster that Jane had been dreading. All the jokes she had made in Nairobi with Alexandra about such things seemed suddenly very pertinent and real. She turned to Meru, all the confidence she had gained evaporating. 'Send one of the boys to find the *bwana*,' she said. 'Quickly. Tell him what has happened and ask him to come.' She hoped to heaven that Tom would be close by and not in one of the top fields miles away. She watched one of the *totos* set off, his long skinny legs scudding across the pathway at great speed.

So now it was up to her, she supposed. She turned back to Meru. 'Do you know where the girl is?' she asked. 'There's no time to wait for the *bwana* . . .' She kept her voice as steady as she could. Whatever, she must give the semblance of calm.

Meru nodded and shot a volley of questions at the boy.

'It is as I thought,' he told her at the boy's reply. 'They were at the small *boma* where the cow is kept. The boy is in charge there.'

All the time he had been talking Jane had been collecting up things she thought might be of use: bandages for a tourniquet, the scalpel, a pile of potassium permanganate crystals, a box of Epsom salt; and last, but by no means least, the *Medical Hints* leaflet, though the quick glance at *Black's* had told her most of what she needed to know.

She sped out of the surgery running behind Meru and the boy as they headed towards the maize sheds and the small thorn *boma* beyond.

The girl had been moved to the shade of the thorn hedge by the time they arrived. She was lying very still, her face ashen and drawn, her dark eyes upturned in fear.

Jane remembered Tom telling her of the Africans' terror of snakes. So strong was the power of their auto-suggestion that it was sometimes the fear alone which killed them rather than the venom itself.

She knelt beside the girl, cursing the fact that she knew so little Kiswahili: she needed to jolt her out of this frightened state.

'Tell her she will not die,' she said to Meru emphatically. 'Tell her that these medicines will save her.' She kept her voice steady, showing none of her own uncertainty. 'Do they know what type of snake it was?' she asked Meru, as she feverishly began to unroll the bandage.

'Puff adder,' he rejoined after a quick discussion with the boy.

Jane thanked heaven that it hadn't been a mamba. The girl would have stood little chance then.

She glanced down at the small frail figure before her. Her breathing was short and shallow and already there were signs of swelling around the two puncture marks on the lower part of the right leg. Jane gently lifted up the foot and passed the bandage hurriedly under and around, tying it so tightly that the skin wrinkled and puckered under its pressure.

Then, taking a deep breath, she picked up the scalpel. *Black's Directory* had advised making a cut half an inch deep and one inch long, following the line of the bite. She hesitated only a moment, nodding to Meru to keep the girl still.

The little audience of *totos* which had appeared from nowhere and were squatting on their haunches in a tight semi-circle around her fell silent as she prepared to make the incision. The stillness was infinitely more unnerving than their earlier noise and chatter.

Jane pressed the point of the blade against the smooth skin. It was so sharp it needed almost no pressure at all to pierce through. As the knife cut in the girl let out a loud scream of pain, her eyes widening, and she started to roll from side to side in agony.

Jane fought desperately to keep her hand steady. 'Keep her still!' she shouted at Meru, terrified lest the scalpel slip.

A few seconds and it was over. She handed the knife to Meru and hunched over the leg, pressing the skin sharply on either side of the incision. Blood spurted out and ran down the child's leg in thin red rivulets. Jane wiped them away with a swab and pressed again.

Twice she did this and then she leant forward and sucked at the wound as hard as she could. She felt her stomach tighten. The taste of the warm blood in her mouth, coupled with the fear of swallowing any of the venom, made her almost vomit. But she couldn't give in.

She spat out the blood, rinsed out her mouth vigorously with water and wiped it clean. Then she bent back over the leg again, determinedly ignoring the lurching feeling in her stomach. She wasn't sure precisely how long she was supposed to keep up the procedure but after another dozen or so attempts, she stopped. Heaven help me if I've got any holes in my teeth, she thought, sitting up and rinsing her mouth thoroughly.

She straightened slowly, feeling a little unsteady. The sheer effort and concentration of the past ten minutes had taken its toll. She was aware suddenly that the little group of *totos* had started chattering again. It was a good omen, she hoped. A sign of the tension easing.

She called to Meru to bring the water over again and began to mix up a weakish solution of the potassium permanganate crystals, stirring it until it was well dissolved. Then she carefully washed around the wound several times, dabbing gently all the time so as to not pull at the open cut.

It was all finished then, save for the final bandaging. She could hardly believe it. She glanced down at the child, putting a hand to the girl's forehead. It was slightly warm, but certainly not feverish, and the breathing, though still shallow, had quietened at last. She felt a surge of elation stir within her. Too early to tell, of course, but she thought, just thought, she might have pulled it off.

It was as she was giving instructions for the child to be carried up to the surgery for observation for the next few hours that she heard the sound of Tom galloping down the dirt track towards them.

She stood up and raised her hand in greeting as he skidded to a halt beside them.

She saw him glance down at the girl and then quickly across at her. 'Don't say you've managed already by yourself?'

The amazed approval in his voice made her glow with pleasure. 'I have. Or at least I think I have,' she told him with a wide grin.

'Good Lord! I'm impressed. I admit it,' he announced, putting his arms around her waist and drawing her to him. 'How on earth did you know what to do?'

'Didn't really,' she admitted. 'But I had *Black's Directory*, remember.' She put her hands on his shoulders and looked up at him. 'Indispensable for reference,' she said, mimicking his voice at the surgery that morning.

He laughed. 'And I thought it would take you at least two days to become a surgeon!' he teased her.

She reached up to kiss him. 'Oh, one learns fast, Mr Stanhope.'

'Out here, one has to!' Tom returned lightly, linking arms with her. 'By the way, what was it that bit her? It wasn't a mamba or her leg would have swollen up like a drum.'

'Puff adder,' she told him. 'At least I'm sure that's what the boy told Meru.'

'You didn't see it?'

'No.'

'Then the boys didn't kill it?' There was an edge to his voice which made her look across at him.

'Not that I know of.' In the chaos she hadn't even thought of telling them to do so.

'Damn!' Tom stopping walking. 'I'm continually telling them if they see a snake to kill it. But they won't touch the wretched things, dead or alive. I'll have to go and look for it myself, I suppose . . .'

'But what hope have you of finding it again?' she asked.

'If it were a mamba, none at all. But as it was a puff adder quite a good chance actually,' he told her. 'They're incredibly slothful things. Probably hasn't moved that far from where it bit the child. I'll just go up and get my gun and then I'll go back to the *boma* and see if I can find it.'

She clutched at his arm. 'Must you?' She didn't like to think of him putting himself in danger, however slight.

'Yes, I must, I'm afraid. The damn thing will probably bite someone else again if I don't. They're beastly things and easy to tread on when they've got a coating of dust over them.'

They had reached the surgery. Jane would have liked to have gone on with Tom but she wanted to give the girl some sal volatile first to boost her circulation and then she had to remove the tourniquet. It would never do to leave that on too long. Besides, she realised now, she had forgotten the last five patients of the morning's surgery. They were still standing purposefully by the door. She could hardly believe it. They hadn't seemed to have moved an inch since she had so unceremoniously burst out of the surgery nearly an hour beforehand.

She went into the little room and washed her hands carefully in the metal basin which Meru had filled with warm water. She lathered the soap up, rubbing and pummelling at her hands, massaging around each finger meticulously. Down by the *boma* she had rinsed her hands and thought to have got most of the blood off, but now she could see by the colour of the water that that had been merely an illusion. She shuddered a little at the sight of it and took the grey towel which Meru held out to her, drying her hands vigorously. Now she was back in the surgery she felt detached, somehow, from all that had happened down at the *boma*.

She quickly dealt with the girl and then called in the next patient. The cut, which was beginning to fester, might have caused her to cringe at the start of the morning. But not now. She dealt with it almost brusquely.

It was as she was examining the second patient that she heard the gunshot. She'd known it would come, of course, but even so it took her by surprise.

She put down the castor oil bottle she was holding and went to the door to look down towards the *boma*. Just in case. But all was well, it appeared.

She saw Tom almost immediately. He gave her a salute to show her the mission was accomplished and then bent down to pick up a long, dangling, rope-like object which he held out proudly, with arm outstretched, trophy-like. She assumed it to be the offending puff adder and hoped to heaven it was well and truly dead. It looked far bigger than she had imagined, far thicker, too. Involuntarily, she shuddered, glad of the distance between them.

She gave Tom a quick, last, encouraging wave and then ducked back into the surgery. For a moment she stood staring down at the man in front of her, momentarily forgetting what it was he had been complaining of. Then she saw the castor oil bottle still unstopped. Ah yes. Four ounces for this case – at least.

It was only as she was tidying up the surgery after the last patient had left that she realised Tom still had not come back. Curiosity getting the better of her, she asked Meru to finish tidying and to lock up for her and started off down the dirt track.

Tom was now nowhere in sight. She came to the spot where he had been. The puff adder lay in a tangled heap by the side of the track. It was a hideously ugly thing, with a flat head – half of which had been blown away – and a puffy body. Lying there covered with a fine coating of dirt, Jane could see how easy it would be to step upon it when it was half submerged and the chevrons on its back camouflaged by the dust. A moment's inattention and its fangs would hook into your leg. She was glad of the heavy boots which Tom had made her buy.

She glanced about her. 'Tom?' she called out. Still she couldn't see him. 'Tom, are you still down here?'

There was a flicker of movement on the other side of the thorn hedge. 'Over here,' she heard him call.

She came round the edge of the *boma* to the entrance. Tom was in the far corner, crouching over a large, dark, immobile mound. He didn't even turn his head as she started to walk towards him and she instinctively knew that something was terribly wrong.

She quickened her pace. 'What is it?' Tension made her voice sharp and staccato. 'Tom, what's wrong?'

He half stood up then and as he stepped aside she saw at once what had held his attention. His precious prized cow, lying, not with her head up and her feet tucked under her as was usual, but stiffly on her side, with her head turned at an odd angle on the ground.

'What on earth's happened?' she asked. 'Is she ill?' As she came nearer she could see that the cow's belly was so swollen that her skin was as tight as a barrel and that one hind leg was pushed up rigidly into the air as if in some bizarre, distorted salute.

She was still alive, but only just. There was foam on her lips and her eyes were dull and bloodshot, her breath coming in long raspy gasps. She didn't even seem to notice Jane's approach.

It was a pitiful sight. 'Is it as bad as it looks?' Jane asked. She could feel Tom's stiffness, his anxiety, from here. She reached out and touched him on his shoulder. 'No chance of saving her, I suppose?'

''Fraid not. It's just what we don't need right now, as well.'

The loss of the cow, though not a major calamity as would be the return of the locusts, was a blow nonetheless. And with the bank manager breathing down their necks it was one that they could have well done without.

'Is there nothing you can do?' she asked him gently.

'Apart from putting an end to her misery, no,' he told her flatly. He kicked at a small stone and sent it skimming across the *boma*, trying to hang onto his temper. 'Damn bloody snakes!'

'Snakes?' Until this moment she hadn't realised the exact cause of the cow's approaching demise. 'Oh, Tom, not the puff adder again?' She felt a sharp pang of guilt. Perhaps if she had thought to have told the boys to find and kill the snake, this never would have happened. Perhaps if she hadn't been so busy with the girl . . .

Tom stretched out and took her hand in his, sensing by the look on her face which way her thoughts were turning.

'You're not to blame, Jane. Truly. It probably wasn't the same snake anyway. Much more likely to have been a mamba.'

But they would never know, that was the trouble. And Jane's former feeling of triumph in saving the young girl was now ashes to the wind, lost in the midst of this new, depressing turn of events. It didn't matter how much Tom denied it, she thought grimly, she would still blame herself.

The cow moaned again, the unfortunate beast caught in a spasm of renewed agony.

'You'd better go,' Tom said quietly. 'There's no point prolonging this. There's no hope for the poor thing.'

His eyes shifted to her face and rested there. He looked so exhausted, so *old*. Her heart went out to him.

'I'll be waiting just outside the *boma*,' she told him, her voice catching slightly.

He gave her a quick nod and then she saw him walk over to the thorn hedge and reload his gun.

She waited outside the *boma* for what seemed to be an eternity and then she heard the echoing crack of the rifle. A little choking sob rose up in her and she fought to keep it back. Silly to let the death of a cow upset her so, she knew, but it was her first experience of the cruel unpredictability of life out here.

She saw now how quickly fortunes could falter and change and it frightened her a little. She would never admit as much to Tom, of course. If life was tough here, then so must she be.

And she knew then that in the few short hours since she had been here she had changed already. And that the young, naïve girl who had stood with Alexandra on the docks of Mombasa had gone forever, cast aside like a cumbersome coat on a warm summer's day.

7

Fine dust swirled about the small crowd of spectators gathered at the edge of the pitch as the polo ponies thundered past, Robert Dalgleish in their midst, galloping and turning at great speed.

The third chukka was almost over and it was proving to be a fast and exciting game. Almost too fast for Alexandra who had little familiarity with the intricate rules and was trying to follow the complex moves.

Colonel Blake, at her side, had offered to explain the game to her but his interpretation of the rules was somewhat woolly and his commentary peppered by loud remarks of: 'Mark your opponent, why don't you?' and 'Easy shot! Shouldn't have missed that!'

The old boy, greatly excited by the game, had been at pains to tell Alexandra of his own expertise at polo, though his wife had winked at Alexandra at this pronouncement, countering in whispered tones that her husband had seldom been out of the practice 'cage'. This, she explained to Alexandra, meant he could only hit the ball when stationary, and since he had to stop every time he tried to take a swing, it also meant that he was constantly being run into from behind by the other players.

Looking across the pitch at the pace of the game Alexandra could see that this might present distinct problems. No wonder the Colonel had only once won a coveted place on the team.

His enthusiasm for the game remained undimmed nonetheless. 'Good shot! Tricky backhand, that!' he roared out as the ponies thundered perilously close past him. In the general cloud of fine dust kicked up by the ponies' hooves Alexandra saw Robert gallop past. He rode expertly, exerting only the slightest pressure to turn his pony left and right, guiding it on with his legs and his lean supple body. Unlike the other players, he barely touched the reins.

She watched him now as he hared up the field, hard on the tail of one of the players from the Visitors' team. The next minute he had blocked a cut-shot, turned sharply and was taking the ball back upfield, changing direction constantly to fool the opposition before flicking the ball through the posts to score.

'Now that's how to play polo!' cried the Colonel enthusiastically, shouting to be heard above the cheers.

The ponies cantered back and lined up again for the throw-in. There was a great clash and a jumble of sticks and then the ball was tapped out of the tangle and taken off down the field again. For a second Alexandra thought the Home team might score again but the ball went wide, hit the posts and bounced back; and just as Stuart Avery looked about to pop the ball between the posts his pony decided it had had quite enough of the game and shied away, almost unseating him.

'That's the trouble with the game out here,' grumbled the Colonel remorsely. 'The ponies aren't bred for the game.'

In truth, Alexandra thought that the unpredictability of the ponies, most of which had little experience of the game and had merely been taken off their respective farms for the day, added to the excitement.

Watching the players now as they careered down the field, she regretted more than ever that she hadn't been able to persuade her grandfather to come. When the Blakes had arrived early that morning to bring her here, she had thought they might induce Edward to join them. Even Juma had been hopeful that he might change his mind. But he'd stood firm, telling them that the journey was too long and it was too hot and giving a multitude of excuses of why he couldn't leave the farm. A pity, because on her arrival a dozen or so of his old acquaintances had asked after him and obviously had hoped to see him again. She would make a point of telling him he had been missed.

She felt the touch of a hand on her arm. 'Shall we move to the shade, dear?' asked Rose Blake, who'd obviously had enough of the dust and the noise and the heat and was taking the opportunity of the end of the chukka to make a move.

Together they walked back to the awnings which the Averys had put up as extra shade for the spectators, and took a seat at one of the trestle tables. A light breeze had begun to blow now, fingering its way across the treetops.

'It won't be long before the rains come,' said Rose, looking out to where small clouds pitted the horizon. 'A day or two at the most, or so I should say.' She glanced back at Alexandra. 'It's quite a spectacular sight you know. You can see it coming from miles away, this giant black wall of rain advancing across the countryside. I won't ever forget the first time I saw it . . .' She paused to accept a glass of iced fruit punch from one of the houseboys. 'Or the first time I saw the coffee flowering, either.'

Rose smiled, silent for a moment, pale blue eyes staring into the distance as if in recollection. 'That was at your grandfather's place, my dear,' she said. 'Stephen and I had just come out from England and had bought a place north of Thika and I remember we met your grandfather at some party or other and he told us to come over to Kirimangari the next day before dawn.' Her old wrinkled face creased even more. 'Well, you can imagine, we thought he was mad, Stephen and I, but he insisted. He was like that, your grandfather, very persuasive. So the next morning there we were, and just after dawn he took us all up to a hilltop overlooking the estate – your grandmother Amelia and your mother, too, – and we sat there just waiting for the flowers to open. Pop-pop-pop-pop-pop. That's what it sounded like, almost like bubbles bursting. And as we looked down over the valley we could see it all literally turning to white, as the buds burst into flower. Magical, it was. Truly. I shall be eternally grateful to your grandfather for insisting we came. Though, I must say, it made our growing sisal seem very flat and boring in comparison after that!' She gave a soft, reedy laugh and put her hand out to Alexandra's arm. 'So, make sure he doesn't forget to take you up once the rains come, won't you? It's a sight you'll remember all your life.'

'Then I'll make sure I don't miss it,' Alexandra told the old lady, wondering why her mother had never once mentioned such a fairy-tale sight to her. She took a sip of her drink, the ice chinking against her teeth.

Rose Blake leant back slightly in her seat, surveying Alexandra slowly. 'So, my dear, how do you find your grandfather?'

'He . . .' She hesitated, not quite sure how much to say. She couldn't meet the old lady's eyes.

'He's still drinking then?' Circumlocution was not one of Rose Blake's faults.

Alexandra smiled, 'Yes,' she admitted quietly.

'Poor Edward.' The old lady shook her head sadly. 'He never quite got over the loss, did he?'

'No,' admitted Alexandra. 'It was a blow to lose so much of the farm.'

'The farm?' The tired voice was suddenly vigorous. 'Good heavens, child, that's not why he drinks!'

'No?'

'No! It was your mother going back to England that did it. And then losing Amelia. He utterly adored them both . . .'

'If he hadn't been so unkind to my grandmother, she might have come back to him,' Alexandra retorted stiffly, thinking, wrongly, that Rose Blake was blaming Amelia for her absence.

'Unkind to her? What nonsense!' Rose Blake exclaimed sharply, putting down her drink and peering across at her. 'Wherever did you get that notion?'

'She lived with us, remember?' Alexandra pointed out, recalling her mother's oft-repeated tale of providing Amelia with a much-needed haven away from Edward's moody outbursts.

A rousing cheer went up from the spectators close by but Rose's penetrating gaze did not flicker away from Alexandra. 'We spent a lot of time with them, you know,' she said slowly. 'He never was anything other than sweet to her. They were very happy together.'

Alexandra stared down at her drink. She felt she had said too much. The rattle of family skeletons in the cupboard sounded acutely in her ears. 'Well, perhaps I misunderstood,' she allowed, trying to make light of it. She'd gain nothing by exposing the extent of her grandfather's irascibility.

'*Very* happy,' Rose repeated, as if to push her point home. 'And Stephen and I were often over at Kirimangari. Never once was there any *hint* of unpleasantness. Never. Now if you'd said that about Cameron Dalgleish and his wife, I'd have agreed with you. He was *beastly* to Vera, though I have to say she deserved it. Always complaining.'

'Was she?' prompted Alexandra, glad that the conversation had turned away from her grandfather.

'Always,' reiterated Rose. 'So much so that I once asked her if she hated Kenya so much why didn't she just go back to England. But she wouldn't of course and once she'd had the accident there was nothing she could do but stay with Cameron so he could look after her.' There was a faint rustle behind them and a tiny ghekko ran across the wall to a shady corner. 'But she made Cameron's life a misery for him. Lucky for him that he had Robert there with him. I think he would have gone the way of your grandfather otherwise, especially when Robert's parents were killed . . .'

She might have gone on but the loud jangling of the *tengele* sounded across the pitch, setting a flock of weaver birds jabbering into the air from the acacia close by them.

'That's the end of the game, presumably,' said Alexandra watching the eight players, covered from head to toe with red dust, canter off the field.

'And the Home team won by the looks of it,' Rose remarked brightly. 'Though I'm not surprised. Stuart Avery was playing well today, I thought. And young Robert Dalgleish even better.' She paused to brush an insect off her brown wrinkled arm and glanced back at Alexandra. 'You know, it was a shame Cameron fell out with your grandfather over that land. They could have done with each other's support during the difficult times. They were such friends once, too. Both demon riders. My dear, when I think of the early morning hunts we had together. Goodness, the pace those two went!' She glanced up as Stephen came towards them. Despite his advancing years he was still ramrod-straight and his purposeful stride betrayed his army background in every regimented step. 'A good game, darling?' she called out to him.

'Very.' He lowered himself into the seat beside her, declining the fruit punch the houseboy offered him and ordering a gin and bitters instead. 'And such a pace. I'm exhausted from having just watched the match!' He glanced across at Alexandra. 'Did you enjoy it, my dear?' he asked.

'Tremendously.'

'Good.' He sank back into the white wicker chair, stretching out his grey-flannelled legs. 'Of course, I'm afraid it's just the poor man's version of the game here. Not like those fellers on the other side of the Aberdares. They've got the time and the money to build up quite impressive teams there.' There was the merest hint of envy in his voice.

'Stephen!' Rose admonished him. 'You know you wouldn't be happy living like that. You've always said they've got too much money and not enough to do!'

'Whereas we have too much to do and not enough money!' Stephen returned with a laugh.

Alexandra smiled. But she sensed for all his humour there was a core of truth to his words. Everyone was having difficulties of sorts, unless like the Happy Valley Set they had substantial private incomes or the backing of large estates in England to keep them bolstered. Robert had told her that if it were not for the Indian traders carrying some of the farmers financially, allowing them to run up bills against future crops being sold, many more of the settlers would have collapsed than had done so.

'I was just telling Alexandra about the hunts we used to have with her grandfather,' said Rose, quickly changing the subject away from the depressing one of money.

'Oh yes, good times those.' Stephen's thin face visibly brightened at the memory. 'We used to ride with the Makuyu hounds sometimes, too,' he said, turning back to Alexandra. 'Remember it well. Lord! The pace your grandfather set! He'd be up with hounds, don't you know, your mother too, skimming across those plains. Quite took my breath away watching them.' He took a sip of his gin and bitters and set it down on the table again. 'Fearless your mother was. Almost recklessly so at times. But, by golly, every man admired her for her spirit! Such energy . . . Tell me, is she still so wickedly devil-may-care?'

'Devil-may-care?' Alexandra tried, but didn't quite succeed, to keep the surprise out of her voice.

'Yes. All fire and mischief,' the Colonel urged, peering at her eagerly.

She hesitated only a moment. 'Yes,' she ventured. 'All fire and mischief . . .'

It was what he had wanted to hear. He smiled happily at her reply. 'Good. Never do for a girl like that to lose her high spirits, eh?' He drained the last of his gin and bitters and called for another. 'Now, I remember the time when we went out over Naivasha way . . .'

But Alexandra was no longer listening. She felt that a window, hitherto shuttered, had been opened to her. And like Alice, she was no longer sure of what was real and what was not. Images crowded in on her. She had thought all this time her mother to be a rigid, rather purposefully conventional person. But now, it seemed, past certainties were only distorted reflections. And this was so, not only of her mother, but of her grandfather Edward and grandmother Amelia too.

Today, the kaleidoscope of the past had been shaken so fiercely that, even though the pieces were the same in essence, the pattern they now made had been changed forever.

A voice broke into her thoughts. Someone was calling her name. She lifted her head to see Robert Dalgleish coming through the crowd towards her.

'So, Miss Drayton, you couldn't persuade your grandfather to join you, then?' His voice was deep and unhurried and there was something brilliant and appealing in his smile. She felt reassured by his presence.

'No,' admitted Alexandra. 'He was determined to stay at home, I'm afraid. The Blakes were kind enough to bring me.'

'That was good of you, Stephen,' said Robert, nodding towards the Colonel. He propped himself up on the table opposite Alexandra, stretching out his long legs before him. 'So, tell me, how are your intrepid travel plans progressing? Or have they been put on hold for the moment?'

'On hold. For the moment anyway.' She dipped her hat slightly so she could see him through the glass. 'But I'm still hoping to get to Nyeri. And across to Eldoret, too.'

'So things are easier for you at Kirimangari then?' He put down his glass and lit a cigarette, watching her carefully. He had to admit she looked more relaxed then when he'd last seen her. Then, he'd been worried by her pinched expression.

'Much easier,' Alexandra admitted. Her grandfather was still drinking, but not to the extent of those first few days.

'Glad to hear it,' Robert said, reaching out and touching her shoulder very lightly in a gesture of encouragement. 'It must have been rough for you at first . . .'

A swift appreciative smile lit Alexandra's eyes. 'It wasn't easy,' she admitted ruefully. Somehow with Robert she didn't feel she had to pretend. 'But we're getting on rather well now. I think he's enjoying having someone to take around the farm with him.'

The *tengele* sounded again, its harsh sound cutting across the stillness. Luncheon was being served on the carefully mown lawns in front of the house. Beside them the Blakes stirred, tempted by the rich aroma coming from the barbecue pits where the roasting meats had been slowly turning on spits since last night.

'Are you ready to join the throng?' Robert asked Alexandra, stretching out his hand to her.

'There's something I wanted to ask you first.' Green eyes met blue. 'I hope you don't mind.'

'Of course not.' She found his air of imperturbability comforting.

'It's just something the Blakes said.' She glanced down, brushing some imaginary particle from her yellow flared silk skirt. 'Something about my mother.' She hesitated then looked up at him. 'You said you could remember her, didn't you?'

He peered down at her cautiously. 'A bit, why?'

'Well, was she the way they described her?'

'And how was that?'

'All fire and mischief, I think . . .'

He laughed uproariously. 'Pretty accurate, if you ask me!' He glanced across at her, noticing that she didn't smile. 'Why, aren't mothers supposed to be like that?' he queried. 'I thought you'd be pleased.'

'I am, in a way. It's just that she isn't like that now,' she told him. She fiddled with her half-empty glass. 'It's almost as if she were another person here . . .'

'Perhaps in a sense she was,' said Robert. He stubbed out his cigarette and leant back against the table again, pushing his hands into the pockets of his fawn-coloured trousers. 'You've seen for yourself, it's a different world here. It's not like England where everything's stifled by conformity. High spirits and exuberance are admired here. Everything's on the surface – tempers, passions. Not like in England where every emotion has to be shut tightly away . . . Perhaps she had to change. Perhaps that was her only way to survive.'

'Possibly.' Alexandra remained unconvinced, though she could see how difficult it would be for an exotic flower to bloom in such a dark constricting climate. Could see, too, that it might be easier to conform rather than face Grandma Drayton's vituperative wrath. Fire and mischief were not qualities which Grandma Drayton would encourage.

And yet, even if that were so, it still did not explain why her mother had spoken so seldom of her years here: nor why, when she did, it was usually in such disparaging terms. It was as if she had purposely cut herself off from everything here, smothering the memories in their warm cradle before they had a chance to grow.

She stirred, aware that Robert's intense blue gaze was upon her.

'Have I said something amiss?' he asked gently. 'You've gone awfully quiet . . .'

'Have I? Sorry,' she apologised, embarrassed that he might think he was somehow to blame. 'Just thinking . . .'

'About your mother?'

She nodded.

He looked down reflectively for a moment. 'You shouldn't worry about her so,' he said, wondering whether or not he was about to tread on sacred ground. 'She may not be the carefree girl she once was, but we all change. Life demands it of us. And she's happy, isn't she? I mean, from what you've told me your father absolutely adores her . . .'

'He does,' Alexandra had to acknowledge. 'And yes, she's happy.' Content might be a more appropriate word, but secure certainly.

'Then that's all that matters,' Robert told her softly. 'Let go of the past. It'll do you no good. Really. It's a tenacious beast once it's got hold of you.'

Something in his voice made her look up at him. Instinctively she knew he was speaking from experience and she realised now how hard it must have been for him to cope with the death of his parents, to push it firmly into the past and to force himself to go forwards.

She leant over and touched his arm. 'It's good advice. I'll try and heed it,' she said quietly. 'And thank you for listening . . .'

He smiled. 'I'm here, remember,' he said, his voice returning to its mellow lightness. 'Any time you feel like talking.'

Their eyes met. 'I know.'

There was a moment's silence, then he stretched out his hands to hers and pulled her to her feet and together they started to walk up towards the house.

And behind them the shadows of the past flickered in the sunlight and were gone.

8

The rains arrived late, coming with a ferocity which took Alexandra quite by surprise. Not the light refreshing drizzle of England this. Clouds would storm dark across the sky and rain fell in spates, drenching the coffee trees and relentlessly filling the gullies. It would pour down spasmodically, stopping as suddenly as it had started. One moment the rain would be soaking into the hard-baked ground, washing it into a sea of mud; the next the sun would come out and the row of coffee trees which had disappeared so completely behind a wall of water would reappear again, glistening under a brilliant sky.

The countryside changed in a matter of days, too. It was as if it had been marking time these past few months, like Sleeping Beauty awaiting her kiss, and that now, awakened, it had burst back into life with a vengeance. The tawny, dried-out grass quickly pushed up new green shoots, the coffee buds swelled out ready to burst into flower, and even the earth seemed to smell different – fresh and fruitful and alive. It was an unforgettable aroma, powerful, evocative: the essence of survival.

For the farm it was a time when the weeding became even more important. If the insidious intruders were allowed to grow during the wet season they would use up the moisture which the coffee would need in the dry weather. Her grandfather told her that weeds could reduce the yield of the coffee cherry by as much as five pounds a tree.

'And in these times of small enough profit it makes all the difference,' he had explained as they rode round the estate together. 'And it's now, early on in the Rains, that the weeds can do their worst, taking up the plant foods needed by the coffee.'

He was given to passing on these little snippets as they rode around the farm. They had taken to riding out each day, and every time she would learn a little bit more about coffee and the art of growing it.

Considering her legacy, she'd been ashamed as to how little she had known about the subject when she'd first arrived at Kirimangari.

'What! Don't you even know a little of its history?' her grandfather had boomed at her soon after her arrival, appalled by her ignorance.

She'd had to admit that she didn't, apart from knowing that it originated in Arabia.

'Abyssinia!' he'd corrected her quickly. 'In the fourteenth century. And from there it was introduced along the old caravan routes to Yemen.' He'd spoken then of the legend among the Muhammadans that the Angel Gabriel had brought coffee for Muhammad to drink when he was ill. 'Which is all very curious when one considers it was some of the more fanatical Muhammadans who tried to ban coffee in the beginning.'

'But why?' Alexandra had asked.

'On the grounds that it was an intoxicating drink and to partake of it was simply a method of evading the law against wine drinking,' her grandfather continued wryly, his greenish-grey eyes atwinkling.

'But that's nonsense, surely?' Alexandra had retorted and had been surprised when her grandfather had merely shrugged.

'I suppose in some ways it's not so odd,' he'd returned. 'There's some evidence to suggest that because of the sugar in the coffee pulp it became mildly alcoholic when it was allowed to ferment for a short time. And after all, it was known as *gahva*, the Arabic poetic word for wine, so I suspect there were some grounds for their complaint. And you know yourself that coffee certainly is a stimulant, even animals become frisky after they've browsed on the shrubs.' He'd smiled dryly at the thought and then leant back in his chair and stretched. 'But, luckily for us at any rate, the Sultan finally overruled the Governor of Mecca's ban and decreed that the faithful would not lose their place in Heaven if they indulged in coffee. Soon it was to be found from Egypt to the Persian gulf and from Aden up to Constantinople.'

'And from there to England?'

Her grandfather had nodded. 'Via the fashionable Vienna, yes. And from there it more or less spread across the world, though it only came to East Africa in the 1890s with the Roman Catholic fathers and their missions. Strange, isn't it, that it took so long to come here when Abyssinia, where it all began, is so close.'

That conversation had taken place several weeks ago, and whereas at first he'd been cautious, conscious of boring her with an overdose of details, he now knew that her interest was genuine and took pleasure in gradually imparting his hard-earned knowledge to her.

Today, as they rode towards the nurseries, he was busily telling her about the seedlings which were to be planted out during the next few weeks. These he had grown from the seeds from his own estate, carefully pulping the berries by hand, so that the parchment would not be broken. The seed had then been mixed with wood ashes and left under an open shelter to dry, with all the uneven-sized or misshapen beans being removed and only the best-formed seeds being sown into the shaded nursery.

Now the seedlings were about fifteen inches high and ready to be lifted out and transferred to the carefully prepared holes, lined and dug out, in one of the far *shambas*.

Looking at her grandfather as he bent down to examine the glossy-leaved plants, watching how tenderly he handled them, Alexandra could tell how much these new seedlings meant to him. His progeny almost. Certainly they were a measure of his own determination not to give in despite all the odds being stacked against him. They were a symbol of his hope for the future, his pride in them almost tangible.

'So, shall we go and see the new *shamba*?' her grandfather asked after he had finished checking all the seedlings. He took the reins from her and mounted up again, swinging up into the saddle with ease. 'It should be staked and ready for planting now. We should be thinking of getting these seedlings in pretty soon, don't you think?' He paused to glance across at her as if in deference to her opinion, his hand going up to stroke his bay's powerful neck.

'Absolutely,' Alexandra agreed, with a smile. Her grandfather's purposeful use of 'we' rather than 'I' touched her. It seemed to signal that he no longer regarded her as an outsider.

They rode off, side by side, the two long-legged house-dogs trotting happily along beside them. They followed her grandfather everywhere around the estate, almost like shadows. Her grandfather had poohpoohed her idea that it was from loyalty that they did so, telling her that it was much more likely that they were afraid to let him out of their sight for fear of the leopards which roamed the countryside. Although she doubted this reasoning, Alexandra was only too aware that there were indeed still leopards around the estate – the very name Kirimangari meant Leopard Hills in Kuyu – and that they would venture right up to a house and snatch a small dog off the verandah given half a chance. Looking at her grandfather's two shaggy cross-breeds she couldn't imagine for the life of her how they could be considered tasty morsels.

Alexandra and her grandfather started to push their way up the hill along the muddy track, the horses straining forward as the rain-drenched earth moved and slipped under their hooves. Alexandra leant forward, patting Pashka's silky neck reassuringly. She glanced across at her grandfather. His big bay was mired up to his hocks but Edward pushed him steadily on, calming his nervous jog. He was an excellent horseman and Alexandra could imagine him to have been a demon at polo. She told him so once they had negotiated the hill. 'Ah, but polo's not so much about being a good rider as it is about being a good ballplayer,' he told her, reining in his bay and turning in his saddle to look across at her. 'They always say that if a chap can't ride particularly well but has a good eye for a ball, they'll still be able to make a polo player out of him. Whereas even if he's an expert horseman, if he hasn't got the eye, then he'll never make the grade.'

Colonel Blake had said more or less the same to her at the Averys' match, but all the same, having watched the fast and furious antics on the field, she knew the skill of the horseman in manoeuvring his horse counted for a great deal.

'But you've got to be able to bring out the best in your pony, surely?' she commented, stretching forward to ruffle Pashka's velvety ears.

'Of course. But at some of the earliest tournaments I played in out here even the mules were roped in to be ridden, so you couldn't count on your pony helping you much. I was lucky, though, by sheer chance my mare proved to be the most neat-footed turner . . .'

'The Abyssinian cross?' Alexandra asked.

Her grandfather's face creased into a smile. 'Yes. That little mare. How did you hear about her?'

'Robert Dalgleish told me.'

She saw him wrinkle his nose at the name, but at least now

it did not provoke the instant angry outburst of not so long ago.

'He said she could turn on a pin,' Alexandra continued steadily, hoping to draw him back to the pony. She saw her grandfather's face ease.

'So she could,' he agreed. 'Best little mare I ever had.'

She smiled. 'So I was told. Robert said he'd been trying to match her for years and never could,' Alexandra told him. 'Wished he'd had one like her.'

Her grandfather turned his head away suddenly. 'Well, that's the Dalgleishes for you,' he said, his voice showing its old bitterness. 'Always wanting something that's not theirs . . .'

'Grandfather!' protested Alexandra. 'That's not fair! He meant it merely as a compliment.'

'And the Dalgleishes are full of compliments, when it suits them,' said her grandfather tightly. 'Take care, Alexandra. He's trying to win you over, that's all. He's probably trying to inveigle his way into your good books, thinking it'll change my opinion.'

'Robert Dalgleish isn't like that,' Alexandra contended, gathering up her reins.

'Isn't he?' her grandfather challenged her. 'But that's what his uncle did. Pretended friendship and then took what he could. I doubt his nephew is any different. They're one and the same, believe me.'

She was about to protest otherwise but her grandfather ended the conversation by digging his heels into the bay, making the great horse bound forward into a canter.

Alexandra urged Pashka on down the track after him, glad a few minutes later of the sudden appearance of a troop of baboons at the edge of the plantation. Their noisy arrival diverted their attention, and the Dalgleishes were forgotten as Alexandra and her grandfather watched a dozen or so wedge-shaped faces warily turn towards them as the little troop made its way across the *shamba*. One was particularly large, the leader of the pack no doubt; it stopped from time to time, stretching its neck and drawing back its lips over yellow teeth, challenging them to dare to approach its little entourage.

'I've seen them riding on the back of bucks, you know,' her grandfather told her as they watched the baboons move off at a slow march. 'They're cheeky devils and they'll run through the coffee rows, pulling the trees about just for the sheer fun of it. Damned nuisance sometimes.' But Alexandra noted that he didn't reach for his rifle, content to let them move off at their own pace.

It was late in the afternoon by the time Alexandra and her grandfather came back to the house. Juma had been down to Thika and there were two letters awaiting Alexandra.

One was from her father. When Alexandra saw that the letter came from England she secretly hoped it might be from Charles. She had to curb her disappointment when she recognised the handwriting, although to be fair, since Charles had only written a few days beforehand it was rather a lot to expect another letter so soon. But she had *hoped*, nonetheless.

She felt rather churlish as she opened her father's letter. It was so chatty and bright. He started off with what she knew already: namely that Charles was still in Yorkshire and that the inquest was set for the end of the month. He also hinted – and this she had not known – that Charles's trip to New York was now unlikely to take place since the bank for which he had hoped to work had hit financial difficulties. Apparently Lord Kildare was suggesting that Charles take a prolonged holiday in Europe instead. The Press's curiosity about the case having been sated in January, it seemed probable that the inquest would only make headlines in the seedier of the papers and would die down much more quickly than had been expected.

It was welcome news for Alexandra. She had not envied Charles, banished first to the wilds of Yorkshire and then being shut up all day in a bank in New York. She knew how much he loved London and thrived in its environment; he would miss the likes of Monty Buckmaster and the endless social life he embodied.

She read on. It was clear that her letter describing the débâcle of her arrival had not yet arrived, for her father made no reference to it, nor to the fact that Edward had not even known of Hugh's existence. Instead he asked fondly after her grandfather, taking great pains to tell her that her mother sent her love to them both, and then concentrated on the home news. The highlight of this, as far as Alexandra could make out, was the premiere of Chaplin's film, *City Lights*, and their meeting with the white-haired little man himself at one of the parties beforehand.

She skimmed over the rest of the letter. Hugh's achievements for the school term had been condensed to one line, the dogs' antics at a shooting party the week before extended to ten . . . Nothing had changed it seemed. It was wonderfully reassuring.

She folded the letter carefully and picked up the other envelope. The large, bold handwriting she did not recognise at first but when she saw it was from Eldoret she knew at once whom it was from. Jane. She slit open the envelope quickly, eager for news.

It was a cheerful enough letter with wry observations and amusing accounts of her past month or so at the farm; but for some reason Alexandra felt uneasy after she had finished it and reread it again, more slowly this time.

'Is anything wrong?'

She looked up to see her grandfather watching her carefully.

'I'm not sure . . .' She hesitated, not quite able to pinpoint what it was about Jane's letter that troubled her. 'Here.' She stood up and, crossing the room, handed him the letter. 'Tell me what you think. It's from Jane, the girl I met on the boat.'

She watched him as he quickly read through the four pages of the letter.

'Well?' she asked, when he had at last set them aside.

Her grandfather looked up at her slowly. 'It's fairly obvious, isn't it?' he said, with an expressive gesture of his hand. 'She's desperately lonely.'

In truth he had hardly needed to read the letter at all to reach that conclusion. He knew very well of the culture shock that many young wives experienced coming from the comforts of England to the wilds of Kenya, knew of their loneliness and their confusion and their divided loyalty.

Alexandra nodded. It was what she had suspected, too. 'She's asking me to visit her . . .' Alexandra began tentatively, not sure of what his reaction would be.

'Then you must go,' he urged, but he couldn't quite bring himself to meet her eyes. He picked up his ancient copy of the *Standard* and held it aloft, pushing up a barrier between them.

'It wouldn't be for long,' Alexandra began. 'Ten days, or two weeks at the most . . .'

'Go for as long as you like.' The voice behind the newspaper was nonchalant enough, but Alexandra saw that the hands holding the paper were shaking slightly.

She couldn't bear it. She stood up and went to his side. 'I won't be away for long,' she said gently, standing in front of him, her shadow falling across him.

Once she had been only too anxious to leave him, but now there was an irrevocable bond between them.

She leant forward and stretching out took his gnarled hand in hers. 'I'll be back, Grandfather,' she told him softly. 'I promise.'

Looking at him hunched there, his face held rigid against betraying emotion, she felt her throat tighten slightly. And for the first time she realised how much she would miss him too.

Kitale was a little township close to Mount Elgon and the Ugandan border and it was to here, rather than Eldoret, that Jane had instructed Alexandra to take the train.

The journey up was slow but Alexandra didn't mind. It gave her a chance to see the impressive, ever-changing scenery as the train snaked its way northwards: the grandeur of the great Rift Valley, the quiet beauty of Lake Nakuru with its shores lined thick with graceful pink and white flamingoes, the desolate wastes of the great Burnt Forest, the Nandi Hills.

Then at last they came into Eldoret with its buildings recalling the Cape Dutch who with their ox wagons had come to the Uasin Plateau at the turn of the century, on the last of their historic treks. Here the train stopped briefly, then lumbered onwards – leaving behind the plantations of black wattle introduced to provide fuel for the Ugandan Railway – and finally crossing the Nzoia River towards Kitale.

The countryside was now gently rolling, warm enough for thorn trees, with pastures and maize fields. In the distance Alexandra could see the peak of Mount Elgon, the bush seeming to sweep like a sea towards it. Then the train started to slow and with a great shuddering it drew to a halt at Kitale station.

Alexandra saw Jane at once. The train had stopped only a few feet beyond where she was standing, her brown eyes scanning the carriages anxiously. She was wearing a yellow linen shirtwaister with tab pockets and a wide belt and even from here Alexandra could see she was thinner, noticeably so; all her misgivings about coming on this journey vanished in a moment.

'Jane!' she called out, stepping down, and was gratified to see her friend's anxious expression change in an instant.

'Oh! It's too good to be true!' Jane said, rushing over to hug her tightly. 'Thank you for coming . . . I can't tell you what this means to me . . .' She slipped her arm through Alexandra's. 'How long are you able to stay for? You didn't say in your telegram.'

'A week, ten days . . .' Alexandra saw Jane's face fall. 'Perhaps a little longer . . .'

Jane forced a smile. 'Well, whatever, it'll be lovely to have you here.' She led Alexandra out through the station to the waiting box-body car outside.

Alexandra glanced about her. 'Tom not with you?'

'He's just gone to the Standard Bank to collect the wages,' Jane told her. 'We're to meet him there.'

They drove out of the station towards the business district on the other side of the railway from the Indian bazaar, and stopped outside Hopkin's store next door to the brick building of the Standard Bank of South Africa.

Tom was already outside waiting for them. He greeted Alexandra enthusiastically.

'You're a positive sweetheart to come,' he whispered leaning over to kiss her cheek. 'It'll do Janie the power of good to have some company at last.'

He threw his money bags into the back-seat and climbed in. 'So, have you done all you need to do here?'

Jane nodded. 'Yes. I've got all the supplies and I've filled the car up with petrol and bought some more paraffin for the pressure lamps.'

Tom beamed. 'Good girl. Then shall we be off?'

They set out on the Eldoret road, passing narrow side roads leading off to other farms. Most of the land close to the little township had been taken and settled, but further on it became more isolated, farms appearing fewer and further between.

After a few miles more they stopped at a rise of a hill.

'That's Maramanga,' said Tom proudly, pointing out across the green folds of land to the opposite ridge. Alexandra could just see the outline of a bungalow nestling against the jacarandas, and close by the maize fields and the *shambas* and the native lines.

'You can't really see it properly from here,' Jane said, almost apologetically. 'Wait until you get closer. The setting is terribly pretty.'

'I can see that from here,' Alexandra enthused.

'And Tom built the bungalow himself, with bricks moulded from clay dug from the stream-bed . . .' Jane was about to go on, but stopped herself. 'Ah, but I told you all that in my letter, didn't I?'

'You did. And I can't wait to see it all. Is the dam finished yet, by the way?'

'Yes, but only just in time,' said Jane with a heartfelt grimace. 'For some reason they couldn't get the by-pass gates working properly and we were terrified that once the rains came all the vegetation would float in through the feed pipes and block them.'

'One of the little hazards of farm life,' Tom said dryly, not willing to admit that he had been just as concerned as Jane.

They climbed back into the car and a few minutes later had turned off the road towards Maramanga. They crossed a wide wooden bridge which spanned one of the streams that fed the dam and then came to the jacaranda drive leading to the house. Alexandra could well imagine the soft beauty of the place when the blossom was properly out.

They drew up outside in the square courtyard. In her letter Jane had described the bungalow as little more than a backwoods hut, so in truth, Alexandra was almost pleasantly surprised by the roughly built brick house.

Inside, although sparsely furnished – mostly with improvised wooden boxes, the sort in which petrol could be bought two *debis* to a box – it was now at least comfortable. Long hours of hard work by Jane, re-covering the sofa and making matching curtains, had resulted in the rooms now possessing an aura of homeliness which they had never done before.

'You've made it look lovely!' Alexandra exclaimed with feeling as she was shown round the small bungalow. 'No longer a backwoods hut, this!'

Jane laughed and kicked off her shoes, drawing her feet up under her on the sofa. 'Honestly, Alexandra, I can't tell you how dismal it all was when I first arrived.' She glanced over her shoulder a little guiltily, but Tom had already left to go down to the *posho* store from where he always paid the farmhands. 'I nearly died when I first saw it. Truly, I did . . .'

'I can imagine! Kirimangari gave me enough of a turn and Thika's positively suburban compared to this!' Alexandra could smile now at the recollection of that first day. 'So, tell me,' she said, her voice suddenly more serious. 'How are you really managing to cope with it all?'

'Truly?'

'Truly.'

Jane lifted her shoulders. 'Some days I almost think of it as home and can't imagine living anywhere else . . .' She paused, not quite able to meet Alexandra's penetrating gaze.

'And others?' Alexandra prompted. She sensed that behind Jane's stoical front lurked a less sure self.

'And others I almost hate it,' confessed Jane quietly. 'I long for hedgerows bursting with dog-roses and columbine, for crisp winter mornings, long to hear a blackbird sing . . .' She gave a sheepish smile. 'You know the sort of thing. Silly, isn't it?'

'No. Everyone feels the same thing,' soothed Alexandra.

'Do they?' Jane leant forward in her seat. She seemed almost cheered by the news. She had thought it her failing alone.

'Of course,' insisted Alexandra. 'And it must be worse for you here. You're miles from anyone else . . .'

'Oh, I can cope with that,' said Jane emphatically. 'To be honest, Alexandra, it was difficult at first, not seeing anyone for days. A far cry from my Suffolk days, so cosy in retrospect. But I have got used to it now. I can cope with all that, and the insects and the heat and the sheer callousness of the place. But what worries me . . .' She stopped. She had promised herself at the beginning of her time here to keep her misgivings to herself, out of loyalty to Tom. But somehow she knew Alexandra would understand. She hesitated only a moment more. 'But what does worry me, Alexandra, is what this place will do to Tom . . .'

'To Tom?'

'Yes.' Jane's voice was tight. 'We haven't a bean, Alexandra. And every little disaster we have to face becomes a major catastrophe. But even if we were on our knees, he wouldn't give up. He'd go on fighting regardless. That's what worries me. I sometimes think the farm will suck the very life out of him.'

'As bad as that?' Alexandra asked gently.

Jane nodded.

'Then can't you persuade him to leave?'

'Leave?' Jane's head jerked up at her words. 'I couldn't do that to him, Alexandra. He loves it here so much. It's his whole life. I knew that when I came.'

'So what will you do?'

'Make the most of it, I suppose. Support him every inch of the way, whatever the cost.' Jane stopped playing with the tab on her dress and looked across at Alexandra determinedly. 'United we stand, divided we fall. I never truly understood that until now . . .'

'And does Tom know how you feel?' prompted Alexandra quietly.

'A bit. Though I've tried to keep it from him. I don't want to destroy his dream. It's as simple as that.' She forced a smile. 'Besides, for all my moaning today, even in my bleakest moments I have to confess I find this country oddly compelling. Not like Tom, of course. He feels a powerful affinity with this place. That's why he won't give up. It's almost as if the country's caught hold of him and won't let go. Sounds silly, I know, but can you understand that?'

'Yes,' admitted Alexandra, thinking of her grandfather. Thinking of how he would fight to the bitter end, too. 'Only too well.'

'So you'll understand then that since Tom won't leave Kenya and I won't leave Tom that there's only one choice left to me . . .'

'And what's that?'

Jane stretched out her legs and gave an incorrigible smile. 'I'll just have to learn to love the wretched place, too,' she said philosophically. 'Won't I?'

There was no self-pity in her voice, only determination, and Alexandra knew that if anyone could make a success of things here, Jane would.

Jane put out her hand to Alexandra's arm. 'Thank you for listening. I needed to chat to someone. I think half the trouble has been trying to bottle everything up. Tends to blow everything out of all proportion, doesn't it?'

'Everyone needs someone to talk to,' said Alexandra. She knew how lucky she had been to have had Robert Dalgleish to confide in. Without him those first few weeks would have been utterly grim. She would be eternally grateful for his support.

'So . . .' Jane stood up, slipping on her shoes. 'Are you ready for some tea?' She smoothed down her dress and led Alexandra through to the verandah where a tray had already been set out on a small round table. The view from here was spectacular, looking across the stream and the green fertile folds of the valley to where the mountains rose in the distance. 'And after we've downed this, shall I show you this place that's won my husband's heart?'

'Wouldn't miss it for the world,' said Alexandra. 'I want to see everything . . .' She glanced across at Jane. Already the pinched look had left her face. She sat there on the white wicker chair, one leg tucked under the other, beginning to look her old relaxed, easy self again.

'Good.' Jane's eyes brightened with renewed vitality. 'There's so much to show you, so much Tom's done here – ' She paused, giving a rueful smile. 'You see, I confess it. I'm a fraud. Although I profess worse than indifference I'm just as proud of his achievements here as he is!'

The seeming volte face, the complexity of Jane's emotions, surprised Alexandra not in the least. She was only too aware that this country was capable of provoking conflicting impulses, so that it was quite possible to love and hate it at the same time.

Their eyes met at the incongruity of it all and they laughed easily together, understanding, the light sound of their laughter drifting across the valley like a wisp of wood-smoke carried on warm night air.

9

Alexandra was fortunate. Although it rained most afternoons there was yet to be a torrential deluge; the mud roads which had been soaked the night before dried out in the morning sun in time for her and Jane to make sorties out into the neighbouring countryside.

They had had a chance to visit the Saiwa Swamp and the Cherangani Hills and Alexandra had been intrigued by the small groups of women they had passed from time to time travelling to distant markets with their heavy loads. They had the coppery Maasai look about them and wore coils and coils of copper wrapped tightly about their limbs, sometimes so tightly twined that the flesh bulged out on either side of the wire. Some wore heavy earrings which stretched their lobes almost down to their shoulders. Jane informed her that the amount of wire wound round their limbs and their bead ear ornaments indicated the extent of their husbands' wealth.

'Aren't you lucky, Charles is much more likely to deck you in diamonds!' Jane exclaimed with a teasing grin. 'What is he up to these days, by the way? You haven't mentioned him much, bar saying he's well.'

'Haven't I?' There was genuine surprise in Alexandra's voice. She hadn't been aware of the lapse, though she supposed, compared to their time on the *Empress* when she and Jane had done little else but talk about their respective amours, Charles hadn't featured in her conversation overly this time. There just seemed so many other things to talk about: Thika, her grandfather, the feud with the Dalgleishes – which intrigued Jane as much as herself, especially when Alexandra told her of Robert's unfaltering support of her – and Kirimangari itself. She grudgingly acknowledged that the place had somehow wormed its way into her affections. Earlier that morning she had even found herself discussing the intricacies of growing coffee with Tom, a sight which brought Jane to much mirthful laughter.

'So, what to tell you about Charles,' Alexandra mused, glancing across at Jane with a smile. 'I told you he's no longer going to New York, didn't I?'

'You did,' Jane acknowledged with a little nod of her head. She was careful to keep her eyes fixed firmly on the road. There were so many ant-bear holes, even the merest lapse of concentration could be hazardous. 'Though you didn't say where he might be going instead.'

'Paris, possibly. Or Vienna. Daddy wasn't too certain. But he seemed adamant it wouldn't have to be for too long. What with the newspapers being full of the Marquess of Winchester's bankruptcy the business of Kitty Marsden isn't front page news any more.' That much, at least, she had to be thankful for.

'So what about you? Does it mean you could go back to England earlier than planned?' asked Jane.

'Possibly.' In truth it had been mooted but Alexandra had mixed feelings about leaving Kenya so soon. She wanted to see Charles of course, but this was her one chance to spread her wings and she didn't want them to be clipped so soon. She said as much to Jane.

'Quite right, too.' Jane felt strongly that Alexandra's freedom of spirit ought to be encouraged. Marriage would mean her life would all too soon take on an air of predictability. She swerved slightly to avoid sending a guinea fowl to its Maker before its time. 'So, we've all got to put up with you for a while longer, have we?' she teased.

'Absolutely. And it gives you extra time to sort out coming down to Thika,' said Alexandra. 'You will try and come, won't you?' She knew Jane could find such a trip difficult but suddenly it was terribly important to her that Jane should see Kirimangari and meet her grandfather. It was as if by sharing them with her, by imprinting them on Jane's mind as well as her own, they would lose some of their transitory qualities, gaining a sense of lasting substance in some way.

Jane glanced at her, understanding. She could feel Alexandra being torn between two worlds. And more than that. She stretched out her hand and touched her friend's arm encouragingly. 'Of course, I'll try and come,' she said. 'I want to see everything. Meet everyone . . .'

And Alexandra, sitting beside her as they speeded down the muddy dirt-track road towards Maramanga, felt a surge of relief at her words. As if a secret, invisible burden had been lifted off her shoulders.

The following day Jane took Alexandra northwards out of Kitale past Endebass to the foothills of Mount Elgon. They were going, not to walk the summit to see the crater, nor to see the hot springs, but instead to visit the caves which had won themselves such a reputation.

These were the only caves in the world that were frequented by elephants, who came to eat the mineral salts with which the rocks were impregnated. In truth, they were unlikely to see the elephants since they came at night, delicately picking their way in the darkness, using the tip of their trunks to feel their way but Jane still wanted to explore for, as well as other game, there was a chance to see several rock paintings in the nearby caves once inhabited by man.

It was late morning before they had reached the caves. Tom had told them that the only creatures they were likely to encounter inside would be the bats, but it wasn't until they stepped inside the cave and shone their torch around that they realised to quite what extent they would be present. It seemed to Alexandra that a thousand little red gleaming eyes glared down at her as she shone the light onto the roof of the cave. Great colonies of furry-faced creatures seemed to hang there, their squeaks and squawks almost deafening.

'Good God! – I never expected to see so many!' Jane exclaimed, glancing cautiously about her. 'Are you sure Tom said they were harmless?'

'Quite sure,' Alexandra reassured her, yet she had no wish to linger. Amiable beasts they might be, but the acrid smell of them was beginning to make her eyes water.

They stepped thankfully out into the sunshine and took a gulp of forest air. In front of them a few yards away a bushbuck started, crashing through the undergrowth. Although he wouldn't hurt them, his sudden movement startled them both and they were glad that Tom had insisted that Mwangi, who was an excellent shot, accompany them. There were leopards and buffalo up here and both could be unpredictable.

They made their way back down the track. It was cloudier now, the brightness of the morning sun had dimmed and the bamboo and forest seemed eerie somehow.

'I hope it doesn't rain before we get home,' commented Jane. 'It looks devilish just beyond Kitale . . .'

Alexandra took in the dense black clouds which clung to the hills to the east. 'It looks like a downpour doesn't it?' she agreed. 'But maybe it will just miss us. It did last night.'

They'd had crackling thunder the night before but little real rain, the bulk of it falling slightly north of them, just as it seemed to be doing today.

'Just so long as it holds until we get home!' said Jane as they reached the car.

It seemed that her wishes were being granted. Certainly they had reached Kitale before they felt the first spots of rain. As they made their way along the Eldoret road though, the drops became more heavy and persistent, torrenting against the windscreen so fiercely that the wipers on the car could hardly cope with the downpour. The road, though graded and ditched, was becoming progressively more difficult to travel over, as deep ruts formed beneath the deluge.

'I hope to Heaven the stream on our farm track hasn't filled yet,' said Jane anxiously. 'We'll never get over it if it has.'

But Mwangi, behind them, seemed confident enough that they had plenty of time. 'This old car, he go well,' he told them brightly. 'He cross waters, very deep waters, with Bwana Stanhope the rains before last.'

They came off the main Eldoret road and turned up their farm track. It was still some way to the house; the track had turned to mud already and it was slippery and hard to negotiate. They came to the spot where the stream cut its way between the two hills. It had been little more than a trickle this morning but had already risen to nearly a foot deep.

'Heavens, it must have been raining like a demon here!' Jane exclaimed. She glanced out of the window, thankful that it seemed to be easing at last. They needed water, but not a deluge.

She eased the car forwards and it skidded and slithered its way down towards the bubbling water. It was difficult to steer properly but she managed to keep the car on the track, letting it gather up a bit more speed in the hope it would negotiate the hill on the other side without any problem.

The frothing water splashed up against the running-boards and Alexandra was surprised to feel the pressure of the river make the car sway slightly as it nosed its way through.

Jane kept her hands firmly on the steering wheel, her eyes fixed steadily ahead, purposefully ignoring the nudging of the water against the car.

Then they were through and coming up the side of the track on the other side.

Jane turned to Alexandra, a wave of triumph rushing through her. 'Not as bad as I thought it would be, at least,' she said, managing a smile.

But just as she spoke there was a loud clump and they were both thrown against the windscreen as the front right wheel sank into a hole.

'Damn! Ant-bear hole, I bet!' Jane muttered angrily.

They got out of the car and bent down to examine the damage. Luckily, since they had been going so slowly there didn't seem to be a dent, but the front wheel had sunk into the hole almost up to its axle.

'Damn you!' Jane seethed at the long-since departed anteater, who had burrowed into the ant-hill and left the surface crust so vulnerable.

Jane got back into the car and tried to back it out, but the wheels spun in the mud, sending up a thick spray and splattering Alexandra and Mwangi, who were standing at the front trying to help by pushing against the wings.

Alexandra seemed to have taken most of the churning mud and was flecked with it from head to toe.

'Lord! I *am* sorry,' apologised Jane out of the window but even so she couldn't help grinning. Alexandra's face was peppered with mud and she looked as if she had some dreaded disease. 'Why don't you see if you can wash most of it off in the stream while Mwangi and I try to dig this wretched thing out? I think there's a shovel in the back, so it shouldn't take us long . . .'

Alexandra started down the hill, carefully walking along the side of the track against the trees where the land seemed firmer. She reached the stream and bent down, cupping her hands together to scoop up the ice-cold bubbling water.

It was just as she was straightening up that she heard the sound. A distant roar, almost like a landslide. She frowned, trying to fathom what it could be.

Then she heard a shout behind her.

'Run, Alexandra, run!' yelled Jane from above her. 'Get out of the stream, for God's sake!'

As Alexandra turned to see what was happening, the deafening roar seemed to burst down upon her and a great wall of water came churning down towards her. It knocked her off her feet before she could gauge what was happening. She felt it dragging her along into the flood, pulling and pummelling at her body with its swirling mass. The current was vicious, and she was conscious of it tugging at her, trying to draw her under like some monstrous beast grasping at its prey.

Fervently she fought against its great force, struggling to keep her head above water, desperately taking great gulps of air as she battled against the raging torrent. She felt a terrible, searing pain in her leg as she crashed up against a submerged tree branch. Sharp as a spear, it tore open the skin as she was swept past. But she didn't cry out. She was using every ounce of strength to try and keep herself above water.

Again she was dragged under, the blackness seeming to close all about her, not only outside, but this time, frighteningly, surging from within. Coughing and spluttering, she struggled back to the surface, knowing she mustn't give up.

If only she could fight the force of the water, keep above the moving torrent. That was all she could hope for. Pray for.

It was then that she saw it. In front of her where the river seemed to curve to the right a branch jutted out across the swirling mass. It stretched out just above the surface of the water, undamaged as yet by its force, and instinctively Alexandra knew it was her only chance.

She willed herself to focus on that point, every muscle in her body stiffening in anticipation. It was coming up towards her much more quickly than she had expected and she fought against the pull of the water, straining to line herself up with the low hanging branch as best she could, her arms flailing wildly against the swirling mass.

Then, suddenly, it was just in front of her.

She thought for one desperate moment that she might miss it; but then, as if by a miracle, she seemed to gain that last impossible morsel of strength to launch herself upwards and sideways. She grabbed at the branch with both arms, locking them tightly together and ignoring the pain as the branch crashed hard against her, knowing only that she must battle to keep hold against the drag of the water and the agonising ache in her limbs.

There was a muffled cry from somewhere above and behind her but Alexandra didn't have the strength to turn her head. It was Jane, she knew; the very thought that her friend had seen her and now would find her seemed to give the encouragement she needed to try to tighten her grip and hang on. She clung there, her arms stiff with the strain, her lungs half-choked, battered and bruised, but safe. Unbelievably, miraculously, safe.

The voices came closer, she tried to lift her head but the world swung dizzily before her.

'Take our hands!'

Trembling hands were reaching out towards her, and Alexandra forced herself to concentrate. Gradually, she eased herself closer to them and then suddenly Mwangi's strong arms had caught hold of her, lifting her up and carrying her to safety.

'I thought we'd lost you!' Jane was beside them, her face deathly white. 'I should never have told you to go down to the stream . . .'

'It wasn't your fault!' The words came out in a raspy whisper. It seemed that even her voice had no strength in it. Alexandra leant against Jane, her whole body sagging as her friend's arms tightened around her.

'I should have known.' Jane reproached herself. 'I knew it had been raining up in the hills behind us all day.' She hugged Alexandra to her. 'I could never have forgiven myself if something . . .' Her voice caught slightly, the enormity of what might have happened too great to be voiced.

'I'm all right,' Alexandra insisted. She couldn't stop shaking though. It was as if her body, having reached safety at last, was now giving way to all the emotions it had fought against so strongly.

'Most important thing is to get you warm,' said Jane, starting to rub Alexandra's back and shoulders with frenzied vigour. 'Mwangi's gone back to the car for a rug now. And as soon as we're home, I'll deal with your cuts.'

'Cuts?' Alexandra glanced down at her arms and legs. She hadn't even realised she was bleeding. The numbing cold of the water had deadened her senses so much that she hadn't been aware of the cuts and grazes which crisscrossed her limbs.

Jane peered down at her anxiously. 'If we help you, are you strong enough to get back to the car?' She turned Alexandra towards her, wrapping the woollen rug which Mwangi had returned with tightly about her shoulders.

Alexandra nodded. She looked up and was surprised to discover she could still see the car from here. She had felt she had been swept along for miles. In truth it had been little more than a few hundred yards.

'At least nothing's broken,' Jane said as Alexandra began to hobble back through the trees towards the car. 'But I still blame myself. I should have known how fast these streams can change. Tom warned me. I just didn't expect it to come at us like that . . .'

'Neither did I,' admitted Alexandra.

'I still don't understand,' Jane muttered. 'Not really.'

'Maybe the farms up in the hills, maybe one of the dams, it broke,' suggested Mwangi. He'd heard of this happening before and it seemed to him the most likely explanation of the sudden wall-like torrent.

His words brought Jane up short. Her face suddenly drained of colour. 'The dam! Oh, heavens, don't let it be so!' She turned quickly to Mwangi. 'This stream, Mwangi, does it run into our dam?'

'I think so . . .'

Alexandra saw now what Jane was thinking. Could Tom's precious new dam possibly have survived such a floodtide?

'And we're too late to warn them, aren't we?' Jane pressed her lips tightly together, knowing the answer already.

They climbed back into the car in silence. There was nothing anyone could say. False hopes would be no comfort.

Jane started the car and revved it up. Mwangi had already dug out a sufficient slope under the wheel, and Jane backed the car out without difficulty then eased it into first gear.

It was no longer raining, but the car side-slipped slightly in the mud and Jane had to drive slowly for fear of another accident. It was hard for her, though, Alexandra knew. All the time she was thinking of Tom and wondering what damage had been done to the farm.

At last they came to the wooden bridge. Alexandra was surprised to find that the stream here, though swollen, had not risen to anything like the depth of the stream on the other side. She supposed it must be fed from a different hill. That at least was something. The dam might be able to withstand one torrent coming through, but certainly not two.

As they came across the bridge they could see Tom in the distance, surrounded by thirty or so of his *shamba* boys. They were running this way and that, following his instructions, trying to clear the branches and debris which threatened to jam across the gates and block the flow of water.

Jane slammed on the brakes and jumped out of the car running across the mud slopes towards Tom. It was too soon to say, but from here at least, it looked as if the dam had held.

Tom jerked round at Jane's approach. 'Thank God you're safe,' he cried, rushing to her side. His face was pinched and white. 'I've been worried sick about you . . .'

Jane put her arms around him, reassuringly. 'We're fine.' She wouldn't tell him yet about Alexandra. He had troubles enough at the moment.

She glanced down at the swirling mass surging through the dam. 'It's holding then,' she said.

Tom nodded. 'Do you remember we rigged up that gadget so that we could remove the baulk timbers in a hurry if we needed to? That's what saved us. Without that, the dam would have burst its sides in a moment.'

She remembered she had laughed at the makeshift gadget calling it a 'Heath Robinson' affair. Never again.

She glanced about her. They wouldn't be able to tell the extent of the damage until the flood-water died down, but she was hopeful that they had escaped relatively lightly. In the dam itself she could see a few of the smaller coffee bushes and could well imagine how the nursery would have been knocked about.

Tom followed her gaze. 'It's mostly superficial, I think,' he told her. 'Where the stream broke its bank it looks worse, but though the maize is pretty shredded it's not as bad as I feared . . .'

So, they could breathe again.

Alexandra, watching them from the car, felt the tension ease. The dam was obviously intact, and looking at Jane's almost skittish step as she returned to the car Alexandra guessed that so was most of the farm.

Jane climbed into the front seat beside her, slamming the door with gusto. 'God! I was scared,' she admitted, able now to muster a smile. 'I thought we'd lost everything.'

'The dam held then?'

'Yes.' Jane glanced across at her. 'Took its battering better than you, if you ask me,' she said with a grin. 'Come on, let's get you up to the house. A hot bath and a drink is what you need, I'd say.'

Alexandra could think of nothing more appealing. She was beginning to feel stiff now, every bone in her body aching. She glanced at Jane, knowing how relieved she was that the farm had been given a reprieve. They had been fortunate today.

All of them.

10

Alexandra stayed one more week at Maramanga. It was a busy time at the farm with everyone trying to help repair the storm damage. All hands were set to the task; even the *totos* assisted where they could. There was the tidying-up of the coffee to do, repairing the small catchwaters and hoeing up the washes; there was the putting back of half-rooted trees and the careful pruning of any broken branches.

There was the checking of the maize *shambas*, too. At first glance they looked to Alexandra as if they had been torn apart by a herd of wild elephants, but Tom seemed confident that the plants would grow back in time. Then the banks of the stream needed to be built back where the water had broken through. They had to be reinforced in places with sandbags and the drainage ditches had to be dug out and cleared of debris.

Because the rains had now started in earnest they could only work properly in the mornings, so for the past week there had been feverish activity all round from the moment the *tengele* had first sounded. It had paid off, though. The farm was looking almost spruce again.

'Just in time for the next storm!' Tom cracked wryly.

Alexandra smiled. She had grown very fond of Tom during the past two weeks, impressed by his ability to remain unfailingly cheerful, despite everything. Quite simply he was an optimist and a great believer that life's opportunities must be sought out and grasped with both hands.

To be a pioneer was to be a man of enterprise, with all the trials and tribulations that that entailed; and he, unlike some of the others, could accept it. From what Alexandra had heard, Lord

Delamere was like that too, constantly turning over new ideas, eternally hopeful, his advantage being that he had the backing of a vast estate in Cheshire to finance his dreams at Soysambu.

Not that either Tom or Jane complained.

'We'll get there in the end,' Jane told Alexandra brightly as they drove to Kitale at the end of her stay. 'Prices might be dreadful now, but they can't stay like it forever, can they? And Tom says he's got one or two schemes up his sleeve which might help tide us over . . .'

And that was all any of them needed. A few years' grace.

'So,' said Alexandra as they reached the station, 'you will come and see me at Kirimangari, won't you? Before I leave. Promise?'

'Try and keep me away,' teased Jane, hugging her fondly. 'I want to meet your grandfather, remember?'

Alexandra smiled. She had loved being with Jane but she had to admit she was looking forward to seeing her grandfather again. She had missed their early morning rides around the *shambas*, missed his informative chatter, missed the farm even. Strange, how quickly Kirimangari had become part of her life. She wanted to see how the little seedlings were faring out in the new fields, wanted to see the coffee trees, with the blossom now set into clusters of green berries, wanted to make sure it was all progressing as it should.

She hugged Jane goodbye, telling her to write, and then boarded the waiting train. She was grateful now that her grandfather had insisted he meet the train at Nairobi, which meant she would no longer have to wait in town another day in order to catch the Thika train. All she wanted to do now was to get back to Kirimangari as speedily as she could.

The station was its usual bustle when she arrived in Nairobi, the noisy, pushing throng coming as a shock after the quiet of Maramanga. She stepped down from the train and looked about her, unable as yet to see her grandfather in the crowd waiting beside the train.

At first she wasn't unduly concerned but then she saw the tall figure of Colonel Blake striding purposefully towards her and knew instinctively that something was amiss.

'What's happened to Grandfather?' she asked above the noise, as they manoeuvred their way back towards the station entrance.

'Now don't you go worrying yourself, m'dear, but he's not been well,' Colonel Blake said gently, his hand going out to reassure her. 'He's on the mend now, so don't you fret. But he wasn't up to coming to town to meet you, that's all . . .'

She searched his face anxiously. 'But what's been the matter?'

'A touch of the old bronchitis, I'm afraid. If you ask me the old fool got a chill going out in the rains and just didn't bother to take it easy. Soldiering on is all very well, but it invariably leads to something far worse taking hold.'

'He should have sent for me,' Alexandra said. 'Why didn't he let me know?'

'Didn't want to go spoiling your time at Eldoret. We wanted to let you know, but he wouldn't hear of us telegraphing you. Got quite uppity when we suggested it. We've got him staying with us at the moment. He wouldn't do a thing Juma told him, so we thought it easier . . . Went over there quite by chance and found him you know . . .'

'Did you? How fortunate.' Alexandra dreaded to think what might have happened had they not visited Kirimangari. 'I still wish he'd let me know, though.'

'Well, no matter. He's through the worst of it now.' The Colonel started the car and eased it out into the main street. 'Though he isn't an easy patient, I tell you. Rosie has had the most fearful trouble trying to keep him in bed. Keeps on and on about getting back to his wretched seedlings or some such.'

Alexandra turned to him. 'The coffee seedlings, you mean?'

'I suppose so.' He gave a light shrug, concentrating on passing an ox-cart. 'Some business about planting them out.'

Her head jerked up at his words. 'Planting them out? Hasn't he managed to do that yet?'

'No, seems not.' The concern in her voice made the Colonel glance across at her quickly. 'Why, is it so crucial if they're not out by now?'

'I'm not sure,' Alexandra had to admit. 'But I know he wanted to plant them out weeks ago . . .' The delay in the rains coming had put them back a bit. Now this. She was beginning to suspect that her grandfather had not been feeling well those last few days before her trip to Eldoret. But she had been too excited about seeing Jane again to notice and he had been too obdurate to tell her. The stubborn and generous old fool, if only she'd known . . .

It was almost dark as they turned off the Thika road towards the Blakes' sisal farm. The light faded quickly, the sounds of the daytime birds and animals ceasing as abruptly, and Alexandra was pleased to see in the distance the welcoming lights of the Blakes' homestead. The old Riley slushed its way through the rain-filled pools, the round protruding headlights casting a thin stream of yellow light onto the pitted track as they drove slowly down the driveway.

As they pulled up outside the house, Rose Blake came down the steps towards them.

'My dears, I was just beginning to worry,' she told them, kissing them both with great gusto. 'You've taken a positive age to get here, you know, and I can't tell you how impatient your grandfather's becoming.' She turned to Alexandra with a smile. 'He's been asking for you all day, despite knowing that the train didn't arrive in Nairobi until late this afternoon.'

She led Alexandra through the house without further ado and after quickly showing her the small bedroom in which she'd be staying, took her through to her grandfather's room.

Alexandra pushed open the door and went in. Her grandfather was lying there, propped up against the pillows, the covers rumpled about him. She was unprepared for the sight of him. He looked weak and emaciated, lying there, his breathing shallow and his face drawn and pale.

'You took long enough getting here, didn't you?' he muttered gruffly as she came across the room towards him. But even the grumpiness of his voice couldn't disguise his pleasure at seeing her again. 'I thought Blake's Riley was supposed to be speedy!'

'It is,' she told him, coming to his side and planting a kiss on his forehead. 'But it's a thoroughbred and needs to be handled gently.'

'A thoroughbred, eh? By that I suppose you mean temperamental. Don't tell me, it doesn't take kindly to rain or pot-holes!'

She laughed. 'Something like that.' She sat on the edge of the bed and took his huge gnarled hand in hers. 'So, tell me, how are you feeling now?'

'Fit as a fiddle.' But even as he spoke he gave a thick, chesty cough. Their eyes met, his sheepish, hers reproachful. 'Well, what do you expect?' he grumbled. 'Rose won't even let me out of bed, so how on earth are my lungs supposed to clear? But now you're here all that will change. I thought you and I could go over to Kirimangari tomorrow . . .'

'Grandfather!' she admonished him, shocked. 'There is no chance of your going to Kirimangari tomorrow. Or the next day, or the next for that matter . . .'

'Says who?' he asked, scowling at her. 'That's the Blakes talking.'

'That's common sense talking,' she told him firmly. 'It would be sheer madness for you to get out of bed for at least a week, maybe two.'

'But I've got to get back to Kirimangari,' he said. He sank back onto his bed, all his former bravado gone. There was a childlike plaintiveness to his voice. 'The seedlings, Alexandra. They're not planted yet. Stephen doesn't understand . . . But you do. You understand, don't you? They must go in . . . two weeks will be too late . . .' He spoke in short sharp breaths, agitation making his voice a raspy whisper.

'Of course I understand,' she said, her hand tightening about his reassuringly. 'The seedlings must go in.'

A faint smile came to his lips. 'Knew I could count on you,' he said, his glazed eyes half closing in relief. 'Tomorrow you can help me out of bed and take me to Kirimangari.'

'No.'

His eyes sprang open at the word. 'But you said . . .' He stopped, understanding at last. 'Listen, Alexandra,' he said, seeing the grim determination in her eyes. 'There's no one at the farm who knows about planting seedlings. That's the point. Jehru has been called home. Some family business . . .'

That she hadn't known. Jehru was the head-boy and he knew almost as much about the coffee as her grandfather. Without him they were lost. No wonder they hadn't managed to get the task done in her grandfather's absence.

'And you know nothing about planting out,' he told her bluntly. 'If you get the taproots in the wrong position the plants will never take. You don't even know the first thing about it . . .'

She eyed him across the bed. 'Then you'll just have to teach me,' she said, giving him her most beguiling smile. 'Won't you?'

Alexandra drove over to Kirimangari early the next morning. It was still cool and the hush of a fleeting dawn hung over the farm as she turned down the familiar driveway.

As she drew up outside the bungalow the two house-dogs came bounding down the steps towards her, wagging their tails excitedly and pushing their wet noses into her hands. She noticed though that all the time they were searching behind her with their eyes, as if half expecting to see their master, too.

Alexandra lifted her head as the verandah door swung open and Juma appeared in the dogs' wake, a beaming smile on his face.

'Miss Alexandra!' he called out delightedly, coming down the steps so quickly that his *kanzu* flapped around his feet. 'Welcome home! How was your stay at Eldoret?'

'I had a wonderful time, thank you, Juma. But I'm glad to be home.'

Her words made Juma beam even more. 'And the *Bwana M'zee*? He is well, now?'

'Yes, Juma. Getting better all the time,' she told him brightly. 'Though he's a fearful patient. Won't do what he's told at all!'

Juma laughed out loud, pleased that the *Bwana M'zee* was being as difficult as he had been at Kirimangari. It meant the old man still had his fighting spirit about him.

'And he will come home soon, now that you're here, *memsahib kadogo*?' Juma asked, his dark eyes eagerly searching her face.

Alexandra shook her head. 'Not quite yet, Juma. He's not fit to be moved for a while.' She caught his look of anxiety and said gently, 'We have to be careful, you see. If he gets up too soon he could make himself ill again. So he has to stay put for another week or so at least.' She paused, letting her words sink in for a moment. 'And that's why I'm here now. We've got to get the seedlings in. We can't risk waiting any longer.'

'But Jehru's not here,' Juma began, a deep frown creasing his brow.

'I know,' Alexandra acknowledged. 'But we shall have to do our best without him, that's all.' Her voice was steady, showing none of her uncertainty. 'Who's in charge in his absence?'

'Ngora.'

'Good.' Ngora was a careful worker, and although he'd had no personal experience planting out, he'd be ideal for overseeing its intracacies. 'Juma, I'm going down to look at the seedlings now,' she told him. 'If Ngora should call at the house before I get back could you tell him to assemble the boys for me, please?'

'Yes, Miss Alexandra.'

'I shan't be long,' she told him brightly and, turning, made her way down the path towards the river.

A few minutes later though, standing by the nursery, Alexandra felt her confidence waver at the sight of the seedlings spread out row upon row before her. Worse still, she had just picked out one of the twin-leaved plants from its bed and, despite having studied her grandfather's detailed diagram late into the night, it wasn't immediately apparent to her which side had the least number of lateral roots, a matter of prime importance since it determined which side the plant was placed against the vertical side of the hole.

She frowned and turned the seedling round, hoping as she did so that the roots might fall into a more recognisable pattern. But it was not to be.

She bent down and carefully placed the plant back in its bed, delicately removing another. This time the predominant side was more obvious but even as she brushed off some of the soil she couldn't help feeling that the roots looked uneven and distorted. According to her grandfather any plants with malformed roots should be thrown away, but glancing down at the seedling in her hand she wasn't sure if the slight twists in its roots were enough to merit discarding it to the rubbish pile or not. She didn't want to waste any of the precious plants unnecessarily.

She sighed, feeling even more confused. Now she could understand why her grandfather had been so insistent that he be with her.

'Damn!' she said under her breath, and put the second seedling back in place. If only Jehru was still here he'd have been able to advise her. But there was no one else on the farm who knew enough about planting out. Her grandfather had not had new seedlings for almost two decades.

She bent to pick up a handful of soil and thoughtfully let it trickle from one hand to the other. She could at least set the men to digging out the holes this morning, that much she did know about. And the seedlings didn't need to go in until this afternoon, in fact shouldn't, since the sun was out in such force.

It was as she was making her way back to the house that she

thought of someone who might be able to help with her problem. Robert Dalgleish. If she could persuade him to come over for even just one hour, she knew that he could give her all the advice she needed.

The fact that her grandfather had warned her that the Dalgleishes were not to be trusted bothered her not in the least. She thought he was mistaken about Robert anyway but even if he were not, did his coming to Kirimangari really matter as long as it helped get the seedlings planted?

Juma's reaction to her request that he take a chit over to the Dalgleishes was not promising, though.

'Miss Alexandra! I can't!' he protested, his anguish all too obvious. 'What would the *Bwana M'zee* say? You know how he feels about the Dalgleishes . . .'

'Of course I do,' Alexandra admitted bluntly. 'But I also know how he feels about his seedlings. They're his dream for the future. You know that as well as I do.'

Juma shifted his position uneasily. 'But he'd be angry if he knew that the Bwana Dalgleish had been here,' he said, his dark eyes imploring her to call off this foolhardy plan. 'Terribly angry . . .'

'Yes, he would,' admitted Alexandra. It would be useless to deny it. 'But only for a few days. Now, if he lost his precious seedlings, his hope for the future, his anger would last for far longer than that, wouldn't it?'

Juma nodded reluctantly. He didn't like the idea, but he couldn't fault Alexandra's reasoning.

'Then you'll do as I ask?' Alexandra urged him. 'You'll not be held to blame, I promise . . .' She saw him hesitate. 'The seedlings, Juma. Think of the seedlings.'

Juma pursed his lips tightly together and sighed. She knew then that she had won him over.

'I'll write that chit now,' she said, before he could change his mind. 'The sooner that Dalgleish gets here the sooner we can get started with the planting.'

Juma sighed, shaking his head, but he followed her up the steps to the house all the same.

It was almost two hours later when Robert Dalgleish arrived. Alexandra was in the *shamba* supervising the opening up of the holes which had been prefilled and staked out by her grandfather about a month before the rains had begun. She was so engrossed in checking the width and depth of the holes – her grandfather had told her they should be large enough to take a *debi*, a four-gallon kerosene tin – that she didn't hear Robert approaching across the lines. She glanced up to find him standing there, smiling down at her, hands nonchalantly embedded in his pockets.

'I don't know why I've been sent for,' he told her with a boyish grin. 'You look remarkably under control to me!'

She straightened up, brushing a wisp of dark hair out of her face with the back of her hand. 'I wish that I were!' she exclaimed ruefully. 'I'm all right here but it's the seedlings which have flummoxed me.'

There was a glint of a smile in his eyes. 'Have they now?' he said, his voice deep and unhurried. 'And what seems to be the problem?'

'Everything!' She gave an expansive wave of her hands. 'For the life of me, I can't tell which side is which and worse, whether or not the plants are healthy enough to go in, even . . .'

He caught the frantic edge to her voice and said soothingly, 'It can't be as bad as all that.'

'It can,' she insisted grimly.

He raised an ironic brow. 'Oh, I see – like that, is it? Well then, you'd better show me where the seedlings are so that I can take a look.'

There was something very reassuring about his presence. Striding along beside him as he made his way to the nursery she already began to feel her confidence rise again.

It rose even further when she saw how quickly and surely he dealt with the problems she had had. He made them seem trifling.

'Look,' he said, holding up the seedling which had so thrown her. 'Forget the laterals, they can be pruned if necessary. The taproot is the key to success. It mustn't be bruised or damaged or bent in any way, do you see? Now, if you hold the plant like this, and gather all the laterals into your fingers like this, then you'll find planting a whole lot easier.'

She could see that. It was exactly what her grandfather had tried to show her at the Blakes', but somehow Robert had managed to make it all seem so much less complicated.

'All right, so far?' She nodded. 'Good. Then, having got that taped, the next thing to know is how deep do you plant it?'

'Grandfather said you should try and plant it so that the level of the soil is the same as it was in the nursery,' Alexandra told him. That part she'd remembered with no difficulty.

'Bravo!' He shot her a brilliant smile of encouragement. 'Then we're nearly there. You've got your seedlings all ready to plant, taproot hanging straight down – and pruned if necessary – and you gradually start to pack the soil back around the root layer by layer. Firm it up all the time, so that there are no air pockets, like this, and then release the lateral roots one by one so that they fall into their natural position again, all the time filling in the soil firmly about them. Thus . . .' He packed the last bit of soil into place, so that it sloped slightly upwards towards the stem. 'And that's more or less it.' He stood up and slowly brushed the soil off his hands. 'So, is that any clearer? Or do you feel I've plunged you even deeper into the quagmire!'

'No, much clearer, thanks. Though I'm still not absolutely sure as to when to prune or not.'

'Well, that comes with experience, I'm afraid. But in general you prune the laterals when they're damaged and the taproots when they're too long. Then you should cut back to the hard wood. Does that make sense?'

She nodded. 'Yes.' She could visualise that easily. 'Thank you, you've been most helpful. I think I can manage without too many mishaps now . . .'

'Good.' He stood there for a moment looking at her, then he turned to glance back along the nursery. 'So tell me, how many of these seedlings are you hoping to plant out?' he asked with interest.

'All of them.'

'Today?' He couldn't hide his surprise. 'But have you any idea of how many there are here?' he asked her bluntly.

'Enough for two acres . . .'

'Good God! I do believe you're serious!' he exclaimed, a glint of a smile in his blue eyes.

'I am.'

He stood for a moment, looking down at her with a faint gleam of admiration, the smile deepening. 'Well then, I suppose we should get started, shouldn't we?'

Her head jerked up at his words. 'We? I'm not expecting you to help, you know. That isn't why I asked you over here . . .'

'I know,' he said. 'But I can tell you, you haven't a hope in hell of getting these seedlings in today without my help.'

There was neither arrogance nor malice in his voice, only quiet authority. And she knew he spoke the truth.

'But I couldn't ask that of you,' she began, her words coming out in a flurry.

He pushed his hands into his pockets. 'You're not asking,' he insisted quietly. 'I'm offering. There's a difference, you know.'

She hesitated, thinking she ought to turn down his offer but her sense of utter relief at his words was overwhelming. She hadn't needed Robert to tell her that the task she had set herself had been Herculean; she had known it from the start.

'Come on then,' he said, taking her lack of further protest as approval. 'What I need now is half a dozen or so of your best boys. Not necessarily those that work the fastest, but the most fastidious.'

She knew exactly whom to choose. Her rides around the *shambas* with her grandfather, and his idle chatter and comments about the boys hadn't been wasted after all.

While they were waiting for the chosen team to arrive Robert set Alexandra the task of dividing the remainder of the *shamba* workers into small groups. Some would be set to digging up the seedlings and transporting them out to the *shambas*, some to start setting up the necessary shading; and the rest would be paired with those who would plant the seedlings, since Robert insisted it would save time if one person held the seedlings and its roots, while another carefully firmed up the soil around it.

Alexandra did not argue. It all made sense to her. Besides, there was a restless, dynamic quality to Robert which drew others to him, making his leadership seem natural, not obtrusive.

They were to take a row each, ten across, and gradually work up the line.

'It's going to take us a good five hours to plant all these,' Robert told her as they started out towards the *shamba*. 'How's your back, by the way? Not painful?'

She raised her eyebrows quizzically. 'Not painful at all. Why?'

He grinned. 'Because it will be by this evening, that much I can promise you.'

Two hours later she was beginning to realise exactly what he meant. Every time she stood up between planting she had to knead the small of her back with the knuckles of her bunched hand. She could remember as a child watching the farm workers on her grandmother's estate gathering up the potato harvest. The task had been of the same back-breaking nature, except that there they had worked from first light until dusk. How they had managed to, she now couldn't fathom.

'Surviving?' She looked up to see Robert in the next row glancing back at her encouragingly.

'Absolutely.' She wouldn't admit to the seering pain, though she suspected that Robert knew very well of its existence.

'Take a break, why don't you?' he advised. 'It's not supposed to be a race, you know . . .'

'I'm fine,' she insisted, defying him to declare otherwise. In truth it would have been bliss to stop, but she sensed that the task was rather like swimming: the first few lengths were the most difficult and after that the rythmic strokes became automatic, almost taking over by themselves. Besides she suspected that if she stopped now, she would never start again.

It was at about four o'clock that the rain clouds started to appear. Alexandra glanced up at the darkening sky and bent herself more determinedly over her task. There were still a hundred or so seedlings to plant and she had no intention of stopping if she could help it.

The first few drops of rain started to fall about twenty minutes later. Softly at first, and Alexandra found it cool and refreshing against the warmth of her skin, invigorating after the hot sun. She stopped only to tie her sun-hat more tightly into place and kept on planting the glistening seedlings.

It was too much to hope that it would continue to fall so lightly. Half an hour later and it was coming down in a deluge. Within seconds Alexandra was soaked.

'God! But it can rain, can't it?' said Robert, slithering his way across the mud towards her. 'Are you finished yet?'

'Almost.' She nodded towards the remaining seedlings.

'I'll give you a hand then.' He didn't even bother to ask whether she wanted to stop or not. The determined set of her head had told him the answer already.

They worked on, the seedlings slipping in their hands so drenched were they. Rivulets of water started to gather force, channelling their way through the field, making the once-fine soil sticky and difficult to handle. But at last they were done.

Alexandra stood up. Her sun-hat was sodden and her clothes so wet that they clung to her like a half-sloughed skin. Robert, just ahead of her, looked almost as bedraggled.

'I feel like a drowned rat!' he said with a grin, taking off his hat and shaking it so hard that water sprayed off it in all directions.

'But we got them in!' Alexandra returned, facing him triumphantly.

'Yes, we did.'

'And they look pretty healthy on the whole, don't they?' she asked, giving the little coffee trees one last glance before they started back across the *shamba*, their boots squelching across the mud.

'Healthier than we do!' Robert declared with a glint in his eyes. He held his arms out in an expressive gesture, his white shirt sticking to him, contouring the lines of his lean body and emphasising how drenched he was. 'I can't tell you how much I'm looking forward to going home and having a long, hot bath.'

She laughed. 'So am I!' They were on the path now, the going easier. 'Would you like a drink before you go, though? A whisky or something?'

'I think if I sit down I'll never move again,' he confessed. For the moment, though, he still felt energetic, almost light-heartedly so, a state which he knew would wear off the moment he eased up. 'Besides, I've still got things to do at the farm. I only thought I'd be gone an hour or so . . .'

She glanced at him a little guiltily. 'You offered, you know,' she protested, feeling a tinge of remorse at having detained him for quite so long.

'So I did.' There was laughter in his rich voice. 'More fool me!'

She laughed with him. 'Do I detect the sign of mutiny in the ranks?'

'Nonsense!'

She laughed again. She felt easy in his company. The day in the *shamba* had forged a strong link between them, hardship dispelling the false barriers.

They had reached his truck. 'Are you sure you won't come in for a drink?' she asked him.

'I'd love to, but sadly I can't.' There was eloquence in his shrug. 'Another time, perhaps.'

'I hope so.' She put her hand on his arm, briefly. 'Thank you for your help, Robert. I don't know how I would have managed without you.'

'Admirably, probably,' he said. But they both knew it wasn't true. The rain was easing now, a shaft of sunshine glimmering against the clouds. Robert took off his hat and shook it vigorously. 'At any rate,' he said, 'at least Ngora can deal with things from now on. Seems an efficient enough fellow. When do you get back from the Blakes' by the way?'

'In about ten days' time, I suppose . . .'

'Well, make sure Ngora knows to keep the seedlings well watered and shaded.'

'I will, thank you.' A lock of wet dark hair fell across her face and she pushed it back, and as she did so noticed for the first time just how grimy and encased with mud were her hands. The rest of her, she imagined, looked much the same.

'Heavens, what a sight I must look,' she exclaimed suddenly self-conscious.

He took a small step towards her, his eyes never leaving her face. 'Actually,' he said, touching her cheek very gently, 'you look magnificent.'

She thought for a moment he was teasing her and glanced up at him quickly. But his eyes were perfectly serious. He stood before her, tall and dominant, and even as she looked up at him, he leant forward and very purposefully drew her to him and began to kiss her.

It seemed the most natural thing in the world for him to have done and her mouth flowered softly beneath his, warm and searching in response. She could feel the heat of his body burning through his thin shirt, the beat of his heart echoing her own. The simple languorous pleasure of feeling him so close flickered within her, changing almost imperceptibly to something more vibrant. It was a sensation, sensual and thrilling, that was wholly unexpected.

'I think,' Robert said softly, his words drawn out on a breath, 'I ought to go.'

There was a pause, intense, electric in its stillness. Then he said, a slight inflection in his voice: 'Listen, Alexandra, I have to go over to Gilgil over the next few days, but when I get back can I take you up on that drink?'

She nodded. 'I'd like that.'

'Good. We might even go down to Thika to the club, if you'd care to. When did you say you get back from the Blakes'?'

'In a week or so,' she said. 'It depends on Grandfather . . .'

'Ah yes, your grandfather.' There was a heartfelt silence. Robert managed a companionable grin. 'I have to confess that for one glorious moment I'd forgotten about him!'

So had she, in truth. 'Surely he won't object to your calling now,' Alexandra protested, knowing which way his thoughts were running, and rebelling against his conclusion. 'You've just saved his coffee trees, for heaven's sake. He can hardly complain about my inviting you here for a drink after such a magnanimous gesture on your behalf.'

'I'm a Dalgleish,' Robert told her bluntly. 'He can complain very easily.'

'Well, I won't let him,' Alexandra pronounced firmly. She was sure that once she had told her grandfather about Robert's help he would change his opinion of the fellow, at least enough to let him call without fear of mortal combat. 'He'll listen to me,' she insisted, eyes bright with certainty. 'He's all bark, no bite – really, you know . . .'

'Is he indeed?' Robert had to smile. 'And I suppose you've got him wrapped around your little finger?' he teased.

She laughed. She felt certain she would be able to persuade him to let Robert visit.

She felt him gently touch her arm, his long smooth fingers warm against her skin. 'So that's settled then. I'll call. Next week.' She nodded. 'Now you'd better go in before you catch pneumonia,' he urged. 'I never should have kept you out here so long.'

It was only then that she realised how cold she was. Almost on cue she shivered.

'There you are. Go in, for heaven's sake.' His hand came up to brush back the damp hair from her face. 'And you're sure you don't need me to drive you back to the Blakes'?'

'Quite sure. Colonel Blake sent one of his boys with me.'

'Good.' He pulled open the truck door. 'Then I'll see you when I return from Gilgil.'

'I'll send a note over to say when we're back,' she said. She watched him climb into the truck and start the engine. The sound sent a flurry of doves fluttering into the still grey sky from the fig tree behind them.

'Go in,' he urged her with a insistent wave of his hand, as he eased the truck forward. 'You're shivering.'

She turned then and started back to the house, stopping at the bottom of the steps to catch one last glimpse of him as the truck juddered its way towards the crest of the hill.

The sound of the verandah door being closed behind her broke into her thoughts. Juma was standing at the top of the stairs looking down at her sodden state reproachfully.

'Miss Alexandra!' he scolded her, wagging a finger at her. 'You'll go the way of your grandfather, do you hear? You'll have the fever, too, and make no mistake.'

'Nonsense!' She bounded up the steps towards him, beaming. She felt remarkably light-hearted, despite her weariness. 'We got them all in, Juma. All Grandfather's precious seedlings.'

'All of them?' Juma's look of severity melted into one of pleasure. 'None left?'

'None,' Alexandra assured him.

'The *bwana m'zee* will think you a miracle worker,' Juma contended happily. He saw her shiver then and pushed open the verandah door hurriedly. 'Now you come in, Miss Alexandra, do,' he fussed, his voice anxious again. 'You will get cold. Truly now. Come and change into dry clothes and then I'll have Kamau make you a hot cup of tea.'

She followed him in, no longer able to pretend to being warm. Robert had been right to insist that she go in, she thought, for once they had stopped working the damp quickly had taken hold.

She went through to wash and change, rubbing herself vigorously with a towel to get the circulation going again. But despite the cold, when she looked in the mirror her eyes were bright, aglow almost, as if the exhilaration of the day was imprinted in them and burned still. She felt she had never been more vibrantly alive.

She changed quickly into a pair of black slacks and a checked Chanel jumper and came through to the sitting-room. Juma had lit a fire and placed the tea tray on the low table by the hearth.

'I've put the letters by the tray,' Juma informed her as she crossed the room towards the welcome warmth.

'Letters?'

'They came while you were away. I fetched them from Thika . . .'

'Oh.' The word fell like a stone into deep water.

Alexandra stood stock still for a moment, almost as if sensing danger, then glanced down. Lying on the table, foremost on the pile, was a letter from Charles. Juma had put it in pride of place.

She closed her eyes, the breath leaving her in a tight hard rush, almost as if she had experienced a heavy blow to the body. Mortification flooded over her.

Charles. This was the first time since returning from Jane's that she had thought of him. She had been busy, of course, desperately so; but in her heart she knew that was only part of the cause, and she felt a stab of guilt surge through her as she remembered Robert and that kiss.

Instinctively, she rubbed at her mouth as if to wipe away any trace of the kiss that lingered there. Oh, how could she had allowed Robert Dalgleish to kiss her? And worse still, so obviously have enjoyed it? It was a moment of madness, that was all, a moment when she'd lost sight of everything else. It was Charles she loved. Charles she was going to marry.

She picked up the letter, a myriad of emotions running through her. Then, with a long-drawn-out sigh, she slit open the envelope.

The note was short and to the point. It brought news of an utterly unexpected nature. A party of Charles's sister's friends had arranged to come out to Kenya on safari and Charles had persuaded his father to let him join them. 'I've been on my best behaviour, don't you know,' he wrote, 'and it's finally paid off! No more being banished to Europe. I'm due out in Nairobi on the 14th, staying at the Muthiaga Club. Come and join me there, darling, your grandfather, too . . .'

Alexandra put down the letter, unable to read on. A day ago she would have felt sheer elation at the thought of Charles coming to

Nairobi. It was what she had dreamed of, longed for. Now, instead, she only felt misty confusion, as if her senses had been flattened, deadened.

She concentrated on pouring herself a cup of tea, her hand shaking slightly with the effort to calm herself.

It was this wretched country, of course. Somehow it had made England and all its images dim and fade under its exotic power. Here, the blood seemed to course through the veins more quickly, the emotions spring more readily to the fore. It had pulled her this way and that, and had turned her world upside down.

She leant back in her chair, stretching out her legs, feeling the warmth of the fire upon her. So perhaps, then, it was just as well that Charles was coming out. In his presence the soft vistas of home would become real again, extinguishing these fierce shimmering shades of umber and gold. Charles would lead her back to normality, to the safe familiar paths and patterns she had left behind. She would soon forget about the wild appeal of this place. And about Robert Dalgleish.

11

A soft wind was fingering its way through the tops of the jacaranda trees when Alexandra drove with Edward Sinclair into Nairobi three weeks later. The long rains were almost over now and, although her grandfather pronounced there might be a downpour or two still to come, the air felt drier and the sun's shadows were sharp and crisp across the wide avenues.

As they drove towards the Norfolk Hotel Alexandra stole a glance at her grandfather. The look of fragility which had marked him at the Blakes' had disappeared completely, and although his face was thinner than before that seemed to be the only sign of his recent illness. Alexandra could only marvel at his constitution. Although she suspected that he felt less well than he looked, his determination was such that no one could persuade him to take things a little easier.

They edged their way slowly past a procession of heavily laden Kikuyu women. On the other side of the road an open-topped car driven by a smallish, wizened-looking man passed by. But it was not just the driver who caught Alexandra's eye. Standing upright in the front seat beside him was a Maasai herdsman, complete with spear, looking as aloof and imperious as ever he must have done on some distant windswept plain.

Alexandra turned her head to watch them pass by. 'Who on earth was that?' she asked her grandfather as the car disappeared behind an ox-cart.

'The driver is Gilbert Colville,' her grandfather informed her with a grin. 'Now there's an interesting man. Potentially one of the richest men in Kenya and practically a recluse. Lives alone in a ramshackle hut with only a pack of undisciplined dogs for company. But he's one of the most innovative cattlemen out here, by heaven! Been experimenting with Boran native cattle, crossing them with English imports. A Maasai addict too, just like Delamere. Has great admiration for them . . .'

Alexandra recalled the proud stance of the bronzed figure with his spear, staring impassively ahead as the car had sped past. 'I must admit, there is something very compelling about them,' she conceded.

'Very,' her grandfather agreed. 'They're a law unto themselves though. Very independent. Lives ruled by cattle. Not like the Kikuyu now. They're different. They want land . . .' He paused. Having been encouraged to put down their spears and to pick up the plough, the Kikuyu were now hungry for more pastures. Edward suspected that they would want more than the Maasai in time. Already the Kikuyu Central Association had been organised to press for changes in the British colonial land policies, and one of its members, Johnstone Kenyatta, had left for his second visit to England to petition the British for more land. There had been disturbances too, albeit minor for the most part. Edward was aware of this, not so much that he had been affected by it directly, but because Jehru, his headman, had been involved in a rumpus with one of the minor offenders recently released from prison.

'Is anything the matter?' Alexandra caught the furrowed expression on her grandfather's face. 'You're not finding this too exhausting, are you?'

'Heavens no!' her grandfather snorted. 'I was just thinking about Jehru, that's all.'

'Do you know when he'll be back?' Alexandra asked. She knew of the dispute about Jehru's son's involvement with a girl whom a returning detainee now claimed had been promised to him before his imprisonment. Her grandfather had told her that it threatened to escalate into a nasty affair, though she couldn't believe that such a matter couldn't be sorted out amicably. Whatever, it had been enough to drive Jehru back to his native village with all haste, the seedlings and their planting forgotten. 'Have you heard from him yet?'

Her grandfather shook his head. 'Only indirectly. I believe he's still hopeful that the village elders will find in favour of his son, but even if they do I doubt the matter will end there. These inter-family disputes seldom do.'

'Then what will happen?'

'Heaven knows,' said her grandfather, with a light shrug of his shoulders. 'If Jehru is lucky he may be able to placate the other fellow's pride with a promise of cattle or land. If not . . .' He gave an eloquent shrug. The natives had their own way of sorting out quarrels. 'We'll just have to hope that it sorts itself out and that Jehru can come back to us soon enough.' He blew his horn at a pi-dog which threatened to run out from the side of the road. 'But we're fortunate in having Ngora, he's proved indispensable these last few weeks, especially with planting out the seedlings.'

'Yes.' Alexandra let the matter rest there. She'd told her grandfather of how much help Robert Dalgleish had been that day, but he preferred instead to pass the credit on to Ngora. Perhaps it was just as well, Alexandra thought. Her feelings toward Robert were still confused. In many ways she was thankful he had been detained over at his farm in Gilgil these past few weeks so that they hadn't had a chance to meet again. It would only have complicated matters. What had happened that day at Kirimangari was in the past, and once she was with Charles again, once he was a reality beside her, she was sure all her turmoil would cease in an instant. Charles was where her future lay. Charles and England.

They drew to a halt outside the Norfolk Hotel, stopping briefly to leave their luggage and to change – her grandfather had insisted on staying there rather than at the Muthiaga Club, saying it would be quieter – and then they drove on to the Club.

As they neared the pink pebbledashed building with its small Doric columns, Alexandra felt the knot in her stomach begin to tighten. What if, during their months apart, Charles had changed? Or worse still, he considered she had? After all, she had come to Kenya to escape the confines of London, to test her mettle against the real world; and although she had come with Charles's blessing, what if her new-found independent spirit did not appeal to him?

'All set?' She glanced up to find her grandfather looking down at her, an anxious crease between his brows. She knew he would sense her nervousness.

'Just about.' She forced a smile, inwardly bracing herself for the encounter.

'Then let's go in. I want to meet this young fellow of yours,' her grandfather said brightly, climbing out of the battered Ford and striding into the Club with spritely determination.

Inside, the Club had a cool air of gentility about it. The walls were cream and green, the floors polished parquet, and with its deep armchairs and loose chintz covers, Alexandra could well imagine many of the settlers finding it reminiscent of 'home'.

'Right,' said her grandfather returning from reception. 'Charles is expecting us in the little sitting-room beyond the bar. Shall we proceed?'

She nodded and started to follow him through, her heart beating like a bass drum. The bar was full, and the sea of unknown faces in the packed room spun in a blur before her. Then, suddenly, she could hear Charles's voice.

'Alexandra!'

She lifted her head, a suffocating compression in her throat. He was there, crossing the room towards her, elbowing his way through the crowd to where she stood. Her heart gave a great lurch at the sight of him, the familiarity of his face, his smile, suddenly overwhelming. She had forgotten quite how handsome he was.

'Charles . . .' She was no longer rooted to the spot but was heading across the room towards him. 'How blissful to see you again!' She meant it too. The reality of his presence flooded through her like a great surge of light. She felt all her old confidence returning. Everything would be all right now, she was sure of it. 'Oh, Charles!'

He held out his arms to her and she almost fell into them with relief, laughing as he swung her around with a great shout. Then he set her down carefully and held her away to look at her.

'Ah, but you're a sight for sore eyes, darling girl,' he told her with a grin. 'You look even more beautiful than I remember, don't you know.' He kissed her again, longer this time, his lips lingering against hers.

All his old assuredness had returned, all his sense of boyish enthusiasm. At their last meeting in London Alexandra had feared that the incident with Kitty Marsden might scar him permanently, but it seemed not the case at all. He looked just the same, just as much the naughty schoolboy as ever.

He smiled down at her, his teeth white against the deep tan he had gained during the voyage out. 'Though I'm not surprised you look so well,' he said, bending his head to hers. 'This country's a tonic for the world-weary. Magnificent place, isn't it?'

'Simply glorious,' she agreed. She was more glad than she could say that he thought so. She desperately wanted him to care as much as she did about this place. She turned then, remembering with a guilty start that her grandfather was still standing abandoned at the bar. 'Come on,' she said, slipping her arm through Charles's, 'there's someone I want you to meet . . .'

She led him across, almost shyly, willing this first meeting to be a success. But she needn't have worried, both Charles and Edward Sinclair were at their most charming, laughing and chatting easily together.

Charles led them through to his table in the corner, where a bottle of champagne stood, already opened. He called for two more glasses. 'Seems a bit early, doesn't it?' he admitted with a wry smile. 'But they all start drinking way before midday here and I must say this champagne is devilish good – though no doubt you've already tried it,' he said to Alexandra, with a sparkle in his grey eyes. 'Dozens of times, I'd hazard!'

'Actually, no,' she admitted quietly.

'Don't say you've got into the cocktails!' Charles exclaimed. 'Not the Bronxes, White Ladies and Trinities!'

'Not even that,' she said. 'Actually, I've not been here before.'

'Not been here! But where on earth do you go in Nairobi, if not here? I thought this was supposed to be one of the "hot spots" of town.'

'It is. But the truth is, we haven't been down to Nairobi much. Haven't had the time, one way or another, have we, Grandfather?'

'Not really, no.'

Charles bent towards Alexandra, eyes wide with genuine amazement. 'Not been down? Then what on earth have you been doing?'

She gave a little shrug of her shoulders. 'Oh, this and that.' Somehow she knew that he wouldn't understand how content she'd been on the farm, nor would he comprehend her interest in the coffee. It was not his world. 'Been taking things rather quietly, really . . .'

He drained his champagne and poured himself another glass. 'So have I,' he said, rather petulantly. 'Enforced by Father. He was like a bally bloodhound, I can tell you. Following me round all the time. Nearly drove me mad, don't you know . . .' He gave them both an impish smile.

Alexandra laughed. 'Poor Charles. Was it really as bad as that?'

'Worse,' Charles said with feeling. He then continued to tell them the awful things he had had to endure in her absence. His manner was animated and engaging and she found herself laughing at his expansive description of his most dire moments. That was what she had missed most about him, she thought – his ability to make her laugh, his sheer capacity for fun. 'So, finally, I knew I just had to do something about it,' Charles was saying with gusto. 'So I persuaded William to have a word with Father about my joining him and Caroline on this safari trip. Had to earn my Brownie points, of course, but in the end Pater agreed. Must say, I was dashed grateful to William. Isn't every brother-in-law who'd step in for a chap.'

'No. But then William and you have always been pretty close,' said Alexandra, taking a sip of champagne. 'So, tell me, when are you off?'

'When are *we* off,' he corrected her. 'You're coming too!'

'Me?' His words had taken her by surprise. 'Oh, Charles, I'd love to, but I'm not sure . . .'

'William's elder sister, Margaret, is with us,' Charles broke in, knowing what Alexandra was about to say. 'And your parents have approved of her as your chaperone. Really, it's all organised.' He glanced across at Edward. 'Alexandra's father was most insistent that she come. Said she might never have another chance . . .'

'I agree.' Edward gave a quick nod of approval. 'Golden opportunity.'

Alexandra was silent. Charles's words brought home to her that her time in Kenya was running out. She felt a little dart of pain stir somewhere within her at the realisation.

Charles slicked back his hair and then leant forward to refill their glasses. 'Of course, we might have to delay for a few days because of this Finch-Hatton business . . .'

'What Finch-Hatton business?' asked her grandfather, straightening, suddenly alert.

Charles glanced up at him. 'You haven't heard then?'

'Heard what?'

'Finch-Hatton's plane came down at Voi this morning,' Charles told him grimly. 'He was killed outright.'

'Lord, no!' Edward's face drained of colour. 'Are you sure?'

'Quite, I'm afraid. I'm sorry, I didn't realise you hadn't heard . . . Was he a close friend of yours?'

Edward shook his head. 'Not close, no. But we knew each other quite well in the early days . . .' He sank back against his chair, devastated. Finch-Hatton dead? It hardly seemed possible. He wondered if Karen Blixen knew. The two had been inseparable over the past few years and although, recently, they had quarrelled and parted, Edward knew how heartbroken the Baroness would be. She was due to leave Kenya any day now and to lose not only the land, but also the man she loved, would be a shattering blow to her. He pushed away the glass of champagne, no longer able to enjoy it.

'Are you all right?' Alexandra stretched out her hand to cover her grandfather's. 'I'm so sorry. What a beastly business . . .' She glanced about her, realising for the first time how quiet the bar was, still, silent. Everyone here must have heard the news, too, she supposed.

Beside her Charles stirred a little restlessly. 'So,' he went on, eager to lift the sombre mood which had settled upon them. 'As I was saying, if all goes well, we should be ready to leave by next week. Not sure yet where we're going, though. Depends on the game.' It was the lions he was really after, of course. Like most hunters, to him they seemed the epitome of challenge. He asked Alexandra if she had seen any yet.

'Only from the train,' she admitted. 'But I've seen a leopard. Quite close to.'

'At the farm?'

'Actually, at a polo match,' Alexandra said, laughing at the incongruity of it all.

She'd been walking with Robert up on the ridge behind the Averys' farm in the late afternoon when suddenly he'd stopped and pointed down into the long grass on the bank of the *donga*. At first she hadn't seen anything at all, and then she'd caught the faintest glimpse of black and gold as the leopard moved forward so stealthily that the grass it parted seemed not even to move. They'd stood motionless, in almost reverent silence, watching as it slipped with cautious deliberation across the grasslands.

Robert had told her it was probably on its way to reclaim a kill it had hidden in some tree close by, and had even pointed out one in the distance which he thought most likely to be its hiding place. He'd told her then about the white spot upon the leopard's tail, saying a leopard would often hold up its tail to expose that spot when walking amongst the wild herds, using it almost as a flag of truce to show them that they had no need to fear him that day. She smiled at the recollection. Robert had said . . .

She stopped herself abruptly, angry that she had let herself drift into this reverie. Damn Robert Dalgleish! How had she allowed him to slip back into her mind?

She turned to find Charles's eyes upon her. He put down his champagne glass and stretched out to take her hand.

'You know, London was awfully dull without you, Alexandra,' he said softly.

'Was it?'

He nodded and then leaned over to kiss her first on the cheek and then on the lips. 'Most awfully,' he murmured, kissing her again.

She felt his breath warm on hers and closed her eyes, determinedly shutting out past memories. Silently defying them – and Robert Dalgleish – to spoil this moment for her.

12

Cold ghost-mists quivered in the grey light of dawn. It was early, only a little after five, but Alexandra could not sleep. She pulled on her clothes and slipped from the green canvas tent, careful not to wake Margaret who lay, swathed in blankets, curled up on the camp-bed opposite.

Outside, the camp was still silent with sleep. Wisps of fragrant smoke from the dying fire curled lazily into the morning half-light as a soft wind sighed through the flat-topped trees overhead.

Alexandra went over to the canvas basin and splashed some cold water on her face and towelled herself dry. In the east the sleeping band of light seemed to yawn and stretch and the first sounds of the day, the cool piping of the doves, began: tiny noises in an immense silence.

Alexandra walked to the edge of the camp, pulling her jacket around her more tightly. At this time of the morning it was bitterly cold, though as soon as the sun slipped over the horizon everything would quickly be baked.

Beyond, the stillness of the African night was lifting. She turned her head at the sound of a high-pitched donkey-like honk and watched as a family of zebras filed slowly past not twenty yards from where she stood. Where they had come from, or where they were going to, she had no idea, but they marched determinedly on with the resolution of Caesar's army. Yesterday they had come across a whole herd and she had taken some wonderful shots with her camera – a new Kodak sent out with Charles from her father – but though that sight had been impressive, it had lacked the intimacy of this purposeful little group. There, the size of the herd had been so great it had given the group an air of unreality.

She turned at the sound of stirrings behind her. The gun-bearers, skinners and boys were all emerging now and she saw Njombo, the cook, busily coaxing the fire back to life, feeding the embers with dry twigs and kindling.

'*Jambo*,' she called out, crossing over towards him.

'*Jambo. Habari?*' he returned cheerily.

Already the fire was beginning to crackle and the water in the *debi* was steaming. He padded softly around on bare feet, rearranging pots and pans over the flickering flames. How he had managed to produce such a tasty supper last night with only these basic utensils Alexandra could not imagine. Back in London, Mrs Thurloe with all her newfangled equipment could not have improved upon the braised guinea-fowl they had consumed last night.

'*Chai tayari*,' Njombo said after a while, handing her a cup of tea. Then, with teacups tinkling on a wooden tray, he set off across the camp to gently awaken the rest of the party, softly rapping on the canvas doors of their tents.

Alexandra sat sipping her tea, watching the sun's sharp rays filtering through the trees. Already the swift African dawn had gone as had the mists which had shrouded the gaunt granite outcrops in the distance. Now, over by those grey rocks, a small pack of hyenas were making their way home after a night's scavenging, their shaggy manes ragged against the outline of their rounded, bear-like ears. How extraordinary they looked, Alexandra thought, with their loping gait, almost as if God had run out of pieces when making them and had stuck different parts of different animals together as a last resort.

'How long have you been up for?' asked a sleepy voice.

Alexandra looked up to see Charles, tousle-haired at her side.

'You look disgustingly bright-eyed and bushy-tailed this morning!' he commented, barely disguising a yawn. 'Don't tell me you slept through those blasted hyenas cackling all night . . .'

In truth, she had. Their noisy laughter was so familiar to her now that it seemed as unobtrusive as the traffic in London. 'It's irritating to begin with, I know,' she sympathised with Charles, remembering her own first few nights at the farm when she'd slept with a pillow firmly over her head. 'But you'll soon get used to it, I promise.'

'Never!' he returned with feeling. 'And as for that lion . . .' He raised his eyes heavenwards.

'Now that I *did* hear!' confessed Alexandra laughing. 'It was so loud at one point, I thought it was almost by my tent.'

'Probably was,' Charles returned laconically. He pushed his hair back from his face. 'But at least it means it should make the tracking simpler. We should be able to pick up its spoor pretty easily, don't you think?'

'More than likely.' Alexandra glanced up at Charles. Standing there in his khaki shirt and trousers he exuded an air of sporty confidence. His grey eyes, hooded with sleep only a few moments before, were now bright with sudden enthusiasm.

'Come on, let's go and get some breakfast,' said Charles, stretching out his hand to her. 'I'm starving.' He moved off towards the table which stood under the acacia trees, set out with its linen tablecloth and best china.

But Alexandra knew that it wasn't just the tantalising smell of bacon which had made him so eager to start the day. It was the thought of tracking down the lion. He was desperately keen to find one, especially since William had been lucky enough to shoot one on their second day out.

It was just before seven that they were finally ready to leave the camp. They climbed into the two converted box-body cars and started out along a trampled game path, six feet wide. As in the previous days, they would take the cars as far as they could and then proceed on foot. Ahead of them, Joro, their lynx-eyed tracker, jog-trotted easily along, his eyes darting from ground to grass to bushes.

After a while, the pug marks became less discernible. Now the signs were more difficult to follow. Joro slowed, bending from time to time to examine a torn spider's web, a bent grass stem, a dislodged pebble: all signs that the lion had come this way.

Alexandra watched him, enthralled. Somehow Joro could read the plain with his eyes and ears and mind. His hearing was so acute he could hear the dry rasp of a snake as its skin slid against the red earth. He was atuned to his surroundings in a way no white man could ever be, the ancient voice of Africa his own.

At last, at the top of a steep grass ridge that looked down onto the ravine of a riverbed, Joro halted. John Stephenson, their hunting guide, signalled for them all to stop, too, and jumped down out of the car. He went over and crouched down beside Joro, examining the ground for a few minutes, then standing up, came back to them.

'Right, there seems to be a choice,' he told them, taking off his bushhat and sweeping his greying hair back from his lined, weatherbeaten face. 'We're still on the trail of that lion, of course, but Joro has come across some fresh rhino tracks leading down to the riverbed. He thinks there are quite a number of them. You've got three on your licences, so if you agree I suggest we try for those first and then come back for the lion.'

There was only a need for a short confabulation. Charles, who was still keen to go after his lion, let himself by swayed by William and Caroline's enthusiasm to find the rhino. So, in single file, they started down the game track towards the river. As they went on the grass became much higher, and at times the reeds were so thick it was impossible to see more than a few feet ahead.

Joro took the lead, followed by William, with Charles and Caroline close behind and their gun-bearers hard on their heels.

Then came Alexandra and Margaret, with John Stephenson, gun loaded ready for action, bringing up the rear.

They walked cautiously through the mud and slush, almost in slow motion, careful to put one foot silently down before lifting the other. Down here in the riverbed with the reeds towering high above them, Alexandra felt more than a little vulnerable, aware that at any moment a rhino bull could come charging at them from out of the cover. She felt her heart pounding in her chest, excitement and fear coming together at the same time.

They were close to the bank now, the thick reeds even higher than before. Suddenly Joro stopped in his tracks and crouched down, signalling to them to be still. Ahead, at the end of the slough of reeds where their path curled round the narrowing stream, there was a slight movement. William, at the front, slipped the safety catch off his gun; Charles and Caroline, one step behind, followed suit.

It was very quiet now. Then up ahead the reeds swayed again, almost imperceptibly. Joro beckoned them on and, hardly daring to breathe, they wormed their way forward.

A few steps on and Joro stopped again. Suddenly through the reeds on William's left they could make out a head with its twitching ears and little myopic pig-eyes. It was a massive rhino with a magnificent horn. It hadn't heard or scented them yet.

William motioned Joro aside; but just as he had brought his gun up to his shoulder, Joro turned gesticulating wildly and grabbed his arm. '*Toto*,' he whispered urgently. '*Toto!*'

William hesitated, not fully understanding Joro's words. He had the rhino in his sights, he had no wish to lose it. He lowered his head again, finger on the trigger.

'Don't shoot!' John Stephenson called out from the back. 'It's a cow with her calf . . .'

William lifted his head and glanced behind him. At the same time they heard a great crashing beside them as the cow and her calf made their way off up the stream through the cover of the thick reeds, the tick birds rising from their backs, uttering their warning chur-chur call.

'Damn!' said William, under his breath, disappointed that he had had to miss such an opportunity at the last minute.

'There'll be others,' consoled John. He understood William's annoyance but it would have been unthinkable to have brought down a cow with a calf. 'Joro thinks there's quite a number in here . . .'

Almost as he spoke there was a great whooshing snort on the other side of the stream. They barely had time to turn before a huge black rhino came crashing through the stream and reeds towards them. Charles, the nearest, brought his Springfield up and fired two shots in quick succession. The rhino swerved and turned, moving with an agility which Alexandra had never thought possible for such an ungainly beast. They could hear him smashing ahead, snorting, as he crashed his way back through the reeds. Then silence.

They waited, half expecting to hear the sound of him starting off once more on the semi-circle round them. He had come at them so fast, charging like a battering-ram, that they had felt the thud of his great feet pounding along towards them. Now it seemed strange to experience such stillness.

'I think you must have winged him,' William said, turning back to Charles.

'More than that,' Charles returned, quickly reloading. 'I think I brought him down . . .'

He had, too. Joro, who had gone through into the reeds to try and find the rhino's tracks came out a few minutes later, gesticulating excitedly. They followed him through the reeds, along the great path that the rhino had cut, to where at last it lay.

'A hell of a shot!' praised John Stephenson, reaching down to the tick-covered hulk. 'Got him just in the hollow between the neck and the shoulder. Surprised he didn't drop at once.'

Charles looked pleased, bending down to examine the carcass and its impressively large curved horn: but William and Caroline, having duly admired his trophy, now appeared restless and eager to be on their way. It was obvious to Alexandra that both were faintly envious of Charles's luck.

'Shall we be off?' Caroline asked, a hint of impatience to her voice.

'In a little while,' John returned, refusing to be hurried.

Caroline sighed, irritated. She was unused to not having her way at once. She went over to stand by William, gun in hand. Small and petite, she was positively dwarfed by William's large frame and somehow Alexandra thought she looked frail and artificial in these wild surroundings.

At last they were ready to leave. It was already becoming hot, and John suggested that they only spend half an hour or so more on the riverbed before heading off. Joro had found tracks of oryx and Grant's gazelles which he thought might be worth following. Then they could head back to the cars for lunch.

This time, however, William and Caroline were adamant that they wanted to continue with the rhino hunt, so they left them with Joro while the rest of the party headed back up the ravine with John.

It was hot now in the open. Later it would be sweltering and the walk back gruelling. Alexandra was glad they had left when they had. Besides, she had a feeling that Caroline and William were so desperate to shoot a rhino that they might take unnecessary risks. She had no wish to be part of that.

They followed the game track back up the hillside. From time to time John would stop to examine the pattern of tracks which dotted the trail, bending down to pick up an assortment of droppings, crumbling them between his fingers to test their freshness. Each dropping was different, too, telling him not only when the animal had been there, but which sort. Thus, the small tan marbles were the gazelles', the one that resembled a grey Brazil nut a zebra's: each a sign which until now Alexandra had not even noticed.

By the time they had reached the top of the ravine Charles was eager to find his lion again, so John and he decided to go in search of it. Alexandra said she'd prefer to stay behind with Margaret. The panoramic scene at the top was stupendous, perfect for their photography, with herds of gazelle and impala and zebra scattered across the plain; Alexandra thought they should be able to take some impressive pictures.

Alexandra was glad of Margaret's company. Although she looked very like her younger brother, William, dark and big-boned, she was quieter, more reflective. Besides, she had as little interest in shooting as did Alexandra and it made a common bond between them.

They left the team of porters setting out their lunch and made their way down a small game trail to a protruding outcrop of rocks. From here it was possible to see down across the ravine to the river and then to the plains beyond.

'There's nowhere on earth quite like this, is there?' murmured Margaret, taking in a deep breath of appreciation. 'What is it about East Africa which makes it so special? It's not just the animals, is it? Nor even the scenery . . . it's something more.'

Alexandra nodded. Strange how potent was the spell of this country. It didn't matter how cruel and unforgiving it was, it still held fast. Why, exactly, she wasn't sure. Perhaps it was the feeling it created, that of stretching back forever, back almost to the beginning of time. An eerie feeling, though by no means threatening: exhilarating, in truth.

'You can still almost see those early pioneers trailing across the plains in their ox-carts, can't you?' said Margaret, edging along the rocks to stand beside Alexandra. 'It must have been a hard life!'

'It was,' remarked Alexandra. 'Take my grandfather, for instance. The tales he has to tell about trying to establish Kirimangari. Every week there seemed to be a new catastrophe of some sort. Though, quite honestly, as far as I can see it's just as difficult now as it was then.' She paused to take a photograph of a party of warthogs, scurrying past, tails held high. 'I told you about my friend Jane, didn't I?'

'The girl you met on the voyage out?'

Alexandra nodded. 'Well, some of the problems she's had to face at Eldoret would make your hair stand on end!'

Margaret laughed. 'Makes us seem rather cosseted, doesn't it?'

Alexandra smiled, remembering London and the constant round of parties. 'Does a bit.'

A group of impala came close and were duly recorded on camera. Alexandra and Margaret stood side by side on the warm rugged rock edge, taking photographs and chatting easily in each other's company. Then, down below them, just to the right on another smaller outcrop, Margaret spotted a cheetah standing out in perfect profile. It was close enough for them to see its tear-stained mask, its loose-limbed slenderness. For a moment Alexandra thought it might start after one of the gazelles which were grazing close by, but after staring out with alert agate eyes, it decided against such exertion and slumped down to rest again, drugged with the heat.

It was as Alexandra was winding back her completed film that she suddenly felt they were no longer alone. She had the eerie sense of being watched. She spun round, half expecting to find one of the porters standing there. But there was no one.

A flicker of tension ran through her. Margaret turned, too, and was about to take a step forward when Alexandra caught at her arm. Something in the long grass had caught her eye.

'Don't move,' she whispered to Margaret sharply. 'I think something's there . . .'

Through the grass she saw a minute movement, almost imperceptible. She stiffened, her mouth suddenly dry.

'Can you see what it is?' whispered Margaret, agitation showing in her face.

'No. But I think . . .' Alexandra stopped, not sure whether to voice her fears or not.

'Think what?' prompted Margaret.

'I think it's a lion.' She was almost sure of it now.

There was a tense silence. Neither of them had a gun and to call out would probably provoke the lion to attack. It was slowly dawning on them just how cornered they were.

'What are we going to do?' Margaret asked in a tight whisper. 'Can't we try and make a run for it?'

'Absolutely not.' Alexandra's voice was fierce. 'We mustn't move at all. Even if he comes out. Not even a muscle. If we don't move he'll lose interest.' Robert had told her that even if a lion charged it was fatal to try and run. Often it would only be a feint and if they stayed still the lion more than likely would give up. Lions, unless mean-tempered, generally only attacked if they were hungry – unlike leopards. The trouble was, Alexandra thought, she couldn't tell from here whether this particular lion was hungry or mean, or both.

'How long are we supposed to stay like this?' Margaret's whisper was plaintive.

'For as long as it takes,' Alexandra told her firmly.

Margaret let out an impatient sigh. 'For heaven's sake, I really think . . .' But her voice trailed away into a strangled gasp as a shaggy-maned golden head appeared above the grass.

He was huge, far bigger than the one that William had shot a few days before, and Alexandra felt the hair on the back of her head rise at the sight of him. He stood there, facing them, with only his rope-like tail moving, swishing backwards and forwards across the grass. His pose was contemptuous, bored almost, but Alexandra knew all that could change in a split second.

He lifted his massive head, as if trying to catch their scent, and then yawned. He was watching them calmly and steadily, daring them to move. He was testing them, Alexandra could feel it. Just waiting for their nerve to break.

Then, with a low growl, he started to move towards them. Slowly at first, then gathering speed into a long loping stride. Alexandra went cold inside with fear. He was about to attack them. For all Robert's words, he was coming for them. She could feel the panic rise within her, swamping her every sense. Beside her, she felt Margaret stiffen and half close her eyes ready for the powerful blow that must come.

But then, incredibly, the moment was over. At the last second the lion veered away, passing so close that Alexandra could feel the faint rush of wind as he brushed by. From the corner of her eye she could see him pass round the back of them, hear his soft paws thudding against the earth as he passed.

He padded determinedly back to his starting place, lashing his tail from side to side. Alexandra could almost sense his confusion. He couldn't understand what animals they were, nor why they hadn't spooked at his charge.

He stood glaring at them for a moment with enraged yellow eyes, unsure. Then, his head went down slightly and his tail stiffened, as he prepared himself for another charge. The great supple body started to trot over the grass towards them, slowly at first, then, just as before, gradually gathering speed. But this time his eyes were full of deadly intent and Alexandra sensed he wasn't about to swerve away.

She felt a scream of sheer panic rise in her throat. But just as she felt she could no longer hold it back, there came the clear and unmistakable sound of the crack of a rifle close by as an unseen Charles tried to bring down his own lion further down the ravine. The lion faltered uncertainly in mid-charge, his head whipping round at the sound. He paused, every part of his lean body alert, as if sensing that here lay a much greater danger. Then another rifle shot rent the air, and a third, and the lion curled back his lips in an angry snarl, looking not at Alexandra and Margaret now, but beyond toward the sound of Charles's shots.

For a moment he stood looking down in the direction of the rifle shots then he swung round and, with one last snarl, hurtled away through the long grass.

As he did so Alexandra heard a faint click and, turning, found that Margaret had coolly raised her camera for a parting shot of their tormentor.

'I don't believe it!' she said with genuine amazement. 'You must have nerves of steel!'

'But I had to, don't you see?' Margaret's eyes were very clear and bright. 'He's our lion . . .'

'What?'

'Our lion,' repeated Margaret, her voice charged with emotion. 'Don't you see? The boys might have shot theirs, but this one is as much ours, maybe more so, than any they might bring down. Oh, I know we won't be carried home shoulder-high like Charles undoubtedly will tonight – the great Simba hunter – but by Heaven I'll remember the moment the lion charged us for the rest of my life, won't you?'

'Absolutely,' said Alexandra with feeling. She found she had even more respect for the Maasai who had to bring down a lion with only a spear to prove themselves worthy of the term Moran.

'We may not have a fine salted skin to show for it,' went on Margaret, a nervous exhilaration in her voice, 'but he was ours.'

Alexandra slipped her arm through Margaret's with a sudden smile. 'Yes, he was,' she agreed. Once you had looked into a lion's yellow eyes that close, she supposed, you could rightly call it your own.

She glanced back to the long grass. The ordeal now over, she no longer felt frightened. Instead a thrilling sense of invigoration tingled through her. That was Kenya for you. It seemed to take a person to the very edge of themselves and then, impossibly, one step further.

13

Jane stood on the verandah looking down over the valley. It was hard to believe such devastation. One moment the farm had been green and fertile and now the fields were ravaged and stripped bare.

She had thought they might just escape the locusts. Tom had been hopeful at least. But they had come in their millions, blackening the sky with their approach, and bringing wholesale destruction with them.

She shuddered at the recollection of their onslaught, at the memory of their whirring seething mass, so thick it almost seemed to block out all breath. They'd closed the doors to them, shut up the house, and all night as they lay in bed they had heard their dreadful noise, their almost discernible munching.

She would never forget that sound, nor the sight of the farm the next day: the empty maize stalks, the paddocks shorn of any grass, the ground thick with their droppings. Only the coffee trees remained – the leaves, she supposed, too tough to be tasty, though even here they had ring-barked the branches or broken them with the sheer weight of their numbers. God! But it was heart-breaking.

She turned her head at the sound of Tom's footsteps as he passed through the house. Then he pushed open the fly-door and came onto the verandah, standing for a moment looking across at her. She couldn't bear to see how thin he'd become, how lined and drawn his face was.

She stretched out her hands to him. 'Any luck?' she asked quietly.

He touched her hand briefly and then crossed over to the table and poured himself a drink from the glass water jug. 'I've staked the claim, if that's what you mean,' he said, sinking down into one of the wicker chairs. He leant forward, his head in his hands.

She hated to see him like this. She came over and knelt down beside him, resting her head against his knee.

After a while, he took a deep shuddering sigh and straightened. 'I'm so sorry about the clock,' he said softly, a flat dullness to his voice. 'If there had been any other way . . .'

She shook her head, not quite able to meet his eyes. 'It doesn't matter.'

'But it was your grandmother's. If we could have managed without selling it . . .'

She took his hands in hers, holding them very tightly. 'It doesn't matter,' she said, almost fiercely. 'Really. If it means we can continue here.' She paused, looking up at him, searching his face. 'It does, doesn't it?'

'Yes. For the time being anyway.' He couldn't promise her more than that. 'And there's always Kakamega . . .'

Her eyes flicked up to his. Kakamega: another false hope? 'Do you really think something might come of that?' she asked, trying not to let her doubt show.

He gave a light shrug. 'All I know is, they *are* finding gold there. That American chap we met, Johnson, swears to it. And we're in there at the beginning, before the rush, that must be an advantage.'

There was such hope in his voice, she couldn't point out all the difficulties to him. Besides, there was no denying it, there *was* always a chance that their luck might finally change. From what Tom had told her, Johnson, before his find, had had even greater misfortunes than they: he'd tried flax and gone bust when the flax boom had collapsed and then switched to maize only to go bust again when maize prices had slumped last year. Now he was said to be staking out claims along the Yala river and successfully panning the riverbeds.

'It's only alluvial gold, of course,' Tom was saying, leaning back in his chair. 'Not many nuggets are being found. But it doesn't matter. I'm not in it to make a fortune, I only want to make enough to give us a breathing space. To keep us going until things pick up . . .'

'I know.' Jane smiled up at him. The tiredness had left his face now. Hope was a great restorative. She only prayed that that faith was not ashes to the wind.

She stood up, biting back a sigh. How different things would have been if only the British Government had acknowledged the settlers' plight here in East Africa, had compensated them for the drastic fall in prices as they had the settlers in some of their colonies. But the British Lion, it seemed, had no intention of helping this particular cub. Why, Jane wasn't sure. Politics and justice often seemed at odds with one another.

She leant her arms against the top of the verandah railings, gazing down the purple tinge of the hills beyond. Behind her she heard Tom stir and a moment later he was standing beside her.

He slipped his arm around her waist. 'We'll make it work,' he said, brushing his lips against her dark hair. 'You'll see.'

There was a steely defiance to his voice which matched the look in his eyes. And as he looked out over the farm, Jane knew, he was seeing it, not in its present desolate form, but as it would be one day: fertile and prosperous. This was his Eden.

She sighed, knowing that every Eden must have its serpents, too.

Charles's penetrating voice cut through the stillness of the camp.

'But you must come with us, Alexandra!' he urged, his tone verging on petulant. 'You'll never have such an opportunity again, you know.'

She looked up at him, her expression guarded. 'I know,' she conceded. 'But all the same . . .' She let her voice trail, giving a little shrug. In truth, she was growing weary of the party being so obsessed with bringing back trophies; but she knew what Charles's reaction would be to her voicing such an opinion and had no wish to be a killjoy.

'But you've heard what Stephenson told us,' Charles persisted, reaching across to squeeze her arm. 'There's a chance of even bigger game where he's intending to take us . . .' He still found it impossible to believe that she preferred to return to Kirimangari for a few days rather than join them on the latest hunting expedition.

'But I've been away from Grandfather nearly three weeks,' she returned, giving him a meaningful glance.

'I don't know why you're so worried about him. He coped well enough without you before.'

He hadn't, that was just the point. But she couldn't admit as much to Charles, for to do so would be a betrayal of her grandfather.

Instead she said: 'But he's been ill, remember?'

Charles leaned back in his canvas chair, stretching out his legs. 'He looked well enough when I saw him,' he insisted, downing the last of his brandy. 'I think you're rather too over-protective about him, don't you know . . .'

Alexandra refrained from replying, knowing it would only goad him further. Instead she concentrated on removing the net, weighted down with beads, from the water jug, carefully pouring herself out a glass. What was wrong with her? She'd so longed to see her friends from England, especially Charles. So why was she now missing Thika so much?

Between them the Deitz hurricane lamp fluttered, a halo of moths and stink bugs hovering against its light. Charles flicked at them idly with his hand, but with little effect.

'You'll miss the elephants. You know that, don't you?' he said, after a while, his voice that of a sulky schoolboy. 'Stephenson says he's had reliable reports of two herds up that way.'

'I don't think I want to see the elephants,' she said quietly. 'At least, not to see you kill them . . .'

Charles's eyes flicked up to hers, hardening slightly. 'For heaven's sake, you're not getting sentimental, are you?' he asked with faint irritation. 'A bit late, isn't it? After all, I didn't hear you complaining much when we brought down that rhino.'

It was true, of course. It was quite hypocritical of her. But there was something about elephants which captured her imagination. She found it difficult to disregard a species which were held to dispose of their dead in secret burial grounds and to carry the wounded or sick hundreds of miles to keep them out of the hands of their enemies.

'Actually, I agree with Alexandra,' said Margaret from the other side of the white-linened table. 'Stephenson was telling me the other day that when Beryl Markham was scouting elephants for hunters by plane, the females grouped themselves about the bulls in such a way that it was virtually impossible to see what sort of tusks they had from the air . . .'

'Oh, honestly, Margaret!' exclaimed Caroline, taking a long drag at her cigarette. 'Next you'll be crediting them with something akin to human intelligence!' She let out a derisive snort. 'Really, it's low animal cunning, that's all. Born of years of being hunted and handed down the generations.'

'But the plane is a new phenomenon for them,' Margaret pointed out. 'I think they are unusually intelligent; besides . . .'

'That's what makes them such a challenge, don't you see?' broke in Charles, as if to make his point. 'Stephenson told me that once an elephant laid in wait beside a trail for days to ambush him because he'd killed his two companions. They *are* thinkers. And they can be especially wily and dangerous once they've been hunted and know something of man and his ways. But that's just the point. Hunting isn't just about squeezing the trigger, it's about outwitting your opponent.'

'Quite right!' William boomed from the far end of the table. 'It's the tracking and stalking that's just as important.'

Alexandra was just about to point out that Joro was the one who did most of the tracking but at that moment Margaret caught her eye and winked. Let it be, she was saying silently. You'll not change them.

Alexandra sighed and leaned back in her canvas chair. Overhead an owl called as it made its way to the clump of acacias close by. She could hear the soft hush of its wings as it passed by, its dark silhouette shadowed against the moon.

Across the table, Margaret stubbed out her cigarette. 'Well, I'm for bed,' she said, pushing back her chair. 'Anyone else going to turn in?'

'But it's so early!' Caroline protested, stretching out to catch up her brandy glass. She caught William's eye over the top of her glass and let out a short sigh. 'Why don't we get out all those records again – set up the gramophone? Last night was such fun.'

'Not for me.' Margaret stretched. 'We've got an early start in the morning.'

Caroline shot her a scornful glance. 'However do you cope in London, Margaret?' she asked pointedly. 'Really, William and I are never in before two – are we, darling?'

'I'm sure you're not,' returned Margaret in a voice which could mean anything. It was clear she becoming irritated with her sister-in-law, finding her shallow flightiness increasingly aggravating. She turned to Alexandra. 'Are you coming?' she asked, pausing by her chair.

'In a minute, yes,' Alexandra told her. 'I thought I might take a turn around the camp first though . . .'

Charles downed his brandy and stood up. 'I'll come with you, too,' he said, careful to avoid Caroline's moody gaze.

'We'll set up the gramophone while you're gone,' Caroline said, not to be outdone. 'Then we can all have a quick spin before turning in. You won't be long, will you, Charles?'

'Shouldn't be,' Charles returned non committally. He bent his head towards Alexandra as they moved away from the table and murmured, 'Infernally bossy, my sister, that's her trouble. Has to be in command all the time. But she means no harm by it.' His tone was almost apologetic.

'I'm sure she doesn't,' Alexandra allowed, knowing in truth how fond Charles was of Caroline.

They walked on past the porters' campfires to the acacias beyond. Charles stretched out and took her hand in his, the earlier tension of the evening gone. 'It's a glorious night, isn't it?' he said, his voice almost hushed.

'Perfect.' She glanced up. The ink-black sky was studded with stars, the canopy seeming to stretch on forever. Tonight there were no clouds to mar its beauty, no clinging mists to cloak its immense expanse.

At the outskirts of the camp they stopped. Alexandra leaned her back against the twisted trunk of an acacia, gazing up past the filigree pattern of leaves to the sky above. About them the stillness of the night was broken by occasional sounds: the cicadas and tree-frogs tuning up, the yak of the jackal, the low grunt of a lion. So familiar were the sounds to Alexandra now that she could identify them all. She smiled, no longer feeling the outsider, the intruder.

In the darkness she heard Charles move. He came to stand before her, placing his hands on either side of her head, looking down at her without speaking. Then he pushed close against her, leaning forward, his mouth closing on hers.

His lips were warm and generous, tasting faintly of brandy. He went on kissing her, pressing her back against the tree, his hands moving over her, moving up to slip inside the silkiness of her blouse. His fingers found their way across to the soft curve of her breast, moving greedily against her skin. He'd had too much brandy and champagne, she realised that now; and somehow, she supposed, he had misinterpreted her signals and believed that this was what she had wanted.

'Charles, no!' The small sound of her resistance was lost amid his murmurings. His tongue was demanding, probing. He was trying to draw her on too quickly. This was not the way she imagined it would be. This was not the slow, sweet awakening she had felt with Robert that day at Kirimangari . . . In spite of Charles, she had not forgotten that . . .

'Charles, please . . .' Her insistence was louder this time. He was pressing so hard against her that Alexandra could feel the sharp bark of the tree biting into her flesh. She could scarcely breathe. It was as if he was trying to impose his will on her.

'*No!*' She wrenched away from him, suddenly angry, giving him a quick hard push. She saw the surprise in his face but before he could speak, a blood-curdling scream rang out far behind them from the camp.

It defused the potentially acrimonious situation in a second.

'What was that?' Alexandra's head twisted in the direction of the sound.

'Not sure.' Charles turned round in alarm. 'It sounded like Caroline!' There was a chilling fear in his voice. 'We'd better get back,' he said, grabbing her arm hastily.

They'd barely left the clearing before they heard another scream. Then the crack of a rifle filled the air. And another. And another.

They were running now, Alexandra's heart pounding wildly as they sped towards the lights of the camp. A thousand thoughts spun through her mind. Caroline's scream had brought back the memory of that day on the rocks: the moment of the lion's charge. What if . . . She shivered, suddenly afraid, a dryness at the back of her throat.

They stumbled on down the dark path. Ahead of them the camp was in chaos. Hurricane lamps flared, the porters had abandoned their campfires and *posho* and were standing confusedly about, chairs were turned over as if abandoned in haste.

'What's happened?' Charles caught sight of Stephenson in the flickering light. 'We heard shots. Where's Caroline . . .'

'It's all right.' Stephenson took hold of Charles's shoulders to calm him. 'Really. She's quite safe. It's all over now . . .'

'What's over? What happened?' Charles was still shaken, his face very white.

Stephenson gave a slight shrug. 'A snake, that's all.'

'A snake?' Anxiety made Charles's voice sharp. He knew how frightened Caroline was of snakes.

'Yes, a bloody snake.' Caroline's hard voice came from behind him.

They turned and saw Caroline standing there in the yellow hazy light cast out from the lantern. Her face looked pinched and tight, and she looked almost waif-like leaning against William's protective shoulder.

'So, what happened?' Charles demanded. 'We heard the scream . . .'

'And the shots,' put in Alexandra.

For a second, Caroline looked vaguely discomfited.

'Well?' Charles probed.

Caroline gave a little nonchalant shrug. 'Well, if you must know,' she said, her voice on the defensive, 'I went to go . . . well, you know where, and as I sat down . . .'

'A snake in the lavatory?' Nervous agitation mingled with relief at his sister's safety made Charles grin.

'Yes,' Caroline admitted crossly. 'And I can tell you – '

She didn't get any further. Charles burst out into hoots of laughter.

'It isn't funny,' she told him angrily. 'It was a huge thing. William, tell him. The damn thing nearly bit me. If it hadn't been for the mere chance . . .' Her voice trailed.

Explanation was useless now. Charles was doubled up in front of her. Worse still, so hopelessly infectious was his laughter that soon Alexandra was joining in, and Margaret, and Stephenson. Even the porters were grinning, sensing the change in mood.

Caroline drew herself up, struggling to maintain some semblance of dignity. 'Well, you may laugh. But I've won in the end, you know. I shall take great pleasure in turning the damn thing into a handbag. One of the boys is skinnning it for me now.'

Alexandra could well imagine Caroline sporting the handbag in days to come in London society. The story of Caroline's conquest of the snake would be suitably embellished – and the place of its discovery presumably left out. Caroline would turn the whole episode very much to her advantage. Still, after such a fright, perhaps she deserved some recompense.

Behind her Margaret pulled her heavy dressing-gown more tightly about her nightdress. 'Well, if all the excitement's over, I'm going back to bed,' she said.

'Oh no! You're not all going to leave me,' Caroline protested. She held out her hand to her brother. 'Charles, you won't go yet, will you? I need a drink all after I've been through . . .'

'So do I,' Charles admitted. 'You gave me an awful fright back there. Thought something dreadful had happened to you.'

'It had, for Heaven's sake,' Caroline said with feeling.

'Come on, then,' Charles said, sweeping his brown hair back from his face. 'Let's go and have a drink or two. Alexandra, what about you? A nightcap?'

She felt it would be churlish to refuse. 'Just one,' she said. 'Then I ought to turn in.'

Charles took her hand. There was a gentleness in his touch now, no hint of his earlier behaviour. Caroline's misfortune seemed to have sobered him up completely. Alexandra was glad. Though she couldn't say why, during these last few days she had felt the affinity she'd shared with him in London start to falter. She wanted desperately to recapture it, making things right between them again. She curled her fingers against the palm of his hand, pressing it tightly.

They walked back to the table. All had been set straight again, the linen cloth back in position, the chairs now upright.

William went over to the gramophone and placed a record on the felt-covered turntable, then he wound the handle and placed the needle on the slowly revolving rim of the record.

The faintly fluted tones of Noël Coward's 'World Weary' floated and crackled across the camp. Alexandra sat there, sipping her brandy, listening to the music waxing and waning through the darkness, watching the bats dive and dart over their heads as if in time to the soft melancholy strains.

From way over the ridge she heard the lion again, and then the cackle of the hyena; the sounds of the bush intertwining with that of the gramophone. And it seemed to her, at that moment, as if the old and new sounds of Africa were moving in unison across the darkened plains, rising and falling together in some strange hypnotic melody.

14

Edward Sinclair was uneasy. Something was wrong. All might seem tranquil enough, but sitting here in the cool shade of the verandah he could feel a shimmer of tension hovering over the *shamba* boys as they worked in the coffee fields below. The hushed hint of expectation, as if they were waiting for something to happen.

He downed the last of his coffee and stood up. He could pinpoint the moment of change: Jehru's return to Kirimangari last week. The elders might have decided finally in favour of Jehru's son in the matter of the girl he wished to marry but Edward had sensed that Jehru's return had not been one of triumph. There was a listlessness to him, a wariness in his eyes, which worried Edward. But although he had tried to extract the reason from him, Jehru had steadfastly refused to be drawn.

Now, this morning, Jehru had not reported for work for the third day running and Edward knew that he would have to confront him. He swept up his bush-hat and, pushing it down firmly on his head, stumped determinedly down the verandah steps.

As he approached Jehru's hut he was aware of how quiet it was. Unusually so, unnaturally so. He frowned. Even the children seemed subdued.

He ducked his head and entered Jehru's house. Wnamba, Jehru's wife, met him by the entrance. She looked strained and tired, no hint of her usual sparkle.

'So, Wnamba, what's this about Jehru?' he asked, forcing a brightness to his voice to counteract the gloom. 'Still not well? We must see what we can do . . .'

Wnamba shook her head. 'There is nothing you can do,' she said gravely. 'Nothing.'

'Nonsense! We'll soon have Jehru up and about. Let me talk to him.'

Wnamba led him through into the hut. Despite himself, Edward's face stiffened at the sight of Jehru lying there. He bit back a loud gasp. It seemed impossible that a man could have lost so much weight in so short a time. Quite literally, he had shrunk, his whole body seeming to have collapsed from within, withered and wizened, like a balloon sucked empty of air.

'Good God!' Edward couldn't hide his shock. 'Jehru, what's going on here? We need to get you up to hospital. Why on earth didn't you send someone up to tell me you were so ill?' He went over to stand by the headman, looking down at him.

Jehru's head moved almost imperceptibly. He closed his eyes as if in weary acceptance of his condition. The death-like mask of his face worried Edward.

He turned and beckoned Wnamba back to the entrance of the hut. 'I'll arrange for him to go to hospital,' he said, his voice still shaken. 'Today . . .'

Wnamba shook her head. 'No, *Bwana*. The doctor's medicine will not be strong enough . . .' Her voice trailed and she looked anxiously over her shoulder. She wouldn't, or couldn't, say more.

But she didn't need to. Edward knew what she was trying to tell him: that black man's magic was stronger than ordinary things. And without doubt the detainee who had lost his girl had resorted to such magic and put a curse on Jehru – and probably his son as well. It would be useless to tell Jehru that the spell hadn't really any power to hurt him, that it was only in his mind. Because if Jehru believed he was going to die, he would do so, and European medicine would be powerless to help him.

'Now, Wnamba, you mustn't worry,' Edward said, trying to sound confident. 'We'll soon get this thing cleared up. Just leave it to me. I'll sort it out . . .'

But, despite his words of confidence, as he started back towards the house, his pace was not the easy stride of earlier that morning.

He passed the barns and then came to the shed which he had allocated to Jehru, as headman, to use as his own. There Jehru kept his records of the men's attendance each day, of the work carried out, of the mulching and planting and pruning. Although Jehru had to share the shed with a workbench and a miscellany of tools and empty coffee sacks it was somewhere which gave him added status and of which he was inordinately proud.

This morning Edward had passed by the shed without a second glance. Now he stopped, some instinct telling him that all was not as it should be. He walked slowly over towards the door, pausing in front of it.

The lock had been broken. It had been set back so carefully in place that from afar it had been impossible to notice. Edward hesitated, then, stretching out his hand, cautiously tried the handle. The door swung slowly open with a groan. Edward stepped forward into the dimly lit room then stood absolutely still.

There was an unnatural icy silence in here. A notion of death. And as animals could sense danger, so could he. He stepped gingerly forward, his nerves quivering involuntarily, the hairs on the back of his neck prickling.

What was it about this place? He could see nothing to account for this dreadful fear which bore into him. Nothing. And yet he knew something powerful was here, something which made the very air pulsate with its force.

He looked round the room. In the slatted half-light he could make out the empty coffee sacks piled up into untidy heaps in the corner, the array of tools set out on the shelves, the spades and forks and scythes propped up against the walls. Nothing seemed out of place.

Then in the corner by Jehru's work table he noticed something swinging in the mottled darkness.

He moved a little closer, his throat catching slightly. For there, hanging from one of the hooks in the beam was the carcass of a white-feathered chicken. Its head had been crudely hacked off and congealed blood covered the drooping, severed head. It had splattered over the wooden work table in a sickening dark-red pattern. Its significance was obvious.

Edward caught his breath. By the smell of the thing it had been hanging there for several days, yet he noticed that it hadn't yet been touched by ants. Odd that.

He straightened his shoulders determinedly and, catching up one of the machetes by the wall, crossed over to where the chicken hung. Then with all his might he swung at the cord just above the point where its feet were attached. The carcass fell onto the floor with a dull thud, sending fine dust curling up into the air.

Edward bent down and picked up the bedraggled remains and bundled it into one of the empty coffee sacks. Then he carefully tied the bag up into a tight knot, his fingers fumbling slightly in his haste. He'd instruct one of the boys to burn the wretched thing as soon as he got back to the house. Then he paused, frowning. No, leave nothing to chance. He would burn it himself.

He sighed. That the detainee was at the bottom of this was now obvious. But how to deal with it, that was the problem.

On any other occasion he might have called in the District Commissioner but there seemed little the DC could do here, in truth. He could hardly run in the detainee on a charge of witchcraft. Besides, even if Jehru died there was no evidence as such. A threat, a dead chicken – not exactly the substance of convictions.

Edward took off his hat and dusted it off thoughtfully. In his experience the only way to deal with black man's magic was on its own terms. Beat like with like.

He came out of the shed into the sunlight, narrowing his eyes against the glare, the sack dangling by his side. He felt like the Ancient Mariner with his albatross, the object he held as much the portent gloom.

So what to do? He paused, remembering.

Once, long ago, he had had a problem down at the village and had needed such help. He had ridden out to see a powerful witch-doctor in the deep country out to the north and the disturbance had been resolved quickly, with mysterious beans and bones and powders. Heathen and strange, maybe, but it had worked.

Now Edward would return to the same witch-doctor to ask him to help cast off Jehru's spell. If he could tell Jehru that the curse had been lifted then he knew his headman would recover. It was all that was needed.

He quickened his pace and strode up to the house, calling for his *syce* to saddle his horse. He was well aware that some of the other settlers regarded witch-doctors as superstitious nonsense and would be appalled that he had resorted to one, but he didn't care. It was the only way.

The ancient voice of Africa ran far deeper than any white man could know. It was strong, primeval, of another world. And it couldn't be ignored.

The wooden slats of the jetty were warm under Alexandra's bare feet as she walked out past the tall rushes which clung to the shoreline. It was beautiful here at Lake Naivasha and Alexandra was glad now that she had let Charles persuade her to stay here with him for a few days before returning to Thika.

She stretched and looked out across the clear deep waters. It almost had the look of a Scottish highland loch about it, she thought, with the mountains encircling it and the grassy slopes running down to its shores. But then, as if to tease her, a hippo raised its head from the cool deep beyond, regarding her with sleepy eyes before sinking back down again amid the floating island of papyrus.

She smiled at the very contradiction of such a scene.

Behind her, from the verandah of the house in which they were all staying, she could hear the muffled strains of Gershwin's music drifting down to the shoreline. It seemed impossible that another party was about to begin, especially after the impressive quantity of pink gins which had been consumed last night; but judging by the sudden swell of loud voices and laughter, that was precisely what was happening.

She heard the soft tread of footsteps and saw Margaret picking her way gingerly across the grass towards her.

'Don't tell me you've had enough already!' she teased her, seeing the pained expression on Margaret's face.

'I had enough last night!' retorted Margaret grimly. 'Heaven knows how they've got the energy for it. You know, they're drinking champagne already and it's not even noon . . .'

Alexandra bent to pick up a small flat white stone at the water's edge and sent it skimming across the shining surface. 'They'll probably all be asleep by lunchtime!' she returned with a mischievous grin. 'Serve them right!'

''Fraid not,' Margaret made a slight grimace, pushing her dark hair back from her face. 'The latest plan is that we all go over to see some friends of Kiki Preston. She says we have to see the house. Quite spectacular it is, apparently. Anyway, William's discovered he was at Eton with the fellow . . .' Her hands moved out expressively, indicating that the matter was fait accompli. 'But it should be fun. Kiki says Joss is a poppet. Quite the most charming of men . . .'

Kiki must have really enthused for Margaret to be so expansive thought Alexandra. But then Kiki enthused about most people, it seemed. She stood for a moment watching a chalk-white egret take off from the rushes on the shoreline, shielding her eyes from the glare as she followed the slow beat of its wings across the lake.

She was struck again by the sheer beauty of the place. It surprised her not in the least that the area around Lake Naivasha was where the most wealthy and fashionable of the settlers had chosen to build their houses. And yet, by the very act of all these lotus-eaters choosing the same spot, it had created an artificial environment.

She had felt it last night. They were all well-bred, rich and charming, but only seemed to play on the surface of life, never attempting to delve deeper nor even wishing to. This was a Kenya at total odds with the one she had experienced so far, out of sympathy with the real world of the struggling farmers and their devastating problems. So far away from the realities of people like Jane and Tom, of Kirimagari or even Robert Dalgleish . . . She couldn't quite come to terms with it.

She heard a shout and turning saw Charles waving at them from the verandah.

'Time to go,' said Margaret. 'Charles seems very keen to get there. I expect he wants to see the sunken marble bath with those black and gold tiles Kiki's been telling us about!'

Her voice was light, and glancing at her Alexandra noticed how much more relaxed she seemed after little more than a month here. She'd changed in looks, too. The London pallor had left her skin and the slight tan seemed to open up her face, making her eyes seem more alive, bright. The change of scene, and of people, seemed to have revitalised her.

Alexandra bent to pick up her shoes and followed her up the grassy slope towards the house. There was already quite a throng of people on the verandah. Alexandra recognised some of them from last night. She found Charles lying on a chintz-covered sofa, feet up, one hand tucked behind his head, the other clutching a champagne glass.

'Did you go for a swim?' he asked, stretching out his hand to her.

She came and sat on the edge of the sofa. 'Earlier, yes. Just after breakfast.'

'I'm having my breakfast now . . .' Charles said, raising his champagne glass with a sleepy smile.

'And your lunch, too,' returned Alexandra, seeing the nearly empty bottle tucked under his arm. She gave him a speaking look.

Charles grinned, unabashed. 'And very nice it is, too,' he said, downing the last of his glass. He sat up slightly and taking her by her thin shoulders leaned forward and kissed her. 'So, tell me, are you glad you decided to stay on?'

'Very. It's so beautiful here . . .'

'Isn't it?' He propped himself up further, a sudden brightness in his face. 'I was thinking,' he said, his voice tinged with enthusiasm. 'Seeing that we both like Kenya so much, why don't we come back next year. A sort of honeymoon . . .'

Her first reaction of delight faded as a tiny speck of anxiety began to stir deep within her. She turned her head slightly so that Charles couldn't see her face, unsure whether the panic she felt was solely about leaving Kenya . . . 'Yes, what fun!' she said, making a great effort to keep her voice light.

'That's just what I thought,' said Charles, missing the change in her. He looked pleased with himself. He stretched out and caught up the champagne bottle, pouring the last of its contents into his glass. 'One of the chaps I met last night had come out to shoot a bongo. They're very rare, I gather, difficult to find. Thought I might try for that next time.'

'Good idea.' Her reply was automatic. She couldn't bring herself to think about their future just yet. 'Next time' seemed an eternity away. She leant over and straightened his glass which was tilting at a dangerous angle, then stood up. 'I suppose I should go and change . . .'

'Suppose so,' agreed Charles, stretching both hands above his hand languidly. 'But there's no need to rush. Time doesn't seem to count for much out here, you know. Different beat and all that . . .'

It was true. No one seemed even to have moved by the time she returned. The only change in Charles was that he had acquired a new bottle of champagne which stood beside him, already half empty. He looked so sybaritically content lying there that Alexandra thought he might never move. But then Kiki came out onto the verandah and with typical American energy whisked around them all, stirring them out of their soporific state and ignoring their mutinous mutterings.

She stood purposefully over Charles. 'You'll regret it if you don't come,' she told him, brushing her fingers teasingly across his hair. 'It'll be tremendous fun. Parties at Joss's always are.' She pushed his feet off the sofa with a playful smile. 'Full of surprises!'

The last phrase was enough to catch Charles's interest. He stretched and stood up, watching Kiki's amused smile, sensing instinctively she was a girl after his own heart.

Behind him Alexandra was struggling with the clasp on Margaret's gold necklace. 'Wretched thing!' muttered Margaret with exasperation, lifting her hair off her neck and tilting her head forward slightly to facilitate Alexandra's task. 'I hardly ever wear it and the one time I choose to . . .' She twisted her head slightly to see what progress Alexandra was making. 'Any luck? I can always ask William . . .'

'Nearly done,' said Alexandra, doubting whether William would be able even to see the clasp, let alone fix it. He'd had even more to drink than Charles and by all reports had only got to bed at four that morning. 'There.'

'Marvellous.' Margaret released her hair and fluffed it back into place.

'All done?' Charles came up behind Alexandra and slipped his arm around her waist. He looked inordinately pleased with himself. 'We're to go with Kiki. All right?'

Outside the cars were cranked up and ready to go and they set off at great speed. Kiki kept up a constant chatter, filling them in with the gossip, mostly about their hosts-to-be.

'Of course, Joss was once married to Idina Gordon. Caused an awful stir when they eloped with each other, I gather,' she told them brightly. 'She was so much older than he and it put an end to his bright future at the FO. Not that he cared . . .' She swung out to avoid a dog on the road, tooting furiously. 'Anyway, all that finished a few years back. He got tired of Idina and took up with Molly Ramsay-Hill. I can't tell you what a to-do there was when Molly's husband, Cyril, found out. Came after Joss with a rhino-whip. Too late by then though. That was that. Molly and Joss were married last year . . .'

She swung into the driveway and ground to a halt outside a huge white-washed Moroccan-style castle, complete with crenellated walls and minaret. 'But Cyril let Molly keep Osterian. The Djinn Palace, we call it. Fun, isn't it?'

It was a house of haunting beauty, set on the edge of the lake with its grounds sloping steeply down to the water. It was one of the most exquisite places Alexandra had ever seen and she knew now why Kiki had enthused about it so.

They went through the house, with its full length portrait of Josslyn in his ceremonial robes hanging at the top of the stairs, and came out onto the verandah.

Molly Hay crossed over to meet them. She was a petite, slender woman with auburn hair. She had a crisp, animated voice and greeted them with the easy charm which Alexandra had come to expect out here.

From the other side of the deep verandah a tall, striking-looking man wearing a kilt waved at Kiki.

'Joss!' cried out Kiki delightedly, beckoning him over.

Alexandra could see at once why he had earned himself such a reputation. Just thirty, with straight pale-gold hair and obvious good looks, he was possessed of a sort of arrogant charm which he used quite shamelessly. But there was something almost licentious in his glance which made Alexandra feel uncomfortable.

She was relieved when Kiki came up and slipped her arm through Joss's, taking his attention away. 'By the way,' Kiki said to Joss, 'has that chap from Gilgil arrived yet? The one whose colt you've got your eye on . . .'

'Just arrived.' Although polo was primarily Joss's sport he was still keen to keep a race-horse or two in his stables. 'But don't you go talking to him and putting up his price, Kiki,' he warned, tapping her on the arm affably.

Molly laughed. 'Actually, I don't think he wants to sell,' she told Joss. 'Not surprised, really. The sire's Archway and if you ask me, the foal's got Leger Cup winner stamped all over it.'

'Perhaps he hasn't noticed,' ventured Joss.

'Much too astute for that, I'm afraid,' said Molly. She turned to Kiki. 'And utterly divine, darling. Though rather aloof and self-contained I found . . .'

'You mean you couldn't persuade him to fall for your charms,' Joss said.

He was teasing, but there was a waspishness to his voice that made Alexandra suspect that at times he might be rather cruel to Molly. She stayed for a while, letting Charles do most of the talking, then on some minor pretext effected her escape.

She pushed her way across the pillared verandah through the throng, exchanging pleasantries with various people whom she had met at drinks the previous night – it seemed to be the same crowd circling round again as far as she could see – and then crossed the lawn to stand at the edge of the garden, looking down to the lake below. Here, away from the crowd, it was almost peaceful and she stood gazing out across the steely glitter, caught again by the myriad of birds hopping and slipping over the broad water-lily leaves.

She didn't hear the footsteps soft on the grass behind her.

'Hello, Alexandra,' said a voice.

Even before she had looked round, she knew who it was.

'Hello, Robert,' she said softly. She felt a sudden rush of emotion at the sight of him. 'I didn't expect to find you here . . .' She was careful to keep her voice even, unwilling to let him see how pleased she was to see his familiar face in so alien an environment.

He gave a light shrug as if to concede this was not his usual scene. 'Joss wanted to talk to me about a colt I've got.'

So it had been Robert's colt. She smiled. 'The Leger winner . . .'

'Absolutely.' His eyes held hers. She had forgotten how piercingly blue they were. 'And you?'

'The people I'm staying with were invited so I came along. I'm actually on my way back to Thika . . .'

'Are you?' He seemed pleased.

'Yes.' She lifted her head to smile at him. She hadn't realised quite how much she'd missed his company until this moment. 'I'm looking forward to getting back. I seem to have been away for ages. Charles wants me to join them on another safari but I told him I'd much rather be at Kirimangari . . .'

She hesitated, aware that her reference to Charles had changed the atmosphere between them.

'I see.' Robert turned away from her slightly, a certain restraint between them now.

There was a silence. Alexandra picked at some imaginary thread on her silk skirt, not quite able to meet his gaze. She wished she hadn't mentioned Charles, but now that she had she felt she must plough on. 'I'm sorry I had to leave Thika in such a rush,' she said, trying hard not to think of their last, fateful, meeting. 'You got my note explaining, I presume . . .'

'Oh yes.'

She looked up at him. His face was closed to her. She had not the slightest notion of what he was thinking. He stood there, hands pushed into his pockets, his stance faintly hostile. She wasn't quite sure how to deal with him. She had never seen him like this before.

She searched frantically for something to say, anything, which might assuage the tension between them. In the past they had been so easy together. She couldn't bear to lose that.

She was relieved to hear Molly's voice floating down across the lawn towards them.

'Oh, there you are, Robert,' she said. 'Joss was getting quite frantic thinking you might have left before he'd had a chance to talk to you about that colt. He's desperately keen to have it, you know.'

Robert's eyes flicked over to her. 'I told him – not this one, Molly. But I've another mare due to foal next month . . .'

'He's set on this one, you know.'

'Well, I'm afraid he's going to have to be disappointed this time, Molly,' Robert said firmly. Joss had a habit of wanting things he couldn't have. It was almost a game to him. 'But the other foal might suit. The dam was out of Clutterbuck's old stable.'

Molly let out a small sigh. 'Ah well, perhaps it might. Joss will probably come up and see it next month then . . .' She turned to Alexandra. 'I can't tell you how pleased we were when Robert moved over this way. We nearly didn't get him, though.' She smiled at Robert. 'Did we? If that obdurate old man next door to you in Thika had given in and sold out to you as you'd hoped, you would never have needed to have expanded out this way. Well, our gain, that's all I can say.' She took a long sip of champagne, oblivious of the havoc she'd just wreaked. 'By the way,' she continued, 'are you still trying to buy him out? Last time we saw you I thought you said you'd a plan afoot to try and get him to change his mind. Any luck with it?'

'No,' said Robert stiffly. He couldn't bring himself to look at Alexandra. 'Things have changed a bit since then . . .'

'Oh . . .' Molly stopped, suddenly aware of the change in atmosphere between them, though not sure of the cause. She looked from one to the other. She was thankful that one of her guests chose that moment to come and bid her farewell and she had a legitimate excuse to beat a retreat.

Alexandra stood very still, struggling to gain mastery of herself. She fixed Robert with her eyes, steady and fierce.

'Presumably that was my grandfather she was talking about,' she said. But for all her determination, her voice was thin and sharp.

'Yes.'

'And you wanted his farm.'

'It made sense.'

No apologies. No denial. She took a deep, shuddering breath. 'And your plans . . .' She hesitated, not quite wanting to go on. There was a slight, awkward pause, then she went on: 'Did I play some part in your plans?'

'To get Kirimangari?' His face tightened. 'Is that what you think?'

'I don't know what to think, any more.' Her voice was whip-thin. 'That's why I'm asking you . . .' She turned her face away, her expression painfully intense. 'I want to know if all the time I thought you were helping me you were really using me to get to my grandfather. He warned me you were, you know.'

'I can imagine.'

She ignored his dart. 'So were you? And that day of the rain . . . when you kissed me . . .' She found she couldn't go on.

'Yes?'

'Were – were you still hoping to persuade me to help you then?'

His eyes bored into her. 'Would it matter so very much?'

Still no denial, she noticed. She felt her world shake. 'So, you *were* using me all that time . . .' Her voice dropped to a whisper.

'We were using each other, Alexandra,' he said, his blue eyes flint-edged. 'Don't fool yourself. You let me kiss you knowing that Charles was coming out all the time. You played me along, aware he'd be with you in only a few weeks.'

'That's not true!' she burst out, angry now.

'Isn't it?' His eyes searched her face.

'No, I kissed you because . . .' She stopped, suddenly aware she might say too much.

'Yes?' he probed.

She took a deep breath, lifting her shoulders in a small, helpless gesture. 'Oh, it hardly matters now, does it?' she said. There was a weary finality to her voice.

'No, I suppose not.' A silence, painful and accusing, hung between them. He turned to look across the lake, watching a pair of black ducks gliding in, their wings a hushed whisper as they passed overhead. 'You know,' he said at last, very quietly, 'I wasn't trying to cheat your grandfather. I offered him a good price.'

Despite the gentleness of his voice she bristled. It was still too raw for her. 'You'll never get Kirimangari, you know,' she said, ignoring his last words. 'Never!'

Despite everything, his mouth threatened a smile. 'You sound remarkably like your grandfather,' he murmured, almost amused. 'No Dalgleish shall have Kirimangari, and all that . . .'

'Nor shall they, Robert,' she told him, her green eyes hard-edged. 'Just remember that.'

'Alexandra, listen . . .' He hesitated, stretching out his hand to her. But she pulled away from him.

'There's nothing more to say between us,' she said, twisting away from his touch, even now not entirely trusting herself. 'Nothing. Just leave, will you?'

There was a pause. 'Is that what you really want?'

She couldn't answer at first. Then she took a deep breath. 'Yes.'

'Very well.' He stood for a moment looking down at her, not speaking, then he turned on his heel and started back up across the lawn.

Alexandra bent down to pick up a small stone and threw it into the lake, watching as it twisted and turned in the air; she was determined not to look round. When at last she did so, he was gone. And for some unaccountable reason, despite the throng, she suddenly felt terribly alone.

15

It was the fireflies Jane would most remember at Kakamega. That first night in the camp she had stood outside their tent watching the little pinpricks of gold fluttering on the dark horizon and somehow they had seemed an emblem of hope to her. A sign. They had hovered over the ridges, as elusive as the glistening gold which she and Tom sought in the earth beneath. Distant, but there nonetheless. Brilliant. And seeing them, she suddenly had been sure that this time their luck would hold.

They had been here for nearly a month now and that assurance still had not faltered. True, they had not discovered anything to cause a stir yet, but, indisputably, there was gold on their claim.

For as long as she lived, Jane would never forget that tight quiver of excitement she had felt that first morning when she had washed through the silty sludge in the pan and had seen the first few specks of gold lying there at the bottom. Tiny pieces, to be sure – and dust, as fine as that on a butterfly's wing – but gold all the same. The roar she'd let out had echoed across the wooded hills to the rocky outcrops beyond and for the first time she could understand Midas's obsession.

Since then, almost every day, they had found half an ounce, here or there. Not exactly substantial, but every find like a sip offered to them from the chalice of hope.

Such was their faith in their continuing fortune that, instead of banking the money that they'd made so far, they had staked out more claims, one even up towards the Isiaho River. It was a gamble, of course, but when Tom had suggested it Jane had instantly agreed. Word was spreading about the finds and even since Jane and Tom had been here two new hopefuls had arrived. Both farmers from the district, both desperate, both seeking their El Dorado. Tom was convinced that over the next year or so the floodgates would open and then the big companies would step in and most of the area would be pegged out.

Jane never ceased to be grateful that they had heard about Johnson and Stearnes' discoveries so early on. They might not be part of the original Eldoret Syndicate but they were only a few steps behind and that could only be to their advantage. Besides, there was an intimacy and comradeship present at the camp which she suspected would be lost once a tide of prospectors arrived. Everyone here had been so helpful, so willing to share their hard-earned tips, showing them exactly the way to pan, even showing them how to put together a makeshift cradle. There seemed to be no jealousies here yet; perhaps that only started when disillusionment set in.

Jane stretched and looked about her. The tents and huts dotted about the camp stood forsaken in the morning light, their owners already down at the riverbed hard at work. From here she could hear the sharp tick-tick of the picks, the dull thud of the shovels, the rattle and squeak of the cradles. Life at the camp had a rhythm and sound all of its own.

She bent down and picked up the breakfast tins and mugs which she had washed in the *kerai* and started back to the tent. As soon as she had finished here she would go down to the riverbed to work alongside Tom, first puddling then panning.

She was about to duck back into the tent when she heard a voice calling out to her, and, turning, saw a Kavirondo *toto* crossing the camp towards her, laden with home-grown produce. Yesterday she had bought some vegetables from him and today she could see he was hoping to sell her a chicken, judging by the fowl hanging across his arms.

'*Jambo!*' she called out to him and was greeted by a winning smile.

He walked over and set out his produce for Jane to inspect. He had brought some eggs, too – tiny ones, only a little bigger than quails' eggs – and some bananas. Seeing the bananas she was reminded that Tom had asked her to find out if the *toto* could provide them with suitable thatching grass or banana leaves for roofing the *banda* which Tom was hoping to build. Since it seemed probable that they would be staying here for the best part of the year now, the tent, with its dubious waterproof shell, needed to be replaced with something more substantial. The weather in the district was such that it rained almost every afternoon and Jane found that however hard she tried, she could never quite rid the tent of its smell of dampness.

The *toto* left, promising to see what he could do, and Jane finished the last of the tidying up. From bitter experience she had found she must leave as little as possible to be done when she came in, so exhausted would she be by evening. Then, having completed her tasks, she caught up her hat and started off down towards the river.

She found Tom, back bent, digging out the bed of the river, shovelling the gritty contents in the home-made puddling tub. The half hogshead, brought with them from the farm, was serving its purpose perfectly. But it was still back-breaking work, not only the digging out but the constant stirring of the silt and water, Tom all the while trying to break up the particles with a long-handled shovel to separate the auriferous drift. Bucket after bucket of water had to be poured into the tub in order to change and clear the water as it become charged with floating particles. Eventually Tom would pan or cradle what was left, hoping to find the heavier flecks of gold had settled at the bottom.

At Jane's approach, Tom lifted his head and smiled in greeting, but he didn't stop his work. There was a certain rhythm to swinging the pick which couldn't be broken, for once lost it took a while to recover. Head down, he hacked on.

In those first few days they had stopped at the slightest excuse, so unfit and unused to the work had they been. And their hands! Even now, Jane winced to think how blistered they had been – Tom's to such a degree that blood had streamed from them down the handle of his pick. Now they had healed and hardened into callouses, as had hers. Never again would they look smooth and white and pampered.

She bent down and picked up the panning dish which Tom had set at the edge of the river. At this point, the river was fast-moving but shallow, so she had the advantage of being able to keep on her boots. Last week, she had worked in deeper water and had had to remove her boots so that by the end of the day her feet were frozen and numb, to say nothing of the jigger fleas which she'd had to remove from under her toenails.

She stooped down and filled the shallow pan with water and

gravelly mud, swirling the pan and tilting it slightly so that the light bits flushed away as the water spilt over the edge. A pan took about ten minutes to wash through properly and though it was a lighter task than the digging and puddling, Jane always found her knees and back were aching by mid morning, especially as had happened today, when she had had little reward.

She stopped and stretched. Today there was a steaminess to the air which made even the slightest exertion an effort. She ran a hand over her forehead to keep the perspiration from dripping down into her eyes, her cotton shirt hanging damply against her body. The humidity wafted about her like an invisible sea, seeming to squeeze every breath out of the air.

By the banks of the river, where the sunshine dappled through the tall trees, a group of native Kavirondo children were playing, running naked in and out of the water, laughing and calling to one another in high-pitched excited voices. Jane looked at them a little enviously. How uncomplicated their lives seemed!

'Beastly hot, isn't it?' Tom was watching her from the riverbank. 'Want a break? It's a good moment . . .' His voice was patently full of moral support.

'Are you stopping?' Jane asked, only too aware that Tom, though careful not to push her too hard, always drove himself to the point of exhaustion. 'For a few minutes anyway . . .'

He hesitated, then put down his shovel. 'A few minutes won't hurt,' he acknowledged. He gave a rueful smile. 'Trouble is, once I stop, it's hell getting started again.'

'Isn't it just!'

They laughed and flopped down beside each other on the river bank. 'So, did you have any luck this morning?' he asked, drawing his knees up under his chin.

'Not much.' She shrugged. 'A few grains here and there. Nothing very spectacular. What about you?'

He lit a cigarette, leaning back against the rocks. 'A bit. Though not as much as yesterday . . .' His eyes flicked over to her, noting how tired she was looking, how pale. He stretched out and took her hand in his, rubbing the back of it with his thumb. 'You look done in.'

'It's the heat . . .'

'I know.' He took a drag at his cigarette, watching the smoke curl up into the canopy of trees overhead. 'Look, if you'd find it easier back at the farm, you have only to say,' he told her gently. 'It would be far more comfortable for you there.'

'The farm?' Jane spun round to face him. 'I couldn't leave you!'

'I'd manage. You mustn't think of me.'

She smiled a little. 'I wasn't,' she returned simply. She leaned over, sliding her arms around his neck, and kissed him. 'Things might be tough here, Tom, but at least we're together. I couldn't bear it if you sent me home.'

She made it sound as if she were being banished. 'Darling!' Tom drew her to him. 'I'm not sending you away. Not against your will. I just thought you needed a break . . . A rest.'

She raised her mouth to his. 'When I'm very rich, I'll rest all day.'

He laughed, kissing her. 'Not you! You're not the type.'

'Want to bet?' But she knew he was right. She came from a long-established hard-working Suffolk line – not one heady debutante or lounge lizard among them.

She leaned back, hands behind head. It was very beautiful here, hilly and picturesque, and because of the steamy climate everything was luxuriant and fertile.

She glanced downstream. There the river seemed to move more lazily, as if the sun had exhausted it utterly. At the bend, where a huge craggy boulder rose, it seemed almost to stop completely, turning on itself in a series of small eddies. Above that point, two butterflies fluttered, soaring and turning in the sunlight, their wings like the flash of a kingfisher so brilliant was their colour.

Beside her Jane felt Tom stir. He leant forward and stubbed out his cigarette.

'Time to start?' she asked him, watching him stand up.

''Fraid so.'

She took his outstretched hand and let herself be pulled up. 'So, shall I help with the puddling this time?' she asked, dusting off her trousers.

He shook his head. 'No, stick with the panning. It'll prove more productive, I think.'

'All right.' She watched him turn to pick up the buckets and carry them down to the river for refilling. 'I can always come and help with the puddling later if you need me.'

'Good idea.'

Jane picked up her panning dish and walked a few steps along the riverbank, watching the butterflies as they flitted and dipped along the river's edge. She followed them quietly to the bend of the river, where they hovered over the craggy boulder, turning to drift along the line of a deep gully which led from the hillside to the river. There were many such gullies along the side of the hills, caused by the constant rainfall here; and more often than not they were marked by a line of rich green, where the trees and plants grew in extra abundance.

She stepped over the gully and, moving into the shallow depths of the river, crouched down, leaning forward and cupping her hands together, intent on taking a cooling sip.

But even as she did so, she stopped in mid-action, looking down at the water before her.

Here it no longer glinted silver in the sunlight. Here, it was a different hue, as if the light from the camp-side lantern was reflected across it.

She began to tremble, almost too afraid to stretch out her hand, just in case she be proved wrong.

She hesitated only a moment longer, then with a deep drawn-out sigh plunged her hand into the cool depths. She felt the gravelly mass beneath her fingers and scooped up a handful, clutching at it tightly as she brought it to the surface.

This time there could be no mistake. Amongst the stones and silt, there were several pieces of gold the size of fine gravel. It was as if the river had slowed here to unburden its great weight. It made sense, of course, that between the huge boulder and the curve of the river where the current slowed, this would be the place where its precious load would be deposited. Text-book stuff, really.

She rose very slowly, her mouth suddenly dry.

'Tom . . .'

Her voice was shaky and not strong enough enough to rise above the noise of his shovelling. 'Tom!'

He heard her, this time. He caught the urgency in her tone and spun round towards her.

'Tom, quickly!'

He dropped his shovel and sped across the rocks towards her, his face tight with concern. He thought she must be hurt in some way and it was only as he neared that he saw by her face that he was mistaken. Her eyes were agleam, she was on fire with excitement.

'Jane, what is it?' His voice was tinged with caution. He was afraid to hope for too much.

She held out her hands to him in reply, the gold nestling in her palms.

'My God!' His eyes flicked up to her. 'Where did you find it?'

'Here!' She was laughing, colour flaming her face. 'Right here! I've been practically tripping over it for the past month!'

'I can't believe it.'

He moved over to where she was pointing and stooping down drew up a handful of pebbles and silt. He carefully washed them through, crouching down and letting the water trickle through his fingers. Again, amongst the river sediment were fragments of gold.

'Well, I'll be . . .' He paused, lifting his head to smile ruefully at Jane, his face crumpling into a boyish grin. 'Well, if it goes on like this I'll be able to buy back your grandmother's clock for you.'

'If it goes on like this,' said Jane with some feeling, 'you might even be able to buy back the farm . . .'

Tom's head jerked up. There was a moment's silence. He hadn't been sure if Jane had realised fully how much of the farm was mortgaged to the bank, or how close they were to ruin.

Jane caught his grim expression. 'Of course I knew,' she said quietly. 'It doesn't take much to realise that drought and falling prices and locusts are not a healthy combination. Besides, one had only to look at the other farmers facing disaster to know we were in the same boat.'

'Oh.' And he had tried so hard to shield her from the truth.

She crouched down beside him. 'We *will* be able to save the farm now, won't we?' she asked him, her voice eager. 'I mean, if this holds out . . .'

'If we've found what I think, then yes. And perhaps buy a bit more land besides.' Too many disappointments made him loath to hope for more.

'And here? What about staking out a few more claims here,' Jane asked, straightening. 'It would be worth it, wouldn't it?'

Tom slipped the gold into his pocket for safe keeping. 'Well, it makes sense to buy the piece of land above here, I suppose. The gold's got to have come down from the hills somewhere and it's more than likely that the leads are up that way, with the reef beyond.' He hesitated slightly. The truth was he didn't know enough to be sure. 'But I have to tell you, Jane. I didn't come here to stake more and more claims. I came here to save the farm.'

'I know that,' she said quietly.

'I'm a farmer, not a miner. I don't want to spend my time digging and panning forever, whatever riches are to be found. So, what I'm saying is – I want to work these pieces, spend a year or so here, that's all. Then leave. I want my children to grow up on a farm, not a mining camp, and it's so easy to want more and more.' His voice was almost apologetic, but he knew he spoke the truth.

By all accounts even if one had found a gold strike, trailing it could turn out to be the most heartbreaking trail of all. Once the original lead petered out, he'd heard it was a fine old game digging trenches to find another one. There were false scents and 'pockets' that didn't lead anywhere and were of little value; and always the hope that the next day would bring a chance of luck, or the day after that . . . He didn't want that for Jane and himself.

'I just want enough to get the farm in order,' he said, hoping she'd understand. 'To be able to put aside enough security to see us through the bad years, so that never again will I have to think about getting rid of Maramanga.' He paused, lifting his eyes to hers. 'Do you mind terribly? Do you think I'm quite mad not to want to stay here for as long as the gold holds out? You must say now if you do, it's your life we're talking about, too.'

She came across and put her arms around his shoulders. 'No, I think you're right.' Her voice was gentle. Tom could never be avaricious and that was partly why she loved him. 'You know where your priorities lie and I admire you for that.'

'But I could be turning away a fortune, you do realise that?'

'Of course. But I agree with you. The price we'd have to pay just isn't worth it. We'll give it a year, as you say. Put enough aside for the farm and hopefully a bit more for an income to see us through those rainy days . . .'

Tom leaned over and kissed her. 'And we've seen rather a lot of those of late, haven't we?'

Jane smiled. 'Yes.' She glanced down at her hand, opening up her palm slightly to see the gold. 'So, what do we do about this . . .'

'Put in a claim for the land above here first and then once that's secure, bank the lot with the minimum of fuss.'

'We could hang onto it for a while longer if you wanted.'

'And store it in that Eno's Fruit Salt bottle of yours? No, thank you.' He laughed. 'No, to the bank straight away with this lot. And after that, I suppose we ought to make a trip down to Nairobi. Get some serious mining equipment up here. If we're thinking of sinking a shaft, a puddling tub and cradle just isn't enough.'

'Nairobi?' Jane's face lit up. Money had its compensations after all. 'Oh, Tom, do you think I could have a few extra days to go up to Thika? I'd love to see Alexandra before she leaves.'

'Go for as long as you like.' Tom was only too pleased for her to have a break from Kakamega. He stretched out and ran his fingers through her hair, lifting it lightly back, caressing her. 'My poor darling, you've had so few treats since you arrived out here . . .'

She bent her head into the curve of his neck. 'You never led me to believe that life would be easy out here, Tom,' she reminded him truthfully. 'And honestly, there's been nothing I've missed.'

'You mean money won't change a thing?' he teased her.

'Well, one or two things,' she admitted, laughing. Children for one. Their unpredictable financial situation had been such that she had been terrified in case she should fall pregnant. She had used the ghastly contraptions she had got from the clinic in England, of course, but with losing so much weight she'd been worried that nothing would fit and that she would conceive. All that palaver for nothing. Too awful.

She leaned against Tom, her head against his shoulder. He was right. The mining camp could never be called home. It was not a place for children. The farm was where they all belonged.

Tom looked across at her and saw that her face had changed, her eyes now wide and misty and instinctively he knew what she was thinking about. He tightened his arms about her and, pulling her towards him, began to kiss her.

With a sigh she tilted her face up to his, her arms going out around his neck, the gold falling from her hand in a shimmering trail, forgotten for the moment.

16

Alexandra had intended to stay only a few days at Lake Naivasha before setting off back to Thika. But when William announced he had secured an invitation to stay with the Longs and to meet Lord Delamere, she felt it was too good an opportunity to miss. Now in his sixties, Delamere was folklore among the settlers for having tirelessly battled against politicians and red tape on their behalf, and Alexandra was intrigued to meet him. Her grandfather had often spoken about 'D', always in glowing terms, and she knew he would not wish her to miss the chance of meeting the man himself on his account. So, much to Charles's surprise, it took little cajoling from him to persuade Alexandra to accompany them.

They set off from Lake Navaisha early, heading northwards up along the floor of the Rift Valley. For comfort they took two cars, Caroline and William in one, while Alexandra travelled with Margaret and Charles in the other. Charles was in fine spirits; their stay at Naivasha seeming to have acted as a tonic, and he was now bursting with easy charm and enthusiasm, almost exhausting with his sudden spurts of energy.

They sped on. By late morning it was hot in the valley, blisteringly so. Everything seemed intensified, the light hard and bright, the heat quivering across the long grass. Several times the cars threatened to overheat, and they halted at the little streams which criss-crossed the roads to fill up the radiators and cool off. Small groups of *totos* in their skimpy cloaks paused in between trying to shoo on their herds of shiny-coated bleating goats, observing the foreigners' antics from afar, intrigued.

This was Maasai country, and from time to time Alexandra would see a small group of Morans standing close to the road, spears by their side. They looked impressive, standing like sentinels against the grasslands, impassively staring out across the valley. Handsome, too, their faces finer somehow than many of the African tribes, with high cheekbones, prominent noses and elongated almond shaped eyes, and amazingly flawless skin – born it was said, from a lifetime of only drinking milk into which animal blood had been mixed. They were Delamere's favourite tribe, the Maasai, his respect for them immense. And seeing them standing there, immobile, arrogant, Alexandra too found their natural dignity compelling.

They came down the villainously stony road to pass Elmenteita, where the lake lay long and narrow among rocks and low craggy hills and flat-topped acacias. Here Delamere had lived at his ranch, Soysambu, before moving to Lorensho with his new wife, Gwladys. He had built a simple home on the ridge overlooking the lake, and the area teemed with wild-life since he allowed no game shooting on the ranch. Herds of impala and zebra and waterbuck grazed their way nonchalantly beneath the umbrella thorn trees; Alexandra thought the scene almost park-like.

At last they could see Lake Nakuru ahead, eerily beautiful, set among volcanoes. It was here that the two cars turned off, swinging up the drive to the Longs' ranch, Nderit. As they drew to a halt, Genessie Long came out to greet them. Slim, elegant and rich, it was she who had bought the ranch on Nakuru's shores, and it was she who had designed the shingle-roofed house with its enormous rooms built around a patio with a fountain playing in the middle. A surge of wolf-hounds flowed out in her wake, offering a sea of waving, excited tails.

'You got here in good time. Well done!' Genessie exclaimed, pushing the dogs away with an ineffectual hand. 'Come in, do. You must all be sweltering.'

Her warm hospitality was typical of all the people whom Alexandra had met in Kenya. The connection between William's mother and Genessie's parents had been tenuous to say the least, but it seemed not to matter one jot: the welcome was all-embracing.

Genessie led the way through into the house, telling them that Boy would be joining them in a moment. Inside, it was a curious mixture. Good antique furniture alongside objects made by the local *fundi*; chairs and carpets covered with the enormous wolf-hounds which had rushed back into the house ahead of them to secure the best position. Genessie made little attempt to move them, evidently used to their antics.

By the time they had washed and changed and reassembled on the verandah for cooling drinks, Boy Long had returned from the farm. He had dark curly hair, a ruddy complexion and lively dark eyes; with the bright blue Somali shawl thrown across his shoulders he made a striking figure. He was said to be one of the best stockmen in the country, having been employed by Delamere until he had met Genessie and branched out on his own.

He was amusing company, full of interesting tales of his time with Delamere; the days when Delamere had been much wilder, days when he had hunted with a pack of bear-hounds, days when he'd shot lions from the saddle. Listening to him, Alexandra realised again the appeal of Africa to men of adventure like Delamere and Boy.

Lunch, served by houseboys in dark red *kanzus* with gold-embroidered waistcoats and scarlet turbans, was taken on the patio. Afterwards they went out to see the stables. Genessie was an accomplished horsewoman and kept about seventy horses at Nderi in magnificent accommodation.

Margaret and Alexandra fell into easy step with one another, lingering over each equine beauty. Everything at Nderit seemed a little larger than life, even the horses.

'Father would be so jealous of this,' Alexandra told Margaret, thinking of their own stables – meagre in comparison – at Drayton Manor.

'And not just your father!' Margaret exclaimed. 'I'm really not much of a horse-person, you know, but when I see it like this, well . . .' She nodded in the direction of Boy, who, with Charles and William, had strode on ahead. 'He makes it seem so easy, doesn't he?'

'Boy? Yes. Though I think this is mostly Genessie's baby . . .'

'Most probably,' Margaret agreed. 'Extraordinary, isn't she? Do you know, she was telling me over lunch that she had always wanted to visit Petra. So, once it was possible to do so, she drove out by car and then hired some camels and a guide and two Circassian policemen and went on – on her own if you please – to Shobak and two Crusader castles, sleeping out in the open whenever necessary!'

'Good heavens!' Alexandra was impressed. Seeing Genessie now, immaculate in her beautifully-cut white jodhpurs and crisp white silk shirt, it seemed impossible to imagine her achieving such a journey. It was a major accomplishment and Alexandra's admiration for the woman increased by bounds.

'Yes, quite an achievement,' Margaret agreed. 'And I must say, I think it's awfully good for Charles to meet Boy and Genessie. So motivating. I fear I thought the crowd at Naivasha far too rich and indolent. Charming, maybe, but not a good influence for Charles . . .'

Alexandra glanced across at Margaret. It was the first time she had voiced such opinions.

Margaret caught her look. 'I hope you aren't offended,' she added quickly. 'But I particularly worried over Kiki Preston's influence. She has the reputation for indulging in all sorts, even cocaine and heroin, so I heard, and I thought, bearing in mind Charles's unfortunate little episode . . .' Her voice trailed slightly, embarrassed. 'Of course, I'm *sure* Charles wouldn't, not after, well you know . . . Oh dear, I wish I hadn't said anything.' She stopped, quite mortified.

Alexandra reached out and touched her arm. 'I'm glad you did. The truth is, I had no idea about Kiki . . .' She couldn't quite believe that Charles would have been so foolish as to indulge in any of Kiki's pick-me-ups – not after the Kitty Marsden affair. Surely not. And yet, she was aware of the feeling of intrigue between the two – conspiratorial almost. Aware, too, of his sudden bursts of energy and good humour.

'Well, he's away from Naivasha now,' said Margaret firmly. 'He'll be fine here with the Longs, and on safari. I might have been mistaken, of course. It was just a vague feeling I had . . .'

'I know exactly what you mean,' admitted Alexandra; she was remembering little incidents now.

'Silly boy. He's so easily led, that's the trouble. That's why the family were so thrilled when he fell for you. A steadying influence and all that.'

'Oh dear,' Alexandra was unsure whether to be pleased or not by such an admission.

Margaret caught her look. 'You mustn't be offended, you know,' she said, laughing. 'It was just what Freddie's family thought of me. Quite the normal reaction of a caring family for a slightly wayward son. Though of course we never quite had the chance to test out the theory.'

This was the first time Margaret had spoken to Alexandra about Freddie, whom she had married at seventeen a year before the Great War and had lost less than two years later at Ypres.

'You know, Charles is rather like Freddie in a way,' Margaret went on, her voice softening. 'That's probably why I have such a soft spot for him. He has such potential, Alexandra. Pushed in the right direction he could achieve so much . . .' Despite herself her mind went back to those days gone by, the days when she'd been swept off her feet by the young Lord Frederick Torrington, days made sweet by their shortness. Even now, certain sounds and smells reminded Margaret of him, sixteen years on. Dappled shadows under apple trees, the click of the croquet ball, bicycles – it was with him that she'd learned to ride one – and the smell of new mown hay, for it was in the fields behind the Great Hall that he'd kissed her for the first time. And more. Memories of him, memories of her youth, so tightly intertwined, so fleetingly held.

'So . . .' Margaret took a deep, shuddering breath, breaking her reverie. 'So, all I was trying to say, really, is how pleased everyone is about you and Charles. Even Caroline, though she'd never tell you so.' She laughed. 'Now there's one of the reasons he's so malleable. Caroline. With a sister like that bossing him since the cradle it's hardly surprising he can be so easily led . . . Anyway, you're strong enough to cope with her. That's another reason why Lady Kildare was so pleased . . .'

'Was it?' Alexandra had had no inkling as to the machinations behind the scenes.

'Oh yes. Lady K knows her daughter only too well,' said Margaret with some feeling. 'And her son. Can see Charles is at the crossroads and all that . . . But I've gossiped enough! Let's catch up with the others, shall we?'

The rest of the party had almost completed their tour. Alexandra was sorry to have missed Boy's chatty comments but glad Margaret had confided in her. She felt that she knew not only Margaret more fully in consequence, but Charles also.

Watching him from afar, Alexandra saw how much calmer he seemed here than at Naivasha; he appeared interested in Nderit and all that Boy Long showed him. Now that Margaret had mentioned it, she could see how easily influenced he was, even by his surroundings.

Gradually during the rest of the day, she felt the Charles of old begin to re-merge – the positive, fun-loving Charles she'd known in London. Here at Nderit they laughed and teased each other, and she felt relieved that they were growing close again.

They spent the afternoon on a guided tour of the farm. By the end of the day they were exhausted, more than ready for cool drinks on the verandah.

'Now, for heaven's sake, don't talk to Delamere about his last trip to England,' Boy warned them as they sipped their sundowners. Delamere and his wife were to join them later for supper. 'He was terribly disappointed by how little he managed to achieve on the Land Reform issue last year.'

They all solemnly agreed; but of course, when Delamere arrived less than a hour later, so emotive was the subject that it was one of the first they plunged into. Land settlement was still a raw issue for the settlers in Kenya. The British Government's sentiment toward the white settlers had changed dramatically over the last two decades.

'They can't see that colonisation no longer follows the old nineteenth-century lines,' Delamere said with disgust, pushing an angry hand through his once-red hair. 'They can't see that it is the making of a new country where two races should be able to progress together without enmity. They see colonisation as the ruthless exploitation of resources and people, that's all. Heavens, more people have lost all their money out here than have made a penny out of the place!'

And Delamere should know, thought Alexandra, recalling that he was said to have drained his estate in Cheshire dry in order to feed his dreams in Kenya.

She watched him now across the table – small, stocky, with a beaky nose, his lively face belying his age. Yet some of the vital energy for which he was so renowned had definitely faded. His lack of success in England had shaken him; he blamed himself for having failed to sense the new wave-length of Labour sentiment.

'But they were determined not to listen, D,' said Boy Long placatingly. 'Probably nowhere in the world are relations between employers and employees better than in Kenya, but one wouldn't think so to listen to the outcry in England!'

'Not everyone feels that way!' insisted William, feeling he should at least say something in their defence. 'It's such an emotive subject, that's the trouble. Public opinion can be whipped up by the likes of Wedgwood Benn at the drop of a hat.'

'But they don't get their facts right,' complained Delamere bitterly. 'Look what they said about reserve taxes. Said we were using that money to pay for European services. Nonsense! Every penny is spent on direct native services.'

'Of course it is,' agreed Boy Long, his dark eyes brooding. 'And the whole relation between the settlers and natives rests on a basis of goodwill. Labourers are housed and fed – on rations laid down by the Government I might add – and every farm has a dispensary to deal with minor ailments, some even provide a school for their employees' children . . .' Ironically, these were probably better conditions than most employers provided for their workforce in England.

William, at the other side of the table, was leaning back in his chair. 'But the whole issue of Land Reform, that's the core of it, isn't it?'

'That's what the Labour Government would like you to believe,' commented Delamere dryly. 'But the point is, Africa has to be brought into the twentieth century and can the Africans do it alone? I think not. And that takes us back to my original argument, that Kenya is the making of a new country where two races can progress together. Look at the achievements of the white settlers, for heaven's sake! Look at all the crops they've introduced which are now the backbone of Kenya! Tea, coffee, pineapples,' he paused there to nod at Alexandra, for it was in the Thika area that the Harries had established their thriving pineapple plantations, 'blackwattle, sisal, maize, wheat. No acknowledgment of any of that, of course. Nor of the sheer effort every settler puts in to make his farm work. Forever trying new ideas, whatever the disappointments, whatever the cost. Take that chap, Dalgleish, out Gilgil way. From what I've heard he's doing a splendid job experimenting with pyrethrum. Very enterprising. Dammit,' Delamere brought his fist down sharply on the table, 'the Government's turned its back on chaps like that. Whatever will it try next? Reneging on its nine hundred and ninety nine year leases?'

There was uneasy laughter around the table. The idea that the Government would pull back the leases was unthinkable, of course; but nonetheless the Longs and the Delameres knew that the chance of the settlers having a say in their own future now looked very slim. Listening, Alexandra could only feel it was a mistake. If one took away the settlers' sense of responsibility towards the country's future it could change the whole pattern and encourage an entirely different type of settler to come out. And whatever she might feel about Robert now – she had to concede that Delamere's admiration was not unjustified.

Delamere drained his whisky and leant back in his chair.

'And of course, the fools back in England don't understand the Africans anyway,' he said bitterly. 'They talk about the natives looking after their own affairs, but they haven't even considered the effects of tribalism. Anyone out here could tell them the Maasai wouldn't pull in the same direction as the Kikuyu or the Kavirondo, nor the Nandi with the Wakamba and the Turkana. I don't think they've even any idea of how many tribes there are out here! So, let's say they give the leading rein to the Kikuyu – and with all the noise that Kenyatta and Tom Ngolo and Harry Kinkardu are making, that's probably where the power will go – what then of the other tribes? What then of the Maasai, their sworn enemies of centuries past? Don't tell me that they'll welcome them into their midst and share their power with them? Of course not, they'll drive them out of their lands with far more subtle means than just spears!

A murmur of agreement ran round the table. Tribalism was one of the great problems of Africa, but to ignore its existence would be stupidity indeed.

'So, we've got to go on pushing!' Delamere declared, fiercely. He coughed slightly, and Alexandra saw Gwladys Delamere put her hand on his arm, anxious lest he be exerting himself too much. Not that she would be able to stop him, of course. Delamere would die in harness with no slackening of activity if he could help it. He was still passionately involved in politics and only this March had been reelected in the fourth general election as Member for the Rift Valley. But all the same, Gwladys would protect him as best she could from the rigours of the life he led.

Now she carefully guided the conversation away from that of Land Reform, turning to ask Charles in her wonderfully deep, husky voice about the hunting safari. She herself had originally come out to Kenya on safari with her first husband and the Prince of Wales's party in 1928. She had fallen in love with Kenya, and out of love with her husband, and had returned to the country on a visit, only to become enamoured with Delamere, some thirty years her senior.

Alexandra heard Gwladys give out a throaty chuckle at Charles's description of his lion hunt, her gaiety permeating the atmosphere. Soon everyone was laughing, much more at ease, caught up by Gwladys's vitality.

Watching her from across the table, Alexandra could well see why Delamere adored her. With her chalk-white skin and jet-black hair, she made a striking figure. But it was her personality, positive, dynamic, which had captured him. A man like that, with so much energy himself, would have been drawn instantly by her air of sheer vivacity.

They talked late into the night. The Delameres were staying at Nderit, too, their intention being to visit Soysambu the following morning on their way back to Loresho, so they lingered over their nightcaps on the verandah, unhurried.

It was an evening of immeasurable charm. The clear African moon poured down its light on them. In the distance they could hear the whistle of a night bird, the screech of a hyrax, the infinitesimal sounds of the night.

Alexandra, sitting there, watching Delamere's animated face as he spoke to Charles, watching the smoke from Gwladys's Turkish cigarette curl across the light from the hurricane lamp, felt the moment stretch in time. This was the feeling she had in Africa. A sense of no beginning and no ending. It was more than a sense of belonging, it was a sense of being.

And she knew now why people like Genessie and Gwladys had risked all to come back.

They spent one more day at Nderit before leaving early on the Thursday morning. The sun was barely up and the grass was silvered with dewdrops as the two cars started on their way back to Nairobi. A runner had brought Alexandra a telegram to say that Jane would be there from the 8th onwards, and hoped to come up to Thika thereafter. So the plan was that, having spent the night at the Muthiaga Club, Alexandra would meet up with Jane while the others set off on their elephant safari with John Stephenson.

They sped their way southwards. Having met Delamere, the Rift Valley took on a new meaning to Alexandra now. As he owned so much of the land, Delamere had had a pipeline laid from the springs on the escarpment above to bring water to this almost treeless valley. He had had the plain surveyed into five hundred-acre sections, and planted on each a patch of quick-growing wattle for firewood; then he had leased out, on very easy terms to encourage the settlers, the little homesteads which now dotted the area like new shoots in a carefully dug bed.

It was just outside Gilgil that William's car started to cause problems. It began to overheat, steaming alarmingly. They all stopped while William refilled the radiator but when he tried to start the engine again the car refused to oblige.

'Damn!' William sighed with exasperation, folding back the bonnet and staring helplessly at the pistons. He could see that the trip back was threatening to be full of mishaps. Charles's car had already had a puncture. 'We'll just have to wait for it to cool down, I suppose . . .'

'Here? In the middle of nowhere? You have to be joking, William!' Caroline protested. She remained steadfastly in her seat, refusing to budge, as if to do so would be an admission that the car had well and truly broken down.

'We can't just stay here, you know, William,' she fretted, her back arrow-straight with annoyance.

William gave her a cold little smile. 'Have you any better suggestions?' he asked somewhat sourly.

'Well, for one we could all go back to Gilgil in Charles's car and wait there,' Caroline returned. Her mouth tightened slightly. She was not one who took kindly to plans going awry. 'Or better still, doesn't that chap we met at Joss's live somewhere around here? The one Delamere was mentioning the other night . . .'

She turned to Alexandra, gesturing impatiently. 'You know the one I mean – the one who's got a place out Thika way as well. What's his name. Robert —'

'Dalgleish, isn't it, Alexandra?' put in Margaret helpfully, much to Alexandra's dismay. 'Isn't he the one with the colt that Joss has taken such a liking to?'

'Yes, that's the one!' Caroline smiled, warming to her theme now. 'He was supposed to be only a few miles out of Gilgil. He must be around here somewhere.'

'There's so many side turnings, he could be anywhere,' Alexandra protested, hoping that her voice didn't sound too high-pitched and frantic. She had no intention of seeing Robert Dalgleish again.

'But he said just outside Gilgil on the road to Naivasha. This *is* the road. It really can't be far . . .'

Alexandra made a moué. 'Could easily be. In Kenya they always talk about places being close to each other – near-neighbours they say – and they're usually miles away!'

William lifted his head from the engine for a moment. 'Actually, I think Caroline's right. I seem to remember he said about five miles out. And Mr Dalgleish struck me as a pretty precise man.'

'Oh . . .' Alexandra ignored Caroline's triumphant look. She felt like a trapped animal, fighting against the inevitable, knowing there could be no escape.

'And if that's the case,' said William, straightening up and closing the bonnet decisively, 'then I suggest we tow this car there as well. I've got a frightful feeling that the problem's not just the radiator. Something must have worked its way loose . . .'

They all groaned. But having made the decision to locate Robert's farm, the probability of finding help there seemed to lessen the enormity of the problem.

Charles opened the boot of his car and took out a rope – they had been forewarned to take such a precaution, motoring in the country roads was renowned for its hazards – and feeding it around William's fender lashed it to his own as securely as possible. Then, with supreme optimism, he told them to get in.

Their progress was slow but sure, Charles's car creaking and groaning under the strain; but thankfully after little more than a mile they found the turn-off to Robert's farm, the signpost simply marked 'Dalgleish', as if defying the need for further information.

At the end of the dirt track stood a creeper-covered stone bungalow with a wide verandah built around it. As they drew up a slim wiry man in his early forties appeared from the nearby stables to greet them.

'Spot of bother, I see then,' he commented, crossing over to shake hands with them. 'I'm Jack Bryne, by the way, manager here.'

'I see.' William glanced around the yard. 'Is Robert Dalgleish about? We hoped to find him in . . .'

Jack shook his head, pushing a hand through his dark wavy hair. 'Not here at the moment,' he said. Alexandra tried, but failed, to look as disappointed as the others. 'Be back in a couple of hours, I suppose,' continued Jack. He paused, giving William a direct look as if summing him up, then nodded in the direction of the car. 'What's the trouble? Any idea?'

William lifted his shoulders in a helpless gesture. 'Overheating, I think. But it could be more complicated . . .' His voice trailed, implying that that was more than likely. 'But seeing that we were so close to the farm here, I thought it might be best to come here and for the girls to have a bit of comfort at least while I tried to find out what was wrong with the bally thing!'

'Can't say as I blame you,' agreed Jack, beaming. 'And as it happens, you've come to the right place . . .'

'Oh?' William's face brightened. 'Know something about motors, do you?'

Jack shook his head. 'Not me. But my son, Peter, does. Only sixteen, but what he doesn't know about cars . . .' He turned and took a few paces in the direction of the stables and called out: 'Peter, over here! Double quick!' Then he turned back to William with a quick, reassuring nod. 'He'll have you sorted out, no trouble. Got a real knack, has Peter.'

A mini-version of Jack Bryne appeared at one of the stable doors – same dark hair, same beaming smile.

'Ah, there you are, lad!' said Jack, gesturing him over. 'Think you can do anything with this?' He jerked his head in the direction of William's car.

'Try.' It was clear by the way Peter's face lit up that it was no task his father was asking of him. He opened the bonnet and bent over the engine, peering inside for a moment. 'Ah yes, I see. Carburettor's chock full of grit and sand . . .'

'Can you fix it?' William asked eagerly, scrutinising the engine before him. Not in the least bit mechanically minded, it was all a complete mystery to him, but he thought he should at least show interest.

'More than likely,' said Peter cheerfully. 'Just a bit tricky getting at it, that's all. Needs to be taken out and cleaned. Wouldn't hurt to tighten a few nuts and screws either!'

'Well then,' said Jack, looking as relieved as any of them – after all, having pronounced that Peter could mend anything he felt his son's honour at stake – 'I suggest we leave Peter tinkering away here and you can either go into the cool of the house or

I can show you around a bit. Take a look at the stables, if you like . . .'

William nodded enthusiastically. Racing was one of his passions. 'The stables, I think, if you don't mind. I'd like to see that colt I've heard so much about.' The others murmured in agreement.

'Right,' said Jack. 'Come and have a cool drink first then I'll show you around.'

Ten minutes later, refreshed, they came through into the stables. The moment they saw the foal they could see instantly why Josslyn Hay had been so taken by it.

He was a bright chestnut with a white star with big eyes and an impish expression, and that bold head which was so sought after. Only a few months old he still had his fluffy baby coat but the sleek lines were already apparent.

'He looks almost like a rug on stilts!' said Margaret, stretching out to touch his teddy-bear-like coat.

'Doesn't he?' agreed Alexandra. But for all that, there was nothing bearish about the way he stalked about his stable. He had that swing of the quarters that marks a real athlete and there was no mistaking, with that bright eager head, that he was a study of co-ordination of muscle and bone and nerve.

'Not bad, is he?' said Jack with obvious pride. 'We think he could be another Camciscan. And from a small stable like this too. But Mr Dalgleish has an eye for them, you know. Picked up the mare cheaply. Been written off, she had . . .'

'Had she? Can't think why,' remarked William, looking the brood mare over. 'She looks a beauty to me.'

'Well, so she does now,' returned Jack. 'But she's been with us for over two years now. Changed out of all recognition, she has. Tendons had been jarred, mishandled by her first trainer, but we brought her back to form.' He ran a weatherbeaten hand gently along the mare's neck. 'Little cracker, she is now. And so are some of the others . . .'

He led the way through the stables, stopping at every box to tell them a little about each horse. Although nothing like the size of Genessie's elaborate stables, nor nearly so grand, Alexandra nonetheless was impressed by what she saw. Each horse had about it something that caught the eye – looks, movement, character, something that made one stop and linger for a moment.

'Of course,' Jack was saying as they came out into the open again. 'This isn't really what the farm's all about. The stables are just a little sideline. You should see what else Mr Dalgleish is up to here. Cattle interbreeding; trying out new crops. There's one he's getting going at the moment – pyrethrum – he's only got a few acres planted but it looks like a winner . . .'

'Pyrethrum? I think Delamere mentioned the other night that Robert was experimenting with that one,' William said, shielding his eyes from the sudden glare. He furrowed his brow in an attempt to recall what Delamere had said precisely. Certainly he had mentioned Dalgleish – full of praise too, but more than that he couldn't exactly remember. Delamere had said so *much* that evening.

Jack nodded his head, approvingly. 'Yes, Delamere's been over a few times,' he said. 'Interested in what's happening here. Particularly interested in the mill, he was. I'll take you down there, if you like . . .'

'Is it far?' asked Caroline. She feared Jack's enthusiasm could mean miles of walking.

'Just across the way,' Jack said, with a nod to a building just beyond the stable block.

'Pyrethrum's an insecticide, isn't it?' asked Charles. He seemed to remember Delamere saying as much.

'It is indeed,' said Jack, leading the way across the yard. 'Pretty daisy-like plant, but with a kick like a mule! Another chap out Nakauru way got a few seeds some years back and gave Mr Dalgleish a few to experiment with as well. See what effects the different altitudes might have. Well, it has certainly thrived here. And it works a treat on those coffee pests, I can tell you. Mr Dalgleish tried it out on his farm over at Thika last year and it worked wonders on those antestia and capsid bugs! Thinks he should be able to find a good market for the ground-up flowers. Should be able to sell everything he can grow . . .'

'It's that good, is it?' asked William, faintly sceptical.

'Of course,' said Jack with conviction. He pushed open the door of the mill and took them inside. 'Mind, you've got to be careful to preserve the toxic elements of the flower. That's the trick. That's what's made the Japanese flowers so sought after. Now Mr Dalgleish thinks we can win the market from the Japanese if only we can produce a higher level of pyrethrins – that's the toxic bit.'

'And how can you do that?' Charles asked, looking down at the jar of powder Jack held out to him, not sure whether he was supposed to sniff it or not.

'That's the tricky bit,' admitted Jack with a grin. 'But Mr Dalgleish has been experimenting and he's found out that if you wait until the flowers are fully open before picking them then they seem to be more toxic than if you pick them when they are closed or half-closed. Early days yet, but if it's true then it'll make all the difference . . .'

He showed them the rest of the mill and then, just as they were crossing the yard back to the house again, Peter appeared, grease-covered but triumphant. 'Running like a bird now!' he announced with a beaming smile.

'Terrific!'

'Well done!'

'Wonderful!'

Everyone spoke at once enthusiastically, full of praise.

Peter led them back round to the cars. William's car stood juddering in the driveway, its engine purring again.

'Good man!' said William, slapping Peter on the back. 'What luck for us you were here. An absolute wizard, eh, Caroline?'

'Absolute,' agreed Caroline, smiling for the first time since the break-down. The Muthiaga Club, with its cool drinks and fans and convivial company, no longer seemed an impossibility. She brightened considerably.

William turned to Jack. 'Is it worth our waiting for Robert Dalgleish, do you think? I should have liked to have seen him —'

Jack shook his head. 'He'll be gone a good hour yet, I should think,' he told William, sweeping his dark hair back from his face. 'And if you're intending to make Nairobi by nightfall I shouldn't risk the delay. He could be longer, of course. Depends on how this meeting has gone. He's trying to fix up a cooperative of all the coffee planters and you know what people can be like when a new idea's put to them . . .' He lifted his thin shoulders expressively.

'I do indeed,' William acknowledged with a laugh. He glanced round at the others. Caroline in particular seemed anxious to depart. 'Well then . . .' He had to admit it seemed pointless to wait. 'We'll take your advice and be off. And thank you again.' He shook hands with Jack and his boy and then started back to the car.

There was a commotion in one of the trees in the paddock close by.

A flock of weaver birds burst into the sky in a yellow cloud, flapping and squabbling noisily.

'It's pretty impressive, all this, isn't it?' William said, turning to Charles as they neared the cars. 'I mean, all the things that Dalgleish gets up to. How on earth has he the energy for it all?'

'Beats me,' said Charles. 'And he's got that place over at Thika to run, too!' He glanced over to Alexandra. 'And by all accounts he runs that pretty well, too.'

'What?' Lost in a reverie, Alexandra was suddenly aware of being spoken to.

'We're talking about Robert Dalgleish,' repeated Charles. 'I was saying, even though he has this place, he still manages to run the place over at Thika, too.'

'Yes, he does.' Though Alexandra's voice was matter-of-fact, her emotions were anything but. She hadn't wanted to come today, hadn't been in the least bit interested to see what Robert was doing here at Gilgil; but having done so she couldn't help admitting she was immensely impressed.

From the moment she had seen that spirited long-legged colt to the moment Jack had finally closed the door of the mill, she had been full of admiration for Robert's every achievement. The farm had revealed yet another side to him. The sheer energy of these enterprises, the sheer conviction of the man: no wonder Delamere had sung his praises.

And suddenly, standing here with his achievements about her, she was sorry to have quarrelled with him that day at Naivasha, sorry to be parting as enemies rather than as friends. It should not have ended like that.

She hesitated, ignoring Charles's chivvying, and on an impulse turned back to Jack Bryne.

'I wonder, would you be so kind as to mention to Robert Dalgleish that I called? Alexandra Drayton's the name . . .' She hesitated, a little unsure under Jack's quizzical eye. 'Could you pass on the message that I'll be at my grandfather's at Thika for the next three weeks? Tell him if he's over that way he's welcome to call in for a drink. Tell him that I still owe him one for that day . . .' she paused, remembering, 'for that day we planted out the coffee . . .'

There. It was done.

If Jack noticed her anxiety he made no sign of it. He merely beamed his concurrence. 'Right, Miss Drayton. My pleasure. I'll pass on your message,' he said. 'Like as not he'll be over Thika way in the next few weeks.'

'Good.' Alexandra heard Charles call out her name again, impatiently this time. 'Thank you, Mr Bryne.'

She turned then and made her way back to the waiting car. She wasn't sure what had prompted her to leave Robert that message. But having done so, she felt no regret, only a sense of light-headed relief.

17

'It's blissful here.'

'Isn't it?'

Alexandra and Jane were sitting on the paddock gate, looking down across the valley which stretched out before them. Below them, in their neat rows, the coffee trees were heavy with shining green berries, ready soon for harvest.

Alexandra swung her slim brown legs against the wooden gate, the sun warm on her back. She was glad now that Charles had not accompanied them up to Kirimangari; for while Jane was full of enthusiasm for the place, she suspected Charles might have been disappointed by Kirimangari's lack of grandeur. After Naivasha and the Longs' immaculate Nderit, the farm looked a little run-down and shabby, even she could see that. But oh, so achingly familiar – she had felt her spirits rise as soon as they had turned off the main road down the murram drive.

She let out a sigh and turned back to Jane. 'So, is there nothing I can do to persuade you to stay longer than a week?' Though they had exchanged gossip and news way into the night it was hard to think that after these few days they might not see each other again for a very long time.

'I'd love to, but I can't. Really.' Jane's voice showed all her regret. 'I don't like to leave Tom at Kakamega for too long by himself. He's hopeless if I'm not there. He'll work all hours, not rest, forget to eat and then wonder why he's fallen ill. Strange, isn't it? Men are so organised in some things, so hopelessly shambolic in others!'

Alexandra laughed. 'So true!'

In the cool shade of the trees close by a pair of red-eyed doves cooed their tone soft against the harsh sawing chirrup of the crickets.

Alexandra stretched contentedly. 'So, what will you do now that you've made your fortune?'

'It's hardly a fortune!' protested Jane. She made a tight little grimace, screwing up her mouth. 'Most of what we'll find will be used to pay off the farm. I doubt we'll have that much left over . . .'

'I see, so it's not Park Lane here we come!'

'Absolutely not, I'm afraid.' Jane smiled. 'But at least it's out-of-the-woods here we go! Feels almost as good.'

'As bad as that, was it?'

'Worse.' Jane raised her eyebrows expressively. 'Awful, in truth. Like being stuck in a tunnel waiting for the inevitable collapse. So tense, so claustrophobic, every step a struggle. I must say, though, it's taught me a healthy respect for money! You don't know how lucky you are marrying Charles. You'll never have to go through all that!'

'I know.' Alexandra slipped off the paddock gate, leaning her back up against it.

There was a silence. The crickets' chirruping seemed very loud at that moment. Jane came to stand beside her, putting out a hand to touch Alexandra's shoulder. 'What's the matter?'

Alexandra leaned her head back and closed her eyes for a moment. 'Oh, I don't know. Nothing really.'

A flicker of a smile crossed Jane's face. 'I see . . .'

It was only two words, but the way Jane spoke them made Alexandra open her eyes slightly and peer back at her.

'And just what is that supposed to mean?' she asked, a hint of suspicion in her voice.

'Nothing.'

'Nothing?'

Jane's shoulders lifted the merest fraction. 'It's just that I've been expecting something like this ever since you started talking about Robert Dalgleish . . .'

'Robert Dalgleish? What's he to do with it?'

'Everything.'

There was something distinctly speculative in Jane's tone. 'Well, you're wrong, Jane,' insisted Alexandra emphatically. 'As it happens I don't even particularly like the man . . .'

'No? Then why does his name come up in conversation once every five minutes?'

'It doesn't!'

'Does too. For every once you mention Charles, you mention Robert at least three or four times.' Jane smiled

'Really – what nonsense!'

'It isn't nonsense,' Jane went on, a hint of laughter in her voice. 'You were just the same when you visited me in Eldoret. Robert this, Robert that. Why don't you just admit the truth to yourself. I can see it, even if you can't. You're jolly well smitten by the fellow. Have been for months!' She knew now that when Alexandra had invited her to Kirimangari it wasn't just her grandfather she had wanted her to meet, although she could see Alexandra hadn't admitted as much to herself.

'Well, you couldn't be more wrong,' protested Alexandra, almost sharply. 'As it happens, we had a blazing row last time we met!'

'That proves nothing,' said Jane unperturbed.

'Besides, you've forgotten, I'm in love with Charles.'

'Ah . . .'

Alexandra's eyes flicked up to Jane's. That one word spoke volumes. Then she bent down to pluck at a long-stemmed grass, twirling it reflectively between her thumb and finger.

'So,' Alexandra said after a while. 'You met him. What do you think of him?' Her voice was deceptively airy, only her fingers restlessly turning the grass-stem gave away her unease.

'Charles, you mean?'

'Yes.'

Jane paused, gazing out across the *shamba*, wondering how truthful to be. 'Well,' she began, 'he's impossibly handsome, of course. Great fun, charming . . .'

'But?'

'But . . .' Jane hesitated, then decided that honesty was crucial at this point. 'But it's as if he hasn't been tried and tested yet, if you know what I mean. I know he's young, but when I think of what Tom had done by Charles's age, the challenges he'd had to face . . .' Her voice trailed slightly. Of course, the Muthiaga Club wasn't exactly the place to judge a man, she admitted; but even so, amusing though Charles had been, she'd come away feeling something had been missing. Perhaps, liking Alexandra as she did, she had hoped for too much. Yet she sensed Alexandra was finding him far more shallow than she'd remembered. 'There was nothing wrong with him,' she insisted carefully. 'It was just that I felt he was sort of at the crossroads. Might float on inconsequentially forever, might not. If he married you, he wouldn't of course . . .'

Alexandra gave a helpless shrug. 'Margaret said that too.'

'Did she?' Jane looked surprised. 'Remember though, Alexandra, he's not your responsibility. He's got to make it on his own, you know. He's got to face up to the real world by himself one day.'

'That's the trouble, I don't think he can,' admitted Alexandra. She thought of him at Naivasha. She wasn't sure he wanted to face the real world. Certainly there he'd been content to skate across the surface of life, along with the others. Perhaps that's all he would ever want.

'You know,' she said, looking at Jane, 'that's what I liked about Robert Dalgleish when I first met him. There was no pretence, no veneer. He was so open about his feelings, even his weaknesses. It made such a change . . .' She paused, remembering the first day at Thika.

'He even told me about his parents' death. Made no attempt to hide his sense of loss, his vulnerability. I don't feel that with Charles.' Her eyes held Jane's, for the first time admitting the truth. 'Do you know, he hasn't even talked to me about Kitty Marsden's death. It's almost as if the incident never happened. I suppose it's stiff upper lip and Charles just trying to hide his feelings, but sometimes I wonder if it really meant nothing much to him after all . . .' She made a helpless gesture. There was a silence.

'The trouble is,' she said at last, 'I just don't know any more. Everything's suddenly so complicated.'

'Just remember, you don't have to decide here and now,' said Jane gently.

'But I do. It's only two weeks or so until we leave.' Alexandra sounded almost desperate.

'Don't rush your decision, Alexandra,' Jane said, her hand gently touching her shoulder. 'That would be the worst mistake of all. Just remember, if the worst comes to the worst, you can still go back to England with Charles, without committing yourself to marrying him. It wouldn't be the end of the world. It might even be easier for you to decide back in England, away from here. You can always come back, you know . . .'

Alexandra thought of Genessie and Gwladys, both of whom had returned to Kenya after their divorces. 'Yes, I know,' she said. Still, she wasn't sure what pressures would be brought to bear by her parents. Already her mother had written saying how much she was looking forward to her return and to their sorting out the engagement plans together.

'Of course,' Jane was saying, thrusting her hands into the deep pockets of her cotton skirt, 'when you see Robert again, you may feel there are no decisions to be made . . .'

'Listen, I don't even know what he feels about me,' protested Alexandra. 'Besides, I very much doubt I'll see him again . . .'

'But I thought you told me you'd left a message for him at his farm at Gilgil,' said Jane.

'I did.' Alexandra made a little gesture with her hand, all pretence at indifference gone now. 'But he probably won't come. I told him at Naivasha I never wanted to see him again.'

'Oh, he'll come,' said Jane, putting out a cool reassuring hand to Alexandra's cheek. 'From all that you've told me about Robert Dalgleish, I know he'll come.'

But for all Jane's confident assurances, by the end of the week Robert still had made no appearance at Kirimangari. Gradually, as the days went by, Jane ceased to insist he would come; by tacit mutual agreement they busied themselves in the farm's activities and tactfully avoided the subject.

Alexandra was at pains to hide her disappointment. She had no wish for his absence to cause any tension between herself and Jane, especially since they had so short a time left together. She assumed a careful light-heartedness which, although it pleased her grandfather who knew nothing of the situation, did little to fool Jane.

On the day before Jane was due to leave, Jehru came up to the house to ask them all to come down to the village that evening to join in the festivities to celebrate his son's marriage to Wanjiru. The marriage had taken place a few days earlier at Wanjiru's village, where there had also been celebrations: but Jehru – for reasons that escaped Alexandra but obviously not her grandfather – felt that there should be a *ngoma* at the farm as well.

Late that afternoon, when all the work on the farm had been completed, the drums started. Alexandra had never heard them in full force before and was struck immediately by their compelling beat. *Tum-atum-a-tum-tum*, *tum-atum-a-tum*: the sound seemed to permeate every corner of the house. Although the African drum was primarily used for ceremonial music, it was also used to send intricate messages hundreds of miles in only a few minutes; listening to the carrying cadence and rhythm of the drum cutting sharply across all other sounds, Alexandra was not surprised. From where they stood on the verandah the insistent beat seemed to rise in waves about them, dominating all else.

Alexandra turned her head as the verandah door opened behind them. Her grandfather came out and leaned up against the white-painted railings alongside of them.

'Amazing sound, isn't it?' he commented, looking out across the paddocks towards the *manyatta*. 'Always reminds me of Conrad's *Heart of Darkness*, though: I expect to see Kurtz running out of the forest.'

'I know what you mean,' agreed Alexandra with a grin, having had precisely the same thoughts herself. 'Something very earthy and elemental about them, isn't there?'

'Absolutely,' smiled her grandfather. He turned his gaze back to Alexandra. 'I expect you two want to go down there straight away . . .'

'If possible,' admitted Alexandra, catching Jane's look of concurrence.

'That's what I thought,' said her grandfather. 'I'll be ready soon enough, but why don't you two go on ahead? I'll be down in about half an hour or so, but if you go now you'll probably catch the last of the preparations. All rather interesting . . .'

'Are you sure you don't mind?' Alexandra didn't want to feel that they were deserting him, but she had to admit that ever since the drums had started she had been itching to be down at the village.

'Of course,' said her grandfather with a perceptive smile. 'Not something to miss. I'll be down as soon as I can . . .'

He gave them an encouraging wave of his hands, shooing them on their way, and without further protest they set off.

The air was hazy with woodsmoke from the bonfires as they came down the narrow track leading to the village. Already most of the preparations were in hand, everyone putting the finishing touches to their attire. Men attached clappers to their ankles, secured elaborate head dresses aloft, and adorned themselves with beaded belts and necklaces. The women, less ornate, wore oiled grass-coloured skirts, decked up with masses of brightly coloured beads. Alexandra had never seen them look so splendid.

Jane and Alexandra threaded their way past the mud and wattle buildings. As soon as they came into the centre of the village, Jehru came across to greet them. He still looked frail after his illness, thought Alexandra; though considering her grandfather had told her that he had been close to death, his recovery was remarkable. Certainly his spirits seemed buoyant enough.

He led them to where the seats had been placed for them at one side of the great circle. Everyone sat facing inwards, the women facing them, the men and boys to the left and right.

Wnamba brought them two wooden bowls and poured some home-made maize-meal beer into them from a huge gourd. Alexandra thought even the smell was intoxicating enough, though she had to admit it was preferable to the sour milk they had been offered in the past.

The sound of the drum changed slightly and twenty or so male dancers sprang into the centre, dancing around the fires with earth-shaking leaps and steps of feverish energy. Soon they were joined by the women who jumped up and swayed with equal intensity, rotating their hips and their bodies in perfect time to the drums. The sound of the drums and the movements of the dancers seemed to fill every sense – the chants, the swaying motions, the leaping fire, almost hypnotising in their effect.

So intense was Alexandra's concentration that she failed to hear her name being spoken at first. It was Jane who had to nudge her to bring her back to reality. She turned, half expecting to see her grandfather there. But it was Robert Dalgleish who stood before her. She felt her heart skip a beat.

'I was on my way to Kirimingari but I heard the drums and thought you might be here,' he said, bending down slightly so that his voice could be heard above the noise. 'Jack Bryne passed on your message . . .'

'So I see. I'm glad. I – ' She stopped. She felt at a distinct disadvantage sitting down while he towered over her. She nimbly pushed herself to her feet. Eye to eye, she felt more confident. 'I didn't want to leave without thanking you for all you did for me while I was at Kirimangari. I fear I was rather ungracious at the Hays' . . .'

'I think we both were.'

She noticed he hadn't contradicted her. No appeasement. No pretence. It was typical of him. She found herself smiling. 'Anyway,' she said, 'I wanted to apologise. I didn't want us to part as enemies.'

'Oh, never that.'

There was a lingering tone to his voice which made her look up at him. There was no mockery in his face now. She gave him a sidelong glance. 'I shouldn't have reacted the way I did at the Hays',' she said softly. 'I lost my temper, I'm afraid . . .'

'Don't blame you,' returned Robert. 'I behaved appallingly. All lies, too . . .'

'What?'

'About using you to get to your grandfather. Nonsense, of course. Stupid of me to say it.' His eyes met hers, piercingly blue and intense. 'Pure jealousy, that's all.'

His admission made her head jerk up. 'Jealousy?'

'My own fault.' He turned slightly to stare out across the dancers, watching as they moved and swirled around the fire. 'You'd made it clear from the beginning about Charles. Can't think why I let myself think otherwise. And that day of the rains . . .' He gave a light, apologetic shrug of the shoulders. 'I don't usually behave so abominably. Kissing another chap's girl . . .'

'Oh, it was just as much my fault,' she protested quickly.

'Hardly.'

'It was. I wanted you to kiss me that day.'

His eyes flicked across to her face. 'Did you?' He was suddenly very still.

'Yes.' There, she had said it. The relief she felt was enormous. 'Very much.'

He caught the desperate longing in her voice and hesitated no more. In two short steps he was beside her, his arms encircling her. Strong arms, gentle and sure. Her head tilted up to his, her mouth flowering beneath his cool soft lips. She felt the ardent strength of him, her head falling back beneath the hungry force of his kiss.

A wave of longing surged through her body, her breath catching in her throat. About her the drums' pulsating beat seemed to echo the fast throbbing of her own heart. Never before had she felt like this, faint almost with desire.

'Alexandra . . .' Her name was almost a sigh, as his mouth moved again against her smooth skin. 'You can't leave with Charles . . .'

'I know.'

'We have to talk.' He broke away from her, bending his head to hers, foreheads touching. 'Is there somewhere we can go?' His lips met hers very gently. 'Somewhere quiet, away from all this . . .'

'I –' She paused. She was conscious suddenly that her grandfather might come at any time, precipitating disaster. 'Robert, we can't talk now. Grandfather's due here any minute . . .'

'He's going to have to know sometime,' Robert told her. He pushed his fingers through her dark hair as he tilted her head back and looked into her face.

'I know.' A small speck of anxiety stirred within her at the thought. Both of her grandfather and of Charles . . . 'But not now. Not tonight.'

'Then when?' He looked down at her with searching eyes. He knew better than to rush her. He had waited all these months, after all; but even so, there was a hint of impatience to his voice.

'Come tomorrow. Late afternoon.' Earlier she was taking Jane to Thika to catch the Nairobi train. 'I'll prime him that you're coming. That way he won't mind.' She hoped to heaven that would be true. Things would be difficult enough without her grandfather's irascible temper.

He stretched out and touched her cheek. 'You're sure that's the way you want it?' he asked.

'Yes.' She leant up against him. Enclosed in his arms she felt all her doubts and fears slide away. There'd be an awful fuss she knew, recriminations from Charles and her parents; but here, safe with Robert, she felt nothing could harm her.

'You'd better go,' she told him softly. 'Grandfather – remember?'

'How could I forget?' His voice was light, his expression a mixture of amusement and accusation. 'Now stop looking so worried. This thing is easily sorted out, you know.'

He made it sound so simple. 'I . . .' She opened her mouth to protest but he bent down to her, his mouth closing on hers, allowing no more words.

Then at last, reluctantly, they drew apart. He held her face between his hands. 'It will be all right,' he whispered, willing her to believe him. He bent down to kiss her one last time. There seemed a magnetic pull between their longing mouths, as if having joined together they were reluctant ever to part. 'Tomorrow then . . .'

'Yes.' She nodded. His hand went out to her hair, lifting it slightly to caress her neck. She felt a deep-rooted physical craving stir within her again, frightening in its intensity. If he didn't leave soon, she knew she'd beg him to stay. 'You must go,' she urged softly.

He stepped back from her then, hands dropping to his sides, as if steeling himself for the parting. He had to leave, he knew it, but these past moments had had a sweetness he could hardly bear to lose. He took a deep, shuddering sigh, his eyes boring into hers. 'Tomorrow . . .'

The word hung between them for a moment and then he turned and walked quickly away through the darkening trees.

Alexandra stood there, watching him, unable to turn away until he had disappeared from sight, conscious already of her sense of loss.

There was a movement a few yards away. 'So,' said a teasing voice. 'That, I presume, was Robert Dalgleish!'

Alexandra started guiltily. She had forgotten Jane. Forgotten everything in truth.

Jane was on her feet and by her side in a moment. She glanced at Alexandra's face and grinned. 'No need to ask you how it went, of course . . .' She squeezed her friend's arm. 'I'm not surprised, though. As soon as I saw him I knew what all the fuss was about.'

'Did you?'

'Ah, yes,' continued Jane happily. 'A rare breed, that one.'

There was a silence. They stood for a moment, side by side, watching the dancers, the men twirling faster and faster, the firelight catching the sheen of their greased and painted bodies. Beside them, the young girls swayed to the compulsive rhythm, their bare breasts glistening in the flickering light.

The drums seemed to beating louder and quicker, deep and high, deep and high, like the sound of the waves on a distant shore. They were throbbing with a passion that Alexandra, with new-found awareness, found almost overwhelming. The sound seemed to echo in the very core of her being. The physical craving which Robert had stirred within her seemed to be captured by the frenzied beating of the drum, lifting her up and up with each terrifying beat.

So strong was the feeling, so undeniable, that, when her grandfather arrived a few minutes later, she had to turn her head away. She had no wish that he should see the look in her burning, bright eyes, see her desire, and somehow guess at the truth.

18

Alexandra went with Jane to Thika station the next day. It was a parting of mixed emotions. Though Jane was looking forward to seeing Tom, she couldn't but help feel she was leaving her friend when she most needed her and told Alexandra as much.

'Nonsense,' Alexandra returned firmly. But in truth she could have done with Jane's support; for despite her meeting with Robert last night, she felt torn by a conflict of powerful loyalties – Charles, her grandfather, Robert. She had to face the many difficulties and decisions still ahead before she could be confident as to precisely where her future lay.

'Don't forget, don't rush into anything,' Jane insisted, as they waited for the train to arrive. 'I know you've more or less decided not to marry Charles, but you can still go home with him, you know, if things get complicated. Margaret's there to keep an eye on you . . .'

'I know,' agreed Alexandra. 'But I feel so positive about things at the moment.'

'So do I,' said Jane with a knowing smile. 'But I sometimes feel you're so alone out here. Got nobody to turn to. And I'm not much help now Tom and I are up at Kakamega.' If they had still been at Eldoret Jane would have offered her a potential safe haven there but now they were encamped at the gold-fields things were not so easy.

'I'll be fine,' insisted Alexandra, kissing Jane fondly. 'I've just got Grandfather to deal with, that's all.'

'But I thought it was only with Robert's uncle that he had this feud problem,' said Jane, looking up suddenly. 'That's what you told me . . .'

'Well, it is really,' said Alexandra. 'But in his worst moments my grandfather is prone to tar all Dalgleishes with the same brush. Robert just as much as his uncle . . .'

'Oh dear.' Jane sounded slightly flustered. 'Well, if that's the case I think I'd better tell you I may have made a faux pas . . .'

A little nub of anxiety stirred within Alexandra. 'You didn't tell Grandfather about Robert and me, did you?'

'Well, not exactly.' Jane paused, making an apologetic grimace. 'He'd sort of guessed anyway. Asked a few questions, that's all. I never thought not to answer them.'

Despite her predicament, Alexandra smiled. Jane's honesty was one of her fine qualities. She put a hand out to Jane's shoulder. 'Listen, he has to know sometime. Really. I shouldn't give it another thought . . .'

'He didn't seem displeased,' Jane told her hurriedly. 'As I said, it was almost as if he knew . . .'

'Probably did,' Alexandra acknowledged. If Jane had guessed her feelings for Robert, doubtless her grandfather had done so, too.

They heard the train coming down the line. Its approach sent a bevy of partridges bursting noisily into the sky.

'Write and let me know what happens, won't you?' Jane said, raising her voice slightly to be heard above the noise of the train drawing to a halt. 'Promise?'

'Of course.'

They embraced fondly, the air heavy with emotion. Jane climbed up into the carriage. 'I hope I didn't blot your copy-book with your grandfather,' she said again, turning back to Alexandra.

'Don't give it another thought,' insisted Alexandra. She had no wish for this last moment with Jane to be spoiled by speculation. 'You've probably done me a favour . . .'

'I hope so.' Jane pulled the door to, then lowered the window and leaned out. 'Lord, I almost feel as nervous as you! You'll have to tell me how it goes. Write?'

'Promise . . . send my love to Tom.'

The train started to edge forward. Jane waved, still leaning out of the window. 'And come and see us at Kakamega when you've got the energy!' The words came out in a tumbling rush. 'Goodbye . . . goodbye.'

Alexandra stood watching as the train snaked on down the track. When it was almost out of sight she turned at last to go back to the truck. The station was empty now and looked rather forlorn. It was like a wind-up toy, one minute full of action and life, the next run-down and abandoned. She found the swift change rather disconcerting, and was glad, when she stepped out into the main street of Thika again, to find it bustling with life.

By the time she had reached the truck, Juma had already returned with the supplies they had ordered, and without further ado they started back towards Kirimangari.

The house was very quiet when they arrived back at the farm. As Alexandra pushed open the door she was conscious of a silence, heavy and all-consuming, enveloping the rooms. Yet she was sure her grandfather was in.

'Grandfather!'

She came through into the drawing-room. He was there, slumped on the settee, looking tired and half asleep. His head was tipped back, eyes half closed, his booted feet up against the cushions.

'Grandfather, there you are!'

She came eagerly towards him across the room, then stopped, suddenly aware that he had made no move to greet her. She could almost feel his hostility. It was then that she saw the whisky bottle tucked beside him. Apart from that very first day, he had hardly touched a drop. What had started him now? She glanced quickly down at him, searching his face.

'Grandfather . . .' There was concern in her voice, not anger this time. 'What are you doing?'

He waved a contemptuous hand. 'What does it look like?' he threw back at her bitterly, his words slurred.

He reached out for the whisky bottle again, clattering it noisily against the glass which he held in his other hand. It slopped over the edges, spilling over his shirt front and running down onto the settee.

She walked over and tried to take the bottle from him, trying to steady it, but he snatched it back, grasping it to his chest like some treasured prize.

'For God's sake, girl, leave me something,' he said, his voice tart. He clutched the bottle to him, even tighter. 'You've left me nothing else . . .'

'Whatever do you mean?'

'Of all the things you could have done to me . . .' He gave a harsh, almost wild, laugh. 'You knew what I felt about the Dalgleishes. I told you. I warned you about their perfidy. But would you listen? I told you they would do anything to get Kirimangari . . .'

So this was the core of the matter. Robert Dalgleish. Alexandra bit back a sigh. She should have known he would not have taken it so easily. 'This has nothing to do with Kirimangari, Grandfather,' she told him quietly.

'Hasn't it?' His voice rasped on the words.

'No. Robert hasn't even mentioned Kirimangari.'

'He will.'

'I think not.' She closed her eyes tightly, trying to remember Robert's touch. He had kissed her because he loved her, it had nothing to do with the farm. 'You misjudge Robert Dalgleish.'

'Do I?' His eyes met hers in a hard stare. 'You think I'm an old fool, but you know nothing about the Dalgleishes. I've had years of dealing with them. I know only too well of their greed and deceit.'

This was too much. 'For heaven's sake, Grandfather,' she said, rounding on him. 'You can't go on blaming the Dalgleishes forever for losing Kirimangari. If you hadn't gambled so unwisely you would never have had to sell the land. It wasn't Cameron Dalgleish's fault you incurred so many gambling debts.'

'There *were* no debts.'

There was a silence. She glanced at him, confused. 'I don't understand . . .'

'There were no debts, Alexandra.' He closed his eyes, leaning back against the cushions for a moment. 'I let people believe that story because it suited me to do so. The real story was not something I wanted people to know. Cameron Dalgleish was a blackguard, plain and simple. He found out something about our family that no decent man would have used to his own advantage.' He almost spat out the words as he shakily refilled his glass. 'He held it up against us and tried to destroy us.'

She looked at him. 'He was blackmailing you?' she asked slowly, her mind in a haze of shock. 'But why? I thought you were his friend.'

Her grandfather snorted, his face tightening in contempt. 'He did it for the land, Alexandra.' He took another swig of whisky. 'I told you, the Dalgleishes are a ruthless lot. He needed the river that ran through our land at the top and he didn't care whom he hurt to get it.

Me, Amelia, your mother . . .' He leaned forward, covering his face with his hand. 'Especially your mother. Threatened to expose us all. Even her. Though how he found about the baby I'll never know . . .' His hands were shaking so much the whisky splashed against the glass dribbling over its sides.

'What?' Alexandra couldn't quite grasp what he was saying. She was sure she must have misheard him.

But then he glanced up at her and she knew by his eyes that she had not been mistaken.

There was a long silence. Then slowly she came across the room towards him and sank down on the settee beside him. 'I think, Grandfather,' she said softly, taking his hand in hers, 'it's about time I heard the truth, don't you?'

His eyes were dark, beseeching her for understanding. 'I hadn't meant to tell you,' he said. If he hadn't had so much to drink, it never would have slipped out like that: a trust betrayed.

'I know.' She took the whisky bottle from him and placed it on the floor beside her. 'But I think I have a right to know now, don't you?'

He looked across at her, then took a deep, shuddering breath and nodded.

'It wasn't her fault, you know,' he said quietly. 'She was young, seventeen only, and oh, so beautiful. She had only to walk into a room and all the men would turn their heads to watch her pass by. I should have guessed, of course. Should have known what was coming, but I didn't. Fool that I was . . .'

The words came tumbling out. He was talking now and nothing would stop him. The secret held so tight for so long had burst out of its bars. Now he needed to speak of it.

'I remember Amelia coming to me that day to tell me what had happened. God! how I raged. Useless then, of course. There was this young chap, you see, she'd met him at the Muthiaga Club, fallen for him head over heels one New Year's Eve. There was no chance of marriage, though. He was killed in an accident up Eldoret way. Never even knew about the child. Sarah wouldn't talk about it.' He gave a shrug, his eyes bleak. 'Anyway, at first she wanted to keep the baby but Amelia and I persuaded her to have an abortion. To have a child at her age – it would ruin any future chances. So, it was agreed she would go to Cairo – there was a good French doctor there who dealt with such things – and then Amelia and she would go on to London to recuperate.'

He paused, glancing at her. 'It was there she met your father, of course. A miracle. They fell in love and he proposed. Everything seemed to be working out for the best. I can't tell you how happy I was.' He did not speak for a moment. His eyes had an inward look as if he were thinking of the past. 'But then Cameron Dalgleish came to me. He said he knew the truth about Sarah and the abortion and said he was sure the Draytons would not be so happy with the marriage if they knew the truth. I had no doubt he was right. Grandma Drayton was being difficult enough about her darling son marrying a nobody from the colonies as it was. I knew she'd stop the marriage given half a chance. So I let Cameron Dalgleish have what he wanted.' He sighed, his shoulders slumping forward. 'It was only a few fields at first – one with the river running through it, of course – it seemed an easy enough thing. But it didn't stop there. An abortion was illegal and it meant that he always had a hold over me, even after Sarah was safely married.'

He spread his hands out in a helpless gesture. 'I wanted to expose him, but how could I? Sarah would have suffered. So on it went. And the more difficult things became here the less I wanted Amelia to come back lest she become involved in some way. She begged to come back, but I wouldn't let her. Things were going from bad to worse at Kirimangari. And all the time Cameron Dalgleish wanted more and more . . .'

Alexandra looked up at him. His eyes were blank with pain. 'Oh, Grandfather, was there nothing you could do?'

'Nothing.'

She felt for his hand and folded it in hers. 'If only my mother could have known the truth . . .' How ironic it was, she thought, that all this time her mother had been blaming Grandfather for the ruination of Kirimangari when in reality it had been her actions, not his, that had brought the farm to its knees.

'Your mother must know none of this!' Her grandfather's head jerked up, his eyes suddenly alert. 'Besides, it would make no difference, she still hasn't forgiven me . . .'

'For what?'

'For making her have the abortion,' he said. He drained his glass. 'Oh, it was all right at first. She had you. But then she had several miscarriages, each time a boy. She started to have this absurd idea that God was punishing her for getting rid of the baby – that, too, had been a boy, you see. If Amelia had been alive she would have told her it was just nonsense, but Sarah was all alone by then. Alone and consumed by guilt. She told me I'd killed my grandson.' He gave a little shake of his head, as if almost to rid himself of that terrible thought. 'I don't think I was truly to blame. I did what I thought was right at the time . . .'

'Of course you did,' said Alexandra, squeezing his hand.

'But Sarah didn't see it that way. She became quite set that it was my fault. I think that's why she never told me about Hugh. Still didn't think I deserved to have a grandson . . .' His voice caught, then fell to nothingness.

Alexandra could hardly bear to see his pain. She saw now how much he had suffered to protect her mother. He had tried so hard and had lost everything in consequence. There seemed to be no justice in this quiet corner of the world.

'I'm sure she doesn't blame you now,' insisted Alexandra. She smiled at him comfortingly. 'I think I was supposed to be the bearer of the olive branch . . .'

Her grandfather patted her hand. 'I hope so,' he said quietly. 'I'm too old for any more battles.' He adjusted his position slightly, peering down at her. 'Though I suppose your desertion of Charles will provoke a few fireworks. And no doubt Sarah will hold me in some way responsible.'

'Surely not!' protested Alexandra, though in truth she thought it might be so. 'That would be so unfair . . .'

'Wouldn't it?' agreed her grandfather with a wry half-smile. 'Especially since I don't approve of the man one bit!'

'You would if you knew him,' insisted Alexandra softly, catching at his arm.

'No. The Dalgleishes have caused me too much pain, Alexandra. They took away everything I held dear. Everything. They destroyed me . . . They're not a family to trust, Alexandra. I wish I could make you see that.'

'But Robert isn't like that. You're not giving him a chance.'

Her grandfather's eyes met hers in a hard cold stare.

'There's no need to, Alexandra. He's a Dalgleish,' he said. 'Mark my words. Cameron will deny everything I've told you and Robert will stand by him. You'll see.'

'Talk to him again, Robert. Please.'

'What's the point? I've asked him about it already. He denies it flatly.'

'And you believed him?'

'Yes.'

Alexandra turned her head away. It was just as her grandfather had said it would be. She had thought, believed, that Robert would take their side in the matter but she couldn't have been more wrong.

True, when at first she had told him of her grandfather's accusations he had driven back to Mitubiru at once to tackle his uncle on the subject. But now, having spoken to Cameron Dalgleish and been assured by him of his innocence, he was steadfast in his support for the man.

'But Grandfather wouldn't have made the whole thing up!' protested Alexandra. 'What would have been the point?'

'I would have thought that would have been quite obvious.' Robert's voice was ice-cold. 'He's been quite determined to put a wedge between us from the beginning.'

'But not like this! If you could have seen him, Robert, he sounded so utterly devastated, you'd have known it was the truth!'

'But it doesn't make sense, Alexandra, surely you can see that?' Robert said. He turned from her, looking down across the coffee fields, trying hard to hold onto his temper. He had come this afternoon expecting to find the loving and receptive girl he had left the night before. But instead he'd been confronted by a very different creature.

He stretched out his arms to touch her. She was stiff and unyielding, as if the resistance of the mind had extended to that of the body.

He felt his exasperation grow. 'It's nonsense, you know, your grandfather's story,' he said sharply. 'Oh, it might have been true about your mother, but that bit about my uncle . . . pure malice. I mean, think about it. Why should he go to all that trouble? It doesn't make sense. There's better land elsewhere. And to go on being so vindictive, to take the land from your grandfather bit by bit – why would any one behave like that? It's certainly not my uncle's style. He might be a cantankerous old fool at times, but he's not malicious. Besides, they were friends; why should my uncle suddenly turn against him?'

Her shoulders lifted almost imperceptibly. 'That's what I wanted you to find out. That's why I wanted you to speak to him again . . .' She looked at him unhappily. She could almost feel the gap widening between them. Yet she couldn't leave the subject, couldn't thrust it aside unfinished. 'Won't you talk to him again?'

'Alexandra, we've been through all this. His answer will be the same,' Robert returned, irritated now. He kicked at a stone with the toe of his shoe and sent it scudding down the driveway. 'You're determined not to see things straight. You won't even try.'

'That isn't true!' she retaliated, appalled at how he saw the situation. 'It's you who won't confront the issue, not me!'

There was a silence. They stood facing each other, their anger so strong it was almost tangible.

'Oh hell!' said Robert, folding his arms across his chest and turning away from her with a despairing gesture. 'We just seem to lurch from crisis to crisis, don't we?' He shook his head slowly and let out a long, regretful sigh. 'I don't want that, Alexandra.'

'Nor do I,' she said softly.

'Then why are we fighting?' he asked. 'Why are you pushing me away?'

She drew a breath. 'I'm not. But we can't hide things, Robert. This business between my grandfather and your uncle will come back to haunt us if we don't kill it now. I can't have a relationship built on doubts . . .'

'So what are you saying? That this isn't going to work?'

'Not at all!' She was dismayed that he had so misunderstood her. 'I want this to work as much as you do.'

'Do you? I'm not so sure.'

The finality of his words sent an icy chill through her. She stood there, looking down at her hands, unable to meet his piercing gaze.

All the tensions of the past few days rose up within her. She was only too aware of the effect her decision would have on her family, and she felt guilty beyond measure at letting Charles down too. She was having to struggle against all these fears and now this, Robert's intransigency . . . Like Damocles' sword, it hung over her.

There was a silence, tense and brittle.

'Listen, Alexandra,' he said, after a while. 'Perhaps we should call a truce for a few days. What do you say? Go back to Kirimangari. Go back there and think about Charles, me, your grandfather, and decide what you really want.' He pushed his hands deep into his pockets, balling his fists. 'I love you, Alexandra,' he said. 'I have since the moment I first saw you at Thika. But I'm tired of being picked up and put down again. If you can't trust me as a woman should trust someone she loves then I want no part of it any more. It's all or nothing with me . . . you decide.'

'Robert!' She put out her hand to him but he brushed it aside.

'I'm going to Gilgil for a few days,' he said, his voice flat and void of expression. 'I'll be back on Friday. You can let me know your decision then . . .' He pulled open the door of his truck and climbed in.

'Robert, we need to talk!'

'There's nothing more to say, Alexandra,' he said, with unnerving calm. 'The decision is yours.'

He slammed the truck door then and drove off, the murram drive crunching and spurting beneath the violent swerve of his tyres.

She watched him speed off, painfully aware of the abyss which now yawned between them. Aware, too, of how fragile a thing their love was, and how easily it could be laid waste.

19

Alexandra turned off the main road and began to drive slowly down the tree-lined driveway towards Cameron Dalgleish's farm. Her hands were shaking but she refused to turn back, despite the strong temptation. Last night, as she had tossed and turned sleeplessly on her bed, she realised that, if she were to discover the truth, she would have to confront her grandfather's enemy face to face. Sooner or later.

She drew to a halt outside the low white-washed homestead and climbed out of the truck. For a moment she hesitated, then, taking a deep breath, she started up the verandah steps, her hand on the rail to steady herself. She could hear a dog barking inside the house, but apart from that there was little sign of life.

She stepped onto the shaded verandah, her nerves a-jangle. As she did so, the door was pushed open and a houseboy in a khaki shirt and shorts came out to greet her.

'*Jambo*,' he said, with a slight nod of welcome.

'*Jambo. Habari?*' she returned, pushing her hands into her skirt pockets to still them. 'I came to see Cameron Dalgliesh. Is he here?'

The houseboy wavered slightly. 'Yes,' he said, lifting his shoulders in a slight shrug. 'But *Bwana sana*.' He moved uneasily from foot to foot. 'Not good. The *bwana* is resting. He not well. See no one.'

'But he must see me!' Alexandra insisted, aware of a certain shrill determination to her voice. Having steeled herself for this encounter she was not going to let it slip away. 'I must see him. Please,' she said again, her voice calmer this time. 'I shall only be a few moments.'

The houseboy hesitated an instant then, with a little nod, pushed open the verandah door and indicated for her to come into the drawing-room. 'Wait here,' he told her. 'I'll go and find out if the *Bwana* feels well enough to see you . . .'

'Thank you.' Relief flooded through her. She stood just inside the doorway, looking about her.

The room was still shuttered but looked homely enough with a hotch-potch of furniture and a piano gracing one corner. Several pieces of music lay on its polished mahogany top and as she walked over, two caught her eye: one by Mendelssohn, the other by Gershwin. If nothing else, Robert had catholic taste.

She smiled. She hadn't even known he could play, but standing here she could very well visualise him at the piano, his long fingers skimming across the notes with infinite ease. She leaned forward, about to pick up one of the pieces, when suddenly a man's voice sounded loudly behind her.

'Who the dickens are you?' the sharp voice demanded. 'And what in Hell's name are you doing prying around in here?'

She knew before she swung round that it was Cameron Dalgliesh who spoke. She took a deep breath to steady herself and then turned slowly. 'I'm Alexandra Drayton,' she said. 'I came to see. . .'

But her voice died in her throat as she took in the man before her.

Face to face with Cameron Dalgleish she felt only confusion. For the man who stood before her, blocking the light from the hall, was far removed from the ogre of her imagination.

She had thought he would be the same age as her grandfather, but he was far, far younger – barely fifty, she guessed. He was tall, with wide arrogant shoulders, a dark brooding face, thick dark hair, hardly even tinged with grey, and the same impossibly blue eyes as Robert. He was a strikingly good-looking man, more like the prince of the piece than the villain. She found it rather disconcerting.

Still, if she was surprised it seemed he was too. There was something in his face which showed his confusion, a flash almost of distant recognition in his eyes. He put his hand out to the doorway to steady himself, a hint of uncertainty about him, then he stiffened and his face hardened again.

'I think you'd better leave,' he said. His voice was quiet, but none the less dangerous for that.

She lifted her eyes to him. 'You don't understand . . .'

'I understand only too well,' he said, glaring at her. 'I know what you've told Robert. Lies, I tell you. Damn lies. And I don't want you on my property.'

'But Robert – '

'Robert wants little more to do with you, judging by his anger last night.' Cameron stood there, his frame filling the doorway, dauntingly formidable. 'He's gone off to Gilgil and I can't say I blame him. You've stirred up nothing but trouble with your lies.'

She refused to be cowed by him. 'They weren't lies,' she said, her chin tilting up defiantly. 'You and I know that, I think.'

'You understand nothing!' he cried out. 'Nothing!'

He lifted his arm menacingly against her and she thought for a moment that he might strike her but then he let it drop to his side again.

There was a silence. She was acutely aware of his uneven, laboured breathing. It was only then she realised how ill he really was. But she couldn't stop now.

'One day,' she said, 'Robert will find out the truth. Perhaps you'd be wise enough to remember that!'

He stiffened at her words. 'Just go, damn you!' he said. 'Go!' There was desperation in his voice.

There was nothing more to say. She turned and went out of the room and down the verandah steps to the truck.

She didn't look behind her.

She didn't see Cameron Dalgleish slump against the doorway as she left, his eyes no longer angry but suddenly bright with poignant tears.

On the Saturday morning Alexandra came back from a ride with her grandfather to find Charles waiting for them in the house, having returned unexpectedly from safari.

'Charles!' She couldn't hide her surprise to find him sitting there in the drawing-room, cross-legged on the sofa. 'I wasn't expecting you until next week,' she said. Panic loomed large within her.

Her grandfather stretched out his hand to Charles, almost as if reaching for a lifeline, his relief at the sight of him obvious.

'Good to see you again, my boy,' he said, slapping him heartily on the back. 'We've all missed you, you know.'

Alexandra's head jerked round at such obvious bending of the truth, but her grandfather steadfastly refused to meet her eye.

'So, tell me,' he said, settling in the chair opposite Charles, 'how was the safari? Nothing went wrong, I hope.'

'No, the hunting was splendid,' Charles assured him, stretching inside his linen jacket to draw out his silver cigarette case. 'But the damn fool of an agent who made our bookings for us made a mistake about our return. That's why I'm here. He said the boat was leaving on the twenty-sixth, when in fact it's the sixteenth . . .'

Alexandra stiffened. 'The sixteenth? But that's Tuesday – '

'Precisely,' Charles said. 'The sheer incompetence of the man, I ask you. We could have easily missed the ship. Luckily, though, he discovered his mistake just in time. But it means we've had to miss some pretty good shooting. Stephenson said he'd never known the game to be so prolific. Damn shame to have to run out on it.'

'So, what are your plans now?' asked Alexandra's grandfather. His voice sounded casual enough, but Alexandra recognised the caution in it.

'Well . . .' Charles paused to light a cigarette. 'We're staying with Lady MacMillan just a few miles away at the moment – came down last night – but we're due to leave for Nairobi tomorrow. Then we'll stay there for one night and leave for Mombasa on Monday.'

'Monday! But that's impossible!' Alexandra's voice rose, with a break in it. She was aware of Charles turning to her with a startled expression.

'Well, I know it's short notice,' he agreed. 'But we can't cut it any finer, you know. Too risky. Could bally well miss the ship!'

'Charles, I can't come!'

'What?' Charles's cigarette stopped midway to his mouth. 'Alexandra, we can't change the dates you know. It's all been arranged. Margaret . . . everything . . . Look, I appreciate it will be upsetting for you leaving your grandfather, but there really is no choice.'

'Quite right. She really must go,' put in her grandfather with gusto. 'It really wouldn't do to stay on all by herself, you know.' This said pointedly to Alexandra, although he continued to look at Charles.

'I don't want to go . . .' The words were spoken almost in a whisper. There was a desperate note to them.

'Alexandra! This is nonsense!' Her grandfather was on his feet. 'For heaven's sake, child. It's gone on long enough. It will only end in tears.'

What's gone on long enough?' Charles's eyes flicked across to Alexandra. There was a hint of suspicion in his voice.

'Nothing.' Edward walked over to the window and stared out across the sunlit garden. 'Nothing of importance.' He was careful not to look at his granddaughter.

There was a silence. Alexandra took a deep breath. 'Charles, I think we should talk,' she said slowly. 'Grandfather, if you wouldn't mind . . .'

'Alexandra –' he began, then stopped as he saw her look of determination. 'All right,' he said tetchily. He crossed the room, but at the doorway he paused for a moment. 'But I warn you, Alexandra. Remember what I've said. You've got no guarantee . . .'

'Grandfather, please!' She didn't need him to remind her of her predicament.

Edward stood there, feet apart, shoulders pulled back, regarding her solemnly. Then, mumbling his disapproval, he shuffled reluctantly out of the room.

There was a silence. Charles took a long drag at his cigarette, watching Alexandra through the curl of smoke. 'So,' he said, his every movement contrivedly untroubled. 'What's this all about?'

'Charles, I'm sorry,' she said. 'I really am. But I just can't go back to England with you.'

'But you heard your grandfather,' Charles said, trying not to let the extent of his shock be apparent. 'He knows you've got to go home . . .'

'But this isn't about Grandfather,' she said, her eyes meeting his.

The silence that followed seemed interminable. Charles stretched over and stubbed out his cigarette in the onyx ashtray.

'I see,' he said at last leaning back. 'And am I permitted to know whom it does concern?'

She supposed he had every right. 'Robert Dalgleish,' she said softly.

'Who?'

'Robert Dalgleish,' she repeated, though she was certain he had heard well enough the first time.

'The fellow we met at the Hays'?'

'Yes.'

'But I thought you didn't even particularly like the fellow . . .'

She lifted her shoulders almost imperceptibly. How could she hope to explain it to him?

'I see,' said Charles at last. But he didn't and his face showed he didn't. He let out a long sigh. 'Listen, Alexandra,' he said quietly, 'if he's compromised you in some way . . .'

'He hasn't.'

'Oh.' He tried not to show the extent of his relief. 'Well, whatever's happened here, I still think you ought to come back to England with me, you know,' he said. 'Oh . . .' He saw her look, 'not to marry me, necessarily, I understand that. But I feel responsible for you, you know. And it was what was agreed, after all . . .'

'But things have changed, Charles,' she said gently.

'Have they?' His grey eyes flicked up to hers. 'Has this Dalgleish fellow said anything to you then?'

By that she assumed he meant proposed marriage. 'No,' she admitted. 'He hasn't.'

'So it's chance to the wind then, really, isn't it?' Charles went on, not entirely unkindly. 'I mean, if he'd said something it might be different, but dash it all, Alexandra, I can't let you stay in the circumstances. Honour and all that.'

'Charles, it isn't your responsibility,' she said. But she saw by his face that he didn't agree with her.

'And what about your parents?' he said, firing another carefully aimed dart. 'Just to stay on here on some whim . . . it would break their hearts.'

'Oh, Charles . . .' There was anguish in her voice. 'Don't say such a thing . . .'

'It's true, nonetheless,' he said, pressing home his advantage. He sensed he'd found the Achilles heel. If only he could induce her to return home he was sure, with her parents' added pressure, he would be able to convince her still to marry him.

'Come back to London, sort everything out there, why don't you?' he urged. 'You must see that makes sense. Robert Dalgleish will wait for you, surely? And if you truly want to come back here, then at least you can do so with parents' blessing.'

He had more guile than she'd given him credit for. He was being unbelievably calm and reasonable. Not once had he mentioned himself, his own hurt pride. 'Listen, Alexandra,' he went on gently. 'I don't want you hurt . . .'

'I won't be!' she broke in. But even to herself her voice sounded hard and on the defensive.

He glanced up at her, sensing that slight change in her, sensing her doubt. 'So . . .' He leant forward slightly. 'What does your grandfather think then? Is he happy with the arrangement?'

'I think you know that answer,' returned Alexandra, knowing that Charles was remembering Edward Sinclair's welcome and was beginning to put two and two together.

'So he's not,' Charles concluded. 'Ah. And why's that? Doesn't he trust the fellow?'

'Of course he does!'

'I do not!' A voice boomed from the doorway.

Alexandra closed her eyes. 'Grandfather!' she exclaimed angrily. 'This has nothing to do with you.'

'I think it does,' he said quietly, stepping back into the room. 'I care about you, you know. I can't stand idly by and see you throw everything away.' He came and stood before her and stretching down took her cold hand in his. 'If Robert cares about you as much as you say, why hasn't he called to see you even once this week?'

'He's been at Gilgil, Grandfather,' she said, struggling to keep confidence in her voice. She didn't want to tell him about their argument – or about her visit to Cameron Dalgleish.

'All week?'

'Pretty much.' Conflicting emotions tumbled through her mind. The truth was, though, it was Saturday now. Robert was supposed to have returned to Mitubiru on Friday. Yet he'd made no move to contact her.

She felt suddenly like a ship without a rudder heading out across some uncharted sea. If only he would call. If only he would come and sweep away the doubts which had started to gather with such alarming force. If only . . . She stopped, a sudden grey tiredness dragging at her every sense.

Her face must have changed, an admission that she was no longer sure reflecting in her eyes.

'Ah, darling child, you'll see, it's for the best,' her grandfather soothed, sinking down on the arm of the chair and stroking her hand gently. 'You should go home. Charles is right. You'll see . . . If you want to come back afterwards, you can. But go back to England first. Please go back . . .'

Quietly, persuasively, he spoke on, urging her to return. Slowly, gradually, she felt her resolve crumbling.

'You'd be making a mistake to stay, you know that, don't you?'

Her denials and excuses had run dry. She felt like a trapped animal caught in a net, exhausted by the struggle, accepting the inevitable at last. She heard Charles saying something about collecting her the next day. Did she agree? She couldn't quite remember. All she knew was that she was terribly, terribly tired, weariness dragging about her like a heavy cloak.

But, alone again, after Charles had left, some of the old fighting spirit returned to her. She knew she couldn't leave without at least trying to see Robert one last time. Even if he rejected her it would be preferable to this searing doubt which seemed to eat into her very being. Rejection might be painful, but silent abandonment was more so.

She called for Juma and asked him to take a note to Robert for her. She would have gone herself but she feared that her presence at Mitubiru might provoke an angry outburst from Cameron Dalgleish again. It would be tense enough without that. And, she decided, if Robert was not there she would send a telegram to him at Gilgil. She would give him every chance.

She knew she was laying herself open to humiliation. But it was a risk she had to take.

Time was running out.

Robert Dalgleish stepped out of his truck and stretched wearily. It had been an exhausting last few days at Gilgil, beset by minor mishaps. First one of the tractors – inevitably the new American one for which they had waited almost nine months – had broken down and he and Jack Bryne had spent the best part of the day trying to find the fault.

Then, just as he was about to set off to Mitubiru, the brood mare had started to grow restless and lactate, sure signs that she was about to foal. He'd thought it would be a short affair, for it was not her first; but by late evening it had been clear that the second stage of labour would be prolonged and that there was a problem.

He'd spent the night towelling her off, trying to make her as comfortable as possible, but it had concerned him to see her in such distress. She'd stand up, move a few paces, then lie down again, as if trying to adjust the foal's position inside her. Then, at last, she'd settled and the front legs had started to come through.

It should have been a matter of course for the head to follow, but no muzzle had appeared. Robert had suspected the head had been pushed to one side, twisting back along the body, obstructing the foal's exit. Head back and no room at all was not a healthy combination and, as he'd pushed and wriggled his arm inside the mare, he'd found it exactly as he'd feared. Somehow, he'd have to turn that head if he hoped to save the foal.

It had taken him two hours and then, just as he thought defeat was staring him in the face, the little head had slithered and slipped and he'd managed to guide it into position, resting against the forelimbs. A while later, Robert had been rewarded with a fine bay filly, spirited enough to try and kick him with both back legs two hours later.

He'd thought his troubles were over then. Misguidedly. Barely had he scrubbed off and changed before Jack came in from the fields, his right arm hanging awkwardly by his side. He'd been out riding around the cattle when a puff adder had spooked his horse and he had come tumbling to the ground. Robert had had to take him into Gilgil to have his arm reset and the cut on his forehead stitched up. Although Jack would mend pretty quickly, Robert could see he would have to spend more time at Gilgil over the next few weeks, something he would have preferred not to have done. His time away from Alexandra had taught him he would much rather be at Thika.

All this week he'd tried not to think of her; but inevitably in those long cold nights he'd spent sitting, back against the wall in the stables, waiting for the foal to be born, his will-power had faltered. And having thought of her, he longed to get back to her with an intense, almost physical craving.

Such was that yearning that he'd had to steel his resolve as he drove past the turning to Kirimangari on the Thika road that morning, forcing himself to drive on by. He desperately wanted to see her but at the same time was aware, after their last meeting, that her reaction towards him might be frosty.

The angry frustration of last time had faded now. He had wanted her to be sure; but in so doing, he realised now he had taken a terrible risk. Perhaps arrogantly, in his heart of hearts, he had supposed that her feelings for him were strong enough to combat all else. But what if the pressure brought to bear by her grandfather had been too great? What if Charles . . . He stopped, an acute sense of something already lost engulfing him.

It was a feeling that stayed with him for the rest of the journey. Walking up the verandah steps at Mitubiru he was filled with a sickening cold dread. He had forced her into making a choice. What if he had lost her in consequence?

He came up into the house and was about to make his way into the drawing-room for a cooling drink when he heard his uncle's voice call out to him.

'Is that you, Robert?' came his tired voice from the bedroom.

'Yes, Uncle.' Robert walked down the passageway to his uncle's room. He stood in the doorway for a moment, watching him lying there against the pillows, his long-fingered hand resting against the yellowing pages of his book. Then he crossed over to perch on the edge of his carefully tidied bed. 'Have you been well while I've been away?' he asked solicitously. 'No pains?'

'Not too bad.'

He didn't look well, in truth. Pale, with a sort of empty desolation in his face. Robert peered down at him concerned. 'Not overdoing things, I hope? You remember what Dr Silvester said . . .'

'Ha! What does he know?' Cameron sounded derisive but the fact that he was in bed spoke volumes. Up until now he had defied Dr Silvester with actions rather than just words.

Robert looked down at him, his still-dark hair against the crisp white pillows, sensing something had changed in the days he had been away. There was a new stillness about him, a sense of turning inwards, as if the outside world had lost its importance somehow.

Robert adjusted his position on the bed slightly. 'So, did you manage to get out at all while I was away?' he asked.

'A little.'

'And any visitors?'

'No.' Cameron's hand tightened slightly on his book.

'And no one for me, either?'

Cameron made a great point of turning the page. 'No. Were you expecting someone then?'

Robert's shoulders lifted momentarily. 'Not really.' This was it, then. She hadn't called. He'd gambled and lost. He felt a great black abyss yawning about him. He stood up and moved over to the chess table set up by the window, picking up the pieces and moving them restlessly about the board.

'So, how were things over at Gilgil?' his uncle asked at last, looking up from his book. His voice was steady, as if he had noticed no change in his nephew. 'We expected you back days ago . . .'

'I know. I'm sorry. I was delayed.' Robert told him about the brood mare. 'She was fine at the end of it, though,' he said. 'Exhausted. But she'd produced a super little filly. I've half promised her to Joss Hay but I'm hoping he might not want her because he told me he was really after a colt . . .' His voice trailed a little. Mentioning the foal had brought Alexandra back to mind again. He knew now he couldn't let her go. He would have to go to Kirimingari and sort things out with her. He saw now, with aching clarity, that he wanted her to stay on any terms.

'You all right?' his uncle was saying, peering over his book at him. 'You look done in.'

'I am,' Robert admitted. 'I was up all night with the mare, remember?'

'Of course.'

He picked up a knight from the chess board, turning it in his hand. 'And I'm still at a loss as to what to do about Edward Sinclair . . .'

Cameron Dalgleish's head jerked up, all attention now. 'What do you mean?'

'Well, with all his stirrings, I fear I didn't leave his granddaughter on the best of terms when I went off to Gilgil . . .' Robert gave a light shrug, not sure now whether he should have mentioned anything.

'Best way, if you ask me,' said his uncle, fidgeting with the edge of the pages. 'Stay well clear. The Sinclairs are nothing but trouble. And that young girl struck me as being as difficult as her grandfather . . .'

'Struck you?' Robert put down the chess piece and turned towards his uncle. 'You've seen her then?'

There was a silence.

'Uncle?' Robert urged. 'I have to know. Did she come here while I was away?'

Cameron Dalgleish turned his head slightly and closed his eyes. 'Yes.' It was barely above a whisper.

'When?'

'So like her mother . . .' Cameron spoke as if he hadn't heard Robert's question. 'I couldn't believe it. So like her . . .'

Something in his voice caught Robert's attention. A deep, desperate longing. He sank down on the bed. He felt suddenly icy cold.

'Uncle!' He forced Cameron to look at him. 'What happened all those years ago? You must tell me . . .'

Cameron shook his head, letting out a long low sigh. 'It's in the past now, Robert. Let it stay there.'

'No.' Robert took him by the shoulders. 'Don't you see? It's come back to the present. Alexandra's brought it back to the present.' Blue eyes challenged blue. 'You *did* know about Sarah and the baby.' A statement, that, not a question.

Robert paused, unwilling almost to put his next thoughts into words. 'And if that part was true, was the rest of what Edward told Alexandra true also?'

Cameron's eyes flickered slightly then closed, as if he couldn't face Robert's piercing gaze any more. His silence betrayed him.

'But why, Uncle? Why blackmail Sinclair?' asked Robert, bending down over him, uncomprehendingly. 'Why try and ruin him?'

Cameron Dalgleish lifted his head wearily. 'You don't understand . . .'

'Of course I don't!' Robert threw back, angry now. 'You don't tell me anything. How can I?'

'Oh, God!' Cameron Dalgleish sank forwards, covering his face with his hands.

'Tell me the truth, Uncle,' Robert urged, more gently this time. 'Before it's too late . . .' He thought of Alexandra, thought of the time they had wasted.

'It was always too late,' Cameron Dalgleish murmured between closed hands, his shoulders beginning to shudder.

He spoke only one word then, but hearing it, Robert saw the truth at last.

'Sarah . . .' His uncle spoke the name with a deep, desperate longing, repeating it again and again, almost as a soft incantation.

'Uncle.' Robert gently caught Cameron Dalgleish by the shoulders, twisting him round to face him. 'I think you'd better tell me everything, don't you? The truth about the feud. About Sarah . . .'

And as his uncle lifted his eyes at last to his, Robert saw

that it was not hatred that had been at the core of the trouble at all.

Rather, it had been love.

Nairobi station was full of last-minute bustle and noise. Alexandra sat in her carriage staring out at the colourful groups who stood on the platform making their farewells to their relatives and friends, ignoring the porters' attempts to usher through the travellers with their bags and trunks. With little more than five minutes to go there was a frantic sense of activity as several latecomers pushed their way along the platform, striding purposefully in front of the porters towards their carriages.

Alexandra turned as a burst of laughter from William and Charles cut across the chatter. They were noisily recounting some tale or other, highly pleased with themselves for some reason. She watched Charles's animated, handsome face, heard his light amused laughter. Last night, at the Muthiaga Club, she had seen women's heads turn in his direction as he had come in the dining-room, their glances frankly admiring. She had watched dispassionately, knowing even then that she wouldn't marry Charles when they arrived back in England, whatever the pressures. She couldn't. She had changed too much.

Now, watching him with William, she saw him only as an incurably overgrown schoolboy – utterly charming of course, but without purpose or direction. So much potential, as Margaret had said; but she realised now that he was not her responsibility.

She pressed her face against the window, the glass cool against her skin. There was an air of imminent departure about the station, doors slamming, steam hissing, high-pitched farewells. At any minute the guard would blow his whistle and the train would jolt forwards, snaking its way down the line towards Mombasa.

And Robert hadn't come.

Until this moment she had still hoped, foolishly she saw now, that he might come and rescue her, like a knight in shining armour. But he hadn't. Despair rolled over her like a crushing wave.

She sat here, tautly rigid, her emotions as battered as pulp in a paper mill. She knew that the pain she felt wasn't just about leaving Robert. She didn't want to leave Kenya, either. The double wrench was almost too great.

She pushed back the tears. Don't think, she whispered to herself. Don't think, it will just hurt too much . . .

The train clanged and started to jerk forward, sealing her fate with that one movement. There could be no turning back.

Robert stood on Nairobi station, his face set. Ever since he had left Kirimangari, ever since Edward Sinclair had told him that Alexandra was leaving Nairobi with Charles on the afternoon train, he had dreaded this moment. He had driven at breakneck speed all the way down from Thika only to arrive at the station to find that, for once, the Mombasa train had left more or less on time. He'd hoped for some delay, some miracle, but this time, it seemed, the Gods were against him. The train had gone and only a dark, gaping void awaited him at the station.

He stood, hands jammed into his pockets, looking helplessly down the empty track, defeat staring him in the face. He'd tried and he'd failed. It was as simple as that. He'd had his chances and missed them. He had only himself to blame.

It was too late now. Even for regrets.

He turned wearily and began to walk out of the station.

20

Edward Sinclair walked up the verandah steps and into the house. Behind him, the sun hung like a golden discus, just touching the horizon, casting its warm, almost opalescent light across the coffee fields and garden. Soon darkness would fall, the shadows were darkening even now, and it was a time Edward normally savoured. But not so tonight. He felt Alexandra's absence acutely, more so than he had imagined possible.

He came slowly up into the drawing-room and stood for a moment looking around him. The last of the day's dappled light fell across the room, revealing the familiar polished furniture, the patterned rugs, the stone fireplace flanked by gleaming copper scuttle and irons. Nothing changed, and yet, somehow, nothing the same.

He crossed over the room to the mahogany table by the window. There the little cluster of photographs stood, and, stretching down, he picked up the one of Alexandra. The image of the four-year-old stared back at him, the button-bright eyes sparking with intelligence, the chin tilted slightly in challenge. It was so like the Alexandra of the present that he found himself smiling.

He replaced the photograph on the table, his eyes skimming over the others that cluttered its top, coming at last to rest on the one of Sarah. He extended his hand, and, trembling slightly, lifted it carefully from its place. Sarah . . . his darling child. He clasped the photograph to his chest, closing his eyes for a moment. How little he'd known. How little he'd understood . . .

Still holding Sarah's picture he walked back across the room and sank down into the armchair by the fireplace. He glanced down at the face that stared out at him from the frame: at thirteen, so young and eager, so expectant of happiness, it wrenched at his heart.

His eyes moistened slightly. He let out a deep, shuddering sigh. Perhaps now, he thought, things would alter between Sarah and himself, the healing begin . . . A second chance for them all.

He closed his eyes wearily, half dozing. Dreams mingled with memories, folding together and then drifting apart. Past images stretched out to him, some long forgotten, some so real they almost made him sigh out loud.

When next he opened his eyes it was dark outside. Juma had already come in and lit the lantern, its warm glow illuminating the room. Edward hadn't even heard his soft tread as he'd come in.

Now he heard the sound of footsteps again in the hallway. 'Juma?' he called out, his voice still thick with sleepiness.

A shadow fell across the doorway, faltering slightly.

'Grandfather . . .' The voice sounded hesitant, unsure.

Edward's head jerked round, 'Alexandra!' He stood up and turned towards her, arms outstretched. 'Darling child.'

'I couldn't leave, Grandfather. I couldn't leave . . .' Alexandra flung herself into his arms, her voice choked with emotion. 'I did try . . .'

He pushed back his tears. 'I understand, darling, I do,' he said, stroking her hair. Hadn't he known from the moment he had seen her picture that she was a child after his own heart? Hadn't he instinctively sensed that she would love this wild, uncompromising land with the same intensity as he did?

'I knew you wouldn't leave for long,' he said, tilting up her chin gently so that he could see into her face. 'There is a saying here, you know: He who has tasted the honey, will return to the honeypot . . .' He looked into her eyes. 'I knew you'd come back.'

She put her head against his shoulder. 'I leapt from the moving train . . .' she said, her voice slightly muffled, as if she were stunned still by her own action.

Her grandfather peered down at her. 'What?' His voice was incredulous.

'Well, it was about to move,' Alexandra corrected with a smile. 'One minute to go to be precise. I just suddenly knew I couldn't leave . . .' She recalled Charles's startled face as she had grabbed her bags without warning and pushed open the carriage door and leapt out onto the platform. He couldn't for a moment understand why she was leaving, why she was giving up all he could offer her in

London for a broken-down estate. Being a person to whom material things were paramount, she supposed he never would.

'But what about Robert?' her grandfather was asking, his words cutting across her thoughts. 'He went down to Nairobi to meet you. Didn't he find you?'

'Robert?' She took a step back and stared up at him. 'I didn't see him.' So, he had not abandoned her after all. Her world stood still.

'Then he must have just missed you,' concluded her grandfather, matter-of-factly, missing the tension in her voice. 'Not entirely surprised. Thought he was being amazingly ambitious to think he could get there in time.' He looked down at her, his brow furrowing slightly. 'But if he didn't bring you, how did you get up to Kirimangari?'

'With Stuart Avery,' Alexandra told him. 'By sheer chance I met him outside the Norfolk Hotel. He was on his way up to Thika and offered me a lift . . .'

'I see.'

'But about Robert . . .' Alexandra's heart began to thud. 'You were saying he came here . . .' Her voice hung on a slim thread of hope.

'Just after lunch, yes.' Her grandfather turned away slightly, his hand going out to trace the line of the table beside him. 'He came to tell me about his uncle . . .' There was an imperceptible pause. 'He came to offer me back all the land that Cameron Dalgleish had taken from me.' His voice caught slightly. He turned back to her, stretching out to take her hand. 'I have to say, my dear, I misjudged that fellow of yours,' he said solemnly. 'He's honourable, that one. Said he couldn't keep any land that rightly belonged to me.'

She would have expected nothing less from Robert. 'So he found out the truth at last then?'

'Yes. Came as a bit of a shock for him, I think.'

'I'm sure. He was very fond of his uncle.' All those years that Cameron had taken care of Robert had bound them irretrievably together. Nothing could change that. 'But did he discover why Cameron wanted to ruin you? That's something I could never understand.'

'Nor could I. All those years, nor could I.'

'But you do now?'

'A little more perhaps . . .' Edward let out a long sigh, looking past her as if to some distant object. 'Yes, I understand . . .' Outside, an owl called as it flew through the darkness towards the coffee sheds. There was a silence, then after a while her grandfather said: 'Do you remember I told you that when your mother confessed to us she was pregnant, that she spoke to us about this young boy from Eldoret?'

'The father of the child? The one who was killed?'

'Yes.' Her grandfather nodded. 'That was the story, at least.'

'Story?' Alexandra glanced up at him. 'Wasn't it true, then?'

'No. It seems there was no boy from Eldoret. She told us that to protect the man she loved. He was married, you see . . .'

'Then who was the man?' Their eyes met, and in that moment Alexandra knew the truth. 'Oh, my God! I understand now,' she said quietly. How could she have missed all the signs? 'Cameron Dalgleish . . .'

'Precisely.' Her grandfather sank down onto the arm of the sofa. His face looked suddenly weary. 'I must have been blind. Of course, once Robert had told me, so many things fitted into place. So many incidents, so many scenes. He was a handsome devil then – rather like your Robert – fun-loving, energetic. No wonder she fell for him.'

'And he wouldn't leave Vera? Was that it?'

'He wanted to, but he couldn't. She was a cripple, remember? The doctors had given her only two years more to live. If nothing else, Cameron had too much decency to desert her in her dying moments. I suppose that was his undoing. To begin with, I think Sarah believed they might be able to work something out, but then she saw the impossibility of it all, and she finally agreed to the abortion. Cameron was distraught apparently. He wanted her to somehow find a way to keep the child. He'd none of his own, you see, no chance of one either with Vera . . .'

He lapsed into momentary silence. 'But even then, he had a thread of hope. As far as everyone thought, myself included, Sarah would come back to Kirimangari after her rest. Cameron still had that to cling to. She would return and in time they might marry, or so he believed. But then she met your father. A totally unforeseen occurrence and there was nothing Cameron could do about it. He was broken-hearted. In one fell swoop he'd lost the girl he'd loved and the child he'd never had. It was a bitter blow and he was out for revenge . . .'

'And so he started to blackmail you?'

Her grandfather nodded. 'Robert told me Cameron never forgave me for being responsible for persuading Sarah to get rid of the baby. His unborn son . . .' He bowed his head, his voice faltering slightly. Then he took a deep breath. 'He'd lost everything that was dear to him and I suppose he wanted to make sure I lost all that was dear to me . . .' He paused for a moment, as if he couldn't trust himself to speak further. Then, lifting his head, he went on, his voice steadier now: 'But I still think I did the right thing, you know. About the baby, I mean. I'm not sure how happy your mother would have been with Cameron had things been different. He was too selfish, too volatile for her. She needed someone steadier, like your father.' He gave a slight shrug. 'But of course, who can say?'

Alexandra stretched out and covered his hand with hers. 'You did the right thing,' she told him gently. 'I'm sure of it.'

'And she *is* happy, isn't she?' he asked, his eyes going up to hers.

'Yes, very.'

'Then, that's all that matters, isn't it?' he said softly. 'All I ever wanted was her happiness, you know . . .' His voice caught slightly.

'I know, Grandfather,' said Alexandra, patting his hand. 'I do know.'

Neither of them spoke for a while. Alexandra was conscious of the soft sound of a moth fluttering against the lantern, its wings beating unevenly against the glass.

After a while she saw her grandfather stir restlessly. He pushed himself up from the chair and walked ponderously over to the desk in the far corner, bending down stiffly to pull open one of the lower drawers.

'I want you to have this,' he said, turning back to her and holding out a long, official-looking document.

She crossed over to take the folded piece of paper from his outstretched hand. 'What is it?' she asked.

'The deeds to Kirimangari.'

'Kirimangari?' She stopped, mid-action. 'Grandfather, I don't understand . . .'

'Quite simply, I want you to have it, Alexandra. I'm changing my will. I'm leaving Kirimangari to you.'

The enormity of his gift overwelmed her. 'But Grandfather, I couldn't!'

'Why not? You love the place as much as I do.' His green-grey eyes were dark with emotion. 'I could think of no one I would rather leave it to.'

His words touched her deeply. 'And I could think of nothing I would rather have!' She fell into his arms, pressing his wrinkled cheek against hers. 'Oh, Grandfather!'

He kissed her. From the moment she had come he had known Kirimangari would be hers. 'Then that's settled,' he pronounced happily. 'But I should warn you, there is one condition . . .'

She eyed him half suspiciously. 'And what's that?'

'That if you decide for some reason that you don't wish to run Kirimangari, if you decide to sell it, then I want you to offer Robert Dalgleish first refusal . . .'

'Robert?' She could barely disguise her surprise. 'But I thought . . .' She stopped as he stretched out his hand to touch her cheek.

'You were right about him, Alexandra. And I was wrong,' he said quietly. 'I saw him only as another Cameron Dalgleish. But in truth, I know of no other man to whom I would rather entrust Kirimangari . . .'

She felt the tears prick against her eyelids. She knew it was his way of saying that the battle between the two families was finally over.

Her grandfather cleared his throat. 'I think,' he said slowly, 'I think it's time for a new beginning, don't you?'

It was two o'clock in the morning before Alexandra heard the sound of Robert's truck wheels crunching against the murram drive at last. She thrust aside the book she was reading and was out onto the verandah and down the steps in an instant.

She saw him step from the truck, his fair hair ruffled from lack of sleep; but as he turned towards her weariness seemed to drop from his face as he caught sight of her running, with winged feet, towards him.

'Alexandra!' He swept her up into his arms and swung her round, relief flooding his face. 'I thought I'd lost you.'

He put her down and gently held her head, pulling her towards him until their lips met. He kissed her softly at first and then with a hungry, growing force.

She knew it was she he loved and wanted. She slipped her arms about his neck and pressed herself closer against him, moulding her body against his. In his arms she had the sense of coming home, of reaching a safe haven. Of belonging.

'Alexandra,' he breathed against her skin. Her name was like the sigh of a knight who has found his Holy Grail at last. 'I love you so very much.'

He held her away from him then, stepping back from her slightly, his hand still against her face. 'When I missed you at the station, I thought you'd left with Charles.' His face was still tight at the recollection.

'I couldn't go.' Her voice was steady but quiet, barely above a whisper. 'I knew if I did, I'd regret it for as long as I lived.' She glanced up at him. 'Even though I wasn't entirely sure about how you felt.'

'How I felt? But you must have known what my feelings were for you,' he broke in swiftly. 'Good God, I nearly went crazy when your grandfather told me this morning that you were about to leave with Charles . . .'

'But you didn't get my note? Or the telegram I sent to Gilgil?'

His surprise was obvious. 'Telegram?' He shook his head. 'It never came.' Though he supposed in all the chaos over at Gilgil, what with the brood mare and taking Jack to the doctor's, anything could have gone momentarily astray.

'When you didn't reply, I thought you'd abandoned me,' she said softly, her voice faltering.

His blue eyes took on a deep intensity. 'No, never that.' He stretched out his hand to touch her cheek. 'In fact, I've been on a wild goose chase all this evening trying to find you. That's why I'm so late. I even went as far as persuading Beryl Markham to take me up in her plane to try and catch you at Voi.'

'You did what?' She smiled. She loved him.

'Well, when I missed you at Nairobi station, I couldn't think how I could stop you leaving. I knew I hadn't a hope in Hell of catching up with you in the truck. And then I remembered Beryl. So I drove to the Muthiaga Club and asked her to take me up in her plane. Not that she needed much encouragement . . .' Beryl Markham always had a strong sense of adventure. 'It was all I could think of. I couldn't just let you slip away out of my life . . .'

'So what happened at Voi?' she asked, leaning her head against his shoulder.

'Well, actually Beryl buzzed the train way before Voi,' admitted Robert with a grin. 'Caused an enormous commotion when she landed. But in truth I have a sneaking suspicion that the train driver was actually rather pleased to have the journey so dramatically interrupted. It's rather a dull trip these days, no stopping even for the lions now . . .'

Alexandra couldn't help but return his smile. She could imagine the stir they had caused. 'So what happened then?'

'I went looking for you. And all I found was an extremely irate Charles.'

'Oh dear.'

'Even tried to take a swing at me.'

'Charles?'

'Yes, Charles. Very upset he was. Told me I was ruining your life. Very pompous about it. Said if you were to have married him you would have been assured of a respected place in London society and would have owned one of the finest houses in Belgravia, an estate in Yorkshire and a few thousand acres in Scotland, whilst all I had to offer you were a few dried-up acres in Kenya. I must say, he made me feel almost guilty . . .'

'Well, don't!' she said emphatically. 'Charles has never learnt that life runs beyond the material things.'

'As long as you have no regrets . . .'

'None.'

'Good.' He tilted her face up to his and kissed her gently. 'And now, I suppose, we must face the music. Your parents . . . your grandfather . . .' He raised his eyes heavenwards.

'No, not Grandfather. He's had a change of heart. He'll not oppose you now.'

'Won't he?' Robert's face showed all his surprise.

'No. I think he wants to forgive and forget. He's had enough of feuding.'

'Sensible man.'

'And what about your uncle?' Alexandra asked tentatively. 'Do you think he'll let bygones be bygones, too?'

Robert pushed his ruffled hair back from his face with a slight grimace. 'To be honest, I don't know, Alexandra. He was in a very queer mood when I left – which reminds me I ought to get back there before too long. I think he was discovering that all these years he's been fighting for revenge and for what purpose? The farm and all that extra land he stole from your grandfather has gained him nothing. It's merely a symbol to him of all his past bitterness. It must be a depressing sensation to think one has wasted one's life like that.'

Alexandra looked up at Robert. 'I almost feel sorry for him,' she said quietly. 'If he hadn't treated Grandfather so fearfully, I would . . .'

'Ah yes, your grandfather. I hope to rectify that as much as I can,' Robert said. 'I've already told him he must have all the land back.'

'I know.'

'Then you know the whole story too? About my uncle and your mother?'

'Yes, Grandfather told me,' she said, her eyes meeting his.

'It explains so much. Do you remember that day at the Averys' when I told you about my mother and how confused I felt because she seemed to have lost all her sense of joie de vivre? I couldn't understand why. But now I know. It was the baby, the guilt about that. Mother wasn't made for deceit . . .'

'I know that.' He looked down at her clear fresh beauty, his hand brushing against her cheek reassuringly.

'But I'm glad I know the truth, Robert,' she said, looking up at him. 'I understand so much more now.' It had brought her closer to her mother, that knowledge. She knew the dreadful burden her mother must have shouldered and at what cost. 'Promise me that we won't have any secrets between us, Robert. They only destroy . . .' There was a measure of desperation to her voice.

'I promise.' The pressure on her hand was swift. 'I love you,' he whispered. 'Nothing will destroy that.'

He took her hand and began to gently lead her back towards the verandah. 'Now go in and have some rest. I'll be back in the morning to claim you.'

'You're not going to Mitubiru?' She wanted him to stay, wanted never again to be parted from him.

'I must. I don't want to leave my uncle for too long,' he said. 'If you could have seen him yesterday morning . . .'

'I understand.' Whatever her own feelings towards Cameron Dalgleish she acknowledged Robert owed him loyalty and support.

'And I'll be back. Early.'

They had reached the verandah. Robert put his hand under her chin and tilted it gently towards him. In the half moonlight her face had a pale luminous beauty, a frailty, which touched him anew.

He bent to kiss her and then stopped abruptly, his hands dropping stiffly to his side.

'What is it?' She felt his stillness, like that of an animal which spies an enemy from afar. 'Robert?'

He was staring over her shoulder into the distance. She turned then, and saw something, a glow almost, like the first tinge of sunrise on the horizon.

'Come on!' he said, grabbing her arm in his.

'Robert, what's wrong?' she asked, following him down the steps.

'Just get in the truck. Hurry!'

She heard the sharp tension in his voice. 'But why?'

He was running now. 'It's Mitubiru,' he said, a dark desperation in his eyes. 'The whole damn estate looks as if it's on fire!'

21

The flames already had started up through the roof of one of the outbuildings by the time Robert and Alexandra reached Mitubiru. Tall fiery columns were spiralling into the night sky and as Robert leapt from the truck he could see the flames moving along the vulnerable line of beams in the adjacent outbuilding, flickering like serpents' tongues as if feeling their way forward.

Robert glanced about him. The voracity of the fire surprised him. He hadn't expected it to take hold so quickly. The fierce sound of crackling was almost deafening.

He ran towards the house. Ahead of him, amid the confused mass of people, he could make out Oudo, the headman, valiantly wielding the hosepipe into the flaring jungle of flames, a great hissing cloud of steam rising up about him as the water evaporated in the fierce heat. Beside him, a hastily organised water-line was struggling to quench the flames; but Robert could see it was difficult for them to get in close enough, such was the intensity of the heat.

As he came closer to the house Robert caught sight of a figure slumped up against the stone garden wall. With an old worn rug draped around his shoulders, Cameron Dalgleish sat hunched forward, his head in his hands, immobile, defeated.

'Uncle?' Robert crossed over to where he sat, bending down to put a hand out to his shoulder. 'Are you all right?'

For a moment his uncle didn't move, then he lifted his face slowly upwards, despair showing in every line. There were great shadows beneath his eyes, his face was pinched and drawn, with an air of hopelessness.

'What a waste it's all been,' he said, a weariness dragging at his voice. 'What an utter waste.'

'Nonsense, we can save most of it,' Robert told him firmly. 'It looks far worse than it is.' He hoped to heaven he was right.

'But I'm going to have to get the boys to concentrate on the outbuildings rather than the house, I'm afraid. The machinery is crucial. Without it the harvest will be lost . . .' He would be able to move some of it, of course, but the heavier parts would be impossible to shift. He would have to work quickly if he hoped to save them. He'd already instructed Alexandra to start dousing the area down in the hope of preventing the flames spreading further.

He glanced down at his uncle. Cameron had made no move, no acknowledgment of his words. His face had stiffened into a hollow, expressionless mask.

'We have a very good chance of saving it, Cameron,' Robert encouraged him, squeezing his shoulder. 'Don't give up. It's only the store house that has gone so far . . .'

Cameron closed his eyes, seeming to discard Robert's comfort like an unwanted piece of clothing.

There was a brief silence. Robert sensed Cameron's need to be alone and turned to go. But as he did so, Cameron spoke at last.

'There should have been a wind,' he said quietly, almost as if speaking to himself. 'A good strong wind would have carried it through. The night's too still, that's the trouble. Too still.'

Robert stopped in his tracks, an icy chill running through him at Cameron's words. Realisation flooded through him in that moment.

He had wondered how the fire had spread so quickly from one building to the other, wondered how it had achieved so firm a grip in so short a time. Now he knew the answer. This had been no accident. Cameron Dalgleish had meticulously set fire to it all himself.

He spun round, peering down at Cameron with confusion. 'But why?' he asked, taking hold of Cameron by the shoulders. 'For heaven's sake, why destroy everything you've spent years trying to build up?'

And yet, even as he spoke he knew the answer.

He could see the despair in Cameron's eyes, that clear knowledge that whatever revenge had gained for him, it had not won him the one thing he had so desperately wanted. He could never recapture those years, never bring back those precious moments with Sarah.

Robert let out a sigh. He stretched out his hand and touched his uncle gently. 'It's time you tried to put it behind you, Cameron. It's the only way . . .' he said, looking down at him with understanding. 'You have to start looking forward now . . .'

'Forward? To what?' returned Cameron bitterly. He turned his head slightly, unable to meet his nephew's penetrating gaze. He'd tried to destroy the farm because it meant nothing to him now. All these years he'd struggled to build up Mitubiru, to prove what? That he would have been worthy of Sarah? All meaningless now. All ashes to the wind. He only felt contempt for what he had achieved at Mitubiru. He pushed Robert's arm away and pulled the worn rug tighter about himself as if erecting an invisible wall between them.

Robert took no offence at Cameron's action. He sensed his mood, sensed also that for the moment he could do nothing to help his uncle. Later, perhaps, he would be able to offer him hope and consolation. But not now.

He straightened up slowly, leaving his uncle sitting with his back propped up against the garden wall. In the distance he could see Alexandra battling with the second hosepipe, drenching the outbuildings. At least she seemed to be keeping the fire at bay for the moment, but Robert knew that if he were about to go in and retrieve the machinery he would need extra cover. It was time to bring across Oudu and the water-line.

He called to the boys to concentrate their attention on the outbuildings, trying not to dwell on the fact that such an action was probably sentencing his home to rubble and ashes. He couldn't afford to be sentimental at such a moment. It had to be done. The machinery had to be saved.

He crossed over to Alexandra's side and bent to kiss her. Her face and hands were scorched scarlet, so intense was the heat from the flames.

'Do you want to stop for a while?' he asked gently, seeing the exhaustion in her face. 'One of the boys can take over . . .'

'I'll survive,' she said stoically. 'How long before you can start moving the machinery?'

'Any minute now,' he told her, brushing at a black sooty flake which had landed in her hair. 'I'll take the tractors out first. Then we can start on the rest of the heavier stuff.'

'Can I help?'

He squeezed her hand. 'You are already. If you can stop the fire from spreading then that's more than enough. If it flares up we'll be in trouble . . .'

It took almost an hour to move what they could from the outbuildings. The very fact that there was no wind saved them. With more wind the outbuildings would have burnt down to the ground in an instant. As it was, with constant heavy dousing from Alexandra and Oudu, the fire seemed to be abating at last. Only the main house was still ablaze and even there the flames appeared to have lost their ferocity.

Robert stretched stiffly and put his arms about Alexandra. 'What a night! Bearing up, little one?' She nodded. 'I ought to take you home, you know. We're more or less done here . . .'

'I don't want to go. Not without you.'

He smiled and kissed her. 'It'll be a good few hours yet.'

'I don't mind. I'd rather stay,' she insisted, leaning up against him.

Robert smiled and stroked her soot-grimed cheek. He loved her more than ever, standing there, dishevelled and exhausted, yet unwilling to give in.

'Come on, then,' he said, putting his arm about her shoulder. 'We'll get the boys to move back to the house again. We might still be able to save some of it.'

He was careful not to allow any of his doubt to show, but in truth he wasn't sure how much could be salvaged. The air was full of smoke, the whole dark frame silhouetted against the fiery glow of the sky. It had an almost haunting beauty about it now, but Robert knew that the cold light of day would reveal a blackened smouldering ruin, a scarred battlefield.

How his uncle was taking this steady slow destruction he hated to think. Was he regretting his mad impulse? Robert glanced over towards the stone wall. But only the rug lay abandoned on the lawn in an untidy heap. Cameron Dalgleish was nowhere to be seen.

'Damn!' Robert swore under his breath. It would never do to have his uncle wandering about in his present state in this mayhem.

A speck of anxiety stirred within him. He spun round trying to make out Cameron's figure amongst the moving crowd in the courtyard, straining his eyes in the half-light to try and find his familiar form.

But there was no sign of him. Robert turned back with a grimace.

It was then that a movement caught his eye. A flicker, no more. But it was enough. He knew then where Cameron Dalgleish had gone. Knew the terrible truth.

He started forward.

'Robert?' He felt Alexandra's hand upon his arm. 'What is it?'

'It's Cameron,' he said grimly. 'Lord only knows why, but he's gone back into the house. I've got to go after him.'

'No, Robert. No!'

He felt her hand tighten on his arm. 'I have to,' he said, removing her arm as gently as he could. 'I can't just leave him in there.'

'But he'll come out of his own accord . . .'

'But what if he can't? What if something's happened to him?' The fact that Robert had seen no further sign of his uncle alarmed him.

'But . . .'

Robert gently placed a finger against Alexandra's lips to silence her. 'I must go,' he said quietly. 'You know that.'

He brushed his fingers lightly across her forehead, his eyes looking at her steadily for a moment. Then he turned quickly and pushed his way back towards the house, stopping only to pick up the rug which lay discarded on the lawn, plunging it into one of the water buckets as he passed up along the line.

Inside, the flames rose and snapped about him. It was difficult to see anything for the heat was so intense he had to screw up his eyes and the thick smoke clung about him like a heavy cloak. But he pushed on, groping his way along the passageway to the drawing-room.

'Cameron!' he tried to call out, but the acrid smoke filled his mouth and nostrils, choking him.

He coughed, fighting for breath, but forced himself to keep on moving, a sense of urgency driving him on. He had to find Cameron. And quickly.

'Cameron!'

He stumbled on, past the drawing-room and down towards his uncle's bedroom. Here at the back of the house the smoke seemed worse, the flames less so. Robert supposed that Cameron's dousing of petrol had not been as heavy this far, so that the fire merely spluttered moodily rather than blazed.

His eyes were smarting in the curling smoke as he came into Cameron's room. He edged cautiously forward, about to call out his uncle's name again, then stopped, his mouth suddenly dry.

There was no mistaking the sight before him.

Cameron Dalgleish's body lay slumped on the bedroom floor just beyond the doorway.

Robert didn't need to touch him to know he was dead. He didn't need to feel his heart, nor listen to his breathing. Cameron lay where he had toppled, mouth agape, eyes wide, a look of almost surprised relief on his face – as if, even though Death had taken him unawares, it had not been entirely unwelcome.

Robert crouched down and closed his uncle's eyes, a sense of utter helplessness washing over him. What on earth had prompted his uncle to come back to the house? What madness?

He leant forward and took his uncle's hand in his, in a last gesture of farewell, letting out a shuddering sigh. Whatever else, Cameron had been like a father to him over these past few years. He felt a dull aching pain twist inside him, knowing his life would be the poorer for this loss.

He stooped to pick up Cameron's body, straining to take his weight upon his shoulders, and as he did so something fluttered out of Cameron's hand to the ground. Robert frowned and bent to pick it up.

It was a photograph.

He lifted it closer, and as he did so, a wave of shock ran through him. The face that stared up at him was so achingly familiar. But then he realised his mistake. Not Alexandra this, but Sarah – though at eighteen they had been touchingly alike, both hauntingly beautiful.

He stared down at the photograph in his hand. Was this why Cameron had come back so impulsively? Obviously he had not realised the danger of such an action and yet Robert sensed that even if he had, it wouldn't have stopped him. He'd been compelled by a force beyond reason. And Cameron had been quite prepared to die. Had welcomed it, in truth.

Robert slipped the photograph into his pocket, bending down to scoop up Cameron again, coughing with the effort. Even in the few minutes he had paused here he was conscious that the smoke had worsened. He knew now he would have to go through the front of the house, despite the flames, for it was the asphyxiating smoke which was his real enemy.

He adjusted Cameron's weight and then, pulling the damp rug down over them both, he started back through the house, moving as fast as he could along the passageway.

He was almost there. Almost by the door. A few steps only.

It was then that he heard the groaning crash of the roof caving in about him.

'Robert!'

Alexandra screamed out his name into the darkness. She had seen his figure almost in the doorway and had thought him to be safe; but then she had heard the terrible sound of the timbers collapsing. Now there was no sign of him.

She ran closer to the house, calling again. But this time her voice was small and muffled, almost as if fear had crushed the sound out of it.

And she was afraid. Dreadfully so.

She pushed her way forward. Already Oudu and several of the boys had gone in after Robert, acting without thought of their own safety. She could hear the sound of timbers being thrown hastily aside, could see the dim outlines of their figures.

She felt the tension rise up within her, so forcibly that she could scarcely breathe. An eternity seemed to have passed and still they had not come out. Delay could only mean one thing, surely?

She ran forward. 'Robert!' she called out frantically, fear almost choking her.

Then a figure appeared at the doorway, supported by Oudu and one of the boys, slowly stumbling out into the cold night air.

'Robert!' She felt tears of relief prick at her eyelids as she surged forward to help Oudu support him. 'I thought I'd lost you . . .'

'Me? Never!' He managed a smile, but she saw the effort of it made him cough. The smoke seemed to have filled every part of him. He slumped down against the garden wall, exhaustion etching his face.

She knelt down beside him. 'And Cameron . . .' Her words hung tentatively on the unasked question.

She saw Robert shake his head.

'Oh, my darling, I'm so sorry.' She drew him close to her, holding him tight against her. 'So terribly sorry. If only he hadn't gone back in . . .'

She felt him shudder against her with emotion, but when he lifted his head, his eyes were steady and calm.

'I think,' he said quietly, 'I think he almost wanted to die.'

Alexandra saw him glance back to the house. She touched his hand, knowing his pain. But perhaps it was fitting that Cameron had died thus, the house and its memories going with him. It was the African way, after all.

Perhaps it was not wise for dreams to outlive the dreamer.

She let out a long, low sigh.

'But what on earth made Cameron go back into the house?' she asked, searching Robert's face.

'This . . . ' Robert put his hand into his pocket and drew out the now crumpled snapshot. 'I think he wanted this . . . '

She took the photograph from him. For a long moment she did not speak. Then she said quietly, still staring down at the picture in her hands: 'He never stopped loving her, did he?' Her voice caught slightly. 'All these years, he never stopped loving her.'

'No, he didn't,' said Robert softly.

She covered her face and drew a deep breath. 'But he was so bitter . . .'

He stroked her hair. 'Only because he lost sight of that love over the years. It became buried in a mound of other emotions: hate, anger, the obsessive need for revenge.' He looked down at her and touched her cheek. 'But he found it again, I think. Over the last few days, I think he remembered that first true feeling. That's what drove him back into the house again.'

'Yes.' She could see that.

A myriad of emotions flooded over her. She felt tears welling in her eyes. Impossible not to pity Cameron Dalgleish now, not to feel with him in his heartbreak. She pressed her head against Robert's shoulder, finding comfort there.

'A powerful thing is love,' said Robert quietly, pulling her closer to him.

'I know.' She slid her arms around his neck, lifting her face to his. 'I do know.'

She felt his lips on hers, lifting her into another world, felt his heart beating hard against hers. How strange it was that love, carried alone, became a heavy lifeless burden; but shared it was a lightweight joyous thing, capable of bearing one through all life's hazardous pitfalls.

She closed her eyes, feeling the safe haven of Robert's arms about her. She felt the dependable strength of his presence. Together they could rebuild Mitubiru. Together they would go forward. She felt momentarily invincible.

She let her head fall softly onto his shoulder. To the right of her the house continued to smoulder, its blackened walls and frames skeletal against the smoke-filled sky.

But it was not there that Alexandra turned her gaze.

It was to the east, to where the first wraiths of white morning light hung on the horizon. Soon dawn would break across the hills, and it would be a new day. A new beginning. It was as her grandfather had said. Now was the time to put the past behind and start again.

She looked at Robert, filled with a formidable, desperate longing. She felt his arms tighten about her, strong and unyielding, and as his lips touched hers, she felt the weariness lift from her. It was as if she were being revitalised, brought back to life again, by his passion and love.

She stretched out her hand to him and together they began to walk away from the smouldering ruins.

She knew now she could face whatever the future might hold for them. Because he would be beside her always.

And nothing else mattered. Nothing at all.

And behind them the last of the night's shadows faded and were gone as the sunlight came streaming across the plains.

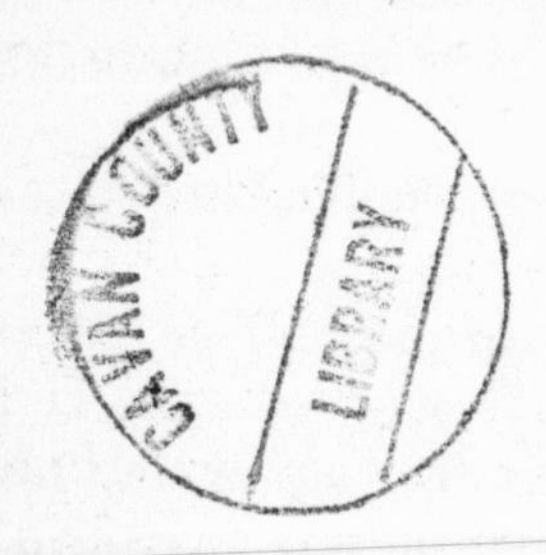